D0250834

THE QUEEN IS DEAD!

"Good gracious!" exclaimed Princess Margaret in her low voice. "Lilibet, come and see," she added excitedly as the Queen walked up behind and the rest of us parted to give her space.

Her Majesty frowned down at the figure.

"She's asleep, isn't she?" asked Princess Margaret. "Wake her up, somebody!"

It was easy to think she was asleep. The eyelids were closed, the hands were clasped meekly over her midriff, and her face had that healthy pink 'n' powdery appearance of the Sovereign in her more public moments.

From behind his hands, Davey whimpered and shook his head to answer HRH's question. Faces dropped. With a sense of foreboding, as well as a chilly sense of déjà vu, for I had had occasion to do the very thing at Buckingham Palace only a year earlier, I extended my hand to touch the woman's throat, searching for a pulse. "Don't!" HM's bodyguard commanded. But it was too late. My hand touched flesh. There was a strange oily feel from the makeup, but there was no pulse, and no warmth at all. She was quite dead. . . .

❖

Also by this author

DEATH AT BUCKINGHAM PALACE

❖

And look for:
DEATH AT WINDSOR CASTLE

HER MAJESTY INVESTIGATES

Death At Sandringham House

C. C. Benison

BANTAM BOOKS

New York Toronto London Sydney Auckland

DEATH AT SANDRINGHAM HOUSE

A Bantam Book / January 1997

JAILHOUSE ROCK. By: Jerry Leiber and Mike Stoller. Copyright ©
1957 by Jerry Leiber Music & Mike Stoller Music (Renewed). All rights
reserved. Used by permission.

JAILHOUSE ROCK lyrics excerpts (page 94) by Jerry Leiber and
Mike Stoller. (For Canada Only.) Copyright © 1957 by Elvis Presley
Music, Inc. Copyright Assigned to Gladys Music (Administered by
Williamson Music Company). Copyright renewed. International
Copyright Secured. Used by Permission. All Rights Reserved.

MANCHESTER, ENGLAND, (from "Hair"), by James Rado,
Gerome Ragni, and Galt MacDermot. Copyright © 1966, 1967, 1968
(Copyrights Renewed) James Rado, Gerome Ragni, Galt MacDermot,
Nat Shapiro, and EMI U Catalog, Inc. All Rights Reserved. Used by
Permission. WARNER BROS. PUBLICATIONS U.S., INC. Miami,
FL 33014.

Grateful acknowledgment is made to Samuel French Ltd. for
permission to reprint lines from the play "The Queen of Hearts, a
Pantomime" by John Crocker and Eric Gilder.

All rights reserved.
Copyright © 1996 by C. C. Benison.
Cover art copyright © 1996 by Tim Raglin.

Maps designed by GDS / Jeffrey L. Ward.

No part of this book may be reproduced or transmitted in any
form or by any means, electronic or mechanical, including
photocopying, recording, or by any information storage and
retrieval system, without permission in writing from the publisher.
For information address: Bantam Books.

ISBN 0-553-57477-9

Published simultaneously in the United States and Canada

Bantam Books are published by Bantam Books, a division of Bantam Doubleday
Dell Publishing Group, Inc. Its trademark, consisting of the words "Bantam Books"
and the portrayal of a rooster, is Registered in U.S. Patent and Trademark Office
and in other countries. Marca Registrada. Bantam Books, 1540 Broadway, New
York, New York 10036.

PRINTED IN THE UNITED STATES OF AMERICA

OPM   10 9 8 7 6 5 4 3 2 1

❖

In memory of Nancy Turriff
and for Jeanne Allen,
who, we trust, will be amused.

❖

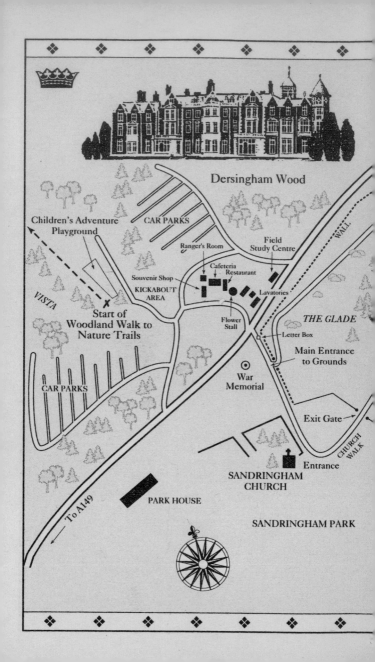

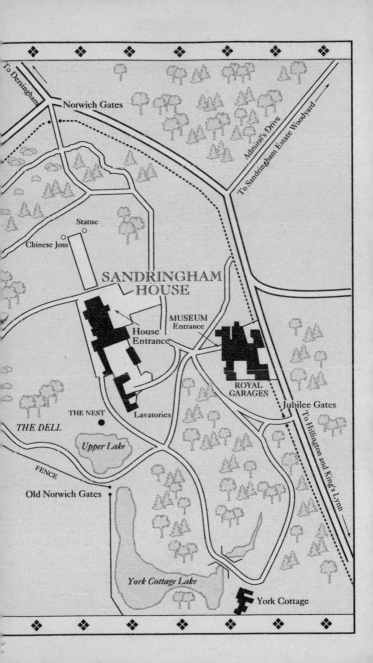

AUTHOR'S NOTE

Though this novel is set at Sandringham House and features the Queen and certain members of the Royal Family, it is nevertheless a work of fiction. With the exception of the Queen and the other Royals, all of the characters, both central and peripheral and whether or not said to occupy certain positions in the Royal Household, are purely products of the author's imagination, as are the actions, motivations, thoughts and conversations of everyone in the novel, including the Queen and the members of her family. Moreover, neither the characters nor the situations which were invented for them are intended to depict real people or events or organizations.

Introduction

OF HER MAJESTY'S five principal residences—Buckingham Palace, Windsor Castle, Holyroodhouse, Balmoral, and Sandringham—I suppose I would have to say I like Sandringham the least. Not that it isn't a smashing place—the house, that is. It's really a big red-brick funny-ugly rambling English country house, much cosier than Buckingham Palace, which is more like a large hotel than any place you'd ever want to call home. The Staff quarters at Sandringham House, as it's more properly called, are a step up from the bolt-holes on the attic floor of Buckingham Palace. The rooms actually look like they were decorated in this century, which is rather nice since I, Jane Bee, housemaid, have to live in one of them. Meanwhile, the rooms that the Queen and her family inhabit at Sandringham are more human in scale. You're not bowled over by the size although there's a lot more of that English country-house clutter, endless knickknacks and gewgaws such as Queen Alexandra's collection of Chinese figures in the Main Drawing Room that people like yours truly are obliged to clean without breakage.

The Queen's grandfather, King George V, once wrote, 'Dear old Sandringham, the place I love better than anywhere else in the world.' Easy for him to say. His idea of fun was to collect stamps and shoot things. The former has always struck me as the single most boring hobby in the world. As for the latter, well, you should see the quantity of pheasant brought back after a shooting party. The word 'slaughter' comes to mind, and, I'm told, it's nothing like the days of George V and his father, Edward VII, when Their Majesties and their aristocratic friends blasted away with their Purdey guns for hours at just about anything with wings.

You can tell I'm not dead keen on this huntin' and shootin' lark. But it's not that that's off-putting about Sandringham. And, as I've said, it's not the Big House itself. It's just that Sandringham is so *isolated*. It's about 110 miles northeast of London, in Norfolk, in the middle of this huge twenty-thousand-acre estate, much of which is farm and forest. I'm told it's quite lovely in spring, summer, and fall but I've never seen it in the spring, summer, or fall when the gardens are in bloom and the fields are ripe. I've only ever seen Sandringham in the winter, which is when the Royal Family decamps for Christmas and afters. I can take winter. I'm Canadian. *'Mon pays ce n'est pas un pays, c'est l'hiver,'* we sang ardently in our junior high school French immersion classes back in my hometown, Charlottetown, Prince Edward Island. *'My country isn't a country, it's winter.'* But winter in Norfolk is different than sparkling-snow'd Canada's. It's a concentrated dose of English winter weather. Ripping winds roar across the North Sea from Norway. Rain drills into your face. The chill claims your very bones. Sometimes the sky appears almost bowed with cold and wet when I glimpse it from a window at the Big House.

My first winter at Sandringham, I have to admit, I

felt a bit blue. I had been away from home for almost a year and a half, in Her Majesty's service just under one year of that time. It was my second Christmas in Europe while my family was gathered 'round the tree inhaling turkey at my grandmother's home in Charlottetown. True, my aged parents, Steve and Ann Bee, were cruising to Splitsville at that point, but my elder sister, Julie, spouse-of-potato farmer, had produced my parents' first grandchild just before the holidays, which ushered in a period of peace and goodwill—highly appropriate given the season and all—and I'd had a hankering to hop a plane at Heathrow and join in the Kodak moment.

Alas, I was low in seniority at Buck House. Worse, I was one of the few non-Brits in residence. Lots of the others in the lower orders had excuses why they should be in the holiday bosoms of their families in Barnstaple or Wolverhampton or Glasgow. They could always be back in uniform in a day or two, if need be. Not me. A trip back to North America, particularly to a place like Charlottetown, was a big deal. I had hoped I might be able to spend Christmas Day that year with my great-aunt Grace, in Long Marsham, a village near the north-west fringes of London, but that was not on, either. So, with some of the other housemaids, like a bunch of girls off to convent school, I went up to Sandringham in a clunky old bus a few days in advance of the Royal Family, who arrived in somewhat more luxurious vehicles.

That was the first winter at Sandringham. The next year I was able to get Christmas Eve and Christmas Day off to spend with Aunt Grace and, as it happened, with my father, who decided my malingering in England instead of being in Canada where I belonged needed investigating. However, Boxing Day, the day after Christmas, I was to report back to work in Norfolk. I wasn't really looking forward to it. As I said, Sandringham House is so isolated. There's not enough to do. Oh, there's enough to do *workwise*, although the resident Housekeeper, our boss, is nowhere near the slave-driver Buck House's assistant Housekeeper, Mrs. Harbottle, is. It's the after-hours that get to you. You can hang out in the Staff lounge. Or sit in your room and read. But if you want to go out you face a half-mile walk through the cold and the dark to the pub in Dersingham, the largest of seven villages on the Estate. King's Lynn, the nearest big town, is fifteen miles away, and finding someone with a car who's willing to take you to the Chicago Rock Cafe or one of the other clubs isn't that easy. Sometimes, after the sun has set, I find myself staring from the window of my aerie past cold-bright patches of wet snow illuminated by security flood-lamps into the black trees and black sky, praying for some constitutional crisis to force the Queen back to London, taking the rest of us with her.

That second winter at Sandringham, however, wasn't anywhere near as grim and dull as I'd thought it would be. As it turned out, there was a bit of a crisis. Not constitutional. And not something that obliged us to hop it back to the Capital. But it was rather, as Her Majesty might say in one of her moments of formidible understatement, interesting. Tragic, of course. But certainly interesting.

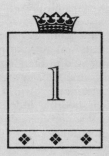

IT ALL BEGAN the morning after Boxing Day. Following several hours of the usual skivvying—hoovering, dusting, bedmaking, and the like—I found myself suddenly assigned a task foreign to my job description. Right time at the right place, I guess you could say, although the seeming serendipity of it all was aided and abetted by one important factor—a 'flu epidemic that had put half the Staff in their beds. Just as the Plague in the fourteenth century helped bring an end to the feudal system, so the 'Flu at Sandringham that winter in the late twentieth century was having an unsettling (though impermanent) effect on the rigid Palace hierarchy, which is rather feudal on the whole. In short, one found oneself doing things one wouldn't normally do.

That's why late that morning I found myself not finishing up a bed or two at Sandringham House, but in the village hall at Dersingham. "You'll do." A finger had pointed at me as I passed by the kitchens just off the Gun Room, and though Mrs. Benefer, the resident Housekeeper, had voiced an initial objection, she soon gave in and I found myself hurtling past the Norwich Gates, down the Dersingham road in one of the Land Rovers with an insulated bag holding a hamper of jacket potatoes and a box of crystal glasses that had somehow been forgotten in the original convoy to the village hall where the shooting luncheon for members of the Royal Family and their guests was to take place.

"Why is it being held in Dersingham?" I asked my driver, Tony Annison, an officer in the Royalty & Diplomatic Protection Department. "Aren't luncheons usually set up at that timber shooting lodge Her Majesty had built on Flitcham Hill some years ago? That's where it was last year, if I remember."

"The anti's got to it," Annison said.

"The aunties?" Two of my mother's sisters flitted through my head.

"Yeah, the anti's. Those so-called animal-liberation types. Bloody terrorists is what they are. Smashed the windows. Spray-painted obscenities. The lot."

"Oh," I said in a small voice, but in a louder one thought: *Oops!* Another security breach. Although the Queen's shooting lodge was some few miles southeast of the Big House it was behind a stone wall, well within the protected security area of the Sandringham Estate. "Was anyone caught?"

"No," Tony replied grimly.

Oops, again. Some of the animal-rights types were a clever bunch, to be sure. I actually wasn't completely unsympathetic to them, but there was an element with a rather frightening zeal that led them, in the name of protecting one thing, to destroy something else, rather like those anti-abortion people in America prepared to shoot the born, a doctor for instance, on behalf of the *un*born. Stunning illogic. During the holiday season the anti-blood sports protesters put much of their effort into disturbing the traditional Boxing Day fox hunt in

Gloucestershire and such places with demonstrations and hoax bombs and the like. Shooting pheasant and woodcock in Norfolk similarly raised their ire. When my father and I drove to Sandringham from Long Marsham on Boxing Day we'd passed a colorful clutch of protesters making their way from the roadside to a nearby field complete with denouncing signs and noisemakers to disturb the shooting.

"Why move the lunch to Dersingham? Why not Anmer? There's an old village hall there. Or Wolferton?" I asked, mentioning other villages on the Estate.

"I wish they would hold these things at the Big House," Tony said sourly, not really answering. "It would be easier on all of us. I don't know why they have to hold a shooting lunch in some damned village hall at all."

I did. The Royal Family fell into occasional bouts of Trianon-ism. Like Marie Antoinette pretending to be a milkmaid in her idealized peasant cottage at Versailles, the Queen and her family liked to play from time to time at being ordinary folks. In late summer, they throw their own steaks on the barbie up at Balmoral, their home in the Scottish highlands. In winter, during shooting luncheons, they like to nibble *poulet au riz* while seated on plastic chairs in a village hall amid notices from the District Community Health Council and schedules for the local camera club. That they are served by footmen and don't have to do the washing-up afterwards never seems to strike them as incongruous. Well, the Royals have their foibles, too. I'm sure you've read about them in the papers.

The village hall in Dersingham reminds me of the village hall in Long Marsham, so often my community-minded Aunt Grace's destination, which leads me to the conclusion that English village halls must be fairly standard in design. They're simple, functional structures, really; in the case of Dersingham, of brick and local carrstone, a rusty red ironstone, with a nod to Tudor-style timbering along the gabled roofline. The village hall was built, I noted from a brass plaque as we drew up to the entrance, in 1911, King George V's coronation year, and it has an appearance as solid and unassuming as His late Majesty himself.

That didn't mean some changes had not been made to the interior in the ensuing years, I discovered after I'd darted across the gravel parking lot through the chilling drizzle with my warm and aromatic bundle of potatoes. To my right, I noted smart clean white walls and freshly painted blue doors to the gents' and ladies' loos; to my left, the hall kitchen, which looked as spruce and modern as the one at the Big House, though of course much smaller. Eric Twist, one of the Buck House scullery hands, a cigarette suspended on his lower lip, wordlessly snatched the box from my hand at the doorway and began rapidly unpacking each foil-wrapped potato onto a baking tray. Tony Annison squeezed past me and placed the box of fragile glassware on a ledge of a service opening into the hall itself through which I could see a table in the process of being set with white linen, napkins, and silver.

"Anything I can do?" I asked as Annison squeezed past me once again and headed back into the drizzle to the Land Rover, cell-phone in hand.

"You can stop dripping all over the bleedin' floor is what you can do," Eric said crossly as he grabbed a mop and proceeded to blot the pool that had gathered at my feet.

"Oh, for heaven's sake. Do you think Her Majesty and the whole pack of them aren't going to drip on this floor, too? And you're getting fag ash all over. Look." I yanked off my damp jacket and gave it a provocative shake as he stubbed his cigarette in a coffee cup and wiped the front of his uniform.

"Just go and help those two buttercups set the table," he snarled.

I put my jacket on a chair by the doorway, took the box of glassware from the ledge, and headed for a table that had been set up opposite the kitchen, between two sets of doors that looked as though they led to smaller meeting rooms or offices.

"What's the matter with Eric? He's being tetchier than usual," I said *sotto voce* to Nigel Stokoe, the footman nearest me, who was looking dubiously at a spotty knife.

"Hangover, darling," Nigel replied, wiping the offending utensil on the sleeve of his waistcoat.

I laid the box on the table and began removing the glasses carefully from their cloth sleeves and layers of bubblewrap—whisky glasses, I noted. You'd need a bracing snort after a day mucking about in the cold murdering pheasants. Nigel and Davey Pye, two of the fifteen footmen in Her Majesty's service, were following each other around the table methodically laying out knives and forks. Because they were dressed in their usual black tailcoats, black trousers, white shirts, and scarlet waistcoats, and, perhaps because both of them were growing a bit tubby, they reminded me of Tweedledum and Tweedledee. However, Davey, normally voluble, was unusually silent, laying out the cutlery like a mechanical toy with dying batteries.

"Davey, you're weaving," I said finally, after observing him for a few moments. He had suddenly grasped the edge of the table, closed his eyes, and begun to sway.

"I think I must be getting this 'flu," he said.

Nigel rolled his eyes extravagantly. 'Hangover,' he mouthed.

"I heard your lips move, Nigel. I am not hungover."

"You were completely squiffy last night, Davey," Nigel retorted merrily. "You were potted. Embalmed. Legless—"

"Spare me the *Roget's*."

"—Sozzled. Paralytic. Drunk as a newt. Your arse, as I recall, was on backwards."

"Language!" Eric's muffled shout came from the kitchen. "What if Her Majesty walked in this minute?"

Davey groaned. "Oh, dear. I must be bright for Mother."

"What were you guys up to this time?" I held a glass up to the window. It looked cloudy, completely unwashed. I set it aside.

"We were trying to call in to that Talk Radio program last night. The topic was 'Who would you most like to shag over the Christmas hols.'"

"Hmmm. George Michael, off the top of my head."

"Fancy! That was Davey's choice, too. Only . . ." Nigel started giggling. "Only Davey got so tiddly—his mother, his *real* mother, Sylvia that is, sent him a bottle of Laphroaig for a Christmas prezzie—that he couldn't punch in the numbers on the phone anymore. Oops."

A fork fell from his gloved hand to the parquet flooring with a high-pitched ring.

"I didn't have that many drinkie-poos, Nigel." Davey was getting cranky.

"The bottle's finished, old dear." Nigel rose with the fork and rubbed it on his sleeve.

"What! I didn't drink it all. That was a gift—"

"Well, you ate half the nice chockies *my* mother sent me!"

"I did not!"

"You did, too!"

"Sharrup!!" growled the kitchen.

"Oh, my head," Davey moaned.

Silence ensued but for the light patter of rain against the window and the delicate pings of the coppered heaters around the room valiantly trying to conquer the chill. Unlike the entranceway and kitchen, the hall was quite plain, even a bit depressing under fluorescent lights, with its dull brown wood siding up the bottom half of the walls, ancient black-and-white photos of long-dead village nobs lining the top half, and faded coronation portraits of the Queen and the Duke of Edinburgh on either side of a stage at the far end of the room. The place looked like a DIY reno from the 'sixties, reminding me of some of my friends' parents' basement rooms back in Prince Edward Island. One thing looked new and fresh, however—a heavy scarlet curtain drawn across the stage.

"Have they been doing a play or something here?" I asked no one in particular.

"Panto, I think." Nigel adjusted a spoon's placement with one hand and stifled a yawn with the other.

"Oh, what fun!" I exclaimed.

Having heard what novel and peculiarly British performances pantomimes were, I had managed to slip away to a presentation of *Cinderella* at a London theatre the previous Christmas. It was a major hoot. Prince Charming was a woman dressed as a man. Cinders herself was a man dressed as a woman. The Ugly Stepsisters, named Anorexia and Bulimia, were also men dressed as women, in their case the gaudiest and most outrageous costumes. The sets were marvels of ingenuity. There were sensational pyrotechnics when the pumpkin turned into a coach and the mice into footmen. Actors and audience engaged in this constant banter. Bits of current pop tunes and topical references were thrown in. Was it fun? Oh, yes it was.

But I couldn't imagine the same glitz in a rather poky village hall. And said so.

"Well, that's London." Davey awoke from his brief torpor. "This is the country, after all. Lots of little places have pantos. We used to have them when I was a kiddie at Stratford. Besides, this one's for charity, isn't it, Nig?"

"Mmmm. The British Something Something Trust, or something. Got an outside director, too. Can't be too awful."

"What play is it?" I had finished unpacking the glasses and was amusing myself popping the bubblewrap.

"*Queen of Hearts*. There's a poster for it on the vestibule bulletin board, next to the sign that says you can't wear stiletto heels in the hall. You'll never get to do your Bette Midler act here, Davey, ha ha."

"*Queen of Hearts?* Of she-made-some-tarts fame?" I asked.

"The very one."

"I do wish you wouldn't mention food!" Davey put a gloved hand to his mouth and belched quietly.

"Is the mention of it worse than the smell of it?" I thought it was hard to avoid the pleasing aromas of Scotch broth and hot mince pies which had managed to waft towards us from the kitchen. It was certainly better than the faint odour of mice and moulds which tended to pervade old buildings in the English winter.

"My nose must be stopped up. Oh, dear, I think I'm going to *die.*" Davey's hand had moved from his mouth to his forehead in a melodramatic gesture.

"Oh, stop wanking on," said Eric testily as he came through the hall carrying a silver dish of hot food enclosed in a padded container. "And stop buggering around with that bubblepack, you. You're making my head ache."

"Language!" I scolded. "What if Her Majesty walked in this minute?"

"Sod off."

In fact, I agreed: Davey did look a bit peaky. His normally plump and pink face had the pale yellowy sheen of the elephant tusks that stood in the lobby outside the Dining Room of the Big House.

"Actually, now that I think of it . . ." Nigel regarded me quizzically. "Why *are* you here?"

"Is this one of those existential questions?"

"Eh?"

"Never mind. I'm here because everyone else at the Big House is either busy or ill."

"You weren't here over this Christmas weekend. I thought you might be sick, too."

"I got the two days off. I was with my great-aunt in Long Marsham. My father's over, which is sort of nice," I added, wondering why I said 'sort of.'

"Over from the colonies?" Davey interjected.

"Yes." I sighed. There are days when I would like to kick these British imperialists. "He came with many beaver pelts. Fortunately, the barque didn't sink in the North Atlantic storms, though the scurvy got to them a bit. It was an awfully rough crossing."

"Does anyone wear beaver?" Davey paused over a salad plate, oblivious to my sarcasm. "Maybe if Vivienne Westwood dyed it orange—"

"—she'd still find the anti's throwing pig's blood on whoever dared wear it," Nigel finished the thought.

Davey shut his eyes and groaned. "Pig's blood! *Must* you, Nig!"

"You're wobbling again, Davey," I said.

"Then would someone *please* change the subject."

There was a moment of silence as we groped around for other conversation. Eric, finished fiddling with a hot plate on the side table, glared at us all, reached for his cigarettes, and dragged himself back to the kitchen.

"Okay, then," I said when he had gone. "How were *They* this Christmas?"

Davey and Nigel regarded each other across the table.

"Do I detect a capital letter swimming about in the middle of that question?" Davey said, brightening a little.

"You do. *And* italics."

"Well, *They* were brilliant."

"Oh, awful, I think," argued Nigel.

"Brilliant."

"Awful. Di was obliged to flee to London Christmas Day. Fergie was banished to Wood Farm, three miles away. She didn't even show at church."

"That's why it was brilliant, Nig. Life is always better when those tension-making daughters-in-law-from-hell pop off somewhere else."

"Poor Diana," Nigel sniffed. "Another Christmas Day alone in front of a lo-cal frozen entrée from Bird's Eye."

"Nonsense. She could have stayed over. It was her own choice."

"And spend the day with her in-laws doing the 'if-looks-could-kill' bit."

"What . . ." I said, wearying of this—listening to Davey's and Nigel's views of Royal Family contretemps was like listening to some headache-making heckling in the House of Commons. "Excuse me, you two . . . what about the Queen?"

"Her Majesty was serene, as usual."

"I beg to differ, Nigel. Mother has become *more* serene in the absence of the Princess of Wales. I should know."

Davey had lately risen in the ranks to become one of two personal footmen to the Queen, assisting the Pages of the Backstairs, members of Staff who are in direct attendance on HM, tidying her personal apartments, serving meals and the like—high-toned skivvying, when you get right down to it. The appointment was a bit of a surprise: Davey wasn't the most responsible member of Staff. But it seems Her Majesty discovered he had a way with the corgis. They didn't lunge for his ankles the way they did with other footmen who are, to corgis, what postmen are to other breeds waiting in front gardens in less palatial British homes. The corgis—Fable, Myth, Kelpie, Pharos, Spark, Joan, Diamond, and Phoenix—actually liked him.

"I don't know why!" he wailed to me after he received news of his promotion. "I don't even *like them*."

I thought at the time that he did protest too much. One way to Her Majesty's heart is through her dogs, and the way to her dogs' hearts, of course, is through their stomachs.

"Are you sure you haven't been running around with a lamb chop in your pocket?"

Davey had coloured slightly at that point. "Of course I haven't. Such a thing would spoil the line of my uniform."

But he was pleased at the appointment, even if it did mean having to walk the corgis when Her Majesty was otherwise engaged, which is often enough.

Recalling this, I failed to pay full attention to what Davey now went on to say: ". . . and I'm sure not even the Thringys will spoil the peace this Christmas week."

"Oh, no!" I couldn't help but exclaim. "Not the Thringys again!"

"And this time, they're *staying* at the Big House even longer than the usual three-day shoot," Nigel explained with glee, noting my distress.

The Thringys, or more properly, the Thrings, were dear old friends of the Queen. Actually, that's not correct. Alfred, the Marquess of Thring, was a dear old friend of the Queen. He was a Norfolk neighbour with lands adjoining the Sandringham Estate, a lover of dogs and shooting and the whole traditional country-life routine HM so enjoyed. Alfred's wife, Pamela, the Marchioness—his second wife, that is; known as Pamela II because, coincidentally, the Marquess's first wife was also a Pamela—was perhaps not quite so dear. I couldn't tell you what HM's feelings were toward the Marchioness because, of course, that's not something she would let be known to any but the very few; however, I had heard from some of the other downstairs crowd that other members of the Royal Family were apt to pull a face when the Marchioness's name was mentioned.

I had only had the briefest encounter with Lady Thring last January during the Thrings' three-day stay at the Big House. She reminded me of certain unrelaxed and demanding American tourists who patronized Marilla's Pizza, the Prince Edward Island restaurant at which I was, once upon a time, a waitress. This was not completely surprising as she was, in fact, American. But it was not the presence of the Marchioness that bothered me. It was the presence of her son, Buchanan, spawn of an earlier marriage or liaison or pass of ships in the night, who was wont to rub up against you if he found you in a corridor bent over your Hoover. He had no idea how to behave in front of servants, or Staff as we're more properly called, and heaven knows how he behaved in front of HM and family. I guess he thought he was cute, but he was more of a boor. Or perhaps 'lout' is the word since I tend to think of boors as old lechers and louts as young lechers. Buchanan—or Bucky, as he was called—was young, about nineteen or twenty, not much younger than I. Mrs. Benefer, the resident Housekeeper, was the recipient of several complaints about him—one from me—but her suggestion to us girls was to keep out of his way for the period of the visit—grin and bear it, in other words.

"Why," I asked mournfully of the two footmen, "are the Thrings staying longer this time? And why Christmas week? I thought Christmas week was for the

Family. Guests usually arrive after the New Year, don't they?"

"I think it's what you Americans refer to as 'a window of opportunity,' " Nigel said snootily. Also provocatively, as he knows damn well I'm not American. "As I hear it, the Thringys are to be away for some longish time in America right after New Year's Day. I think his lordship is doing a few of those dog-judging whatsits he does. And then they're off to the Caribbean somewhere, isn't that right, Davey? Davey?"

Nigel's would-be interlocutor burped and nodded, covering his mouth apologetically.

"Then why can't the Things just stay at Barsham Hall and . . . and *commute*," I moaned, thinking of Bucky.

"To the Caribbean?"

"No, you treacle brain. To Sandringham House. Barsham's only about twenty miles from here."

Nigel pouted. "I should imagine most of Barsham's been put to bed for the winter with the Things going to be gone and all. I think they spent Christmas Day in London. Anyway, the renovations at Barsham still aren't complete."

"What! It's gone more than a year. Davey and I were looking at pictures of various rooms in *Tatler* or *Architectural Digest* or *Hello!* or whatever the hell it was we were looking at."

"Those pictures were merely a tease, Jane. Lady Thring has barely begun her mighty task. Oh, dear!" Davey belched again. "I do beg your pardon . . ."

" 'Flu, you say," Nigel said archly.

The Marquess, though close to the Queen in age, had only become the Marquess about fifteen months earlier. Alfred's father, a sort of titled hermit, had not been keen to join the daisy support scheme—to die, in other words—and had lived on and on in Barsham Hall well into his nineties. And when the Marquess of Thring did, at last, snuff it, the first thing the new Marchioness did, with barely a nod to the customary mourning, was begin redecorating Barsham Hall from attic to cellar, making the place nearly unlivable in the meantime.

Their London home, Thring House, was in Mayfair but their country home after their marriage and prior to Alfred's acceding to the marquessate (in the days when he went by the courtesy title, Earl of Chudleigh) had been Anmer Hall, which had been vacated by the Duke and Duchess of Kent in 1990. About three miles east of Sandringham House, Anmer Hall was a six-bedroomed Georgian mansion Edward VII sometimes used to house the overflow of guests at his fabled Sandringham house parties. The Thrings vacated it soon after the late Lord Thring's death. What with the renos at Barsham, the Thrings had been, in effect, without an operating country home for over a year.

"Anyway, Her Majesty has invited the Thringys to stay until the New Year," Nigel continued.

"Mother's too kind," Davey interjected.

I'll say, I thought. But HM does tend to be very loyal to old friends. "Are they with the shooting party this morning, then? The Thrings?"

"Of course, the ladies don't join the shoot until the late morning, before luncheon," Nigel explained in a patronizing tone.

"I know that, Nigel."

"Well, anyway, I understand her ladyship's begged off the luncheon. Migraine—a likely story. I assume Bucky's with the guns. His mother's so intent on him learning all the bits that go into making a proper English gentlemen. Ha! He's a better chance of being an aristocrat than he does a gentleman. He's a bit of a yob, don't you think?"

"Of course, Affie is with them," said Davey, ignoring the question, referring to Lord Thring by his pet name. "Isn't he the second-best shot in England?"

"I thought he was the second-dullest man in England?"

"Lost the crown to you, did he, Nig?" Davey smiled.

Nigel looked down his nose and drawled: "I thought you weren't feeling well?"

Davey's smile faded. He touched a hand delicately to his brow. "Too true. I am feeling rather poorly."

Silence reigned for a few moments as Davey and Nigel surveyed their handiwork, fiddling with this and that plate as if to assure themselves. Of what, I don't know. The plates were plain and white, a simple setting for a simple meal. Sort of. I started counting the number of place settings.

"Who else is here for luncheon?" I asked.

"I'm not sure," Nigel said. "We were told sixteen. Charles, I expect. Wills and Harry. Or at least Wills . . ."

"Father," Davey chimed in, using his pet name for Prince Philip. "Edward. Andrew? Or did I hear he's down with 'flu, too. Peter Phillips, Princess Anne's son. The Thrings, of course. One or two of the local aristos perhaps . . ."

"Fewer this year, I think."

"The 'flu curtseys not to great kings, nor to members of the aristocracy," Davey retorted, flourishing a silver salver.

"Epigrams R Us? Shakespeare?"

"A hash of, more like," said Nigel.

Davey's brow crinkled. " 'Nor custom stale her infinite variety . . .' " he muttered. "No, no, that's not it. Great kings, what is it? . . . customs . . . 'Nice customs curtsey to great kings.' That's it. *Henry V.*"

Davey's being Stratford-upon-Avon-born was a curse. We were unimpressed.

"And the women?" I queried, turning to Nigel.

He surveyed the table and counted on his fingers. "I don't know about the ladies. Besides Her Majesty . . . well, the Queen Mother is much too frail these days. The Marchioness has ducked out, so to speak. The Princess Royal, of course. Zara Phillips, likely. Perhaps a few other wives . . ."

"A fiver says Margo turns up," Davey interrupted, using the name close members of the Royal Family have for Princess Margaret and which we below-stairs types use out of earshot.

"Never," Nigel tut-tutted.

"I thought she hated blood sports," I said, surprised. "Not to mention the idea of tramping about on a damp cold winter day."

"Ah, but you haven't accounted for the effect of male pulchritude on Her Royal Highness." Davey turned a leg daintily outward as though he planned to hitch a ride on the A149.

"You *must* be ill." Nigel stared at him. "You're hallucinating."

"I don't mean *me*, you nit. I mean Paul Jenkyns."

"Ah," I said, enlightened. Inspector Paul Jenkyns was HM's new minder, her Personal Protection Officer, one of a team of four. He had recently come into Her Majesty's service after a stint with the Kents. "He is a babe, to be sure."

"Oh, really." Nigel contemplated the ceiling. "You're being ridiculous."

"Who? Me?"

"No, Davey. Paul is, well, rather gorgeous, but . . ." He paused and pursed his lips. "All right, you're on, ducky. A fiver says Margo *is* at the Big House. Right this minute she's sitting up in bed with a purple peignoir on, sipping a cup of Lapsang souchong, and reading a trashy novel."

A little smile crept across Davey's plump face. And then he started. He gripped the table end with one hand, and fingered his stomach tenderly. "Ooooh," he groaned. His smile collapsed. "I just felt a wave of something run through me."

"Probably single-malt scotch sloshing through your veins."

"Oh, do shut up, Nigel." Davey grimaced. "Oh, dear, oh, gosh, I must lie down for a moment." He looked around forlornly. There were chairs along the walls but in great orange stacks, waiting for the next performance of the panto. The doors to the smaller rooms revealed themselves to be locked when I rattled them.

"There's probably something to lie on backstage," I suggested, thinking of the coach in the Cinderella panto I'd seen.

The rumble of a Land Rover drawing up on the

gravel outside the hall filtered through the walls, alerting us to the imminent presence of some members of the shooting party, but Davey was already headed toward one of the two doors on either side of the stage. My own presence suddenly concerned me. I wasn't needed to serve lunch—it's hardly part of my job description though I wouldn't have minded—and I was dressed in my boring white housemaid's uniform. I looked quite out of place. At Buckingham Palace, some housemaids still dart into empty rooms if they hear the scrabble of corgis just so they don't have to confront HM. I don't know why. I've never felt that way. On the other hand, a housemaid at a shooting luncheon seemed as unwelcome as a nun at a wedding. Nigel suggested I duck into the loo.

But my progress was halted by a sudden and strange conjunction of events. From behind the curtain, we could hear Davey mutter, "Oh, wherever is the bloody light switch," and then, in a small startled voice say, "Your Majesty?" We turned to stare at the curtain and then Davey said in a somewhat louder voice, "Ma'am?"

This was very peculiar because at precisely that moment, at the other end of the hall, Her Majesty stepped into the room, tugging at her Hermès headscarf with one hand while the other reached for the zip on her Barbour jacket. In her wake were Princess Margaret, in a quilted blue jacket and a tweed skirt, and Paul Jenkyns, HM's detective, in a black coat that nicely set off his curly silver hair. But just as we swivelled heads to take in the Presence & Co., our heads swivelled again as a terrible shriek came from behind the curtain, cutting the air with almost physical force. It was followed by a fearsome and rattling intake of breath and then the incredible words:

"THE QUEEN IS DEAD!!!"

The Queen, who had entered into the hall smiling and apparently invigorated from her morning outdoors, continued smiling as though determined nothing could ruin her day.

"I've never felt better in my life, thank you very

much," she said cheerily, shaking the moisture from her headscarf.

I can only presume that HM thought that this, ghastly as it seemed, was another one of the jokes and pranks they like to play on each other over the holidays at the Big House. Or else it was an excellent example of her remarkable ability to remain nonplussed in any situation.

Unfortunately, the rest of us were completely nonplussed by Davey's unearthly scream. Prankster he might be from time to time, but Davey's devotion to Mother, as he calls her, was inviolable. This weirdness was beyond reasoning and, like automatons, we found ourselves moving inexorably toward the stage with utter disregard for the niceties of protocol. Nigel, Eric, who had stepped from the kitchen to greet HM, and I stage left, Princess Margaret and Inspector Jenkyns stage right.

"Lilibet! Are you coming?" Her Royal Highness called impatiently as the Queen, unmoved, continued unzipping her coat.

There was really very little room behind the curtain. It was crowded with a series of painted sets, the one most visible a scene vaguely reminiscent of the Ballroom at Buckingham Palace. But in the middle of the stage, both hands covering his mouth, his eyes goggling, was Davey, spotlit, pale as an albino frog. And what he was gaping at was truly remarkable. Indeed, so remarkable that none of us bothered to inquire after Davey's condition, for there in a pool of light on a fanciful gilded litter, as if in sleep, was a woman who was a dead ringer for Her Majesty the Queen.

The figure, however, was not dressed in a ball gown with sash, or a crown and a mantle, or even in one of those highly colored outfits worn to be seen in crowds on public occasions—clothes most readily identifiable with the Queen—but in a costume remarkably similar to that of the monarch whose very footfalls we could hear mounting the steps—Wellington boots, green overtrousers, a waxed Barbour jacket, and a headscarf with horsy designs on it.

"Good gracious!" exclaimed Princess Margaret in her low voice. "Lilibet, come and see," she added excitedly as the Queen walked up behind and the rest of us parted to give her space. "Quite remarkable."

"It's never Jeannette Charles, is it?" Eric whispered, his usual surliness lost in apparent wonder.

Her Majesty frowned at the figure. "No. No, I've seen Mrs. Charles." HM did not whisper. Her eyes moved from the wellies to the owly eyeglasses and then, at the same moment as everyone else, caught the one anomalous note in the figure's costume: On top of the headscarf was a tiara. Her Majesty's frown grew deeper. Though I was already feeling shock, surprise, anxiety, and curiosity, I had to add another emotion: embarrassment. The tiara was a note all too reminiscent of *Spitting Image*, a British TV comedy featuring puppets that savagely caricatured the rich and the famous and the great and the good. When the program had been on air, Her Majesty was routinely shown wearing a housewifely headscarf with a great tiara perched on top.

"How rude!" Princess Margaret fumed. "She's asleep, isn't she? Wake her up, somebody!"

It was easy to think she was asleep. I could see from the unlined skin that the figure on the litter was a much younger woman than the real Queen before us, but makeup had been expertly applied so the face had not only a semblance of age but that healthy pink 'n' powdery appearance of the Sovereign in her more public moments. The eyelids were closed, and the hands, that of a younger woman, were clasped meekly over her midriff like a choirgirl's.

From behind his hands, Davey whimpered and shook his head to answer HRH's question. Faces dropped. With a sense of foreboding, as well as a chilly sense of déjà vu, for I had had occasion to do the very thing at Buckingham Palace only a year earlier when a footman was found dead just outside HM's private apartments, I extended my hand to touch the woman's throat, searching for a pulse. "Don't!" Paul Jenkyns commanded. But it was too late. My hand touched flesh. There was a strange oily feel from the makeup, which, but for a smear on her left cheek, extended smoothly down toward the chest, but there was no pulse, and no warmth at all. She was quite dead.

The others didn't need me to say anything. A frisson of horror shot through us like electricity in a thunderstorm.

"Does anyone know who it might be?" The Queen looked around but gathered no intelligence from her impromptu Court. I was silent. I thought there was something faintly familiar about the figure, once you focused your attention past the looky-likey thing, but I figured I was just fooling myself. Everyone else shook their head to the negative.

"Ma'am, I think we'd better—" began Paul Jenkyns in a patient, authoritative voice, but he was cut off by two contiguous events. Davey, whose face had been turning from the colour of parchment to the colour of French Canadian pea soup, darted toward the back of the stage, knocking over a props table and sending, among other things, a rolling pin, tart pans, and a tray of plaster tarts clattering and shattering to the floor. We heard him clumber down a set of steps, then a door opened and closed. Immediately after, a big black dog tore into the room like some netherworld familiar, leaping and whimpering, forcing everyone to dodge out of the way. Concerned for Davey, and without a care for protocol, I fled the Presence and raced backstage to see if I could do anything for him, since there was obviously nothing I could do for the deceased. I left a minor pandemonium: Eric, unpractised, trying to restrain the dog, Jenkyns advising withdrawal, Her Majesty agreeing, the hound barking, and a crowd of other, fresh, mostly hearty male voices, coming in at the other end of the hall.

I went down a few steps, opened the door against a gust of damp cold wind, and peeked outside. Davey was leaning against the carrstone wall gasping for air.

"Are you all right? Are you going to be sick?"

"I'll be fine, darling." He put one gloved hand to his chest. "Oh, but whatever will I say to Mother? I'm *so* embarrassed."

"Don't be silly. It's a mistake anyone could make." As I said it, I didn't believe it. The Queen having a snooze backstage at Dersingham village hall was too impossible. But I suppose in Davey's condition . . .

"You're sure you're all right? You haven't a coat on."

"I'll be fine, really." He waved me away with his hand. "Just leave me be a moment. I need the air."

"If you're sure. Did you let that dog in, by the way?"

"Darted right past me."

I closed the door and made my way up the few steps. I could hear the others moving back down into the hall.

"Come along, Margo," I heard the Queen say. From behind a cardboard tree I could see HM's back disappear from view, Nigel and Eric following her with Jenkyns bringing up the rear, restraining the frenzied dog by its collar. I was about to step forward into the penumbra of light but something about Princess Margaret made me hold back. She seemed to be hesitating and then, to my astonishment, just as Jenkyns's back was fully turned, she did something I would never have expected, something that sent my jaw Argentina way: With one deft movement, Her Royal Highness whisked the tiara from its resting place on the dead woman's head and enfolded it in her jacket.

I HAD ARRANGED to have dinner with my father that evening at the Feathers Hotel in Dersingham where he had booked a room for the duration of his stay. Given the weather—since the morning the rain had become, if anything, worse—and given the hour of the day—the sun had well and truly set by four-thirty, leaving the countryside beyond the perimeter wall of Sandringham's private grounds in utter blackness—the half-mile walk from the Big House did not promise to be a pleasant one. But then, it rarely was. Quite often a few of us struggled down the road and round down the hill to the Feathers in the evening, the wind billowing our coats, the rain slapping against our cheeks, one of us with a torch guiding us the first half of the journey until the feeble street lamps along Manor Road marked the way into the town. You had to dress wisely and I did. In my Mountain Equipment Co-op jacket over a fleece and with my Docs on my feet, I was able to trudge through the countryside without too much discomfort. Indeed, there were occasions—rare—when I almost thought I could get used to it.

Besides, the walk was an opportunity for a think. Witnessing Her Royal Highness whisk that tiara off the head of the deceased woman had left me a little perplexed. Her action wasn't quite the same as rooting around in the pockets of a dead man for his wallet. The tiara was only a bit of costume jewellery, after all, and it was perched within easy reach, so her taking it was hardly a major act of looting. But taking it at all did seem out of character. I tried to rationalize the act: HRH knew the costumer who rented the jewellery. (Far-fetched) Or, the tiara was actually *hers*, a paste copy. (This had a pinch of logic, given the identity of the deceased). Or, more likely—and this was the reason I settled on— HRH was so ticked off by the sight of this mockery of her sister, she angrily snatched away the offending article. When those of us who had found the body behind the curtain were briefly questioned by the Dersingham branch of the Norfolk Constabulary, I had dreaded being asked about the tiara. I didn't fancy saying, 'Oh, Princess Margaret took it.' Fortunately, the tiara never came up, although later I was to think that rather odd.

The reason I say there was a pinch of logic behind the tiara belonging to HRH lay in the deceased's connection to Staff at Sandringham House. It turns out the woman we'd found lying so peacefully on the gilded litter onstage at the Dersingham village hall was Jackie Scaife, the younger sister of Aileen Benefer, the resident Housekeeper at the Big House. It was, I think, why the dead woman's face had seemed familiar even under the makeup and royal paraphernalia. There was a certain family resemblance: Both sisters had faces broad and full at the cheek narrowing to a chin that was somehow just a Valentine's Day away from being heart-shaped. Jackie's features were the more delicate, however. She was—had been—the prettier. That, even the regal getup couldn't disguise.

It was a bit of a shock, to say the least, and I felt terribly sorry for Mrs. Benefer, who is pleasant enough to work under most times, though she does tend to be a bit overanxious and pinched in manner. Since Mrs. B. had been taken away to identify her sister and begin the other inevitable duties that attend a death in the family, there was no opportunity to express condolences.

But, of course, there was the usual buzz below stairs in the wake of this tragedy. Jackie Scaife, it was said, had been gone ever so long in America and wasn't it strange that she'd come back after all these years and then not do much of anything except this silly panto, living with Aileen and Tom, her sister's husband, in one of the gamekeepers' cottages on the Estate where of course it hasn't been all beer and skittles—terrible rows lately, don't-you-know—but, well, it's Christmas and all that peace and good will always put people in a temper, and did you ever clap eyes on her? Oh, of course you didn't, you poor dear. I saw her in Sainsbury's in Lynn, tramping about in this astonishing fur coat like a Hollywood starlet who didn't get the part but got the prize, if-you-know-what-I-mean. And someone else was telling me they saw her sitting in the Feathers pub cadging drinks from everyone, well, she was like that as a teenager she was, always wanted the fast life, ambitious sort of girl, not in quite the proper way; well, it just goes to show, oh yes . . . and so the talk went.

But the farther I walked from the Big House and the closer I got to Dersingham, the more my thoughts turned to my father. It wasn't that I wasn't happy to see him. I was. I hadn't clapped eyes on anybody from my family in ages, and Christmas with him at Aunt Grace's had been really very nice, on the whole. Because he hadn't seen Grace since he and my mother honeymooned in England nearly thirty years before, and because he was seeing me for the first time in over two years, the conversation seemed to jump like electricity between the two poles, then and now, while certain events in between received only brief notice. After the turkey and before Grace lit the plum pudding, I told him about my adventure helping solve the murder of a footman at Buckingham Palace the year before. I knew that he, being a Royal Canadian Mounted Police officer and, well, being my dad, would never blab the details to anyone if I made him promise. Unfortunately, he didn't believe me, especially when I told him of the Queen's involvement. "You've always had a great imagination, Bird," he said, tucking into the pudding, having resuscitated the unenviable family nickname for me. Aunt Grace backed me up, but my father's response was of the yeah-and-I-saw-Elvis-at-Burger-King variety.

It was, I suppose, the beginning of a certain strain that was to follow. At Grace's on the Christmas weekend there had been other people about—some farther-flung members of the extended Bee family, friends, neighbours, and the like—but once we squeezed into Dad's rental car at Long Marsham, hit the M25 en route to Sandringham and found ourselves alone together, certain inevitabilities crept into the conversation. Topic A, not in the form of a question: 'Why aren't you back home, in school.' It was difficult to get across to my father that the world he knew, the world of JFLs (Jobs for Life), was over. I could slog my guts out in halls of higher learning and find myself at the end with a sheepskin in one hand, yeah, but a dustcloth just as likely in the other. I wasn't ruling school out, but I didn't know what I wanted to do, or be, and I couldn't see the value of taking an arts degree and landing $25,000 in debt. And I didn't want to go back to Prince Edward Island, an island with fewer souls than an average London borough. I liked life in the big city, I argued. I had good mates inside the Palace: It was like a little village with its own social clubs and sports teams. And I had good mates outside the Palace, too. So what if I was a skivvy? I wasn't going to change Her Majesty's bed linen and dust Her Majesty's china for the rest of my life, for heaven's sake. I was shouting by this point. The weather all weekend had been unusually dry, the Boxing Day traffic light on the eight lanes of the M25, and my father, growing comfortable with driving on the wrong (left) side of the road, was picking up speed as he headed toward the M11, the main route to Cambridge and the northeast. The wind whistled past the car windows and the tires on the pavement kept up a dull roar that discouraged conversation.

My father was silent for a time, as he is apt to be anyway. He doesn't shout. He's always *reasonable,* gratingly so sometimes. I thought about what I couldn't really explain to him, he whose life had been so straight-arrow, who had left school, gone straight into police training school in Regina, Saskatchewan, then into a series of predictable postings with the RCMP, methodically rising through the hierarchy. I couldn't tell him that what I savoured about London was the promise and the unpredictability—the role that chance could play in your life, the endless permutations and combinations arising from living among eight million people in a cosmopolitan, multicultural, multilingual city, the possibility of some weird and wonderful thing happening to you out of the blue. Yes, I spent a lot of each day skivvying, but the work wasn't hard; there was adequate free time, and I always felt something exciting was just around the corner.

At last, after we got onto the slower A10 past Cambridge heading for Ely, my father broke his silence. "Anyway," he said, trying to make it sound lighthearted, which was interesting, "I hope you're not staying away because of what's happened between your mother and me."

Ah, Topic B. I sighed inwardly. No, I told myself, that's nothing to do with it; besides, I'm not 'staying away.'

"No," I said out loud to my father. I must have sounded a little defensive because he took his eyes off the road for a moment—we were tailgating a removals van—and gave me one of his cool, reasonable police-type stares. "You're sure?"

"Of course I'm sure." In truth, I did feel a strange pang of guilt. I knew my parents' breakup was not my fault. And yet I couldn't help but regard the sequence of events—my leaving for Europe and their separating—as meaningful. I was the last to fly the nest. Jennifer, my oldest sister, had left years ago to study science, then medicine, in Halifax, Nova Scotia. Julie, daughter number 2, married Mr. PotatoHead and moved to PotatoHead Acres on the Island. Had my departure coincided with some bad patch the aged parents, Steve and Ann, had been going through? Had I stayed, might they have stayed? Together, that is?

Truth is, I hadn't paid a huge lot of attention to them during my last year at home. I had been going to university and working part-time at various McJobs and going out with my friends so that home was almost more of a pit-stop than anything, a place to catch up on sleep and do the laundry. But, I suppose, if I thought about it—and I *had* thought about it since they had announced their separation not long after I had left for Europe on the Grand Tour that led, ultimately, to Buck House— my parents had seemed to be growing apart in recent years. Of course, with parents, you can never quite understand what the attraction was in the first place; it's hard to imagine them your own age. But when I think, for instance, about their jobs—his with the RCMP, hers with the Charlottetown *Guardian*—and move backwards through time, I can see where the seeds of doom might have been planted. A cop and a newspaperwoman are not seeing the world through the same lens. I remember certain dinner-table disagreements and think now, as I only half wondered then, that they were really arguing about something else.

"Perhaps," I said to my father, "I should ask you more or less the same thing: Was my leaving home the . . . what's the word? . . . catalyst?"

"Bird, we were well down that road anyway. The answer is no."

"But would you have split, or what I mean is, *could* you have split when I was thirteen or fourteen? Did you want to, but only hung on because of us kids? That's what Julie thinks. If she isn't giving me a dissertation about my nephew, she's giving me a blow-by-blow of you guys, Mom and you."

"Brendan's a great kid. You should go home for a visit."

"I get a picture with every letter. You didn't answer my question."

"We weren't miserable. This isn't an acrimonious separation. We just . . . grew apart."

"Funny that you're in the house."

"Why 'funny'?"

"Just—I don't know—fathers usually move out. That's what happened with all my friends whose parents split."

"Your mother wanted the change."

"She hasn't got, like, a toy boy, has she?" It was startling to even think of.

"No." He laughed.

"And you, Dad? Have you got what they call around here a 'fancy woman'?"

". . . No."

Slight hesitation, I thought, or was I being hypersensitive? Oh, well, hell, I thought, it's their lives. I'm here. They're there. We're all adults. At least I'm not on the verge of teenagerhood, like a certain young prince I could think of, and have to read about my parents' acrimonious relationship in the papers and be teased remorselessly by my mates.

Ahead the octagonal tower of Ely Cathedral, visible for miles across the flat fenland of Cambridgeshire, rose like a beacon in a grey veil of mist. The arresting beauty of the scene diverted me to a more ordinary and immediate worry: What in heck was I going to *do* with my father for a week in Norfolk in the dead of winter?

"Oh! You should visit that cathedral while you're nearby," I enthused, pointing at the windscreen toward the church, the inside of which I had never actually seen.

"It's a thought," he said noncommittally.

"There's a nice one in Norwich, too."

"Mmm."

I suppose the Bloody Freezing English Church Tour was not on, even if Norfolk had more churches per square mile than just about anywhere else in England. Stately homes open-to-view such as Holkham Hall, home of the Earls of Leicester, or Houghton Hall or

Blickling or any of the other great piles littering the countryside would all be closed for the season. I didn't think there was a whole lot to see in King's Lynn, the region's major centre. And Hunstanton, the beach town I assume would be a treat in summer, would be a misery in winter's driving rain.

"Ooh, watch it, Dad," I said suddenly.

Too late. I twisted around in my seat and saw through the back screen a pillar of feathers soar into the air.

"Oh, Jesus, that's never happened to me before," my father said, glancing into the rearview mirror and grimacing. "All my years of highway driving and I've never killed anything."

"Really, they're the stupidest birds, pheasants! You see them squashed all over roads around here. They'll flop out of a hedgerow right in front of you just when another car is coming the other way. And it's worse at night. They get mesmerized by the car beams."

Actually I'd only heard this. I had never been in a vehicle that actually hit one of the large game birds. Now I found it upsetting to be in a car that had run one over. And it was odd to be upset because the poor things were being killed in droves anyway. Even as we spoke, shooting parties in selected parts of East Anglia were out for Boxing Day with pheasants their prime target.

"It's all right, Dad," I said, noting his eyes lingering in the rearview mirror. "We forgive you."

". . . and that," I said to my father not half an hour later, "was how we found her."

We were sitting in the saloon bar at the Feathers, me warming myself next to the fireplace, each of us drinking a pint of Woodforde's Norfolk ale. It was early in the evening. We were the only ones in the room. The barman and patrons were more preoccupied with the television in the public bar next door that was blaring *Brookside,* the Merseyside soap.

"Are you okay about it, Bird? It's no pleasure to come across a dead body."

"It was a little creepy, I admit. But it's not the first. And at least I didn't know this woman the way I knew Robin," I added, referring to the footman I had found dead in Buckingham Palace the year before.

"The security work's pretty poor. Didn't someone check out the stage area?"

"I guess not."

My father folded his arms across the canary-yellow sweater Aunt Grace gave him for Christmas and shook his head. "Terrible," he pronounced.

"Well, I guess it was all done on short notice. They only discovered the lodge on Flitcham Hill had been trashed that morning so they had to make new plans quickly. Ruined the luncheon. We had to pack it all up and move back to the Big House."

"Could have been a bomb behind that curtain." He looked pensive. "The people who wrecked this lodge of the Queen's could have known the village hall here in Dersingham was the logical next choice for this lunch of theirs . . ."

"Anyone able to break into the Flitcham Hill lodge undetected could just as easily have left something like a bomb there, too."

"True." My father gave me an appraising sort of look. Then he smiled. "Very good."

"And it's not the first time security have dropped a brick, or even the worst screw-up," I continued. "Remember that incident years ago? I was just a kid then but I remember Gran clucking about it. The one where some guy found his way into the Queen's bedroom at Buckingham Palace? There've been others. Nothing quite as bad . . . well, nearly as bad . . ."

"Like your episode last year with the footman?"

"Yes," I sighed, noting the touch of skepticism in his voice.

"Who exactly was the 'we' who discovered the deceased, Jackie Scaife, in the village hall?"

"Davey Pye, as I said. Nigel Stokoe. He's another footman. Eric Twist, who works in the Sandringham kitchens. Paul Jenkyns, the Queen's new Personal Protection Officer and . . ." I shifted uncomfortably in my chair and added quickly the detail I had avoided in my earlier telling, "The Queen and Princess Margaret were there, too. They happened to come at the very moment Davey sort of lost his head."

"I see." My father took a slow draught of his ale. "Pretty strange, this woman being dressed up as the Queen."

"How did you know?" I exclaimed. "I hadn't got to that part yet."

"Your old dad's no slouch." He grinned over the top of his glass. "As it happens, I met the director or producer or whatever he is of this show they were doing at the village hall."

"Pantomime."

"Right."

"Where did you meet him?"

"Here." He took another sip. "We're the only guests. Name's Pryce. I talked with him briefly after dinner . . ."

"Upset, I'll bet. Back at the Big House, they said Jackie was one of the leads."

"No, he didn't seem upset. Anyway, he said he'd be back down from his room, so you'll probably meet him. Likes to talk. I think he's bored stiff being here."

A sudden pang of guilt went through me.

"So," I said, running my finger idly over the top of my glass, "what did you do today?"

"Walked."

"Dad, it's awful out. It's been pouring since early this morning."

He shrugged. "It's no worse than the Island some days. Look, Bird, I know you're worried there's nothing for me to do around here . . ."

"But . . ."

"I'll be fine. I walked in the Country Park, whatever it is, that part of the Estate open to the public all year 'round at Sandringham. And I think I'll get some binoculars. They say there's some good bird-watching in Norfolk."

I studied my father as he contemplated his half-empty glass. Bird-watching? In the winter? Ugh. And what an un-Dad thing to do! My father's previous interest in birds ran more to domestic varieties plucked and roasted in a hot oven.

"It's never too late to start a new hobby," he declared as my mouth opened to voice an opinion. "Oh, and here's Hume Pryce. Join us," he called across the room with what sounded like a measure of relief in his voice.

Hume Pryce did not look the sort of man my father would normally leap to engage in conversation with. I say this because of the hair, which was flax-coloured, kempt, and luxuriously long. My father has a thing about men's hair. If it isn't short-back-and-sides like his (or what's left of his), then he becomes immediately suspicious of motives, morals, lifestyle, and a whole range of phenomena. He denies this, of course. But all the sensitivity courses they've had to take at the RCMP have not changed him; they've merely obliged him to keep his opinions to himself. This time, however, there wasn't even that barely perceptible narrowing of the eyes that used to occur when I brought certain boys with unsuitable haircuts home.

Pryce did a thumbs-up gesture and then, eyebrows raised, did a little circular movement with his index finger to ask if we wanted another round.

"Just a half for me, ta very much," I said. I didn't fancy a squat in the dank and dark Dersingham woods on the way back to the Big House.

A moment later he had joined us with drinks.

"My daughter Jane," my father said by way of introduction. "Hume Pryce."

"Your father tells me you work at Sandringham." He arranged the three glasses in front of us on the tiny table and sat down. "He didn't say what you do."

"I'm a housemaid. A skivvy."

"How interesting." This is what nearly everybody says, either because they can't think of anything more *un*interesting or because they think I'm a fount of gossip about the Royal Family only too happy to be primed and pumped. Hume Pryce was a little different, however.

"It's the ugliest house, isn't it?" he said cheerfully,

beaming at me behind a pair of oval-shaped glasses. "It reminds me of a grandiose Victorian seaside hotel. Or a railway station, like St. Pancras Station, only with a rather nice garden in front. And the inside—hoo!—like a set for *Charlie's Aunt*.

"Do you clean in the dining room? I was invited to some drinky-do at Sandringham one summer some years back with Prince Charles—no, really, it was nothing important, some Prince's Trust thing of his; there were dozens of people there—and we went into the dining room and I couldn't believe it! It was green, and not just green, but the sort of green you'd find in a kitchen in a council estate in the 1930s. The sideboard, pilasters, wainscotting, all of it I'm sure of walnut or some rich dark hardwood painted the most unattractive shade of *green*. Appalling! But the Royal Family are a bit, well, vulgar, I suppose."

I bristled a little. One does become somewhat attached to one's employers.

"And how," he continued without pause, "did a Canadian come to work at Sandringham?"

"At Buckingham Palace, really. They just cart us around to whatever home the Queen happens to be staying in." And I proceeded to tell him how I had come to Europe to do the Grand Tour, ran out of money faster than expected, answered an advert for live-in domestic work in one of the London papers, then—total surprise—received a reply from the Lord Chamberlain's office in Buckingham Palace and ended up as a housemaid in Her Majesty's service.

"Ah," he said, "a youthful adventure. I remember hitch-hiking virtually around the world when I was your age, working in a kibbutz in Israel, staying in an ashram in Katmandu, a sheep station in Australia, and so on. Wonderful days! I think it's just the best thing to do with your time when you're your age."

"See," I said to my father, who was holding his own counsel behind his glass of ale. "My dad," I said, focusing my attention on Pryce, "thinks I should be back in Canada knuckling down to the study of something gruesome like computer engineering or nuclear biophysics . . . or, worse, home ecology so I can be a better catch for some man."

Pryce glanced at my father. "Well, I suppose it is a colder world out there."

"See," my father retorted.

"Apparently I've landed myself in the middle of some family contretemps," Pryce murmured diplomatically. "Well, it's true there aren't the opportunities there used to be. For instance, I read classics at Cambridge in the early 'seventies and there was evidence even then— if I had chosen to look at it, *stare* at it, perhaps—that the ability to read Plato in the original Greek had little currency in the so-called real world. On the other hand, I'm inclined to think you should do what feels right to you and then see what happens. Things may turn out quite marvellously." He blinked at us tentatively over the rim of his glass. "I'm not being helpful, am I?"

"I take it, then, that the study of classics didn't land you a job in the theatre," my father said, frowning slightly.

"Oh, no. I only dabble in theatre. I was once a tiny bulb in the Cambridge Footlights. An avocation, I suppose, I do wish they'd lower the volume on that television!" He glanced through to the public bar as the goggle box burst again into canned laughter.

"And what is your vocation?"

"I don't really have one. I'm rich. Well, rich-ish." He laughed. "I'm what they call in this country a 'Trustifarian.' You see, my great-grandfather invented a very clever device to package tobacco that saved all kinds of labour costs and he became enormously wealthy. He set up trust funds for his family and so . . ."

"You dabble," I supplied.

"Dabble I do. Trustifarians are regarded as aging hippies wandering around aimlessly through life on the cushion of a healthy bank balance. Well, aging hippie I may be, but I'm not aimless in my pursuits. I keep busy. I have all kinds of interests, theatre being one of them. And I'm very grateful to my clever great-grandfather who made all this possible." He smiled broadly. He had a square face with features so firm and angular, his skin seemed to be stretched taut, except for the eyes where a web of fine lines gathered behind his spectacles.

"Of course," Pryce continued, the smile fading a kilowatt or two, "I don't always make the wisest decisions. Coming here, for instance, putting on a panto. And now, as I was telling your father earlier, my star's gone and made her final exit."

My father glanced at me. "Jane was among those who found her," he said.

"Really! But how . . . ? Oh, the shooting luncheon, of course." Pryce paused, a look of dismay settling along his features. There was a burst of laughter from the public bar. *Brookside* over, the television had been switched over to what sounded like a Fry & Laurie comedy special.

"I just don't understand it," Pryce continued. "It makes one feel awfully vulnerable. Jackie wasn't that much younger than I am. Couldn't be much more than thirty-five. One of those embolism things, I suppose. Or a heart attack? Stroke . . . ?"

"I guess," I said. I kept thinking how placid she appeared in death.

"She looked fine when I last saw her," he said. "Very cheerful, in fact. Oddly cheerful, when I think about it. Given the reaction to the performance, I mean," he added, noting our quizzical expressions. "Well, the response was a bit cool. The kids loved it, of course. But some of their parents . . . oh, dear. Nobody said anything, mind you, but the applause was tepid from the older folk. No encores."

"Probably impersonating the Queen didn't help."

"Yes, I suppose it wasn't quite the best tack to take in these parts but . . . have either of you seen a panto? Ah, well, as Jane will know, there are always bits of topical humour, rather mild stuff, harmless fun usually. I thought after the last few years of scandal about the Royal Family no one would be bothered by a bit of parody. As it happens, I had more or less settled on doing the *Queen of Hearts*, which rather lends itself to incorporating bits of the Chuck 'n' Di saga and such. But it really came together when Jackie showed up.

"Jackie was a marvel really," he continued. "She was about the Queen's size, or height at least. Slimmer, of course. Quite delicate. Although, I suppose the Queen was slimmer when she was young. Well, weren't we all?" He eyed my father's bulk. "But it wasn't that. With the right wig, a tiara, and a little makeup, many women—many *men*, for that matter—can do a passable impression of the Queen. But what Jackie had . . . well, she had two excellent physical attributes—the eyes, *those eyes*, the same startling blue as the Queen's, and she had the voice. People I've heard 'do' the Queen so often make her sound like a . . ." He faltered.

"Like a small animal being gelded," I offered. "High-pitched shrieking and so on."

"Quite," Pryce said gratefully. "Nature didn't endow Her Majesty with a lovely voice—it's light and it's high—but so many impersonators go over the top with it. Jackie could do a devastatingly funny impression but it was all the funnier because it was so much like the real thing. And she could do all the mannerisms, too—the wave, the po-face. Wonderful! Perfected it while she was in America, she told me. Sort of a part-time thing, opening shopping centres and business conventions and the like." Pryce paused. "I'm quite relieved the Queen—the real Queen—never came to a performance. Jackie was so good I was dreading Her Majesty showing up with her grandchildren in tow."

"You invited the *Queen*?" I asked, agog.

Pryce grimaced. "Well, we couldn't very well *not*, being that Sandringham's just down the road. And I didn't think she really would come. But, just in case, I sent the invitation deliberately late so that it arrived at Buck House last week at the same time Her Majesty was decamping here. I had a call Friday from one of the ladies-in-waiting thanking me on the Queen's behalf but declining the invitation. Rather a relief."

"Will you be able to replace this Scaife woman?" my father asked.

"No." Pryce pulled his flax-coloured hair back with one hand and gave it a little shake to settle it. "This was just a little amateur production. There were

no understudies. We were only going to do another two
performances, one tomorrow and the final one on Friday,
but I suppose they will be cancelled now. Just as well, I
guess. As I said, the reaction was decidedly cool. *Lèse-
majesté* doesn't go down well in these parts, I'm afraid.
Besides, my ladyfriend is in the Caribbean, where I normally am this time of year, so I should be able to get an
earlier flight."

"Oooh," I sighed, my mind filled with travel-
brochure images of white sand, azure sea, and hot, hot
sun. "Wouldn't it be wonderful to be in the Caribbean,
this time of year? Just think, Dad, you could have spent
Christmas on some tropical island with—"

"I came to see you, Bird. I don't care about the
weather." He sounded a little surprised and miffed.

Pryce looked sharply from me to my father.

"I have to admit I find the Norfolk winter relentlessly awful, or awfully relentless," he said. "One or the
o' er. I'd forgotten how bitterly cold it can be closer to
the sea. My fault. I should have thought about it when
Pamela induced me to accept this . . . assignment, I
guess you could call it."

"Not Pamela, Marchioness of Thring?" I said, surprised.

"The very one. Ensconced at Sandringham by
now, I suppose, is she? Dear Pamela. A *very* persuasive
woman. I was involved last summer organizing some
theatre performances for the King's Lynn Festival and I
ran into her ladyship, who seemed to have a sudden
yearning for pantomime. Pamela couldn't understand
why pantos mightn't as easily be staged in summer, but
I had to point out to her that they're distinctly an English *Christmas* tradition. I don't know why. They just
are. They wouldn't do in summer at all. She was quite
earnest but, well, Americans never seem to get it quite
right, do they? I hope you don't mind my saying so."

"That's all right. We're Canadians," I said, feeling
as I often do that the English, along with the rest of the
world, hadn't a clue about Canadians.

"Just so. Anyway, she thought a panto in her part
of the world would be a good idea—they had moved out

of Anmer Hall, I think, and were still renovating Barsham Hall, but she was quite keen to maintain her influence in the community. I thought doing a panto would be rather jolly. I loved them as a child and they've been making a comeback of late in places outside London. But, of course, what I didn't think about was being in Norfolk in December. Helen did—that's my ladyfriend—and she went off to Nevis without me. But I had committed myself." He laughed. "Turned into a bit of a debacle, didn't it?"

"Did her ladyship mind the satire of the Royal Family?" I was curious because the downstairs crowd was undecided about the Marchioness's motives. Did Lady Thring involve herself in west Norfolk life to ingratiate herself with the Queen, who owned a significant chunk of the territory? Or did she involve herself to try and outdo the Queen? Either way, the Marchioness was thought to have overstepped her bounds on occasion. Her Majesty was the real guv'nor on the Estate and didn't take kindly to effrontery, though usually she just ground her teeth and said nothing, in this case particularly because Lord Thring was such an old friend.

"I don't really know," Pryce replied to my question. "After Pamela initiated the idea, wrote a very nice cheque, and did a little preliminary organizing, I never saw her again. Until last night, of course. Showed up to play Lady Bountiful, although only at the last minute, really. I had to telephone her last week to remind her to come. We'd arranged the proceeds to go to BERT—the British Epilepsy Research Trust—and she's their patron. Her husband was with her, and their son. Or *her* son, as it happens. He threw a fit, the son. Ironic, when you think about it."

"Really?" I was intrigued. "I wouldn't have credited Bucky with the intelligence to be that critical of a theatre performance."

"No, no. He threw a fit. A *fit* fit. What's the word I'm groping for? A seizure. He's an epileptic, apparently. It's the reason why Pamela's involved in the Trust. Or one of the reasons."

"You're kidding?" I felt bad for my mean-spirited

comment and worse for always thinking so ill of Bucky Walsh.

"It happened near the end of the first act. We had to stop everything—it's not a very large hall, and it caused quite a commotion—and we were able to move him into one of the side rooms . . . um, yes?"

Mr. Temple, who runs the Feathers with his wife, was signalling madly to Hume from the doorwell.

"Telephone for you, Mr. Pryce. In my office."

"Helen, probably," he said, rising. "I tried to get her earlier today to tell her I might be able to get a flight out in the next day or two. Excuse me."

My eyes must have followed Hume Pryce in a provocative way for my father said, left eyebrow at two o'clock: "What are you thinking about?"

"I was just wondering if he uses a special conditioner, that's all."

"A special what?"

"Hair, Dad," I replied, gloomily examining my split ends in the light from the fire. "It's not fair."

"No, I guess it isn't."

"Oh, poor Papa," I laughed as my father patted his pate. In the two years since I'd last seen him, his forehead seemed to have grown larger. "Anyway, I suppose I should think about getting back to the Big House. I have to be up at seven. There's rugs to hoover and beds to make . . ."

"I'll drive you."

"Oh, no. I'll walk."

But Pryce was back in the room before you could say Vidal Sassoon, his earlier look of anticipation faded to one of concern and disappointment.

"Well," he said, hovering over our little table, "it looks as though I won't be going to Nevis immediately. Jackie Scaife isn't just simply dead." He paused, his eyes staring over us through the mullioned window to the darkened garden beyond. Howls of electronic laughter erupted from the public bar. "It seems, of all things, she's been murdered."

I gasped. My father levelled his gaze at me. "No arguments, Bird, I'm *driving* you back to Sandringham."

3

"But," I said to my father as we turned out of the Feathers's parking lot a little while later in his rental car, "except for a smudge on her cheek, she didn't *look* like she had been anything like murdered."

"Meaning . . . ?"

"She looked peaceful; no, not peaceful so much. Composed, maybe, as if she had lain down to think about something and then just slipped quietly away."

"Bird, it's only in novels that murder victims die with expressions of horror frozen onto their features. Even the faces of those who have been brutally murdered settle into a kind of composure."

"Really?" I looked out the rain-spattered window. My father slowed the Vauxhall as he turned and began the gentle climb to Sandringham. Leafless tree branches flared in the headlights like patterns of veins.

"And there wasn't any blood, not that I could see. Nor any wounds. Of course, the makeup she was wearing probably disguised . . . Well, anyway, when I found Robin," I continued, referring to the footman I had found deceased in a Buckingham Palace corridor, "his face had this strange paleness, like nothing I had ever seen before . . ."

"No, the colour is never altogether the same as someone who has passed out, or who's sick."

"Robin's death was awful. This is just . . . *strange.*"

"What about her hands? After time, the lividity sets in. Hands may look very pale but the tips of the fingers will be noticeably discoloured, a reddish-purple usually."

"Let me think— Just a slight left turn here, Dad." The Norwich Gates, with their ironwork flowers and leaves, loomed ahead, but the Norwich Gates, given as a wedding present to the Prince and Princess of Wales in the 1860s, are rarely ever opened. "Her hands were resting on her stomach, her elbows on the litter. But I don't really remember if . . . well, I think the coatsleeves covered most of her hands. Anyway, we were too distracted by her appearance in other ways. I told you about Davey going white at the gills but the scene really was . . . eerie. Poor Queen. I mean, it's not as if she doesn't see her image all over the place—on stamps, on money, in the papers and whatnot—but to come into a small room and see, well, see yourself *dead* must be really frightening."

"Did she look frightened?"

"No. You know the Queen. Well, you don't, but you know what I mean. She doesn't exactly wear her emotions on her sleeve in public. Oh, stop here."

We had followed the road around the high brick-and-stone wall surrounding the grounds and stopped at the Jubilee Gates just past the Sandringham Museum, which contains the Royal Family's collection of big-game trophies, vintage cars, and displays of gifts—china and such—that HM gets with regularity from various nobs.

"Why don't I phone you around noon tomorrow," I suggested. "Will you be at the Feathers?"

"If I'm out I'll be back for lunch. There's not many places for lunch around here."

"Too bad you can't join us in Servants' Hall. On the other hand, you probably wouldn't want to. Anyway . . ." I leaned over and gave my father a daughterly peck. "Probably see you tomorrow."

"Put your hood up."

I stepped into the rain and waved the car off before presenting my Staff pass to plastic-mac-swathed PC Brian Nesbitt, who gave it and me a cheery smile.

"Wet as fish," he said as I moved past. "Supposed to be clearer tomorrow."

"Bet it isn't," I called back.

"You're on."

Far down the path, above the thorny crowns of the denuded oak trees and the sombre marshallings of pine, I could see the darkened gables and towers of Sandringham House, its eccentric outline silvered by security lights beyond. The wind pushed and snapped at the giant rhododendron bushes and sent the last uncollected autumn leaves skittering across the rain-soaked lawns. The Queen's father, George VI, had died here at Sandringham, I recalled Davey telling me as I quickened my step. It might have been on a night such as this, a winter night, cold and wet. A watchman had seen him fiddling with the latch on his bedroom window on the north side of the house at about midnight. In the morning he was found dead by his valet. The Queen's grandfather, George V, had died at Sandringham, too, on a winter night. I shivered in the cold and once again thought of Her Majesty and the body backstage at Dersingham hall. No, the Queen hadn't looked frightened. I really couldn't imagine her frightened. She had said little, of course; she had been a little short with Eric Twist about Jeannette Charles (whoever she was). But, just for a moment, there had surely been a fleeting expression of shock and dismay, as if she was being granted a . . .

But, no, I thought, oddly grateful to be at last in a

pool of warm light at the Staff entrance, I was letting my imagination run away with me.

I had trouble getting to sleep. First, Heather MacCrimmon who rooms next to me wanted a bit of a natter since, of course, the news of the murder had spread swiftly through the corridors, upstairs and down, of the Big House that evening. Then, lights out, uncharacteristically distracted by the wind roaring and whistling down the Elizabethan chimneys, I found my mind returning to the conversation with Hume Pryce in the Feathers.

"Do they know who did it?" I had asked Pryce after he had given my father and me the startling news that Jackie Scaife had been murdered.

Pryce seemed to look through me. "Um." He blinked. "Um . . . no. Or at least they didn't say."

"Who was on the phone?" my father asked.

"The police, actually. The local branch of the Norfolk Constabulary. They want me to 'help them with their inquiries,' as the sergeant put it. I thought the police only used that expression on telly." He laughed weakly. "Sounds ominous when you hear it said to you."

My father regarded him speculatively. "When are you supposed to give them this 'help'?"

"I'm supposed to go around tomorrow."

"Then I wouldn't worry. If they needed your . . . help more urgently, they would probably be here right now."

Pryce caught my father's eye. "Before I do a bunk, you mean?"

"Presuming you were guilty of something, and they knew you were guilty, and you knew they knew."

"Well, then," Pryce said, resuming his seat. "I have nothing to worry about." He released a sigh and smiled broadly. "Another round?"

"I think my daughter has to be getting back."

"You have one, Dad. I could sit for a bit." As I said this I felt guilty for appearing anxious to leave one minute and keen to stay the next, as if the old man's company wasn't completely appreciated.

"Okay," he said reluctantly, "but maybe just half. I have to drive." He edged out of his seat. "My shout, I think the expression is."

"Get a packet of crisps, would you, Dad? Bovril-flavoured, if they've got it."

"Bovril-flavoured!"

"And could you ask them to turn down that bloody television?" Hume added. "Thank you."

While my father was collecting drinks and etceteras at the bar, I asked Pryce whether he thought there was anybody who would want to murder Jackie Scaife, anybody among the pantomime actors, say.

"No," he replied, shaking his head adamantly. "We were rather a merry band. Most of the principals are people I've known for ages in Cambridge, amateurs all—decent actors, though. They'd drive up for rehearsals and such. The few locals who turned out to participate in the panto fit in quite well, and didn't seem to mind when the production began to take a turn toward satirizing the Royals. Everyone got along. There was none of the unpleasantness I've witnessed with other troupes. Everyone knew it was just a lark, anyway. There were no galloping egos and fragile personalities. Well, except for Jackie."

"Oh . . . ?"

"No, no, I mean Jackie was the exception because she was a class above amateur. 'Semiprofessional,' I guess you could say, although I guess you could really only extend that designation to her ability to impersonate the Queen. I don't think she did any other performances. I assume her ego was healthy enough." He paused in thought, then sighed. "I'm sorry she's dead. She was really quite vivacious. Had a certain . . . spark about her. Didn't give a tinker's what other people thought. Wearing that outrageous fur coat for example . . . oh!"

The glasses of ale my father placed on the table would certainly be attractive to the thirsty imbiber but I wasn't sure they rated Pryce's exclamation.

"Oh, what?" I inquired, shifting slightly to accommodate my father's poundage, noting he had brought back boring old plain crisps and the volume of the television next door had been lowered a notch.

"I just remembered something. The letter. She showed me this letter she had received. It was quite ludicrous, or at least it seemed so at the time. Rather like something in an old film, you know, letters cut out from magazines and pasted on a piece of paper saying— oh, I can't remember exactly what, but the gist of it was something like, 'we'll get you, you dirty rat.' Along those lines . . ."

"But why would . . . ?" I struggled with the top of the crisp packet.

"Not 'you dirty rat.' Sorry, I seem to have gone into a Jimmy Cagney impersonation. More like, 'you animal murderer.' It was signed the A.R.F."

"Oooh." I sucked in my breath. "The Animal Rights Front. Not exactly a ladies' sewing circle."

"Yes. Quite."

"They're apparently behind the trashing of the Queen's lodge over at Flitcham Hill last night. And while another group has already claimed responsibility, I gather last month Prince Charles was sent some booby-trapped parcel with razor blades all over it after the papers featured Wills and Harry at a fox hunt in Gloucestershire."

Pryce grimaced, whether at the assault on the Wales boys or the hurricane of crisps I'd inadvertently released on the table, I didn't know. "I said at the time she really should take the letter to the police," he continued, adding mournfully: "But Jackie just laughed it off. I should have been more insistent."

My father lifted a crisp from the pile. "Why— presuming these animal-rights terrorists are behind this murder—would they target this Jackie Scaife if their usual habit is to target high-profile types like members of the Royal Family?"

"I'm not sure that is their habit," I countered. "I think they get up to all kinds of things: 'sabbing'—sabotaging—hunts, and raiding animal research centres, attacking meat-packing plants and so on. I remember reading about a bunch of shopkeepers somewhere in England who got threatening letters just because they happened to advertise a circus."

"But all this woman was doing was wearing a fur coat!"

"Dad, you don't see much fur worn in England, even among the gaudy rich. I don't think I've ever seen anyone in a fur coat in London, not that I'm invited to a lot of gala premieres or anything."

"It's true," Pryce added, snapping a crisp in two. "The animal-rights lobby has been rather effective. I've a fabulous leather coat I bought in America that I've stopped wearing because I'm never sure if it won't provoke someone on the street. And it's only leather, not fur. I'm certainly eating less meat these days, too. I've even got one of Linda-bloody-McCartney's vegetarian cookbooks. I deplore the tactics of these ARF people, but what some of the anti's do go on about does make you think. Still, if they're behind this . . ."

He paused in thought. "Jackie had had a letter printed in the King's Lynn paper about all this. I wonder . . . ? You see, there'd been a feature about animal rights, pro and con, and Jackie had decided to add her two-pence-worth. They're country folk around here and so most of them have little sympathy with the anti's, but I think Jackie had been getting a comment or two about her coat nevertheless and so she decided a get-knotted gesture through the newspaper was the order of the day. Not wise, in retrospect, I suppose."

"Like waving a red flag."

"Mmmm. And of course her name was on the posters for the panto dotted around the community."

"And this coat . . ."

"It was something, I must say. Not just some bit of mousy brown mink. Lynx, I think it was. Or fox. Something like that. I don't know fur. But it shimmered, silvery-white. A gift from an American admirer, as she put it. Wink wink, nudge nudge. *Her* winks and nudges, by the way. I happened to run into her one morning at a cashpoint in Lynn practically smothered in the thing and heads just swivelled. It was really too warm to be wearing fur in the fall—and awful, I should think, in the dreadful rain we get here—but she looked to be enjoying the effect enormously. Seemed to cheer her up anyway that morning."

"Did she wear the coat to the village hall for last night's performance?"

Pryce's eyes narrowed with the effort of recall. "I think so. Jackie was hardly without it. But I was rather busy."

"I wonder if the same bunch who messed up the Queen's lodge might have targeted Jackie Scaife. Or, perhaps, the other way around—Jackie first, lodge second."

"I think you're getting a little ahead of yourself, Bird," my father interrupted. "There's no evidence the two events are related."

But visions of intense terrorist-types with spray cans of paint and carpetbags full of murder weapons charging about the Norfolk countryside were filling what I'm pleased to call my brain. Which prompted me to ask Pryce: "How did she die?"

"I don't know. The police didn't say." He fingered a strand of hair that had slipped over his shoulder.

"Odd," I mused, thinking of the supine figure I had witnessed.

My father asked: "What happened after the performance? Did she stay behind? Or would she have gone back to the village hall later in the evening for some reason?"

Pryce contemplated his glass of ale for a moment. "Whether she stayed behind, I know that—she said she was meeting someone. But whether she and that someone went out somewhere, I don't know. She was still in costume when she died, so I assume she didn't go anywhere."

"Who was she meeting?" I asked.

"Didn't say."

"You didn't ask?" my father chimed in.

"I say, you two could be a Starsky and . . . Lacy or Cagney and Hutch." He regarded us benevolently.

"Well, Dad *is* a plod."

"I'm a what?"

"A plod. A copper. A police officer."

"Doesn't sound exactly complimentary."

"You said you were with the government at dinner."

"A branch of."

"Royal Canadian Mounted Police," I added helpfully.

"Oh, do you wear those red uniforms and the Boy Scout hats?"

"Now you know why I tell people I'm with government."

"Ah."

Of course, the other reason Dad prefers to dodge questions about his occupation is that people tend to come over all funny when he tells them, as if he's the figure of comeuppance finally arrived to do them in for that unpaid parking ticket or that chocolate bar nicked as a seven-year-old in a frenzy of sugarlust and self-assertion. Or worse, of course. Any or all of which is apt to put a chill into social intercourse, rather like now. Pryce didn't freeze up the way I've seen some people do, but a certain reserve had entered the atmosphere. Happens all the time.

"Well," he continued, his smile fading, "as to your question, I didn't ask Jackie who she was meeting because . . . well, I suppose it was none of my business, really. Anyway, there's always much to do after the performance. Striking the set, collecting the props. Some of the actors did their makeup and costumes at home—the facilities at the hall are minimal—but some didn't, so there was that to deal with. And so on.

"Everyone was anxious to nip down to the pub, too. Here, to the Feathers. Me included. Needed a drink. You always do, after opening night."

"When did you leave the hall?" I asked.

"Oh, five-thirtyish, I guess. It had already gone dark. The panto ended at four-thirty. Most of the audience had cleared out quickly. Needed to get their kids home and begin the evening meal, although, as I said, there was a certain *froideur* from those past the age of consent. Pamela stayed back a while, and I was expecting to chat with her, but she and her son seemed to be having a rather heated discussion about something—the boy appeared to have recovered from his seizure—and then the next time I looked, they were gone.

"Anyway, I was keen to lock up but Jackie had this appointment or whatever it was, so I left a set of keys with her."

"Doesn't the hall have a caretaker?" my father asked.

"Normally, but he had been knocked out by this 'flu bug, so I was left with the responsibility."

"Gosh," I told Pryce. "Maybe you were the last person to see her alive. Well, second-last."

"Third-last, at best, I should think."

"What do you mean?"

"Jackie had someone with her when I left. Her sister. Works on the Estate, I believe."

"Aileen Benefer. The resident Housekeeper. My boss, as it happens."

"Oh?" He regarded me with sympathy. "I don't think she was very pleased with Jackie's performance. Fairly lit into her. I hope she's not like that with you housemaids."

"No, not usually," I said, surprised.

"Anyway, I didn't feel like hanging about listening to them argue so . . ."

"You left."

"Yes," he said unapologetically, finishing the dregs in his glass. "And speaking of leaving"—he glanced at his watch—"I really should try and telephone Helen. Siesta must be over by now and she'll be thinking of going down to the beach for drinks. Will you excuse me?"

We excused him. I could hear sonorous strains announcing the late news on telly. It was time to leave.

4

Oʜ, ᴛʜᴇ ʟɪꜰᴇ of a housemaid! Early to bed (sometimes), early to rise, et cetera. Perhaps such a schedule makes one healthy. But wealthy? Ha! And wise? I'm not sure wisdom will ever be the result of a life crawling out of a warm bed before seven o'clock in the morning. Early rising I have gotten used to, after a teenagerhood of comparative sloth, or creative malingering as I like to think of it, but rising in the dark, at the darkest time of year, in the dark English countryside, does tend to make one's resolve flag a bit from time to time, as it did the next morning when my alarm went off and I found myself shaken out of a dream of peace. I must have dozed off because my next waking moment featured the alarm clock with Mickey's arms at 6:56 looming two inches from my nose, conveyed by a hand attached to a limb that seemed, to my hazy consciousness, in the dim light from the hallway outside my open door, to belong to Heather MacCrimmon.

"You're going to be late, Jane," the blurry face on the far side of the limb said with a soft Scots burr as my bedside lamp burst into sudden illumination.

"Bugger," I moaned. And then, as I flopped over in a futile act of denial, recognized a certain fuzzy yellow material that had been covering the unwelcome alarm-clock-conveying arm. "You're going to be late, too, Heather. You aren't even out of your housecoat."

"I'm not well, Jane. I must have a wee bit of this 'flu that's going around. I was wondering if you could tell Mrs. B. I'm going back to bed. That's if she's not taking bereavement."

I slid one leg out of my own bed and let my foot touch the icy floor. "You're not skiving, are you, Heather?" I whimpered, jolted by the cold into something resembling full consciousness.

Heather regarded me as dourly as her plump pink face would permit. I confess the pinkishness did appear to have gone into retreat. I relented. "Okay, I'll tell her. Will you be all right? Can I bring you something from Servants' Hall?"

A futile gesture that. I barely had time to splash a little water about my person, hop into my incredibly attractive white uniform and ever-so-alluring black flats, tie up my hair, and dash down to Mrs. Benefer's office without so much as a sip of coffee or a piece of dry toast to alert Mrs. B. to Heather's ailment and receive changes to the rota that were sure to come in the wake of the increasing number of 'flu victims.

Mrs. Benefer lives with her husband Tom, one of about a dozen gamekeepers on the Estate, in one of a pair of truly adorable little gamekeeper's cottages a couple of miles from Sandringham House, near the village of West Newton. But when Her Majesty is in residence, as she is from Christmas until the end of January, Mrs. Benefer takes up residence in the Big House in a small suite of rooms off the housekeeper's corridor on the second floor, including a small office from which she organizes the unending cleaning program and oversees the laundry and the linen rooms and decides which guests shall sleep in which bedrooms and arbitrates the inevitable crises *du jour* among her staff and so forth. A fairly demanding job on the whole which Mrs. Benefer seems to fulfil admirably, but sometimes I wonder if these periods of royal inhabitation don't take their psychic toll.

On the surface Mrs. B. appears to be a model of rectitude. She's very controlled, if a bit dour, and takes everything *terribly* seriously. She couldn't even crack a smile last year before the Royal Family trooped down to Norfolk when she caught some of us housemaids wandering around the Main Drawing Room wearing the furniture dust covers as if it were a ghosts' cocktail party. Unlike Mrs. Harbottle, the redoubtable Assistant Housekeeper at Buckingham Palace who straps on her Boadicea breastplate each morning and thrills to cracking the whip around us girls when the Court is in London, Mrs. Benefer prefers the martyr's mask, giving us such shattering looks of disappointment if we underperform we feel we've only added another board to the coffin that will eventually carry her to Sandringham churchyard. Mrs. B. is a perfectionist. And perfectionists, I think, must always find themselves thwarted by the imperfection that is life itself. This continual disparity, I'm sure, is the source of her tension. And she is never more tense (so permanent Sandringham staff tell me) than when Her Majesty is in residence. I think Mrs. Benefer believes HM has a gimlet eye out for wanton dust and will have her head on a platter garnished with vacuum cleaner hose if she sees a speck.

Still, old Aileen, as we sometimes call her (she's not really that old—early forties; she just *seems* old), manages somehow to get through the whole worrisome holiday (the Royal Family's, not hers) without popping a gasket. I was concerned, however, that the sudden death of her sister might be the straw that broke, etc. I was already fascinated by Hume Pryce's mention that Mrs. B. had 'fairly lit into' her sister after the panto. I'd never seen her manifestly angry with anybody.

At 7:15 that morning, however, in the wake of her sister's untimely death, Mrs. Benefer's usual habits appeared on the surface little changed. When I pushed through the door and stepped into the room, I found her behind her desk engaged in paperwork. Or so I thought at first. I quickly realized Mrs. B. was not reading anything pertinent to housekeeping, however; instead, it was a Bible she had before her. She was running her index finger over the text and moving her lips silently with the words, oblivious to my presence. Feeling like an intruder, I stood for a moment letting my eyes wander over the miscellany of the room: the paperwork in wire trays on either side of her desk, the reference manuals dedicated to domestic science within arm's reach on nearby shelves, the typewriter table with its old Selectrix and desk-size photocopier and the extra glass display case containing small items awaiting the conservator's attention: a leatherbound book, a vase that had been chipped by one of us housemaids (not me!) and a miniature with a damaged frame. Her office was, as usual, neat as a coffin, almost depressingly so.

" 'Let not your heart be troubled, neither let it be afraid,' " Mrs. Benefer said finally, her mouthings rising to an audible whisper. She sighed softly, carefully drew a marker of red ribbon down the page, and closed the Bible, setting it beside the great bundle of keys which was, to her, like the Lord Mayor's chain of office.

"Oh, ah, there you are, Jane," she said, looking up, and removing a pair of large pale-rimmed glasses, rather like HM's. She regarded me with pursed lips, then motioned for me to sit down opposite her.

"Oh, Mrs. Benefer," I said wretchedly, for I felt quite sorry for her at that moment. "I'm so sorry."

She nodded in receipt of the condolence, and drew her blue-ribbed cardigan tighter around her shoulders. On closer inspection, her plump pallid face did betray strain. Her grey-blue eyes were opaque and faintly red about the rims. Her hair, mouse-brown with grey streaks, shampooed-and-set in a fussy style that made her look years older, was as spruce as could be, however.

"I wasn't sure you'd be here, Mrs. Benefer, with what's happened and all."

"I'm sure I don't know what you mean, Jane."

"Well, I mean, it must be a shock," I sputtered. "I thought you'd probably be taking a few days off."

"That wouldn't do at all."

"But . . ." I tried to imagine how I'd feel if either of my sisters, Jennifer or Julie, had died so unexpectedly. Pretty incapacitated, I thought. If there was bereavement leave in our Staff agreements—and there was—I'd be taking it sure as God made little green apples for the Princess Royal's horses.

"I would be remiss in my duty if I wasn't here while Her Majesty is in residence," Mrs. B. remonstrated. The very mention of the august title seemed to stiffen her backbone. She straightened in her chair, reached for her clipboard, and cleared her throat. "You are, by the way, late, Jane."

"I'm very sorry, Mrs. Benefer." I shifted in the hard seat. "I had a poor sleep."

There was a painful silence. "So did I."

"Oh. Right. Of course. Sorry." I shrank to about the height of a Barbie doll only without the preposterous horizontal proportions. "I can imagine you did."

Mrs. B. continued consulting her clipboard.

"I mean," I babbled on, about to pile on the *gaucheries* in that relentless way you do in such moments, "I mean, it's just so . . . terribly awful, Mrs. Benefer. I don't understand. As I was saying to my father last night, she looked so peaceful, so composed, when we saw her."

Mrs. Benefer looked up, stony-faced, reminding me suddenly of her sibling in slumber. "*You* saw my sister?"

"Yes. Remember? I had to take the potatoes and the box of crystal to Dersingham, to the village hall. I was there when Davey Pye . . . well, when Davey made the discovery. We never thought for a moment about it being . . ." I gulped it out: "murder."

Sometimes curiosity overcomes any sense of the propriety I should have cultivated by my advanced age,

and besides, I was already in for a penny in the mal-
adroit sweepstakes. "How . . . ?" I persisted. "I mean,
it didn't look like she had been . . ."

Mrs. Benefer took a ragged breath. "It was a blunt
instrument, Jane."

Must have been a well-placed blow, I couldn't
help thinking, ignoring Mrs. Benefer's growing exasperation. Jackie Scaife certainly hadn't looked the way I
imagined someone hit with a blunt instrument would
look. "Did the police find it, whatever it was?"

"No." One hand sought her keys. "No, they
didn't. Or they haven't. Now, perhaps we can . . ."

"Oh, gosh. Then, do they have any idea of *who* did
it? Was it those animal-rights terrorist types after all, I
wonder?"

An alertness came over Mrs. Benefer's face.
"What?" she asked in a strained voice. She was staring
at me. "What did you say, Jane?"

"Well, I guess it is a little early yet." I glanced at
my watch. Hume Pryce had only mentioned the threatening letters from ARF last night. Would the police
know by now? Not likely, I thought.

"What?" Mrs. Benefer repeated. "What are you
talking about?"

"The animal-liberation terrorists, Mrs. Benefer.
The Animal Rights Front, I think they're called. The
ones suspected of messing up Her Majesty's lodge at
Flitcham. You know, the same people that'd been sending your sister threatening—" I ground to a halt. There
was a peculiar expression on Mrs. B.'s face that I could
only interpret one way: "You mean . . . you didn't
know she was getting these threatening letters
from . . . ?"

Mrs. Benefer had turned, to quote a song played
relentlessly on those oldies radio stations, a whiter shade
of pale.

"No, I didn't know," she replied slowly. The keys
began to tinkle softly. Her hand was trembling.

"Mrs. Benefer, are you all right?"

"How do you know this?"

"From the man who put on the panto—Hume

Pryce. I met him at the Feathers last night. He said your sister had been receiving threatening notes or letters signed the ARF."

Mrs. Benefer looked stricken. "What kind of notes?" she asked in a weak voice. The keys dropped from her hand with a clatter.

"I'm not sure." Now I devoutly wished I hadn't proceeded down this path. "Stuff with cut-out letters from magazines, I think. Some sort of intimidating message. According to Mr. Pryce, your sister didn't take them seriously."

"Did my sister show them to Mr. Pryce?"

"Well, one anyway." I shrugged. "But, then, maybe she only got the one."

"The police never mentioned this to me. Was this note . . . this letter with her when you found her?"

"I don't know. I don't remember such a thing. Anyway I think she showed it to Mr. Pryce some time ago. Mrs. Benefer, you really don't look very well."

A tiny moan emitted from somewhere back of Mrs. Benefer's throat. "Oh, my Lord . . ." she whispered, clutching the nape of her cardigan.

"I'm sure the police will catch them soon enough," I said hurriedly. "I know. It's a shock. Maybe you should lie down. Mrs. Benefer?"

"Oh, my Lord . . ." Mrs. Benefer whispered again. I watched her hand flutter into her greying bangs and sweep the hair to the side in a futile gesture. "If only she'd stayed in America. If only I'd never . . ."

Her hand next strayed to her Bible, gripping its edges.

"I'm told she'd been in the States for a long, long time and hadn't been back," I rattled on, under the notion that in times of grief or stress it helps to talk. "It was nice you were at least able to have your sister here with you in England this last little while." Cold comfort, but, oh well.

"Yes, it was . . ." Mrs. Benefer responded vaguely, staring over my shoulder toward a set of barrister bookcases topped with Christmas cards. "Nice."

"How long had she been back?"

"Since September," she replied hollowly, some of her composure beginning to return. "She just appeared one morning at our cottage."

"Oh! No warning, then."

"No." Mrs. Benefer absently rubbed her fingers over the gold embossed lettering on the Bible's grainy leather surface. "No warning. Jackie wasn't much for writing or telephoning. A call at Christmas occasionally. A change-of-address card, and sometimes that arrived long after post I had sent had been returned, marked address unknown."

"But *you* kept corresponding?"

"Oh, yes. Of course."

I felt a twinge of guilt. My sister Julie, aka Mrs. PotatoHead, somehow managed to maintain a flow of chirpy correspondence to me at regular intervals between her wifely, farmly, and motherly duties to which I replied at somewhat less regular intervals. There were times, however, when I wondered if Julie, older than me by only seventeen months and my chief sisterly competition through childhood, didn't find this faithful letter-writing business a way of oneupmanship, oneup-womanship, rather, proving herself the better sister.

"What did your sister do in the U.S.?" I asked, stifling my guilt twinge.

"I don't . . . really know. Temp work of various sorts, I think. She said very little." A blotch of color appeared on each of Mrs. Benefer's cheeks. Something—fury?—flashed in her eyes and faded as quickly. "She wasted her substance with riotous living is what she did. Luke," she added sombrely, tapping the Bible's cover. "Jackie was always restless, always moving, always . . . I had addresses from all over America, New York, Las Vegas, California . . ."

"Seeking the sun, sounds like," I said. And then she comes back to a wet, cold Norfolk winter. Crazy.

" 'Wide is the gate and broad is the way, that leadeth to destruction,' " Mrs. Benefer intoned. St. Luke again, maybe.

"I suppose."

I'm hardly disposed to the notion that death is

some sort of punishment. Besides, at that point, I would have said Jackie Scaife had been an unwitting victim, targeted by ARF extremists as a grim warning to the British public. One couldn't forget that she had been killed while dressed and made-up to look like Her Majesty the Queen. Perhaps, I thought, that was why no mention of the ARF threats had been made to Mrs. B. It was information the police sought for the time being to keep under wraps, to deny the most violent vanguard of the animal-rights movement any pleasure in its 'victory' and allay unnecessary public concern for Her Majesty's safety. If that was the case it was a race against time for the police to make an arrest before the ever-inquisitive press learned all and blabbed all. Few details of Jackie Scaife's murder would be kept for long within the small knowing circle of Estate workers, Staff, and Royals.

"Mr. Pryce said your sister did a bit of looky-likey in the States. That's why she was so good at impersonating the Queen . . . Oh!" It was the wrong thing to say and I knew it the second the soundwaves from my mouth bounced off Mrs. B.'s eardrums. The earlier blotches on her cheeks became ruby stains, and her mouth wrinkled like an apple found after a long winter.

"So insulting to Her Majesty," she murmured. "I was never more mortified in my life."

"You mean you didn't know what she was up to in the *Queen of Hearts*?"

"I had no idea."

"She was quite good at it. At least that's what I've heard," I added lamely, reflecting on this sisterly lack of communication.

Mrs. Benefer said nothing.

"How did she take your . . . critique?"

"Whatever do you mean?"

"After the performance, you went back and had a few words for her. Or so I'm told. Mr. Pryce again. Sorry. He was rather chatty."

Worry tugged at her features. "Yes, I did go back," she said slowly, and then with more assurance: "Yes, I was extremely disappointed with her. I told her so."

And, I wanted to prompt. And? The reaction? But old Aileen's eyes went to a clock on her desk.

"I'm sorry, Jane," she said. "We must get back to the tasks at hand. I shouldn't be taking your time with my problems."

"No, that's all right." She'd done it again. I was the one left feeling guilty. "I really am very sorry," I added helplessly.

"Now," she said dolefully, handing me a sheet of paper. "I think if you—"

"Oh! I'm sorry, I forgot to tell you. Heather's ill. 'Flu. She asked me to tell you."

"Oh, dear." Mrs. B. looked anxiously at her clipboard. "I wondered whether something had happened. Then would you add these few rooms to your rota . . ." She passed over the sheet and stole another quick glance at the clock. "But would you tidy the Saloon first thing, before Her Majesty and Their Royal Highnesses rise? Thank you."

"Mrs. Benefer," I said, getting to my feet, "why did your sister go to the States in the first place?"

Mrs. B. reached for her silver hoop of keys. "I really haven't the faintest idea, Jane," she said stiffly and emphatically. "Not the faintest idea."

5

BY ELEVEN O'CLOCK that morning I was dead peckish.
I hadn't had a bite of breakfast and my stomach was
doing a lively impersonation of some of the larger felines
in the London Zoo. I had, however, been superdiligent
in my work. (How virtuous of me!) The Saloon, the
principal reception room of the house, with its scads of
oak furniture (Queen Alexandra, Edward VII's wife,
who lived on at the Big House for fifteen years after her
husband's death in 1910, hated dark woods) was a relative doddle since Mrs. Benefer had already ensured its
spotlessness before the Royal Family had even arrived
from London. (I don't know why she doesn't wrap the
Big House in one huge paper strip like those used in
hotel toilets—Sanitized for Your Protection—and just
have the Queen cut it with ceremonial scissors.) After
going over the rug with a manual sweeper (quieter!),

whipping round the gewgaws with a feather duster, and plumping up the pillows on the squashy, comfy furniture as the winter light began (finally!) to gather outside the east windows, I plucked some fading blooms off the Christmas flowers, straightened a few of the annual blizzard of Christmas cards, and, in an echo of the grimmer lives of housemaids in a previous era, cleaned out the grate of the only remaining working fireplace at Sandringham. A dirty job, but someone's got to do it, and if you do it properly you don't soil your uniform. I didn't.

There were the usual beds to make and lavs to clean afterwards, but I suppose because I was propelled by the thought of some pastry and a cup of coffee—or something—I got through the morning rota faster than expected and made a Bee-line (ha! joke!) for the fount of all foodstuffs—the kitchen.

The Royal Kitchen in whichever of HM's homes you care to name is very much a world unto itself. It's a tiny kingdom, as it were, ruled over by Terrill Pentelow, the hugely fat and temperamental Royal Chef, who believes constitutional monarchy below stairs is an outrageous affront, a practice only the Queen of England should have to endure in the world above. There's no democracy amid the pots and pans of Sandringham's kitchen, and the mood of the kitchen invariably follows the mood *du jour* of His Culinary Majesty, sullen, acrimonious, or gone bonkers, depending on the occasion or availability of diverting libations. It's an all-male kingdom, military in its organization. Women are about as welcome as a dose of the clap and they are often greeted with a hail of dinner rolls or diced veg or some of the more obscure variations of garden-variety swearwords. Late morning, particularly, is never a good time to make an appearance. HM's holiday residences—Sandringham, and Balmoral, in Scotland—are where the guys really like to kick back, and if they've had baked beans for breakfast, then you're apt to come across them in the middle of one of the less enchanting below-stairs holiday pastimes—the Royal Chef's Farting Competition. Clearly, the Royal Kitchen is no place for a lady.

However, a woman can, and this woman does, occasionally make determined egress without major damage.

"Get out! Get out!" several voices chorused above the clatter and scrape of preluncheon preparation as I pushed through the swinging doors of the south entrance and sniffed the air tentatively. There was a heady aroma of broth and simmering onions. I could detect no methane. Something lobbed my way and I made a neat catch (I've played a little baseball in my time). "Thank you, gentlemen," I called, dropping to a deep curtsey. "This will do nicely." It was a dessert apple, a Cox's Orange Pippin, grown in abundance on the Estate. I turned to make a hasty exit before I was pounded with more fruit, but a voice rose above the din.

"Wait, you!" came the shout. In the kitchen, all nonkitchen staff are known as 'you' unless their position in the Royal Household is more august than that of Royal Chef.

It was Eric Twist carrying a tea tray.

"Take this up," he growled. "Her Royal-bleedin'-Highness has finally shifted herself."

"And to which Royal-bleedin'-Highness might you be referring?"

"How many Royal-bleedin'-Highnesses do you know get out of bed this time of morning?"

Point taken.

"It's not my job," I pouted. Frankly, I don't give a monkey's what jobs I do in the royal homes. I welcome a change. But everyone else is so protective of their perks and privileges and rank in the class-ridden hierarchy that you feel obliged to protect your own sometimes.

Eric shoved the tray in my chest, rattling the teacup and sloshing the teapot so a splash ejaculated from the spout. "Then you find someone whose bleedin' job it is! We're busy!"

"Oh, all right, then!" I pocketed my apple and grabbed the tray.

"She'll be with Her Majesty. In Her Majesty's study. And don't drop the bleedin' thing on your way there!"

"I'll bleedin' try not to!"

.　　.　　.

The Queen's study—her office, really—is on the north side of Sandringham House, on the first floor (second, to North Americans), overlooking an avenue of pleached lime trees, knobbly and hideous in winter, box hedges, and, at the far end, a golden statue of some fat Buddhist deity given as a gift to Edward VII in the 1860s when he was still Prince of Wales. I trotted up the stairs from the kitchen, and down the first-floor corridor, past innumerable pictures of dogs and horses and hunting scenes and the like, toward HM's study, expecting, as I neared, to find someone more highly placed than myself to whom I could entrust the breakfast tray. I hoped Davey might be lingering about, since he had been elevated to personal footman to the Sovereign, but he was not evident. Nor was Humphrey Cranston, one of HM's five Pages of the Backstairs, an even more personal servant, who I thought was scheduled for Sandringham for the duration of the holiday. There was no Corridor Officer about; nor was Inspector Paul Jenkyns, HM's minder, in evidence, either. The only evidence of life I glimpsed as I rounded a corner was the satiny gleam of some gorgeous purple fabric slipping through the door of HM's study.

I sighed inwardly. I wasn't too sure how I, a housemaid, would be greeted when tea service to members of the Royal Family was outside my proscribed duties, but what choice did I have? I shifted the tray to one arm and raised my hand to tap on the door, which had been left open a crack, when I heard the Queen say, aghast:

"*Oh, Margo, how could you!*"

My hand went limp. Oh, jeez, I thought, a Royal Family Spat. What to do?

"I hold Cousin Halifax responsible," I heard Princess Margaret reply. Her voice, mellower and richer than the Queen's, teased.

"It won't do, Margo. At your age, you can't blame an imaginary childhood friend. And if you take things that don't belong to you, you're going to end up like Grannie."

"Really, Lilibet!" The mellow voice turned peevish. "The reason I removed the tiara was because I found the whole thing so insulting. To you, particularly. That woman looked just like that wretched puppet on that disgraceful television program—"

"Yes, I know. I did watch it once or twice."

"—and to think this is happening under our very noses on our family's Estate. We are *not* amused."

"I believe that's my line, Margo."

"It's Great-great-grandmother's line."

"*I* inherited it."

A corgi yapped. Another joined in. The sound of doggie scuffling ensued.

"Margo," HM said in frosty tones once canine order was resumed, "that woman was *murdered*."

"Yes, I know that now. But I didn't know that at the time. If I had known, I'd never have removed it. I'd only intended to put it down somewhere in the hall . . ."

"But this tiara might be important, don't you see, Margo? It might be useful to the police in their inquiries."

"Yes, well, what I was going to tell you was this: I had intended to put the tiara down somewhere but the moment I lifted it, well, I realized . . ." Princess Margaret's voice fell to a stagey whisper that I could scarcely hear. "Lilibet, it's *genuine*."

"Oh, don't be silly. How could it be?"

"Well, it is. Here, look for yourself."

"Margo! What about fingerprints!"

"Too late now, I'm afraid. I've been trying it on . . . er, rather, I was examining it earlier. Here. Are you going to take it or not? And where's my tea, I wonder?"

Right here, Your Royal Highness, I said to myself, still hovering by the door like some geeky adolescent on a first date. My arms were starting to ache but it seemed an impossible juncture at which to make my entrance.

"My goodness," I could hear Her Majesty exclaim. "Cartier. I recognize the hallmark. But how . . . ?"

"And that's not all, Lilibet. There's something else."

"What?"

This time PM's voice was ringingly clear: "It's Aunt Wallis's!"

I heard a gasp of incredulity. And then a throaty laugh. I nearly dropped the tray. Aunt Wallis? Wallis Simpson? The Duchess of Windsor that was?

"What nonsense!" declared the originator of the gasp.

"It is!" said the laugh, laughing.

"It isn't! How could it be?"

"I'm sure it's Wallis's, Lilibet. I've seen it in photographs. Don't you remember? Uncle David had Cartier make Wallis a tiara as a wedding gift. I don't think she ever wore it at the wedding, though. Too insulting to Mummie and Daddie, I expect."

"Margo, it's so unlikely. Didn't we view Sotheby's catalogue together? When that sale of Wallis's things was held in Geneva after her death? I don't recall a tiara made for their wedding in any of the lists. And if it did slip my attention, it's not likely the sort of thing this poor murdered woman could possibly have afforded. She's the sister of our Housekeeper here at Sandringham. I think she'd been living in America for many years. She's—"

"Never mind all that, Lilibet. That tiara was stolen!" PM cut in, her voice animated.

"Stolen? From whom?"

"From Wallis and Uncle David, of course! Don't you remember? It was a year or so after the War. They came back to England for a visit and were staying with the Dudleys at Ednam Lodge—you know, not far from Windsor. I think they'd gone to London for the evening and a cat burglar climbed a drainpipe, broke into Wallis's room, and took her jewel case. I'm not sure of the details . . ."

"Yes, I do seem to recall something . . ." HM's voice sounded dubious.

"I think you were too besotted with Philip at the time to be paying much attention . . ."

"Really, Margo! I remember the theft well enough. But none of it explains how this tiara could come to be perched on the head of this poor slain woman. It's too odd. Perhaps it's a copy of something *like* Wallis's . . ."

"I'll wager twenty pounds it *is* Wallis's."

"Oh, Margo, that's much too much." There was a pause from the thrifty billionaire monarch. "Ten pounds, then. Ten pounds, it *isn't* Wallis's."

"Make it ten pounds in National Lottery tickets, just for fun. The draw's Saturday. I might win."

"Or I might win, Margo."

I believe you've already hit the jackpot in life, I thought. They're funny about money, the Royal Family. You'd think they hadn't got any. But they do love a flutter.

"Verification is going to be difficult," I heard the Queen say next and then in a sharper tone: "But, Margo, this really should go to the police investigating this murder. I just . . ."

I could easily fill in the words for Her Majesty: Just how was Princess Margaret's imprudent act of theft going to be explained to the authorities? And, worse, what if it should reach a wider public thanks to the tabloid terriers? A shockhorror headline danced in my head:

STICKY FINGERS MARGO!!

"Lilibet, I have an idea," I heard Stickyfingers say. "If we get verification from Cartier's, we can return it to the police having done some of the investigation ourselves! Then perhaps they won't be put out. What do you think?"

"Well . . ." Her Majesty's sigh was sufficiently loud to penetrate the door. "Well, how would we do it, then? Neither you nor I can leave our guests. And paying a sudden visit to New Bond Street would be most unusual in any case."

"Have someone from Cartier come to Sandringham."

"I'm not sure—"

"Command them! You're the Queen."

"Really, Margo!" There was a pause. "I'm not sure it would be wise to have unscheduled guests. With this murder on the Estate, there's bound to be additional press interest this Christmas. And I would rather that interest *not* be focused on one or one's family."

"Yes, of course," PM said cheerlessly. "Who, then?"

Well, if there was ever a cue in the theatre of life, this was it. Besides, my arms were fit to fall off and I couldn't very well linger in the corridor long without someone passing and wondering why I was lurking about.

Enter Jane Bee.

I tapped on the door, waited long enough for PM to say, "Good, here's my tea," and slipped in as unobtrusively as I could.

"Your Majesty. Your Royal Highness," I murmured, bobbing. Bob. Bob. Not easy with a tray.

"*Pas devant . . .*" Princess Margaret said under her breath to the Queen, as if I couldn't hear her. *Pas devant les domestiques.* Not in front of the servants.

HM's eyebrows went up with faintly amused exasperation. "*Trop tard, Margo. Jane est Canadienne. Je suis sûre qu'elle comprend le français. N'est-ce pas, Jane?*"

"*Oui, Votre Majesté,*" I replied, wondering if I had got HM's title correct. Like so many of my generation of Canadians, through most of my school years, I was enrolled in immersion French; that is, I took many of my courses in the French language. I'm bilingual, in a technical sort of way, but I couldn't say I'm fluent.

I endured PM's scrutiny as I crossed the room past the racks for newspapers and magazines and deposited the tea tray next to a vase of yellow mums on a table the Queen had silently indicated. As I did so, I cast my eyes about the room, eager to catch a glimpse of the tiara, hoping I wasn't being detectably impertinent. But where was it? Disappointed, I turned and waited for HM to dismiss me.

But the Queen seemed to be lost in thought.

"*Vous êtes la jeune femme que j'ai vue dans la salle hier matin à Dersingham,*" PM said. *You're the young woman I saw in the hall yesterday morning at Dersingham*. Her eyes narrowed. Like the Queen's, they are a startling blue. I have to report, however, that in the accent department, Princess Margaret is head and shoulders above the Queen, who speaks French like an English tourist ordering *frites chez* McDonald.

"Oui . . ." What was French for Your Royal Highness? *Altesse* something. "Ma'am," I finished lamely.

"Hmm. Lilibet?" PM shot her unresponding sister a look of annoyance. *"Jane, du thé, s'il-vous-plaît."*

I hurried to serve her her tea. Although it smelled wonderful—Lapsang Souchong has a dense smoky fragrance—the *thé*—tea—looked dreadfully stewed. Its unlovely state made me anxious to skedaddle. I don't know why I was doing the tea-pouring in the first place. Such refreshments you normally left to whichever member of the Royal Family or upper echelon of the Household you were serving to help him or herself. Then, as I again picked up the tray, I realized where the missing tiara was. Princess Margaret was swaddled in a voluptuous dressing gown of violet silk damask. The diadem, I was sure, was concealed in the folds. She didn't dare rise from the settee and the Queen's mind had evidently flown from the mundane task of pouring tea.

Princess Margaret regarded me coolly as she took the cup from the tray and stirred a teaspoon of sugar. *"Vous avez quitté la scène avant nous, n'est-ce-pas?"*

"Shall we speak English?" the Queen interrupted, evidently returned from her reverie.

"You left the stage before the rest of us," Princess Margaret repeated coolly, lifting the cup to her lips.

"I went out the back to see if Davey—David Pye—was all right, Ma'am."

"And how did you return? Oooh!" PM's mouth made a moue of distaste. "This tea is tepid."

"I, uh, came back through the stage."

Princess Margaret looked at me sharply, then at her sister. But the Queen's attention had turned to the door to her study.

"Margo, did you leave the door ajar when you came in?"

"I'm sure I don't know."

"At least at Sandringham, the kitchens aren't far off," HM mused. "Tea or coffee doesn't usually arrive cold."

Her Majesty gave me one of those famous looks of hers that make you wish the earth would open and swallow you up. I could feel my face flush and my lips wobble in their search for a contrite expression.

And then a little twinkle supplanted the ocular ice chips and a smile erased the lines around her mouth.

"I think Jane may be able to help us with the tiara," HM said, to my surprise and shock.

"Lilibet, have you gone mad?"

"Jane, did you witness something backstage at Dersingham Hall . . . ?"

"Lilibet!" PM gasped.

"And do put that tray down, Jane. I think you'll be staying for a time."

"Yes, Ma'am." I crossed to the table. "I saw . . ." I deposited the tray and turned toward Princess Margaret. I gulped. "I saw Your Royal Highness remove the tiara . . ."

"And you were listening at the door," HM continued.

"Yes, Ma'am. I'm very sorry, Ma'am."

Princess Margaret looked thunderous. The Queen raised her right hand as if to stave off any protest and studied the watch on her left wrist. "There's bound to be a train leaving King's Lynn for London around one o'clock. Let me see. You'll be able to get to Cartier's by three or a little after, I should think, Jane. That will give you enough time—"

"Lilibet!"

"I'll make a telephone call to Cartier's and I'll provide you with a letter. Now Margo . . . Margo? Bring it out. Come along now."

"Lilibet! This young woman is—"

"—completely trustworthy," the Queen provided. "Do you recall me telling you about the incident last year just before the State Visit of the Malaysian King? About the poisoned footman? And about the housemaid who helped one with one's inquiries?"

"Yes . . ." Princess Margaret answered in a dubious tone.

"This is she."

PM looked me up and down like fresh goods at a market stall. She didn't appear wholly convinced. Absently, she lifted the teacup to her lips and once again her mouth crinkled in distaste. Impatiently, she set the cup on its saucer and thrust the offending china at me. I quickly took the cup from her as she drew aside with a dainty hand a fold in her dressing gown and lifted the tiara to the light.

"And you intend to entrust her with *this*, do you?"

I gasped. The circlet of diamonds—four large centre stones and three curved upright fingers of smaller diamonds set in platinum—blazed as if fuelled by a cold white fire within. Rainbow colours flashed, darted, and dazzled the eye. Seeing the tiara as a thing apart from the distressing circumstances of its discovery, knowing now something of its authenticity and possible provenance, I found myself entranced—no, that's not the right word—*seduced* by its breath stopping beauty. I suddenly had a taste of the passion that has driven men— and women, of course—to acquire diamonds. So mesmerized was I, I barely heard HM's reply to her sister:

"Yes, I do intend to entrust Jane with this. You wouldn't run off to Brazil with it, would you, Jane? Jane?"

"Gosh, no, Ma'am," I stammered, still agape. "But it is . . . brilliant, isn't it? And to think Her Royal Highness might actually have owned it and worn it. It's—"

I stopped in mid-sentence. Princess Margaret snatched the tiara to her bosom. There was a sudden inexplicable chill in the air. The Queen frowned.

"'Her Grace,' Jane," HM said gently. "The Duchess of Windsor is styled 'Her Grace.'"

"Oh, I see," I responded, not seeing. Apparently, in opening my mouth, I had merely changed feet.

"Just something to keep in mind," the Queen added without explanation. "Now," she continued briskly, "we must get you to King's Lynn somehow."

"Oh, Ma'am, that's easy. My father's staying in Dersingham. He came over for a Christmas visit. He can drive me to Lynn, I'm sure." I just hoped he would be back at the Feathers for lunch.

"He's with the RCMP, I believe you told me once. How very useful."

Princess Margaret rose from the couch with a silky rustle and thrust the tiara at the Queen. "I'll leave this in your capable hands, Lilibet. Remember, now—£10 in tickets. I'll ring for some hot tea from my room. And some breakfast."

"Margo, the kitchen will have begun luncheon preparation."

"Oh, they won't mind."

The hell they won't, I thought, as PM glided out the door.

There was a sigh but I think it might have come from one of the corgis gathered in a heap around HM's desk. The Queen stepped around a few, added the tiara to the controlled clutter of papers, books, and framed photographs, and reached for a pair of glasses.

"Now," she said, adjusting the frames, and switching on a brass table lamp. "I'll prepare something in writing—some bona fides—and . . . let me see, we'll need to package this somehow." She gestured toward the tiara.

"Perhaps just a plastic carrier bag, Ma'am."

"Oh, I see. Anonymity. Very good." She glanced at my white uniform. "You get yourself ready—I don't think you should appear at Cartier's in that—and I'll have everything sent to you at the back entrance in half an hour."

"Very good, Ma'am."

"Have you completed your other duties? I'm not going to get you into trouble, am I?"

"I'm pretty much done, Ma'am. Besides, Mrs. Benefer isn't—" I hesitated, not wanting to make it seem as if Mrs. B. didn't have control over us girls, because she did, in her way.

"—quite as formidable as Mrs. Harbottle?" Her Majesty supplied with a knowing smile.

"Exactly, Ma'am. I'll just tell her that something's come up." But what? I wondered.

"That poor woman. She really must rest at home. We'll get by for a few days, I'm sure."

"I think Mrs. Benefer feels she would be letting Your Majesty down if she didn't stay at her post."

"Very commendable, but I think I must have a word with her. Now, on your way, Jane Bee."

"Yes, Ma'am." I backed toward the door.

"Oh, Jane. One other thing: Would you purchase ten tickets for the National Lottery on my behalf . . . ?"

I was half expecting this. The Queen never carries any money.

"I never carry money, you see." HM smiled.

I returned the smile and curtseyed. "Of course, Your Majesty," I said and thought as I departed the Presence: Ten pounds says I'll never see that ten pounds again.

I called my father from the Staff lounge. Hallelujah, he was in at the Feathers and was not only willing to drive me to King's Lynn, which was great, but to accompany me to London as well, which was less great. I wasn't sure what I was going to tell him.

Then I darted down to Mrs. Benefer's office prepared with a toothache-must-see-a-dentist-emergency only to find her gone, and Caroline Halliwell, the Marchioness of Thring's lady's maid/personal assistant loitering about. Caroline is one of those cool, blond, leggy Englishwomen you expect to be efficiency-plus and a total snob who turns out to be ever so cheerful and relaxed and uncomplicated, which is, perhaps, how you have to be if you're going to work closely with someone as demanding as Pamela II.

"Oh, hello," Caroline trilled as I barged through

the door. "Another Christmas gone by. Did you have a pleasant one? Lots of swag?"

"It was fine, thanks," I said, sorry to be a bit impatient and not ask after her Christmas. "Do you know where Mrs. B. is?"

"Just left, I'm afraid. I'd come to give my condolences when she had a call from the police." Caroline grimaced. "More questioning, I'm afraid. She's gone to Dersingham."

"Oh."

"Her ladyship had a call, too." Caroline looked practically mirthful. "Well, I expect the police will be questioning everyone who was at the panto. Still, her ladyship was none too pleased."

"Perhaps they think she saw something. I'm told she was one of the last to leave the hall."

"Oh, was she? Well, she was certainly late getting back to the Duke's Head. I had expected her before five-thirty but she didn't arrive until after seven. His lordship was late, as well.

"You're in some sort of hurry, aren't you, Jane? I can read it on your face."

"Yes, actually." I laughed. "Should you see Mrs. Benefer in the next few hours would you tell her . . . I've had to see a dentist in King's Lynn."

"Oooh," Caroline cooed sympathetically as I held my hand up to a *faux* throbbing jaw. "Poor you. Bite into something?"

I wish. The last thing I'd bitten into was a crisp at the Feathers last night. My stomach growled.

Shortly afterward I was down at the back entrance, about to bite into my apple, wearing my hound's-tooth A-line skirt with a little black cardigan sweater over a white blouse, my to-die-for 'sixties mod black leather jacket (bought at an antique clothing shop in Camden Town), and, of course, my serviceable Docs—not quite the best sort of gear for a trundle around Cartier's but better than a housemaid's uniform by a long shot. But before I had even set my teeth into the fruit Davey dashed up, out of breath.

"Mother's had me racing all over trying to find a Tesco carrier bag or a Sainsbury's bag or something like—certainly one of her more peculiar requests. Here, Jane. I hope this will do." *It* was a Marks & Spencer bag, white with dark green printing, and it had a nice heft to it, thanks to the contents.

"I thought you had 'flu?" I asked him, taking the bag and once again pocketing the apple.

"Twenty-four-hour variety, I guess. Oh, all right," he added testily when I rolled my eyes. "Perhaps I'd had a few too many drinkies. It could have been 'flu. Everyone else seems to be getting it. I think Nigel's getting it. Ha!" This prospect seemed to brighten Davey up considerably.

"Did you get your fiver off Nigel?" I was referring to the bet over Princess Margaret's attendance at the aborted shooting luncheon.

"Not yet, but I will."

Betting suddenly reminded me of my conversational *faux pas* earlier in the Queen's study, and Davey, fount of arcane lore about the Royals might, I thought, be able to clarify.

"Quicky protocol question, Davey: King Edward VIII was styled 'His Majesty' when he was King, of course. And when he was made Duke of Windsor he became 'His Royal Highness,' demoted, sort of. Right?"

"Yeessss," Davey drawled.

"Then wouldn't his wife, the Duchess of Windsor, be 'Her Royal Highness'?"

"Oh, nooooo."

"But doesn't a wife take her husband's status? I thought it was some English common law thing. Every king has a queen, every duke a duchess, every earl a countess, every mister a missus. And so on. Wouldn't the wife of a Royal Highess be a Royal Highness?"

"Well, you've hit upon one of the stickier wickets in the Windsor chronicles, Janesy. You'd think old Wallis Simpson would have been elevated to HRH but the Family *loathed* her. They *reviled* her. In another age, they would have had her locked up in the Tower. She was an *arriviste*, a *parvenue*, an adventuress, a divorcée, an *American . . . !*"

"Yes, yes, I get the point."

"Ghastly woman! Nice taste in clothes, though. Very chic. Smart jewellery, too . . . er, what was your question?"

"Title."

"Oh, quite. Well, Mother's father—you know, George VI, Edward VIII's brother—simply denied old Wally-poos the title HRH, when he came to the throne after the Abdication fuss in 1936. Some legal fiddle-faddle was found, and there were heaps of cranky letters back and forth, but His Majesty couldn't be shifted. So that was it. Wally was stuck with 'Her Grace,' the style for a non-royal Duchess. Of course, Edward—David, as he was known to the Family—was in a snit about it for the rest of his life."

"Seems a bit mean-spirited, on the whole. Denying her the title, that is."

"Yes, even I, a most loyal servant of the Crown, have to agree. Anyway, Mother was too young to be involved. It's all so long ago now. And why . . ."—he put a gloved hand to his mouth to stifle a yawn—"dare I ask, are you so interested in that silly old fag hag, the Duchess of Windsor, dead lo these many years?"

"Just something I overheard."

Davey arched his eyebrows. "And I suppose I mustn't ask why Mother obliged me to bring you a Marks & Sparks bag?"

"You didn't look in, did you?"

"I was tempted. But Mother gave me one of her rare 'the Tower for you, laddie' looks if I didn't obey her command sharpish. I did note plenty of tissue paper, however. And something pointy inside kept jabbing my leg."

I must have given him one of my goofy, apologetic, 'sorry-I-can't-tell-you-much-as-I-would-like-to' looks, for he said, eyes narrowed, referring to last year's murder-solving episode at Buck House: "You were like this after Robin died."

"Davey, I'm just running a small errand for Her Majesty, that's all."

"Uh-huh. Well, *don't* tell me. I don't want to know. I want nothing but the peace and good will of the season to continue unabated . . ."

"A quiet life, in other words."

"After yesterday's unpleasant episode, quite frankly—yes!"

6

ABOUT HALFWAY THROUGH the train journey from King's Lynn to King's Cross Station, London, I finally gave in to temptation. I just couldn't help myself. I tried to be nonchalant when my father collected me at Sandringham in his hire car and asked me the predictable questions about why I wanted to go to London. I maintained my composure as the train left King's Lynn station. I was able to distract myself for a time by devouring the cheese and chutney sandwich and the carton of milk Dad shelled out for when the food trolley came by. (The apple had turned out to be brown inside, eliciting the evergreen 'one bad apple in every bunch' adage from my wise papa.) For a time I was even able to hold up my end of the conversation as the train passed through Ely and then Cambridge. But finally I could stand it no longer. On the Marks & Spencer bag on my lap was a crest, one that looked as though it had been patched together from bits left on the cutting-room floor at the College of Heralds. A shield dominated, held on one side by a skinny lion, on the other by an astonished owl. Beneath this unlikely duo was written: STRIVE ❖ PROBE ❖ APPLY. Words to live by, I thought as I stared, but then the letters scrambled and I knew, finally, I had to do something.

"I'm just going to the loo, Dad," I explained hastily and dashed up the aisle as though the cheese sandwich had contained a nasty surprise.

I ducked into the WC, then carefully laid the bag and its contents on the toilet cover. The letters under the crest had realigned themselves properly, but for a moment back at my seat they had spelled one thing: TRY ❖ IT ❖ ON ❖ JANE and I had felt compelled to obey.

Well, what was a body to do? Just what were my chances of ever being this close to such fabulous jewellery again in my life? I suppose it didn't help having been eight years old when Diana Spencer became Princess of Wales and sparked a bout of princessmania among the Bee sisters back in Charlottetown, PEI, or having watched the *Sleeping Beauty* video about a million times, or owning Ballerina Barbie. Girls absorb an awful lot of princess palaver in their early years and I suppose I was no exception, though, of course, you do grow up and like to think you've packed away that sort of baggage in the furthest reaches of your mental attic. Still, things have a way of slipping out. There have been occasions—and I attribute this strictly to working in a royal palace—when I've caught myself humming under my breath, ironically I like to think, 'Someday My Prince Will Come.' I've plunked my bottom onto certain pieces of furniture in Buck House and pretended to receive Top People, and stretched out on a few royal beds (before making them) and made believe *I* was the one being awakened with tea. So this may go a ways to explaining why, that winter afternoon, as the train rattled through the English countryside, I found myself removing the mass of tissue paper from the M & S carrier bag and carefully, with trembling fingers, pulling back each fragile leaf like the petals of a pale lotus to reveal the glittering prize at its centre.

All right, I admit a cramped loo on the Intercity to London is not exactly the Robing Room at Buckingham Palace. And a toilet seat is not a crimson velvet-covered spotlit repository. But, for the moment, for this commoner, it would have to do. Even in the pallid light through the frosted window, the diamonds sparkled with a radiance surpassing even crisp new snow under a Charlottetown street lamp, my only previous experience of what one might call radiance on a grand scale. I gloated for a moment, my heart filled with a kind of wonder, then, with both hands, gathered up the tiara, briefly running my fingers over the cool, glittering surfaces before turning to the mirror above the sink and raising the circlet high over my head like the Archbishop of Canterbury holding aloft St. Edward's Crown over the Queen on Coronation Day. Slowly I allowed the diadem to descend, feeling a strange warm flush come over me as the weight of the diamonds and platinum settled upon my head. And there I was, in all my splendour, the one, the only, the undoubted, the true: Her Royal Highness, the Princess Jane.

I wish I could say I looked dead princessy but, in truth, I looked more like an idiot. Particularly as the train lurched suddenly and sent the tiara tumbling over my eyes onto the bridge of my nose with a painful bang. The Duchess of Windsor—if this tiara indeed had been the Duchess of Windsor's—must have had a biggish head, I thought as I pushed the priceless bauble back on top of my own. Or perhaps there was some special way of securing such jewellery unbeknownst to me. I sighed. The reflection staring back at me wore an expression of the goofiest solemnity, and then there was this growing welt on my nose. Did you actually have to be born to the purple to wear these things? I wondered. Or was it my hair? I had been growing mine longer—it was about shoulder-length when taken out of its housemaid's knot—but, due to my late rise, shampoo and conditioner had not whipped it into its highest achievable state. Maybe you needed your hair up in a certain way to properly set off a tiara. Or would it have helped if I had worn some makeup? Better lighting in my ersatz robing room?

I had to acknowledge that I was probably not the stuff of which princesses are made, whatever that might be. I also had to acknowledge a certain tapping on the door of the loo which had lately grown in insistency. I quickly flushed the toilet and ran the taps while removing the tiara from my head; then, with a sense of disappointment for the stones seemed to have lost their lustre, rewrapped it in its bed of tissue paper and reintroduced it to the Marks & Sparks bag.

"Sorry!" I apologized to an anxious elderly woman as I exited past her and scuttled down the aisle.

"You okay, Bird?" My father looked up from his newspaper when I took my seat.

"Yeah."

"Something happen to your nose?"

"The tiara fell on it."

"I see."

He went back to his paper. I rubbed the sore spot. I had worried about explaining my errand in London. The tale of my previous adventure with HM at Buckingham Palace had already been greeted by the aging parental-unit with something akin to incredulity. I didn't expect him to embrace this story, either, but, when in the car at the Jubilee Gates he had asked me the question—'what's in the bag?'—I decided I might as well be forthright but in a casual sort of way.

"A tiara," I replied as I buckled up.

"Returning it?"

"No, I'm just having it checked out."

"I see."

And that was it. I'd hoped his curiosity would be piqued. I had decided: Well, I might as well tell him, he's a Mountie, he's not going to blab, and, besides, it might be sort of fun to involve him, although I reasoned it might not be wise to mention the source of the tiara, the head of Jackie Scaife. But he didn't bite.

My father has great reserves of male obtuseness. Maybe, I reflected, as I stared out the train window at the grey veil of mist over the landscape, he thinks I really do own a tiara. Maybe he thinks all his daughters own tiaras, that the tiara was part of a rite of passage into womanhood, only he never paid much attention, and thinks in today's political climate it wouldn't be wise to reveal the depths of his ignorance. Maybe he thinks I really am going into London to have my tiara serviced, the way he might take the car in for a tune-up or have someone in to look at the furnace before winter set in.

"What are you looking so fierce about?" he asked, breaking away from his paper and into my thoughts.

"Oh . . . nothing!"

We separated at King's Cross, my father to spend a little time in the British Museum, me to take the Underground to Cartier on New Bond Street, with plans to regroup later at the Maple Leaf pub in Covent Garden.

The staff at Cartier seemed to be expecting me, which is an awfully nice sensation. I had half anticipated being barred at the door because I hadn't cruised up in a Roller or because I wasn't dressed in Lacroix, but everyone was all smiles as I was escorted past the display cases aglow with gardens of jewels into a dark-panelled office presided over by a short, thin, impeccably dressed man with an almost hilariously anachronistic pencil moustache onto which my eyes locked immediately. He greeted me very formally, sepulchrally actually, received HM's letter from my hand as if it contained the ashes of his late mother and perused it as I removed the tiara from its crumpled folds of tissue and, at his invitation, sat down.

Mr. Rose, as he informed me he was called, was brisk. After reading the contents of the envelope, he quickly examined each stone with his jeweller's loupe, rotating the tiara with short sharp movements. He scrutinized the hallmark and consulted a series of sketches that appeared to have been pulled from some archive. On paper with faintly yellowed edges were pen-and-ink drawings of views of a piece of jewellery, with tiny notes in a crabbed hand that appeared, from my (disad)vantage point across the desk, to be written in

French. Then, with barely a moment to reflect, he made his pronouncement.

Well, what can I say?

Margo 1. Lilibet 0. National Lottery tickets would cross a royal palm before long, and that palm wouldn't be HM's.

"But how . . . ?" I stammered to Mr. Rose. I suppose I was a little nonplussed, though I wasn't completely surprised—those Windsor women do know jewellery.

Mr. Rose's moustache twitched. "But how . . . ?" he echoed helpfully.

"Um." I had nearly asked out loud, 'How did the Duchess of Windsor's tiara end up on Aileen Benefer's sister's flippin' noggin?' Of course, it was a question Mr. Rose could not answer.

"I was just wondering how . . . how valuable it is."

Mr. Rose's eyebrows played counterpoint to his moustache. "You are," he allowed, "certainly one of Her Majesty's more unusual couriers. I'm not sure, however, the Queen is seeking an evaluation . . ."

"Er, no. I mean, I'm sure it's worth hundreds of thousands of pounds, in any case."

"That would be a somewhat understated assessment."

"I see. Then can you tell me something about its history?"

"There's little to tell, I'm afraid." Mr. Rose glanced at the tiara, resplendent in the soft light of a desk lamp. "The Duke of Windsor commissioned this for Mrs. Simpson, as she was then. To wear at their wedding, I believe." He paused and added sombrely, "You must realize this is well before my time."

"Of course."

Did I sound insincere? There was a flicker of doubt on his face. Old people—well, middle-aged people—like Mr. Rose always think people my age have no chronological perspective.

"Apparently, according to information I've managed to piece together in the last few hours, it was decided the tiara shouldn't be worn at the wedding after all," the jeweller continued. "Because there is a tradition of associating tiaras with royalty, it was thought Mrs. Simpson's wearing one would be viewed as provocative, as a deliberate affront to Buckingham Palace."

"They weren't exactly keen on her, were they?"

"The Royal Family, you mean?" He frowned and assessed me with his sharp little eyes. My hand went to the welt on my nose. "No, they weren't. That's certainly common knowledge. At the time of the wedding, there was particular acrimony between the Duke of Windsor and Buckingham Palace. The wedding was in France in 1937, about six months after the Abdication, and, I believe, no members of the Royal Family were in attendance.

"Now, let me see . . ." He paused and ran a finger along the band of the tiara. "I understand this exquisite piece was only worn by Her Grace in private, but it does come to public attention through an unfortunate theft which took place after the war—"

"At a place called Ednam Lodge," I interrupted, rubbing the bridge of my nose. The sore was getting rather tender.

"Yes. You know about it?"

"Only a bit." Only what I had overheard, actually.

"Ednam Lodge, then home of the Earl and Countess of Dudley, was offered to the Windsors during a visit they made to England. As I understand it, the Windsors travelled up to London one evening, and while they were dining, their bedroom at Ednam Lodge was burgled. The Duchess's jewel case was taken—"

"—by a cat burglar."

"Mmm." Mr. Rose made demurring noises.

"Not by a cat burglar?"

"Well . . ." He cleared his throat. "It's rather interesting. I don't believe the case was ever solved but, according to my sources—at the time of the theft the insurers had reason to consult with Cartier, as we had created much of Her Grace's jewellery—there were a number of anomalies. The thieves seemed to know precisely where to look. They climbed up a rope into Lady

Dudley's daughter's bedroom—I think it was—before sunset and made their way down a corridor directly to the Duchess of Windsor's bedroom. They ignored other items of value in the Duchess's room and in the room next door, which contained Lady Dudley's jewels. Instead the thieves went straight for the Duchess's case. The servants heard nothing—it was their evening meal. And—most interesting—the Windsors' dogs, which were upstairs, didn't bark."

"An inside job, do you mean? The dogs recognized the intruders?"

"Possibly. This is mere speculation. As I said, the theft was never solved."

I glanced about the windowless room, not really taking in the details. The notion of an 'inside job' was certainly intriguing.

"What usually happens in the case of stolen jewellery?"

"Well, the pieces are most often sold through another party—fenced, in other words. Almost invariably the stones are removed from their settings, recut and placed in new settings. The original settings themselves—gold, platinum—may be melted down. In a sense, unlike valuable paintings or sculpture, distinctive pieces of jewellery, such as those belonging to the Duchess of Windsor, can simply disappear." He sighed, perhaps mourning the lost tiaras, brooches, and necklaces of yesteryear.

"On the other hand, there are cases where the theft is done to order; that is, a collector may have a particular passion for paintings or silverware or porcelain of a certain period or by a certain artist, so he hires the services, usually third-hand, of someone among the . . ."—he sniffed and pulled a handkerchief from somewhere below the edge of the desk—"criminal element. This happens rather less often with jewellery. Excuse me, I think I may be getting a cold."

He dabbed fastidiously at the end of his nose.

"Might this," I asked, nodding at the tiara, "have been stolen to order?"

He pursed his lips. "It's possible. Certainly, that's

suggested by the fact that this piece is here, now, un-damaged, in its original state. But, as you might imagine, the number of serious collectors of jewellery of this cali-bre has always been small and select, indeed. I can think of two elderly collectors who favor the designs of the 1930s, the Art Deco period—the era of their youth I suppose—but I'm sure neither of them began collecting in earnest until long after the Ednam Lodge theft, and both of them I know to be utterly incorruptable. As for jewels associated with the Duchess of Windsor, I've never heard of anyone with such a specific taste, at least not going back to those early post-war days." He seemed to search his mind. "Yes, I'm quite sure.

"Anyway, after Her Grace died in 1986, her jewel-lery was sold at auction in Geneva. While there were those eager, I suppose, for the cachet of owning some-thing that once belonged to the Duchess, no one singu-lar collector emerged, to my knowledge. Curiously, among the pieces at auction were some of those listed by the Duchess as stolen in the Ednam Lodge bur-glary."

I reflected on what he had said earlier. "You mean the Duchess of Windsor was involved in an insurance fraud?" The notion seemed rather astonishing.

Mr. Rose waved his handkerchief dismissively, as though at an imaginary insect, and said with a tight smile: "I think perhaps Her Grace had forgotten which jewels she had brought with her for the 1946 visit to England and which she had left behind in a vault in Paris."

How very diplomatic, I thought. But it made me wonder if the Duchess of Windsor fiddled her income tax, too. (If she had paid any, that is.)

"But what of the pieces that were definitely stolen, that didn't show up later at the auction?" I pressed.

"As I said, none have ever come to light, as far as I'm aware. Because of their association with the Duch-ess of Windsor, the jewels would have been impossible to dispose without breaking them up. Or so I would have thought. I would have assumed, therefore, that they *had been* broken up . . ."

"And yet . . ." I pointed at the tiara.

Mr. Rose's eyes followed my finger.

"It is rather remarkable that this item is in Her Majesty's possession," he said, fishingly, tracing a finger delicately over each moustache.

"Yes, I suppose," I said noncommittally.

"A recent acquisition, I presume?"

"I couldn't really say, Mr. Rose. I'm only Her Majesty's—as you put it—courier."

"And as such, the soul of discretion."

"Of course," I replied evenly.

"Then perhaps I will tell you another story—and you must understand I'm telling you this without prejudice to Her Majesty or to other members of the Royal Family . . ."

I leaned forward in my seat.

"It was said at the time that a member of the Royal Family had arranged the Ednam Lodge burglary—"

"You're kidding!"

"   to retrieve the Alexandra emeralds."

Mr. Rose paused. His moustache twitched. I bit.

"Which are . . . ?"

"A collection of unset jewels belonging to Edward VIII's grandmother, Queen Alexandra, who left them to her grandson, who then gave them to Wallis Simpson. The story is that the Royal Family first tried to reclaim the emeralds through negotiation before the Windsors were married. They failed. Hence the theft at Ednam Lodge."

"You're not suggesting this is actually true, are you?"

"Of course not, Miss Bee," the jeweller said adamantly. "If it were so, Her Majesty would not be seeking a confirmation of the authenticity of this particular piece of jewellery." He glanced at the tiara. "I'm merely giving you what little I've gleaned to help you in your . . . inquiries."

"Yes, of course," I murmured, subdued.

"And, besides, I believe the Alexandra emeralds are a fiction."

The jeweller's expression remained impassive but his eyes twinkled. Was this a wind-up? It was hard to believe an official of Cartier's would be having me on. Were there, or weren't there, Alexandra emeralds? I smiled weakly at Mr. Rose and said, thinking of my tight schedule and trains to Norfolk, that I would need to leave shortly. As I stuffed the tiara back into the M & S bag, Mr. Rose pulled stationery from a drawer, wrote a few lines, and sealed the results in an envelope.

"This has been most interesting," he said, handing me the envelope. He ushered me out the door and back into the showroom that seemed to blaze against the darkening London street on the other side of the window. I would have loved to linger and gawp but it was growing late and I had arranged to meet my father at six o'clock at the Maple Leaf. Mr. Rose looked askance at the M & S bag. "Mind you don't leave that parcel somewhere," he cautioned, and I promised to be especially careful.

As I plodded through a sodden Piccadilly Circus with its dazzle of neon, down Haymarket Street and past the National Gallery toward Covent Garden, I pondered the total awesomeness of life, as I am wont to do, particularly when I am walking through a major world capital toting a million bucks in jewellery, which is not often. In fact, never. What flukes of time and chance had led to this work of the jeweller's art finding its way onto the head of an ordinary, until-recently-expatriate Englishwoman in a village panto nearly half a century after its disappearance? Did Jackie Scaife know the value or history of what she died wearing? And if she did, why would she be so brazen as to wear it in public? While her death might be linked to animal-rights extremists, wouldn't diamonds of great value also be a powerful motive for murder? And yet, if that were so, why had the tiara remained on her head after the killer had struck? Curious, I thought, as I made my way through double doors into the Maple Leaf, London redoubt of homesick Canucks, where my father had snagged a booth and was peeling the label from a bottle of Molson Canadian while frowning at a large Inuit print on the wall.

"Enjoy the Museum?" I asked as I removed my coat, gave it a little shake, and draped it over the side of the pew.

"I'd forgotten how big the place was. I didn't get much further than ancient Egypt. How's your tiara?"

"It's fine, Dad. Jeez. It really is a real tiara," I whispered intensely as I sat across from him. "Here, I'm going to let you take a peek."

I reached into the bag and made a tiny tear in the tissue paper. "There. See that?"

He squinted. "Rhinestones."

"Diamonds."

"I'm not sure you should have a drink, Bird."

"Look, Dad, I'm going to tell you something and you have to believe me. You also can't tell another living soul what I'm about to tell you. Okay?"

My father took a sip of his beer, then nodded. I looked around. Fortunately, the pub was not too crowded and the canned music was just loud enough to make conversations private.

"This tiara," I said with gravity, "once belonged to the Duchess of Windsor. The Duke of Windsor had it made for their wedding."

"Mm. And what are you doing with it?"

"The Queen asked me to check it out at Cartier's—you know, the jewellers."

My father rubbed his face with both his hands and then stared at me. "I'm going back to Canada next week, Jane. I'd like you on that plane with me. You can take some half-courses at university when we get back."

"Dad, this is the truth!" I could have cried I was so frustrated.

"Why would the Queen entrust you with such a thing?"

"Because, well, because . . ." So I told him how, backstage, when the body of Jackie Scaife had been found, I observed Princess Margaret remove the tiara and conceal it in her jacket, and that this had drawn me into the potential dilemma presented by a combination of sticky-fingered royalty, a murder investigation, and an intrusive press. And, besides, the Queen had entrusted me before. I had a track record.

"That could be evidence, you know," my father said darkly. "It should never have been removed from the scene of the crime."

"I know, I know. But no one knew at the time Jackie had been murdered. Margo . . . er, Princess Margaret was just trying to defend the Queen's dignity. It was an impulse."

My father spent a longish while pondering, his eyes wandering from my face, to the A. Y. Jackson print of Lake Superior on the wall, to the flag of Alberta pinned to the booth high above my head, to his beer. Finally, I went to the bar, ordered a Canadian Light and brought it back to the table. I said, "You do believe me now?"

Dad noisily expelled a volume of air. "I'll tell you what. You ask the Queen if she's ever met the King, give me the right answer, and maybe I'll believe you."

"The king of where?"

"The King! There's only one."

"You mean Jesus?"

"Of course not!"

"Oh, for God's sake." I had forgotten the old man's closet passion. "You want me to ask the Queen of England—"

"And of Canada, incidentally."

"—and of Canada, and of Australia and New Zealand and a whole bunch of other countries if she's ever met *Elvis Presley*?"

"And no looking in a book."

"Believe me, there are no books about Elvis in the Sandringham library. I've dusted every one of them."

"Fine, then."

"You're mean."

"I'm your father. Being 'mean' is just part of the job."

·   ·   ·

The Elvis Challenge, as I came to call it, seemed to cheer my father considerably. At King's Cross, at the King's Lynn station, in the car back to Sandringham, he'd fill lulls in the conversation by whistling a few bars of "Love Me Tender" or "Are You Lonesome Tonight." Very provoking, but I refused to be provoked. Instead, in those moments, I mulled over the other information dear old Dad had passed on during our respite from wet wintry England in the cozy confines of the Maple Leaf. It seems he had not been passing the whole morning tramping about the damp west Norfolk countryside or planning an un-Dad birdwatching expedition; he had introduced himself to a couple of the plods from the Norfolk Constabulary who were having an early lunch at the Feathers, and what with them all being jolly coppers together, they gave him some of the poop regarding the late Jackie Scaife.

The cause of death, it seems, was a well-placed blow to the back of the skull with a blunt instrument; indeed, the skin had been barely broken, but Jackie, a relatively petite and physically delicate woman, seemed to have had a paper-thin skull, or so it was surmised. Her body had fallen front-first onto the stage—this was supported by makeup on the wooden floor matching the pattern of the smudged makeup on the victim's left cheek—but had been later moved to the litter. The weapon was not in evidence. Based on the rate of cooling, modified by the Barbour jacket Jackie had been wearing and the temperature in the hall, the time of death was estimated at between five-thirty and seven-thirty Boxing Day evening. The autopsy also revealed the fact that Jackie had been about six weeks pregnant.

Meanwhile, the search had begun in earnest through the web of the Animal Rights Front and its supporters. A menacing note, torn in several pieces, had been discovered in the pocket of the Barbour and reconstructed by the police. Composed of a series of letters snipped from magazines, the note threatened Jackie with reprisals for continuing to publicly flaunt her support for slaughtering animals by wearing the skin of one on her back. Said skin, a fur coat, identified as Jackie's, had also been found off the main hall in a room used for costume changes. It had been shredded, the yoke smeared with red grease pencil to form the letters *ARF*. These strong leads had been greatly welcomed; the scene of the crime was otherwise a hodgepodge, the village hall having been so recently peopled by so many performers, volunteers, and audience it was a forensics nightmare.

"Why didn't you tell me this when we were coming up to London?" I asked my father over some nosh.

"I did try. You seemed to be preoccupied with something else."

"Oh." The damn tiara.

Which reminded me: "I have to buy ten tickets on the National Lottery."

My father shook his head. Seeing as he so often does the seamier side of what are supposed to be bright pleasures, he takes a dim view of the lotteryization of modern life.

"Bird, why are you wasting your money? The odds of winning are something like one in thirteen million. You've got a better chance of being the Prince of Wales's second wife."

"The tickets aren't for me."

"Who, then?"

I hated to say it: "Um . . . the Queen. Oh, look, Dad, they've got a hockey game on the TV. Did you know someone videotapes them in Canada and sends them over? Looks like . . ."—I peered at the screen off in a corner near the fireplace—"the Habs and the Leafs playing!"

" 'Warden threw a party in the county jail,' " my father intoned, ignoring my pathetic diversion, reciting Elvis as if it was poetry. " 'The prison band was there, they began to wail/the band was jumpin' and the joint began to swing/you should've heard those knocked-out jail-birds sing . . .' "

Sometimes he thinks he's funny.

•　　•　　•

And almost spookily prescient, as it happened. One thing I can say definitely—and this is not a lesson in life, but a mere observation—it is easier to take a Marks & Spencer bag out of a royal residence than it is to bring a Marks & Spencer bag into a royal residence. When my father dropped me off at the Jubilee Gates, I was, to my astonishment, challenged by PC Nesbitt.

"Sorry, miss," he said cheerily, when I presented my Staff card, "but we're on amber alert what with the murder in the village and all." He reached for the bag.

"But it's just something I bought at Marks & Spencer. It's nothing, really."

"Sorry. I'm required to inspect every parcel thoroughly."

My heart settled somewhere around my ankles as I obligingly handed the bag over and watched the frown form on his face when he plunged his hand into the mass of tissue paper. "What's this, then?" he said as he pulled forth the bauble, releasing a sheet of tissue paper to the wind. Dispiritedly, I watched the paper dance and swirl its way across the wet grass while Nesbitt grasped the diadem with a meaty hand. He held it up to the light streaming from an antique lamp high atop the gate. The damn thing twinkled and sparkled remorselessly.

"Marks & Spencer doing a line of tiaras, then?"

"It's just something for New Year's," I replied, aiming for nonchalance.

"And here's me without mine. Whatever shall I do?"

"Could I have it back, please? It's not a bomb or anything. You don't have to worry."

"Sorry. The only people I know who wear this sort of thing around these parts are Their Majesties and some of Their Royal Highnesses. I've never known a housemaid with her own tiara."

"It's paste."

Nesbitt weighed the tiara in the prairie of his outspread hand. "It's got a heft to it. Looks like the real goods to me, not that I'm any expert."

"But I'm bringing it *in* to the Estate. I'm not taking it out."

"There is that." He studied my face for a moment. I must have looked a misery, what with the disappointment at finding myself in this pickle and patchy rain splattering my face.

"Look," he continued more sympathetically, "I'm going to have to call someone. Just wait over there." He pointed toward the wooden porch on Jubilee Cottage and pulled out his talking brick, the personal radio with which each officer is equipped.

I leaned against the railing disconsolately, out of the way of the rain, and tried to make out what was being said over the static. But police always sound like they're talking in code.

"Inspector Jenkyns is coming over," Nesbitt reported, after a brief exchange. "Given that this tiara looks like Her Majesty's sort of gear and all."

Normally, I would have greeted the possibility of a personal encounter with Paul Jenkyns with undiluted pleasure. Like that of many women in Her Majesty's employ, my usual, though unspoken, response to the sight of Jenkyns tends to be along the lines of: *Take me. Here. Now.* He's definitely a major muffin. Handsome, to be sure—all Italianate dark good looks, though, of course, he isn't Italian; a local boy, King's Lynn-born, as it happens—but he's got a certain something in addition to physical scrumminess, an aura of total magnetic cool. Only the cream of London's Metropolitan Police are chosen as bodyguards to Royalty, and they have to be superprofessional in the deportment department, never overfriendly with the Royal they're charged to protect. So some of Jenkyns's cool was nurture. But some, I'm sure, was nature. He was just born that way. Since he came on duty about six months earlier as the newest of HM's four Personal Protection Officers (after a stint minding the Duchess of Kent), some of us housemaids have passed idle moments wondering how Her Majesty copes with all this fantabulousness when Inspector Paul comes on for his eight-day shift.

"But Her Majesty's an old age pensioner," was Heather's argument.

"She's a woman!" was mine.

"Don't be vulgar," was Davey's comment when I mentioned this conversation later. "She's the Queen!"

Besides, *he's* married. Heather briefly met Mrs. Inspector Paul Jenkyns at the Staff Christmas Party in the Ballroom (which I missed) in the week before the Big Day. Or Ms. Judith Haverly, as Mrs. P. Jenkyns preferred to be called. She was, Heather reported, a bit posh, daughter of a current Lord Mayor of King's Lynn, don't-you-know, so we imagined her keeping her maiden name less a feminist gesture than a social conceit: Paul must have married up in the world. That, or Judith Jenkyns was a moniker too cute to bear. Anyway, Heather said Ms. Haverly was slim, slight, and sleek, a wintry blonde in a chic black trouser suit, a porcelain doll for the handsome inspector's arm. When he had a free arm, that is. PPOs spend so much of their time with their Royal bosses that wives and children are rumored to have a habit of falling to second place.

The muffin in question was not long in appearing. Dressed, as plainclothes officers around the Queen usually are, in civvies, on this winter evening in a trim black overcoat, Inspector Jenkyns strode past me without a glance, pretty as a stallion, his thick, curly, prematurely silvered hair glistening with rain. After talking briefly with Nesbitt and being handed my M & S bag, he returned and gestured for me to remain standing inside the wooden porch of Jubilee Cottage. I had never been inside Jubilee Cottage before—it's an adorable little house with Tudor-style timbering and bay windows and great chimneys, which I've always fancied—but I knew I wasn't going to get a chance that night.

"Hi," I said sheepishly, searching the Inspector's face for some indication of mood. With his square head and faintly olive skin, he looked like my imaginings of a young Roman senator; in this case a senator faintly annoyed with troubles in Gaul. He has grey-green eyes—noted earlier by our housemaids' male pulchritude assessment division—but in the golden light of the porch, the irises seemed all the greener, quite emerald. I should have melted. Alas, emeralds are hard stones and the Inspector's eyes were hard.

"You are?" he asked.

"Jane Bee, sir," I gulped, feeling dithery.

"You were at the village hall yesterday morning, I believe." It was more of a statement than a demand for confirmation. "And it seems you've got something with you that has PC Nesbitt concerned."

Like his colleague, Inspector Jenkyns thrust his hand into the M & S bag, but he didn't pull the tiara forth. There was only the rustle of tissue paper being turned aside and then silence as he stared down into the bag.

"What is this?"

"A tiara, sir."

"I can see that. What are you doing with it?"

The $64,000 question. Approximately £42,000 at current rates. But, before I could give a prize-winning reply—not that I had one—the Inspector's chiselled jaw dropped an inch or two.

"Where did you get this." It wasn't a question. His voice was suddenly terse, icy; his dark green eyes under fine black brows bored into me. Jenkyns knew exactly where *he* had seen the tiara last. And here I was in the extremely awkward position I'd hoped I wouldn't find myself in—having to decide whether or not to shop Princess Margaret. And to decide in double-quick time.

"At Dersingham Village Hall," I replied. "Yes, I know. I shouldn't have taken it, but I didn't know at the time that the woman had been murdered."

I had made my decision in that instant and my rationale was courtesy PM herself.

"I thought the way she was dressed seemed so insulting to Her Majesty, like that Spitting Image puppet," I continued, practically gabbling with nerves. "So I just snatched it off without thinking." Then I added in a rush, "I'm really sorry. Really."

Jenkyns greeted this improvization with frigid silence. On the other side of the security wall, a speeding car's tires hummed as they slashed through the puddles pocking the sodden road. The trees all around rustled and trembled in the unrelenting northeast wind. I shivered and turned up my collar, diverting my eyes from the Inspector's icy expression to the pale cloud-shrouded moon, nearly three-quarters grown, brushing the tops of the wellingtonia trees concealing York Cottage. I waited. When finally he spoke it was with a simmering anger.

"You've behaved very, very foolishly, Miss Bee. This should be in the hands of the investigating officers. What do you think you're playing at . . . ?"

"I know, I—"

"Why wasn't this turned over?" he demanded more sharply, yanking the diadem from the bag. The diamonds glittered accusingly.

"I . . . Well, I thought I could, um . . . help. By getting it checked out myself. I thought it was real, you see. Genuine. I mean, look at it."

"Don't be ridiculous."

"It is, really. Genuine, that is. I took it to London and had a jeweller look at it and he said . . . Cartier's, actually . . ." Jenkyns's mouth opened a crack. I rushed on. "And he said it was real, and not only that, it once belonged to the Duchess of Windsor. It was stolen during a break-in after the Second World War and then it was—"

But something in Jenkyns's face put a stop to my breathless explanation, a flash of fury that warned of potential storm. The muscles along his jaw worked fiercely. At the same moment, the tiara dropped from his hands. It hit the porch's wooden slats with an ugly little thud.

"I don't believe it, it's impossible," he muttered as I hastily retrieved it. The tiara was undamaged.

He snatched it from my hands and turned it over and over until he found the hallmark. His eyes locked into mine. "Who knows you have this?"

"Er, just me, sir, and, well . . . just me."

"And? And who?"

"Well, the man at Cartier's, of course."

Jenkyns's gorgeous eyes narrowed. "And he wasn't

suspicious of a young woman carrying jewellery of this value?"

"No, I don't think so. I mean, I don't know." It was a good question and my answer was as lame as a horse headed for the glue factory. "I said it had passed into our family . . . unexpectedly, and I gave my name and everything, and identification, and he seemed to accept that. Jewellers are supposed to be discreet, I think, and besides—"

"But you're Canadian, are you not? A Canadian walking into Cartier's with this?"

"My grandparents are English-born," I said crisply. "Things could have come into our family that way. Could have. In theory. Mr. Rose, the man at Cartier's, seemed to accept it." It was truly one of my more atrocious lies; Jenkyns appeared barely convinced.

"Sir," I continued in earnest, "I'll return it to the investigators tomorrow an. . . ." I shrugged to indicate I would take the consequences.

"No! No, you most certainly will not. I will. There's risk you would be charged with impeding an investigation—which is exactly what you've been doing. But a Staff member charged with even a misdemeanour in this incident is likely to draw the sort of press attention Her Majesty doesn't need. I'll return this . . . object and have a quiet word with those in charge. And there will be no more said. Am I understood?"

"Yes, sir," I replied contritely. In fact, I felt rather contrite. A shuddering image of me sojourning at Holloway Prison had burst unbidden in my brain and I was anxious to banish the thought. "Absolutely, sir."

7

I REALLY DRAGGED myself up to my room that evening. It had been a long day after a poor sleep and my brush with Inspector Jenkyns hadn't exactly been the conversational equivalent of a nice cup of cocoa before beddy-byes. If the Inspector hadn't lost his cool with me, he'd come close. I wouldn't want to be on the other end of his Glock handgun if he ever saw fit to draw it in defense of his 'Principal,' as members of the Royal Family are called by those in the Royal & Diplomatic Protection Department.

I opened the door and groped with my hand for the light switch while yawning with what seemed like all the force in the universe.

And then my mouth went into clamp mode and I practically jumped out of my epidermis. For there, as the overhead light snapped on and washed my room in a photographic flash, was Bucky Walsh, propped against a couple of pillows, stretched languorously on my bed like a cashmere-sweatered lizard sunning on a rock.

"Hi," the son and heir of the Thringys said, smiling and blinking against the sudden glare.

"What the hell are you doing here?"

"Sir.

"Just kidding. You don't have to call me 'sir.' I think that's so weird, anyway. We're practically the same age. Sit down and talk to me now." He patted the bedcover invitingly.

"I asked you what the hell you're doing in my room!"

"Oh, we were playing hide-and-seek. They really love these kids' games around here."

I pulled back the sleeve of my jacket and gave my watch face very deliberate scrutiny. Nearly eleven o'clock. It was true: The Royal Family liked to play old-fashioned parlour games as generations of Royals had since Edward VII and his wife, Alix, romped with their aristocratic guests around their beloved Sandringham. But, unless I was mistaken, the only reason current members of the Royal Family continued to play Hide and Go Seek was to entertain young Princesses Beatrice and Eugenie. It was now hours since their bedtime and some few miles from Wood Farm where the two little girls were probably tucked into their royal beds while their mother, Fergie, structured an intricate plot for her next volume of *Budgie, the Little Helicopter*. Besides which, if the Royal Family and guests had indeed been playing Hide and Go Seek, the Staff rooms would have been declared well and truly out of bounds. I said as much to Bucky.

"Okay, you got me," he drawled lazily, tucking his hands behind his head and leaning back against the pillows. "I sort of slipped out and came up here to see if I could find you. Look, I'm bored out of my skull in this dump."

Up until about twenty-four hours ago, I would have agreed with him. Now, after my upsetting 'interview' with HM's PPO, I wasn't bored. I was just plain knackered. The last thing I needed was to have to go 'round the mulberry bush with Buchanan Walsh, the Marchioness's immature son.

"You're not supposed to be here, you know," I explained, irritated, recalling I had said the same thing to him last year, although at least that time it had been said out in the corridor, not over my bed. "You're a guest of Her Majesty. We're Staff. There's this great divide. Ne'er the twain shall meet. And so forth. At least socially," I amended, thinking of my own peculiar situation.

"We don't have this kind of shit back in the States. There everyone is equal."

In theory, I thought. But I was in no mood for a political argument. "Anyway, would you mind leaving? I'm really tired. And I have to be up before seven."

"Ah, lemme stay. There's nothing to do here," he pouted, oblivious, moving his hand to my ancient bedspread and plucking at its few remaining tufts. "You're the only other American around here."

"I'm Canadian," I sighed. Note to myself: Get a T-shirt that proclaims as much, with large maple leaf emblazoned, so you don't have to keep reminding people.

"Yeah, yeah, same difference. C'mon, it's early yet." Bucky rolled onto his side as I moved to the narrow wardrobe on the wall across from the bed. "So, like, how was your Christmas?"

I opened the wardrobe door, removed a hanger, and hung my damp jacket on it. "Aren't there any other guests you can *play* with? How about Peter Phillips?" I suggested, referring to the Princess Royal's son, the Queen's first grandchild, who was about seventeen years old. "Or Zara? She seems like a nice kid." Or was, for all I knew. But then the Princess Royal's daughter was just barely a teenager. God save her from Bucky.

"They're stuck-up as hell," he replied sulkily.

"Did the Queen have any other guests tonight? Didn't they bring their kids?" I closed the door and turned to my own guest. Unwanted guest.

"No. Everybody's got the 'flu. Or something."

He looked at me pleadingly. Buchanan has a long, lean face that somehow just misses being handsome. His head is too narrow, the watery-blue eyes are closer set than they ought to be, as if forceps dragging him into this vale of tears had been clamped a trifle too tight. There's a soft droop to the shape of his eyes, which is potentially endearing, and sharp little upturned nose, which isn't. There's one physical attribute of Bucky's that really puts me off, however: his mouth. It's like a pale rosebud. Some women might think it cute and kissable but to me it's just a puckered puncture portending petulance, if you'll pardon the alliteration.

"So," Bucky continued in his lame attempts at conversation, "what did you do today?"

Practically got arrested for jewel theft, I wanted to say. "Cleaned a bunch of lavs," I declared instead, hoping he might be put off and then bugger off. "Including yours, as it happens. And would you stop picking at that bedspread!"

"Mmm."

He wasn't really listening. What a surprise. He was a little prince, a little American prince, an only child. He had probably been indulged to the furthest reaches of F.A.O. Schwarz and Disney World by his doting mother. That is, until Pamela met and married Alfred Morys Addison De'Ath, Marquis of Thring, who, one gleaned during last year's Sandringham Christmas, took a less sanguine view of his stepson's charms. Even if he was, as gossip maintained, absolutely besotted with the boy's mother.

This was part of Bucky's bellyache to me last year: Steppapa was tight as a Scotsman's purse, or pocketbook of the pecunious ethnic group of your choice. Couldn't squeeze a shekel out of him and he was nearly as rich as the Duke of Westminster, owning nice bits of Lancashire that were now part of the centre of the city of Manchester and nice bits of Norfolk that adjoined the Queen's estates and nice bits of other places I knew nothing about. Which had made me wonder at the time: Surely her ladyship, Pamela II, had some lolly in her own right. Was she not from some rich North Carolina family?

I don't know why I was wondering any of this anyway. All I really wanted to do was shift Bucky's Yankee (or was it Confederate?) carcass out of my room so I could crawl between the sheets. Alone.

And then I remembered that Bucky had been at the panto. This thought shored up my flagging energies. Perhaps he had seen something, heard something vis-à-vis the murder or the mysterious case of the Duchess's tiara. Although there was something so self-absorbed about Bucky I'm not sure he was capable of noticing much beyond the needs of his various assorted organs, mostly stomach and parts south. I leaned against the wardrobe, not in a provocative way, mind, but because the room is so small and I wanted to keep a secure distance between him and me. I folded my arms and inquired in an opening-gambit sort of way:

"What did you think of the panto?"

"The what?" He looked up from his coverlet-plucking.

"The pantomime. The play. The *Queen of Hearts.*"

His face darkened. "Oh, yeah. That thing. It was stupid."

"Well, pantos are peculiarly English, I guess. All that cross-dressing. Had you never been to one before? No? Then why did you go to the one at Dersingham?"

"Mom insisted. She's big on family values." He infused the last two words with derision. "So we have to show up at places together every once in a while, smiling like morons. Village stuff, garden parties, openings for whatever. You'd think she was *running* for Marchioness. We had to go to this play thing because she's a big deal in the charity they were giving the proceeds to."

"But you're at school most times, aren't you? I thought you were at Cambridge this year."

Bucky's expression soured. "Yeah. Well, I was. Sort of. But I'm not going back. It's so boring. I can't stand it."

I could understand university being a bit of a bore. I had found it so in my first (and only) year. But Cambridge? I somehow fancied the idea of myself at Cambridge. Punting on the Cam. Attending the May Week balls. (Clearly, academic work was not uppermost in my mind.)

"What do your parents think? Not exactly chuffed, I'll bet."

"Mom doesn't know. Yet, anyway. And I sure don't give a fuck what Affie thinks." The latter was uttered with ruthless contempt. "I can't take England. I've been here for—what?—like, nearly four years now. Everything's so phony. They all look down their noses at you. Use the wrong fork and they freeze up. They just dumped me in that public school in Yorkshire. Ampleforth. The place was full of perverts, I swear. And then here I am stuck in this place at Christmas again with the whitest white people in the universe! Well, the Queen's okay. She's nice. But the rest of them—forget it. They've all got turnips up their asses. I don't know how you can stand living in this country."

"I'm having fun, actually." Well, I was. Despite the occasional encounter with the likes of Inspector Jenkyns. "I think being an American is an advantage—"

"Canadian. You were making a big deal about being Canadian earlier."

"Oh, you noticed. Will wonders never cease? Well, being a *North* American—is an advantage, then. They have trouble slotting you, don't you think? They're more likely to overlook your faux pas—gaffes, I mean. It can work to your advantage, least that's what I've found. You must have got off on the wrong foot."

Bucky shrugged. Of course, I thought, being dragged out of the U.S. and finding yourself suddenly immersed in an upper-class milieu in the U.K. might be a bit more daunting than my freely chosen experience among a mixed bag of working-class and batty old family-retainer types, however obsessed many of them were with their place in the great chain of being, hierarchically speaking. For all I knew, maybe Americans had it rougher in the former Mother Country. Ambiguous feelings about rebel daughters and all. Canadians, Brits know nothing about. They just have some vague memory Canada was once part of their Empire.

"Anyway," Bucky continued, lurching me from this psychohistorical reverie, "I'm going back."

"To Cambridge? You just said—"

"No, to the States."

"So are your parents, I gather."

"I'm going back *permanently*." Bucky pulled his legs up to his chest and rested his chin on his knees. "Come with me."

"To the U.S.? Sorry, I'm booked here to the next millennium."

"Then out somewhere. How about the Feathers? I know you guys go there sometimes."

"Bucky, watch my lips: You're a guest of Her Majesty the Queen. You can't just bug out and go down to the pub with a bunch of Palace employees. It's not done." Besides, I thought, he would cramp our gossiping.

"You've got real pretty lips." His own puckered puss eased into an eager smile then snapped back when I responded with a cold frown. "Ahh, hell," he groaned, "all these people do around here is play cards . . . or charades. I hate charades! They're, like, *sadists* about it. I had to do Blur—y'know, the group? *You* try and act out Blur. And Princess Margaret keeps playing these gawdawful show tunes on the piano. And I'm stuck here till New Year's!"

There's something so attractive about a man who whinges on and on. "My heart breaks for you, Bucky. It truly does," I said, reaching for my toothbrush, hoping it might indicate to him we were definitely not in for an all-nighter. "Your life is hell. Stepson of one of the Queen's oldest and dearest friends, a Cambridge student, rich as blazes, everything you could possibly want—"

"Affie's rich. I'm not. I've told you before. Look, I'm going to have to rob a bank just to get the money to get back home."

"Then what about your father—your *real* father,

your natural father or whatever the term is. Can't you get some money from him?"

Bucky mumbled something into his knees.

"What?"

"I don't know where he is," he cried, lifting his head.

"Oh."

"Or even who he is," he muttered.

"Oh, that *is* crummy."

"I know, isn't it? Really crummy. I always feel bad about it at Christmas." He gave me a pitiable glance. "Y'know, I could use a hug."

Abuse a hug, more like. "Hasn't your mother ever told you who your real father is?" I asked, ignoring his plea.

Bucky sighed. "No. She won't. Won't discuss it."

"Water/bridge analogy here, possibly?"

"Huh?"

"Never mind. But surely people in your family know who your father is," I continued. "It's hard to keep secrets like that."

"Well, they're doing a damn fine job. They've never said."

"And you've asked?"

"You bet."

"Walsh, hmm," I considered, reaching for the toothpaste. "Probably lots of Walshes around. Still, other people find their parents these days against great odds."

"Walsh is my mother's name. We're the Walshes of Durham County. Walsh-Rayner Incorporated? Agricultural products . . . ?"

I shrugged.

"There've been Walshes in North Carolina since around 1700," Bucky continued in a tone that suggested I should know this vital part of American history.

"Then get the money from your rich, came-over-on-the-Mayflower-or-whatever type relatives."

"Yeah, well, anyway . . ." Bucky shifted so he sat on the edge of the bed, facing me. "C'mon, Jane," he pleaded, "tomorrow, let's go to the Feathers. There's a disco in Lynn. I know some places in Cambridge, too."

"Do you have a car?"

"Women! '*Do you have a car?*' You just want us for our money." He chuckled slyly.

"Bucky, oh Bucky—(a) I don't want you and (b) you just said you don't have any money anyway."

"Then *meet* me there. At the pub. It'll look like a coincidence or whatever."

A thought struck me. The Thringys were rich as Croesus. And even though they—or at least his lordship—were apparently keeping Bucky on a short financial leash, it seemed unsportingly non-U to keep him from having his own motor, some expensive little model suitable to his age and class and so forth. I imagined a wire-wheeled roadster. I watch too many period films.

"Is it because of the epilepsy? Not having a car, I mean. Them not wanting you to drive."

His brow darkened. "How do you know about that?"

"The panto, remember? I heard you had a . . ." Was there some polite word for it?

"A fit? You can say it. Yeah, I had one. I don't get them that often. But sometimes something just sets me off, a noise or flashing lights or . . . I don't know. At this play on Monday, there was this sudden bang in the first act and, of course, they had us sitting in the front. Some guy playing a Demon arrives in a car—well, it's cardboard, actually—and there was this awful loud backfiring and, anyway, that did it. At least I didn't have to sit through the rest of the stupid play."

"You were moved off to a side room, I gather."

"Yeah. I usually need to lie down after—sleep a little. Who told you this stuff?"

"Hume Pryce—"

"Oh, him."

"—last night at the Feathers. Do you know him?"

"Who?"

"Pryce." You idiot.

But Bucky's gaze seemed momentarily to turn inward, then his eyes rolled back slightly. I dropped the toothbrush and toothpaste in the sink.

"Bucky?" Was he all right?

He blinked and refocused on me. If this was what they call a petit mal seizure, it was quickly over. "Um . . . Hume Pryce. He was just hanging around afterwards. After the play ended. I think he wanted to talk to my mom."

"But you and your mother were busy arguing."

"Jesus, it's like being spied on," he said peevishly. "Mom wanted me to come back to the Duke's Head with her. And I wanted to meet some friends. I mean, I'm a grown man and she does this shit to me all the time. Like I'm eight years old or something." A sharp infusion of blood darkened Bucky's countenance.

"Bucky," I said soothingly, "she's probably just being a mother."

"She's being a bitch, is what she's being. She thinks I'm going to get drunk. Drinking lowers the threshold. Yeah, yeah, I know. I'm careful, for Christ's sake. Does anybody think I *like* having these *fucking* seizures?"

His eyes blazed angrily. I found myself, almost against my will, wanting to console him, but my all-girl antennae told me Bucky wouldn't be able to tell a comforting gesture from a come-on.

"Sorry, Bucky. I didn't mean to provoke you."

"That's all right," he said, suddenly becalmed in the way of temperamental children. He leaned back on his elbows and regarded me speculatively. Alas, it was as I feared: He was equating a few kind words with opportunity.

"Anyway," I said, groping around for a new topic and annoyed with myself for continuing the conversation, "did you win the argument with your mother?"

"Yeah, of course. Went to a club in Lynn."

"I guess you know about the murder at the village hall in Dersingham." I pulled my Tank Girl T-shirt, my sleepwear, from the foot of the bed. "You didn't by any chance see anything, did you?"

"Yeah, I heard," Bucky replied irritably. "Of course I didn't see anything. Why would I see anything?"

"Just asked. I thought you might find the whole

business interesting. You're American. You must be used to murder."

He scowled. "What's that supposed to mean?"

"Oh, nothing." I wished I hadn't said it. It *was* prejudicial. But I was getting past caring. "Do you think you can get back to your own room now? It's getting close to midnight."

"Aww, you're not kicking me out already?"

"Yes, Bucky. Yes, I am. Good night, Bucky. Sleep tight, Bucky." I waved my fingers.

Bucky didn't shift.

"Bucky?"

"If I go, Jane, will you meet me at the Feathers tomorrow?"

I glared. I hate the bargaining bit. "Bucky, when you're a guest of the Queen of England in the Queen of England's own private residence, you can't just get up of an evening and say, 'Sorry, luv, I'm down the pub to hoist a few wi' me mates, wot includes yer 'ousemaid. Cheers.' There's such a thing as manners. And your hostess is the bloody Monarch, for heaven's sake. You're the envy of millions. How the hell did you get out of the Saloon tonight, anyway? Had Her Majesty gone to bed first?"

This is the usual protocol. No one goes upstairs until HM goes upstairs. Fortunately, she's an early-to-bed, reasonably-early-to-rise kind of monarch.

"I said I had a headache."

"Oh, brilliant."

"They were glad to get rid of me anyway. I probably scare them. They think I'm going to have a fit and fall in the fireplace."

"Her Majesty's had worse scares. Somebody took a shot at her once—"

"No kidding."

"—when she was Trooping the Colour. It was years back. Anyway . . ."

Bucky got to his feet. "Yeah? So, anyway, you'll meet me at the Feathers?"

"We'll see." I sighed.

Bucky leaned toward me. "Oh, look, you've got a little boo-boo."

Instinctively, I touched the welt on the bridge of my nose, dabbing at its tenderness. "I hit it on something."

"Aww. Here. I'll kiss it and make it better."

"Bucky! Don't!"

Too late. He grabbed me by my shoulders and forced my body against his, planting a wet one between my eyes. Instinctively, I pushed at his bony chest and broke the lock he had on me. He fell toward the bed.

"Hey!" he yelped. "I was only being friendly."

"Bucky, it's not welcome. Now, could you go?"

"Ah, c'mon. You like it. You're interested."

Where oh where was my 'No Means No' button when I needed it? "Bucky, go away. Or I'll tell the Queen." Now that was an interesting threat.

"Did anybody ever tell you you were beautiful?"

"Yes, regularly, about half an hour before they call time at the pub."

"Hey, you're pretty funny."

"A laff riot. Now *go.*"

"C'mon. I might have to take my *droyt de signoor* then . . ." He rose again from the bed, grinning an insipid grin, and sort of wagging an imaginary tail.

"Droyt de . . . ?" I was momentarily confounded. "You mean *droit du seigneur*? Look, Bucky," I said heatedly as he took a step toward me. "You're not the signoor of Sandringham. And even if you were, believe me, you don't have that kind of droyt anymore. Nobody does."

But a kind of obsessive glaze had come over Bucky's pale eyes as he reached toward me. His right hand dug into my left shoulder. I tried to brush his arm away with my free hand, but to no avail. Skinny he might be, but the boy's hands were strong.

"Bucky, cut it out, you're hurting me," I cried, taking a step backward, momentarily loosening his grasp. I wasn't frightened even when he began making these strange crooning baby-talk blatherings. But I was very angry. My room may not be big enough to swing a cat, but it's big enough to swing a few other things. As Bucky lunged toward me, I did something I had never done before. I moved so quickly, I was barely conscious of what I was doing, or even if I should be doing it, but my palm was flattened and my fingers squeezed tight, and before I knew it, my arm was slicing the air and my eyes were stinging with tears of pain as flesh assaulted flesh. A sharp crack rent the air followed by a yelp of surprise from Bucky as he tottered, then nearly fell, righting himself only by grasping the handle of the wardrobe at the last second. He gasped and blinked rapidly, his free hand rubbing his cheek where a red welt the size of Wales was subduing the winter pallor. Then, to my surprise, Bucky didn't say anything, didn't curse me or threaten me, or try to hit back. He just gawped at me for what seemed like an eternity and then beat a retreat out my door.

8

EARLY NEXT MORNING, I found myself again in the Saloon, as per schedule, cleaning brushes and Hoover in hand, ready and raring to give the place its requisite tidy. I wish I could say I had spent a restless night, tossing and turning, troubled by images of lurking dirty young men, worried about the consequences of striking a guest of the Queen, consumed with guilt for using violence, annoyed because somebody had short-sheeted my bed as part of the Christmas hilarity, but I can't. True, I was shaken afterwards. I had to sit on the bed and take a few deep breaths. Then Heather appeared. My cry had awakened her from her sick bed and the sound of the slap had sent her flying into my room. She quickly appointed herself minister of outrage, fulminating against men and all their calumnies with a zeal that belied fatigue wrought by 'flu. However, I found that though my hand continued to smart, a sensation less painful began to bloom inside—almost a kind of elation. There had been something powerfully cathartic about giving Bucky whatfor. It felt good. Maybe I was being naïve, or I had become de queen of denial, but I don't think there was ever any true danger from Bucky Walsh. He mostly lacked couth. A poorly house-trained puppy, he was, and a firm slap was just the sort of discipline he needed, although I must confess I would be less sanguine about this if my response had provoked him further.

At any rate, word had got about, as it tends to do below stairs, and when I arrived in Servants' Hall the next morning for my wake-up coffee and a quick bun, there had been a burst of applause from my female peers in the lower orders—which I accepted with great humbleness, of course—followed by demands for the 411, to which I graciously acceded, with, of course, some judicious editing. Frankly, I think there's a couple of my professional colleagues here in the royal housecleaning biz who would have fancied their chances with Bucky, if Bucky had fancied his chances with them, but then there's no accounting for taste.

Thinking about this, I paused in front of the green baize-covered table holding one of the jigsaw puzzles HM likes to work on during her occasional idle moments. I had just finished tidying a stack of sheet music someone (probably Princess Margaret) had left in disarray on Queen Alexandra's oak grand piano and was, as a consequence, humming one of the tunes the title of which my eyes had glanced over ("I'm Just a Girl Who Can't Say No" from *Oklahoma!*), when a couple of my brain cells discerned the soft patter of tiny feet along the Axminster. Alas, it was not Princess Eugenie. She was at Wood Farm playing quietly in the dawn with her new Christmas toys. The sound emanated instead from one of those harbingers of the approaching Presence—a corgi, a breed beloved by Her Majesty and regarded askance by those of us who treasure unbroken skin around our ankles and unladdered tights. The little dog plunked its shaggy bottom down on the edge of the carpet and regarded me wantonly, its wicked tongue lolling from between exposed teeth. Hastily—for I had no business dallying with Her Majesty's jigsaw—I returned the puzzle piece I had idly plucked from the baize just in time to properly turn and curtsey as the Queen entered the room, carrying a copy of the *Daily Telegraph* folded to the crossword.

"Joan!" the Queen said in a low warning tone to the corgi, whose idea of obedience was to rise and move closer to my vulnerable ankles.

"Good morning, Your Majesty," I said, surprised at her arrival, but edging cautiously away from Joan.

Though I had anticipated an audience with the Queen, I had not expected one quite so early and was somewhat startled to find HM up and about at such an hour. Not only up and about, but looking ready for the day. I guess at the back of my mind I expected the holidaying Monarch at 8:05 to have her hair in curlers and her feet encased in furry pink mules, but, wonder of wonders, she was wearing a tweed skirt, with a pastel pink woolly cardigan pulled around her shoulders; more miraculously yet, her now almost completely grey hair was as set and springy as it would be on a day of public appearances.

"Jane?" I heard Her Majesty say. "Jane?"

"Oh, yes, Ma'am," I replied, realizing I must have been gawking. "Sorry, Ma'am."

"Come with me. We'll go into the Drawing Room. There'll be more privacy."

The Saloon, it's true, is somewhat bereft of doors that one might properly close. Bereft of doors, period. It's the largest room at Sandringham, two storeys high, with a gallery across the upper half of the back of the room where minstrels might play if this was another age, with access through three large Romanesque arches of dark oak. It was through the middle of these we walked, past the weighing machine with its leather-covered seat, which Edwardians found so amusing, and past the mahogany circular table with its gizmos to measure speed and direction of the wind—useful I suppose in a windy place like west Norfolk, although I think all you really need do is look out the window to see which way and how low the rhododendron bushes are bending.

The Drawing Room or, rather, the Small Drawing Room—because that's where we were headed—lies just on the other side of the corridor that forms the central axis of Sandringham House. The Small Drawing Room is my favourite room in the Big House and, as HM switched on the overhead lamp, a pink and green Dresden china chandelier to light the darkened room with its soft glow, I understood anew why. It's pretty—'bonny,' Heather calls it—and that's definitely the word; the furnishings are delicate, of such rare materials as satinwood and tulipwood; the wallpaper, a cosy pattern of tiny roses and vines, is silk and matches precisely the needlework on the chairs done by Queen Mary, the Queen's grandmother. There's scads of the most exquisite antique porcelain—figurines, vases, jars—lying about, most of it in a recessed wallcase beside the fireplace, and, fitting in so feminine a room, a plethora of portraits of royal women, Queen Alexandra's mother, Queen Louise of Denmark, for instance, and two of her daughters, Princess Louise and Princess Victoria, King George V's sisters.

The Queen sat down, Joan in a comfortable and nonthreatening heap at her feet, and bade me sit in one of a pair of comfy beige armchairs set on either side of the (alas) unlit fireplace. I did so, and immediately there was this appalling flatulent sound.

"Oh, dear, one of the grandchildren must have left that there," Her Majesty said as I pulled a rubber bladder as red as my face out from under me.

The Queen smiled serenely while I turned and placed the whoopee cushion on an adjacent table. In doing so I could see through the panes of the connecting glass door into the Main Drawing Room, still in shadow at this early morning hour, though the silver light of approaching dawn was beginning a dance along the branches of a great Christmas tree in the recesses of a bay window, the shapes of balls and bows and candles gradually emerging from indeterminate gloom. I felt a pang of homesickness at that moment, remembering the

Christmas tree in my grandmother's own bay window at her little house in Charlottetown. I must have appeared a trifle sad, for Her Majesty, placing her crossword on a nearby lamp table, inquired: "Are you missing home at this time of year?"

I blinked. "Yes, Ma'am, a little. But my father is here, at any rate. Which is very nice."

Thinking of my father reminded me suddenly of the Elvis Challenge he had presented at the Maple Leaf pub, and I could feel a flush creeping anew into my face. Asking HM if she had ever met the King (of rock 'n' roll, that is) seemed too mortifyingly peculiar a question to pose at such an early hour. But the Queen had read the discomfort in my face and, asking after my health, obliged me to confess the source of a rosy face in the dead of winter.

"Ma'am," I said, shifting uneasily in my seat, "can I ask Your Majesty a . . . an odd question?"

"You *may*," she said, granting permission and correcting my grammar in one fell swoop.

Here goes, I thought. Blurt it out, Jane. "Ma'am, have you ever met Elvis?"

"Presley or Costello?" Her Majesty shot back.

I must have looked slightly stunned, because HM regarded me challengingly, her blue eyes twinkling with amusement. "One does endeavour to keep up with the trends, Jane." She paused and smiled, taking evident pleasure in my astonishment. "Now, why would you want to know such a thing?"

"My father, Ma'am. He was keen to know. He's a big fan."

HM raised an eyebrow.

"Of Elvis Presley, I mean, Ma'am. And, of course, of Your Majesty, too," I added hastily, feeling as I said it that I would be better off just putting both feet in my mouth and calling it a day.

"I'm not sure," the Queen said briskly, her smile fading a little, "that I care to think of my subjects as 'fans.' Now, to answer your question . . ."

.   .   .

And she did.

"I do hope your father will find this satisfactory," she concluded.

More than that, I should think, enormously pleased. He would never be able to accuse me of getting that answer from a book.

"Thank you, Ma'am," I replied. "I'm sure it's just what he'd like to hear."

The Queen bent forward and patted Joan, who twisted her head ecstatically to better receive her mistress's attentions. "The question I have for you," HM said, resuming her position, "concerns your mission to London yesterday. Was it at all successful?"

"Well, yes and no, Ma'am." I paused.

How to put it?

"I did buy ten tickets on the National Lottery, but I, um, regret to inform Your Majesty that the tickets must go to Her Royal Highness." Goodness, I sounded portentous. Like some courtier obliged to give Charles I the bad news about the beheading thing.

"Sorry," I added lamely.

The Queen sighed and fingered the strands of opalescent pearls at her neck. "Then that tiara did belong to the Duchess," she murmured. "How very extraordinary." She glanced at the golden clock surrounded by Christmas cards on the mantel, a certain pensiveness smoothing the lines around her eyes. The adjacent lamp cast a gentle glow on Her Majesty's full soft face, which was powdered pink, the only other makeup a blush of red at her lips.

"Well," she said at last, "I, too, had an opportunity to make a few inquiries. Did Mr. Rose at Cartier's tell you anything about the aftermath of the burglary at Ednam Lodge?"

"No, Ma'am. It was his understanding the jewels disappeared without a trace in 1946, although a few apparently came to light at an auction sometime after Her Grace's death."

HM's lips formed a slight moue of disapproval.

"So," I continued, "the gems were assumed removed from their settings and recut. Gone for good. At least until the tiara suddenly appeared out of nowhere."

"The tiara had to have come from somewhere," Her Majesty countered. "But where it's been all these years is the question. I've learned, however, that a thief did confess to the burglary at Ednam Lodge, a certain Mr. Richard Dunphie. He was jailed in Norwich Prison for housebreaking and robbery in the early 1960s, I'm told. He had apparently broken into a number of country homes over the years and had concentrated his . . . talents, such as they were, on jewellery."

"Ma'am, did he confess where any of the jewellery may have got to? Particularly that lot stolen at Ednam Lodge?"

"Apparently not. I understand the jewellery was 'fenced'—I believe that's the correct term—and that Mr. Dunphie didn't reveal who these people might be. And, of course, he's no longer living."

"Oh," I said, disappointed.

"However," HM continued, "the jewels from the Ednam Lodge burglary were apparently kept on a boat at King's Lynn for some time while they were . . . oh, what's the word? It was in a crossword the other day. Short word."

" 'Hot'?" I supplied.

"Yes, that's it. Very good, Jane."

"But isn't that interesting, Ma'am! It means the tiara was in the area for a time. Of course," I added, deflated, "that was nearly fifty years ago. Still"—brightening here—"perhaps it's never been far away the whole time!"

"Odd the tiara has remained intact, though," HM mused. "The custom, as you've said, Jane, is to dispose of jewellery by removing the gems from their settings and recutting them and so forth, such that their provenance is difficult to determine . . ."

"Which suggests the thief—Mr. Dunphie—may have done the burglary to order, Ma'am. A commission, of sorts. Oops." I suddenly remembered Mr. Rose's reference to the Alexandra emeralds.

"Jane, is something the matter?"

"Er . . . well, nothing, really." Oh, why had I oopsed? But Her Majesty was regarding me with a hint of impatience. "It's just . . ." I continued, awkwardly, "it's just that there's this story about something called the Alexandra Emeralds . . ."

"Oh, yes, the Alexandra Emeralds," Her Majesty said dryly, twisting her wedding ring. "A ridiculous story. My great-grandmother, Queen Alexandra, supposedly bequeathed my uncle David a collection of jewels, including emeralds, which he subsequently gave to Mrs. Simpson, as she was then. I don't know why this story has persisted. There are no 'Alexandra Emeralds.' Even if there were, it makes no sense to me that the Duchess would have carried uncut stones from France to this country as part of her travelling collection. You can't wear uncut stones. And there would have been no other reason to bring them. As for the rumour that my family may have been involved in retrieving these fictional jewels, well, I can only say that it is utterly untrue. Did Mr. Rose tell you this?"

"Yes, Ma'am. But he assured me there was absolutely no truth to the story. We were just speculating about the causes and consequences of jewel theft, that's all. I think he just thought I would find the story interesting."

"I see."

Whew, I thought. I had most definitely been schooled about raising royal rumour.

"Nevertheless," Her Majesty continued, "you do raise an interesting point. The burglary might have been done, as you say, 'to order.' "

"Or, perhaps, Ma'am, the fence to whom the jewels were sold knew of someone who fancied the Duchess of Windsor's jewellery, or a piece of it. A collector of some sort. Mr. Rose suggested the tiara may have fallen into the hands of a collector at the time, though he said he's never heard of anyone from that period who would fit the bill. Someone, I guess, rich enough to afford diamonds in 1946 and willing to make a deal under the table. And, for some strange reason, wanting to keep the jewels, or maybe just the tiara, intact."

A faraway look came into the Queen's eyes as I was talking. Absently, she ran her fingers along the strands of pearls.

"Yes . . . yes . . ." she murmured, nodding in response to my conjecturing, or at least that's what it seemed. I waited for Her Majesty to reply, noting as I did that the darkness beyond the lace curtains had separated into more distinguishable forms: the west lawn and, beyond, the sombre massings of oak and pine lining the winding walk to Sandringham Church. A silhouette interceded and then vanished. A security policeman, his footfalls very nearly audible, had crossed on the cinder path in front of the window, a reminder of the ever-present security on the Estate when HM was in residence, and a reminder that security had been intensified.

'A penny for your thoughts, Ma'am,' I felt like saying, turning my attention from another grey winter sunrise back to the Queen, but one—you might imagine—always feels somewhat constrained in conversations with the Sovereign. There are boundaries to familiarity, no matter how relaxed and normal these old master/servant tête-à-têtes can be, and usually are.

Joan yawned one of those squealy doggie yawns and HM, reverie broken, turned her attention back to me, the faintly troubled expression transformed into one of amusement. Even though the redness had receded somewhat overnight, my boo-boo was still sufficiently distinct to capture her attention. I could tell. Her eyes were focused right on the bridge of my nose.

"Tried it on, did you?" she inquired.

I crossed my eyes trying to focus on my nose. Impossible. "Ma'am . . . ?" I said, beginning to sputter.

"One has to learn to affix a tiara properly, or it can come crashing down on one's nose. Quite painful, as some of the women in my family can attest. Still, your red spot is rather exceptional."

"I tried it on on the train, Ma'am," I confessed, blushing deeply. "The train lurched suddenly and that made it worse, I think." I touched my nose delicately with my index finger and winced. It still hurt a bit. "Anyway," I sighed, "it's not likely to happen again."

"I daresay," Her Majesty said.

Suddenly I found my shoes terribly captivating.

"I trust the tiara's safe, Jane," the Queen continued. "I shall have to return it to the proper authorities." She pursed her lips. "One hopes our detective work will make up for the . . . impropriety of removing the tiara in the first place, oh dear."

I don't think Your Majesty is in any danger of arrest, I thought, but said instead: "Inspector Jenkyns has it. The tiara, that is."

"Oh, indeed?"

And I told the Queen of the previous evening's events when I tried to bring the tiara back through security. "The Inspector said he will return it to the authorities investigating the murder."

"Good," Her Majesty commented tartly when I had finished.

"And Inspector Jenkyns said he would have a quiet word so news of the tiara's . . . travels from the scene of the crime don't get in the papers and all."

"I see. Yes, I expect that's for the best. Although"—Her Majesty tapped her chin thoughtfully with one finger—"I must say, it's difficult to see how the tiara will help the police in their inquiries in any case—"

"I know, Ma'am," I interrupted excitedly. This was more interesting. "Priceless jewellery is the sort of thing people are likely to commit murder *for*, don't you think? And yet, there it was, perched on the victim's head. Whoever murdered Jackie Scaife couldn't possibly have known anything of the value of the tiara."

"No, I suppose not."

There was just the tiniest hint of doubt in the Queen's tone. "I understand these Animal Rights Front extremists are the focus of the investigation," she continued.

"A threatening letter was pieced together from torn pieces found in the jacket the victim was wearing. And there had been other letters, apparently. And

Jackie"—how familiar she was becoming; we'd only met once and the woman had been dead at the time—"had been provocative in other ways." And I mentioned Jackie's letter-writing to the *Lynn News* and the flash, and now slashed, fur coat.

There was a set to Her Majesty's mouth that spoke of dissent.

". . . and, of course, these extremist types made a mess of Your Majesty's lodge at Flitcham. And then there's those awful booby-trap things sent to His Royal Highness last month—"

"That's supposed to be confidential!"

"Oh, Ma'am."

'Confidential' meant everyone in the Household and Staff knew. The entire nation would know as soon as some newspaper reporter got off his lazy backside.

"Yes, well . . ." HM responded, eyebrows arched with pique. There are times the Palace leaks like a sieve, and I'm not referring to the plumbing.

"Nevertheless," she continued. "I find it puzzling. This woman, Jackie Scaife, does not seem to me to be an obvious target for animal-rights extremists despite such so-called provocations."

"But, Ma'am," I argued. Surely what I was about to state was the obvious: "Jackie Scaife was dressed as . . . you. As Your Majesty."

"Yes, Jane," the Queen said patiently. "I know security believes Miss Scaife was made a target because she was impersonating . . . One."

"But surely that's the motive! These people thought by targeting her, a woman dressed as Your Majesty, they would really frighten people into stopping blood sports, escalate the whole business, and such. I'm told the ARF is regarded by police as the biggest terrorist threat in Britain today. Maybe they thought Jackie *was* Your Majesty!"

"It's most unlikely I would be alone in a village hall on the Estate in the evening, Jane."

"But, Ma'am, the symbolism of it all! You—the real you—could be next!"

"Jane, calm yourself. I understand the ARF is a

serious threat. I understand its members have stepped up their campaign of violence. But furriers and medical researchers are their usual targets."

"And politicians, Ma'am."

"No one has been killed."

"Yet," I countered. And then backtracked: "Jackie Scaife has been killed." Now who was being de queen of denial? De Queen!

"Jane, the ARF has not claimed credit for this woman's death, which is the usual pattern for terrorists. And . . ."—HM held up a cautionary digit—"the means is unusual. A blunt instrument. Not the common thing, such as a bomb, to lend the sort of spectacle these people often seek."

Hmm, I thought. Her Majesty was certainly determined to dismiss this potential threat.

"And what do the police think?" I persisted.

"The Anti-Terrorist Branch is involved and, of course, they're concentrating on the ARF," she replied in even tones, her familiar face as impenetrable as it is on a £5 note.

She was being circumspect, I could tell. Of course, the police would concentrate their energies on anything that even had a whiff of a threat to the person of the Queen. They had learned a hard lesson in the early 'eighties when an intruder bypassed the security in Buckingham Palace and made his way to the Queen's bedroom—with Queen in nightie and asleep—with no difficulty. A couple of years back another person, a homeless man, made it over the wall into the Palace gardens and walked through an open French window before being arrested in a passageway. And there have been other incidents, each one a nightmare for members of the Royalty & Diplomatic Protection Department, each of whom fancied keeping his head attached to his neck, or at the very least keeping his job. Indeed, I thought, it was just these sorts of concerns and worries which could shift the direction of a murder investigation, perhaps along the wrong path. Was this what HM was thinking? Of course, it was difficult to tell. Not only is she not the sort of woman to wear her emotions on her sleeve, she isn't likely to offer a critique of her security to one as humble as yours truly. And yet . . .

"Ma'am," I braved, "might Your Majesty have a different theory . . . ?"

The Queen pursed her lips. "One does continue to find the notion of the tiara rather intriguing," she replied. An oblique answer, I thought.

"Still," she continued, "I expect the police shall be able to make something of it."

Her eyes caught mine. There was a twinkle in hers and a certain intelligence passed between us. I had been HM's eyes and ears in a previous incident at Buckingham Palace a year earlier. I understood, now, in a tacit sort of way, that my ocular and aural skills might again prove useful. Her Majesty reached down to stroke Joan's golden fur.

Joan sighed.

9

WELL, I THOUGHT, when a little later I had departed the Presence and settled back into my skivvying routine in the bedrooms of the high and mighty, this is a curious kettle of fish, if kettles of fish can be said to be curious. While the investigating authorities in the murder of Jackie Scaife seemed to be barrelling down the M1 of animal-rights extremism, the Queen appeared to have turned onto a B road. No, not even that. A country lane. A winding, hedgerow'd, uphill downdale sort of track leading who knows where. And it wasn't so much as if HM had turned onto the road herself; rather, she seemed to be standing at a crossroad pointing: Castle Rising, this way. Burnham Market, that way. Possible Solution, t'other way. Of course, it's not always easy for the Queen, if her notions are contrary to the Palace bureaucracy, to shift momentum in other directions, and both her constitutional position and her celebrity make it virtually impossible for her to do her own sleuthing. She is obliged to engage in more subtle strategies.

But why she was taking a contrary view on the Scaife murder at all was the puzzle. Of course, Her Majesty does like a puzzle for puzzle's sake. In evidence, m'lud, I present puzzles jigsaw (Exhibit A) and puzzles crossword (Exhibit B), either or both of which are never far from HM's desk. But murder is a game with consequences. The stakes are higher. I had a niggling feeling while we were talking that some other suspicion had formulated in her mind, one that she could not, would not, or should not share with yours truly, full-time housemaid and part-time Nancy Drew, OHMS.

On the other hand—and such hands are always floating about, rather like some Hindu goddess's—I wondered whether HM was resisting the hypothesis of animal-rights extremists because of the shock of witnessing the dead body of Jackie Scaife. Granted, the episode backstage at Dersingham Village Hall was a shock to all of us who were present Tuesday morning, but it must have been particularly disturbing to the Queen. I have no idea what it must be like to see your image everywhere, on stamps and coins, in newspapers and magazines, on television and film, as the Queen is able to. And I can only imagine she has glimpsed at one time or another someone impersonating Herself, even if she only came across it by accident flipping through the channels on telly on evenings when Prince Philip is out making one of his frequent speeches somewhere and leaving his wife back at Buck House dining off a TV tray. But I don't think any of this could prepare you, queen or commoner, for the surreal shock of seeing your own self laid out, as if on a bier, dead as a proverbial doornail. They say everyone has a double somewhere on the planet, but who ever runs into hers or his sauntering down the high street? If you did, you'd be absolutely gobsmacked. If you ran into yourself *dead*, you'd be absolutely gobsmacked with the theme music from *The Twilight Zone* crashing about your head. I had to admire Her Majesty for maintaining her cool that morning. I know she's a pro at sangfroid and stiff upper lip and all, but if it had been me I would have jumped out of my skin like a greased ferret. I said as much to Her Majesty. Albeit in somewhat more refined language.

"I must say, Jane, it's not an episode one would care to have repeated," she replied. "However, I have met my doppelgänger before. Fortunately, she was living at the time."

"That wouldn't be that Jeannette Charles person, would it, Ma'am?" I asked, thinking of Eric Twist's amazed comment when we first came across Jackie Scaife's body.

"Yes, I believe it was she. Or at least I hope it was. One wouldn't care to have whole armies of these people about.

"Jeannette Charles," HM continued, explaining, "does impersonations of one. Or so I've been told." The Queen frowned ever so slightly. I bet her husband was the one who did the telling and had a jolly time doing it, too. "I came upon Mrs. Charles one day when I was on the way to Maldon, in Essex, for the town's eight-hundredth anniversary, I think it was. We were passing through a nearby village, and one was, of course, waving. The car had slowed, I turned my head toward the curb, and there, about as far away from me as you are, Jane, was a woman who bore a striking resemblance to one. It gave me the oddest feeling."

"Spooky, Ma'am?"

"Yes, as you say. Spooky."

"Was she . . ."—how to put this?—"doing a kind of send-up?"

The Queen appeared to consider this. "No, I don't think so. She simply has the odd luck of resembling one. Anyway, I believe this woman near Maldon was Jeannette Charles. And that is my only previous encounter with such a person. Until Tuesday."

The Queen grew solemn. And then, after a moment, reached for her crossword. It was the signal that our interview was drawing to a close. Joan, ever alert to her mistress's habits, got onto her little feet and turned her nose up toward the Queen inquiringly. Absently,

HM ruffled the fur around the dog's neck with her free hand.

"I'm sorry you had trouble returning the tiara to the Estate, Jane," she said, placing the crossword on her lap.

"Oh, it was nothing, Ma'am." I was a little startled. The Queen is not noted for being apologetic. I suppose she feels she rarely has anything to apologize for, since she does her job with such remarkable diligence, and expects everyone else to do the same.

"And you must let me know if anything else seems . . ." She paused, fingering her pearls. "Should not seem quite right. I'm sure you know what I mean."

"Yes, Ma'am."

Her Majesty rose and brushed at her skirt. I rose as well, and made one of my usual inept curtseys.

"And Jane, the National Lottery tickets . . . ?" HM asked as I began to make my way from the Small Drawing Room.

"Oh! I can go get them now. They're in my room. And there's that letter from the man at Cartier's about the tiara's provenance."

"I'm afraid the rest of my day will be taken up. Perhaps if you deliver them to a member of Staff. You're friendly with David Pye, I think. He'll do."

"Very good, Ma'am."

By mid-morning, after all the guests were up and about, doing whatever it is Her Majesty's guests do at Sandringham when they're not shooting small animals for amusement, I was into the donkey work of housemaiding—changing beds, cleaning lavs, tidying rooms. We housemaids usually work in teams. It's more fun that way because you can have a good natter and do the work, such as making toenail-shattering supertight hospital corners on the beds, in double-quick time. But my partner, Heather, was still knocked out with 'flu, so I was stuck on my own.

At least, though, being alone gave me a chance to activate the brainbox along certain lines. If, I thought, as

I lugged my equipment into the Marchioness of Thring's bedroom, the murder of Jackie Scaife wasn't attributable to some demented animal-rights type, then who? Aileen Benefer, our conscientious housekeeper? Clearly, there had been rancour between the two sisters. How about Hume Pryce? He had certainly come over all funny when he learned Dad was a plod—I mean, a member of the Royal Canadian Mounted Police. Even Master Walsh had behaved evasively when I raised the topic of the Boxing Day panto. And where might that blasted tiara fit into all this?

The Marchioness's suite lay, as did some of the other guest suites, toward the south end of Sandringham House, in a wing that had once housed on the ground floor not only a billiard room but, of all things, a bowling alley. It's hard to imagine members of the Royal Family bowling, and maybe it's because the Royal Family hasn't bowled since the days when bowling was a craze among Edwardian aristocrats that the bowling alley is now occupied by a library. Above this are some of the newer suites of bedrooms. I say 'newer' only because they were added after a fire in 1891 damaged a great deal of the original structure.

The Marchioness's bedroom was one of the prettier in the place. The walls were pale lilac, the splendid canopied bed hung with deep violet and gold floral curtains, the chaise longue in a complementary chintz with a floral design in shades of purple and dark green. There was a charming escritoire topped by a vase of fresh flowers, a large dressing table with an enormous gilt-edged mirror, a highly decorative fire screen hiding the vacant grate of the (nonworking) fireplace the mantel of which was laden with various china knickknacks, and the walls had lots of pictures of sporting scenes and local views that the Royal Family seem to collect by the hundredweight. A bowl of fresh fruit and a small dish of Bendick's mints (uneaten) on the bedside table completed the hospitable tableau. All in all a room I wouldn't mind camping in, not that I have any major complaints about my own bolt-hole.

I wondered, though, what her ladyship thought of

the room. Rumour had it she was spending gajillions of pounds refurbishing Barsham Hall, the ancestral pile of the Thrings, repairing, rehanging, remounting, restoring, reupholstering, and regilding practically everything down to the last doorknob so that the place dazzled and shone. Looked at through the eyes of a decorating-mad marchioness, I thought, Sandringham House, including its guest bedrooms, must appear a bit down-at-the-heel, a trifle shabby.

'Tat, Jane dear, is the hallmark of the true upper classes,' Davey had drawled at me admonishingly Tuesday afternoon in the footman's lounge where he was recovering from that morning's shock at the village hall. We were flipping together through a photo-spread in a six-month-old *Tatler* that had devoted considerable space to the ongoing progress of the Barsham Hall restoration (or desecration, depending on your view).

"She's turned the place into a tart's boudoir," Davey sniffed. "Ooh, and look at this! Wall-to-wall carpeting. And beige, too! D'you know there's a seventeenth-century oak floor under that mat of sheeps' curls? Absolutely shocking vulgarity! The late Lord Thring must be spinning."

Why the present Lord Thring, guardian of a great heritage home, allowed his second wife to muck about with said great heritage home, adding gewgaws to the gewgaws, selling off this and that art treasure unsuited to her tastes, and generally causing conniptions in the conservation community, which loves stately things when they are scrumptiously rundown, was a subject of certain chitchat. 'Pamela's much too grand for us,' Davey said the Sergeant Footman overheard the Palace Steward tell the Page of the Chambers that he had happened to hear Prince Philip disclose to his Private Secretary that that was what the Queen had remarked to him.

But, fundamentally, it was said, Lord Thring cared much more for his wife than for his inheritance. 'Besotted,' was the word in constant use. Poor Lord Thring, who had married late to begin with, about age forty-five, had spent nearly twenty years between wives. His first, Pamela I, sometimes known as the Bolter, had run off with a South African cattle rancher after three years of marriage, and the fact that she died about a year later in an accidental drowning was no comfort.

"There's a pattern here," I once said to Davey. "Didn't Di's mother dump Earl Spencer for some Australian sheep farmer? And what about Fergie? Didn't her mother run off with an Argentine polo player? I'm sure there's other examples."

"Tons, my dear. Even the late Lord Thring's wife—Affie's mother—bolted, or so they say. Or did she die young? I can't remember."

"What's the problem?"

"Well, take Lord Thring . . ."

"I don't think I would, actually."

"Well, exactly."

"I mean, he's much too old for the likes of me. Rich, though. I could change my mind."

"But such a bore, Jane! The man is simply a mind-numbing, sphincter-winkling, crashing bore. Shall I spell it? I shall. B-O-R-E. Bore. All he does is go on and on about dogs and horses, horses and dogs. And, occasionally, his collection of porcelain replicas of horses and dogs. It's enough to make one cross-eyed. These country folk give me *mal de mer*. Oh, for the city. Oh, for London." He whimpered into his tea. "How much longer will we be exiled here in . . . in the fens? The wind. The rain. The cold . . ."

"These aren't quite the fens, Davey."

"Near as dammit."

"But the Queen seems to like him," I continued.

"The Queen seems to like who?" Davey struggled to rise from his case of weather-induced sulks. "Whom? . . . Who?"

"The Marquess. Lord Thring. Stop hooting, for heaven's sake."

"Beg pardon. Yes, well, Mother's known Affie for donkey's years. He was her Equerry once upon a time. And besides, she's keen on dogs and horses and such, too."

"But the Queen is interested in other stuff," I argued.

"I think Mother probably finds Affie's mind-numbing, er, *simple* conversation a relief from the end-less Red Boxes, and from Father mithering about the state of the world—how that man does go on!—and from worrying about her children's gruesome marriages, and her mother's declining health, and these new tax demands—"

"Okay, I get your point."

"—and the kingdom's decay and the Commonwealth's irrelevance and whether Maastricht means she'll be out of a job and the fact that her horses haven't won a race since who-knows-when. It's probably just one of those old-shoe friendships—comfortable, you know. Anyway, perhaps Affie fancied her in days of yore before she became Queen. She was rather fetching. You've seen the pictures."

"Doesn't explain this bolting phenomenon among the upper *clawses*," I said, pushing the tip of my nose toward my eyebrows with my index finger.

Davey moved his face closer to mine. "It's the sex," he whispered stagily.

"As in 'gender'?"

"No, silly. As in 'shagging.' It's my hypothesis many of the Bolters bolted because in the end they really weren't up to—how shall I put this?" He made a face. "Meeting their husbands', ahem, *needs.*"

"Piffle . . . !" I piffled. Davey's eyes were glittering with amusement. "Okay, in what way, then?"

"*Engagez votre* imagination, Jane, my darling."

And thence commenced, unbidden and unwelcome, a parade of leather knickers, assorted equestrian instruments and farm animals plus a few other items guaranteed to put one off one's tea.

"You see," Davey continued, "once one of them finds the right woman, he's lost to her, absolutely lost. Gone mad. Besotted. Why, even the throne of England was thrown over for such a woman."

"You refer to the Duchess of Windsor, I presume."

"Apparently Wallis had some quite remarkable methods for keeping the Duke . . . amused. Or so I've heard."

"So, you're suggesting something kinky lies at the heart of Affie and Pamela II's relationship?"

"I don't *know*, Jane, dear. I'm merely speculating. He certainly didn't marry her for her money."

"Why would he? He's got more money than British Telecom's got wrong numbers."

"Quite. But part of the charm of American women for so many of the English aristocracy has been their ability to bring lots of lovely lolly to the relationship, facilitate the cash flow, et cetera . . ."

"You mean *rich* American women."

"Are there others, darling?"

"Well, perhaps Lord Thring married to improve the bloodstock," I suggested as an alternative. "You English are as inbred as hillbillies. You haven't been invaded in nine hundred years. You want invading."

"And has the Thringys' marriage produced a child, you rude colonial?"

"No. But it's not too late. Lady Thring's not yet forty, I don't think."

Davey had shrugged at that point and drained his cup. "I'm sure I don't know the attraction between the Thringys," he said. And we went onto other topics.

The attraction, I thought as I surveyed Lady Thring's bedroom, was likely as simple as loneliness on his side, given that he did seem rather puppy-doggish around her. Perhaps there was a certain venality on her side, given that Lord Thring was awfully rich and titled to boot, but who knew? The two had apparently met at a performance event for Labrador retrievers in the United States, to which the Marquess (or the Earl of Chudleigh, as he was then) had been invited to act as judge, Americans seeking to add tone to their doggie shows by inviting English lords from time to time. As the former Pamela Walsh was at the same event with her own dogs, presumably their mutual canine interest was the spark that led where such sparks so often end up leading.

It's quite easy to go on automatic pilot when you're housemaiding and I was, more or less, on automatic p.

while I tidied the Marchioness's suite. Her ever-so-immaculately-turned-out ladyship has a way of turning her room into a tip, what with clothes and towels strewn about, and makeup-smudged tissues tossed in little heaps on the dresser and so forth. The personal effects I leave to Caroline Halliwell, her lady's maid, but I do have to be careful to maneuver around lest I mistakenly place something somewhere her ladyship can't find it immediately, the theme of last Christmas's unhappy encounter when I foolishly returned to her jewel box an emerald and diamond bracelet carelessly tossed on a night table and suffered an accusation of theft until I told her where to look.

Though the drapes were parted and a lamp glowed bravely on the dressing table, the room that morning seemed to be swallowed in shadow. Outside the window the sky was iron-grey. Eddies of sleetish rain tapped against the glass and dripped, melting, from the filigrees of the ornamental balcony. If this weather continues, I thought as I stepped into the adjoining bathroom, it could put the brakes on the next day's planned shooting party.

The bathroom, by contrast, was radiant. Not radiant clean, for her ladyship had tornadoed through this room, too. But radiant bright, thanks to a light fixture like a bright sun in the middle of the ceiling, making the grotty work of cleaning tubs, sinks, and loos at least a little less cheerless. A little, that is. The illumination was also an aid in another respect. While it's possible to miss a spot or two when you're cleaning on a grey day in a room that has only area lighting, it's difficult to miss anything in a bathroom ablaze. When I lifted a wastebasket overflowing with tissues and wrappers in order to empty the contents into a bin liner, my eyes immediately lit upon a bit of paper that had drifted from its fellows and caught on the edge of the baseboard. I crouched in the space between the sink and toilet to retrieve it, and would have tossed the scrap in the bin liner with the other rubbish, but something about the way it felt between my fingers made me turn the paper over.

What I read on the other side, in normal circumstances, wouldn't have caused me anything more than a moment's pause, either. There were just three numerals—a 6, a 2 and a 7—and two letters above—an *S* and a *T*. Nothing really exceptional. The numbers could have been part of a street address or a telephone number or might even have been three of six picks for the National Lottery. The letters—well, they could have been part of thousands of words. But what made me shift from my awkward crouch and plunk myself on the loo-lid to stare at my funny little find was its, well . . . style, or lack thereof. The numerals were not handwritten or typewritten. Rather, each was composed of a different typeface, of a different size and color, and each was clearly taken from a different source, a magazine or newspaper (I could tell from the glossy or opaque surface; clever me), and glued onto an otherwise unremarkable piece of standard white typing paper. And one might have overlooked even this as little more than a failed example of someone's peculiar hobby (like glueing macaroni on a jar and fashioning a baroque monstrosity with gold spray paint) but for the fact that cut-out letters had recently cleared a space in one's brain pan. Hadn't Jackie Scaife been receiving menacing missives of just such contrivance in the weeks before her death? Was Pamela, Marchioness of Thring, also the subject of intimidation by animal-rights extremists?

I leaned over, snatched the wastebasket by its rim and dumped the contents on the floor. There had to be more bits. It was like a jigsaw puzzle, though a crude one. The piece I possessed had part of one fine clean paper edge—about half an inch left of the letter *S*, but the remaining sides were jagged and shredded where a hand had evidently torn through the paper to leave the *T* and the three numerals intact, just fraying, though not obscuring, the 7 at the corner where the two strokes joined.

I pocketed this piece in my uniform then pushed my hands into the icky mess scattered on the floor and started rooting about. So concentrated was I on this task that I heard no sound above the rustle and swish of churning paper, nor did I notice the outline of a figure slip quietly into the doorwell.

The body may sense a presence, some disturbance in the atmosphere, before the mind makes its acknowledgment, and a cold shiver of fear travelled my limbs before I realized I was being watched. Then, as if someone had turned the other tap, came the hot flush of embarrassment as I lifted my head and saw Pamela, Marchioness of Thring, staring at me, her huge brown slightly protruding eyes glittering, her arms folded across a thick bitter-chocolate wool poloneck jumper.

"What," she inquired in a tone that somehow managed to be languid and icy both, "do you think you're doing?"

It was a darn good question, and I had less than a second in which to find an answer. "I . . . I think my ring might have slipped off . . . my lady," I gulped.

Her ladyship's eyelids dipped slowly in response, as if she was trying to control anger, battle an incipient headache, or indicate utter disdain. The latter, I realized, when she turned back to the bedroom and said carelessly over her shoulder, "Then please hurry up and find it and get out of here."

"Yes, my lady," I replied meekly as I slid off the loo-lid and scooped the trash into the plastic bin-liner. Had she flushed the other bits of paper? Or had someone else done the flushing?

But a moment later the Marchioness again loomed in the doorwell, only this time her angular face was rigid with unconcealed rage. "Aren't you the one responsible for attacking my son?" she snapped, impatiently pulling at a brown velvet ribbon behind her head and loosening a mane of thick blond hair.

"I didn't attack your son," I said from the floor, startled by the accusation.

"Don't lie to me," she continued. "You're Jane . . ." She shrugged irritably. "Whatever your name is. You hit my son." She jabbed her finger at me. "How dare you!"

"Your son came after *me*!" I rose and faced her. There was something rather strange and alarming in the

Marchioness's face which the cruel light of the bathroom could do nought but amplify. Her eyes were glowing like cinders and her hair, eased from its velvet band, seemed to snake across her shoulders Medusa-like. Well, stone me! I was taken aback and leaned into the sink, its cold surface pressing unpleasantly against my back.

"My lady," she prompted, lids narrowing. "Address me properly!"

"My lady," I tried again, in what I thought were reasonable tones, "your son was in my room last night, uninvited. He made certain advances and they weren't welcome."

"No." She shook her head imperiously. "*You* lured Buchanan to *your* room and when he wouldn't do what you wanted, you hit him . . ."

"What?" This was breathtakingly crazy. "Your ladyship," I ventured along the route of rationality one more time, "I would never invite any of Her Majesty's guests to my room for any reason. It would never occur to me. It's not done—"

"Buchanan is a delicate and sensitive boy. He has only just gotten over one of his episodes!"

Delicate? Sensitive? Bucky? And what did his 'episodes' have to do with anything?

"My lady," I continued, somewhat at sea. "Your son was in my room, waiting for me. He was not invited by me or any member of Staff. He invited himself. And when he tried it on, and when he wouldn't take no for an answer, the only thing I could do was defend myself."

"Listen to me, you trashy girl, if you ever touch Buchanan again I'll make your life a living hell."

Extreme politeness is said to be the most highly refined and cleverly diverting expression of one's contempt, a particular achievement of the upper classes. The Marchioness was not achieving. My dander was up.

"I'm sorry, but you have no right talking to me like that," I protested.

"I won't take lip from servants. You will apologize to my son, or I'll have you fired."

"You're not my employer. And I won't apologize."

A kind of thwarted fury turned her honed cheek-bones into ridges of scarlet. She thrust her sharp chin forward and said in a voice husky with anger: "You *will* apologize!"

I met the Marchioness's blazing gaze but said nothing. There was no point in launching a round of childish gainsaying. I would not apologize and that was that. And I did not fear losing my job. Everybody knows the Queen cannot abide rudeness to her Staff; she's gone so far as to admonish her own children for discourtesies. And I think—and I hope I'm not sounding pompous—that over the time I had worked for HM I had managed to gain a modicum of her trust and confidence (not that she does the actual hiring and firing anyway, of course).

Evidently interpreting my silence as assent, Pamela II turned and strode back into the bedroom proper. She began noisily banging hangers, fussing around with her wardrobe, undoing all my good work, I thought, as I continued with my toilet tasks. Some wag below stairs had once tagged the Marquess and Marchioness the Owl and the Pussycat, a tufted old bird and his sleek consort. But 'pussycat,' I thought, was the wrong allusion for the Marchioness. 'Tigress' was more appropriate. As in, protecting her cub. But the cub, in this case, was grown, certainly big enough and ugly enough not to need Mommie for protection against someone like me, a mere slip of a girl. Or even, I thought as I replaced the soap in the basin, a *grrrrl*. The Marchioness, I concluded with last year's bracelet episode in mind as I turned my ear to another voice in the outer room, was nevertheless a force to be reckoned with.

". . . and would you lay out my clothes for this afternoon, Caroline?" I heard the Marchioness say sharply to her lady's maid, followed by the sound of a door banging shut. I waited. And then Caroline Halliwell slipped into the frame of the doorway to the bathroom.

"Her Ladyship has quite the temper, doesn't

she?" Caroline smiled sympathetically, popping a Bendick's mint into her mouth.

"God, yes," I replied more vehemently than I intended. "Is she gone?"

"Don't worry. She's left to visit some of the tenants with Her Majesty. Won't be back until luncheon. Will you be apologizing, do you think?"

"Heard it all, did you? Of course I'm not apologizing. Not on your life. I've nothing to apologize for."

"Good for you." Caroline licked a chocolate-stained finger. "I had a chance to view the state of the young master's face earlier. Lovely bruise, Jane. It's time the little sod had his comeuppance."

"Tried it on with you, did he?"

Caroline laughed. "You're very kind, Jane. No, I'm a little too old for his tastes, I should expect."

"Oh, surely not. You can't be thirty."

"Twenty-eight come March."

"Bucky could still be your toy boy."

Caroline made a face of mock horror. "I'm sure there's other reasons I've been spared Bucky's attentions," she said.

"I think English women intimidate him, for one. Likely why I've been favored with his attentions, oh lucky me."

"You're probably right. Her Ladyship is always thrusting these terribly articulate and rather bossy-boots upper-class girls at him to ill effect. The pairings can be quite hilarious."

Of course, anyone looking carefully at the Marchioness's lady's maid would realize there might be another reason Bucky mightn't have tried to exercise his *droyt de signoor* (as he called it), an aspect of Caroline's appearance that struck me immediately the first time I met her: She bears an uncanny odd resemblance to her employer.

Like Pamela, Caroline is tall and blond. She has large and widely spaced eyes, though they lack the lustre of Her Ladyship's, and her face is comparable in shape, unblemished skin, and small mouth. Yet Caroline, despite the advantages youth should give her (she has to be ten years younger than the Marchioness) comes across as a less brilliant edition of the older original, slightly less slim, less defined, less chic, her hair less carefully coiffed, her clothes less carefully chosen. I wondered if some narcissistic impulse on Lady Thring's part hadn't led to Caroline's employment: Hire someone who looks like you, yet not enough like you to cause you unease.

Well, I thought, the resemblance would probably be enough to cause Bucky unease.

Then I realized I had been lost in my own reverie. "What?" I asked.

"I was saying she treats Bucky as though he was the Tsarvich. Touch him and he'll bleed. It's quite . . . neurotic, really." Caroline shrugged and turned back into the bedroom. I followed with the trashbag and my cleaning equipment.

"Her ladyship's been more than unusually anxious and testy lately," she continued, removing a dressing gown from the bed and folding it. "You can always tell. She seems to fling her clothes about with greater abandon."

I surveyed the room. There looked to be several changes of clothes in different piles, as if her ladyship hadn't been able to decide what to wear. "She can't be the easiest person to work for," I commented.

"In many ways, her bark's worse than her bite, although she can be quite savage when she's in a temper," Caroline replied. "Of course, she's ever so sweet around Her Majesty and the other members of the Royal Family. It's her staff who bear the brunt of her displeasure."

"Why do you put up with it?" I thought: With the exception of Mrs. Harbottle, the deputy Housekeeper at Buckingham Palace, who could be a bit steely at times, most of the overseers in the Palace system were rather harmless, if not indolent. Certainly *la suprema* herself, the Queen, was as agreeable an employer as you could probably find.

"Oh, there are worse jobs," Caroline replied. "Most of the time, her ladyship is pleasant enough to work for. And there's the perks—nice homes, travel and such. Occasionally, she even comes bearing gifts . . ."

"Christmas . . . ?"

"No, I mean after she's had one of her tantrums. She gives one things. This sweater for instance." Caroline twirled around. The sweater was a pale blue cashmere, a perfect match with her eyes, quite lovely enough to give me in my boring white uniform a prick of envy. "Her ladyship becomes rather contrite. She doesn't apologize as such, but . . ." She left the rest unanswered. "It's quite odd: At times, she seems to want to be your friend. She doesn't quite understand the boundaries between employer and staff . . ."

"Neither does Bucky," I said sourly.

"I daresay."

"Perhaps her ladyship will come over all contrite around me. I could use a few additions to my wardrobe."

Caroline laughed. "Don't bet your pay packet. Bucky is the apple of her ladyship's eye."

I thought back to my experience in the loo when her ladyship had been a bit harpie-ish, and about the curious scrap of paper I found behind the wastebasket.

"You mentioned the Marchioness being particularly testy of late," I said. "Is there some reason? Christmas blues? Salmonella turkey? Asked his lordship for diamonds and got a Teasmade instead?"

"If her ladyship wanted diamonds, you have my word there'd be diamonds under the tree." Caroline frowned at the vase of flowers, then gently rearranged a few stems. "I'm not quite sure what's put her ladyship in a mood. She's been less than her energetic self in London the past several weeks. I've wondered if she isn't . . . ?"

"Isn't?"

Caroline shook her head as if to brush cobwebs away. "Oh, nothing, really. At any rate, her ladyship's certainly been a bit peculiar since we arrived here Tuesday morning for the shooting party," she continued. "The Queen had postponed the annual Boxing Day shoot to accommodate Lord and Lady Thring's schedule—a very gracious thing for Her Majesty to do—and then her ladyship announces she has a dreadful head—ache and can't possibly participate."

"The guns are awfully loud," I suggested. "You can hear the whole barrage from the Big House so, I mean, if you're actually *there* among them it would probably make your head swell . . ."

Caroline shook her head. "Her ladyship's head—aches are more of a useful fiction. Her Majesty was very understanding, of course, but really . . . !"

"You said yesterday her ladyship was late returning to Duke's Head after the panto Boxing Day."

"Oh, did I?" Caroline bit her lip and regarded me doubtfully.

"In Mrs. Benefer's office," I prompted.

"Oh, yes. Oh, dear. I did, didn't I?" Worry settled on her face. "Well, she wasn't *that* late," she said at last.

My face must have registered the doubt of an evo—lutionist at a creation science seminar, for Caroline's ex—pression changed from worry to dismay. "Or maybe she wasn't late at all. I don't know." She turned and fid—geted with a cosmetics case on the dresser but I could see her face, like a pale moon, in the mirror. I waited.

"Her ladyship says she arrived back at the hotel at five-thirty," Caroline continued with sigh. "My room was adjacent to her suite, and I could usually hear her moving about. And, besides, her custom is to ring for me almost immediately when she returns from wherever she's been. So when she rang at seven, I assumed that's when she returned. But she insists it was much earlier. She arrived at five-thirty and just lay down, didn't call me."

"Why is she being so insistent?"

Caroline glanced at me in the mirror. "I don't know, really. She finally laughed and said one of us must be on Sandringham Time."

"Eh?"

"You know, moving the clocks ahead on the Estate so there would be more daylight time for shooting."

"How far ahead?" I'd never heard of this.

"Half an hour. But they don't do it now, of course," she added, noting my consternation. "It was

something Edward VII instituted. I think it went out in the 1930s with Edward VIII. I was surprised her lady-ship even knew of the tradition. Her Majesty must have told her, I suppose."

"There hasn't been anyone threatening her lady-ship, has there?" I asked on impulse, the scrap of paper from her ladyship's loo floating through my mind like an autumn leaf.

Caroline turned to face me. She looked almost re-lieved to find some other topic of conversation.

"What a strange question? Why do you ask?"

"Oh, just, you know"—dissemble, dissemble—"the ARF thing. Lady Thring has a relatively high pro-file, she's here at Sandringham for the shooting parties, and there's been this murder at Dersingham of course, so I just wondered . . . ?" I shrugged. "Maybe that's why her ladyship's been so . . . anxious."

Caroline's feathery eyebrows knitted together. "I . . . I don't think so." She cocked her head and looked at me inquiringly. "You *are* odd, Jane. Did the dentist give you some strange new drug?"

"Dentist? Oh, the dentist!" I remembered just in time—my intended excuse for Mrs. Benefer. "Just a fill-ing, nothing really."

10

THE BALLROOM LIES at the end of a long corridor called—no surprise—the Ballroom Corridor, which zigzags from a small lobby off the Dining Room around and through the Gun Room and straightens out past a marshalling of low bookcases (filled with forbidding-looking bound volumes such as Sir Walter Scott's *Waverley* novels, Plutarch's *Lives,* and a multivolume biography of Napoleon—all unread, as I and my handy hogshair dusting brush can attest) on top of which are arrayed a number of bronze statuettes, mostly of Edward VII rigged up in various outfits either naval or equestrian. My favorite is the model of King Edward's 1896 Derby winner, Persimmon, a dinky version of the life-size statue outside the Sandringham Stud on the Anmer road. I always pat its horsy back when I pass, and I did so again, but rather absentmindedly as I made my way toward the great white doors of the Ballroom, because I was pondering Caroline Halliwell's uneasiness over Lady Thring's—did I dare think it?—*alibi*? That bit of paper I had found in her loo drifted through my mind like a single snowflake heralding the first storm of a Charlottetown winter. Something was compelling her ladyship to make a to-do about her ETA at the Duke's Head hotel.

The doors to the Ballroom were closed. At first, given that no sound seemed to be coming from within, I thought I had missed Davey. I had dashed up to my own bolt-hole immediately after doing Lady Thring's room to fetch the National Lottery tickets (plus the letter from Cartier's) to give to him to give to the Queen who, I thought, would probably want them sharpish so that Princess Margaret could have her little gloat over her victory and be done with it.

But, as I pressed my ear to the crack, I could hear murmured voices and the sharper sound of what seemed like metal sliding against metal. So, in the usual 'nothing v. nothing g.' manner, I pushed one of the doors open wide enough to poke my head through and glimpse what was going on.

What was going on was Davey Pye, about ten yards away pointing a shotgun at me. I flinched and snapped my head back like a Benzedrine turtle.

"Blam, you're dead, Jane Bee," I heard Davey drawl in a sardonic way. A roar from another, deeper, male voice quickly followed: "Don't *ever* do that!"

"Ooh! Beg pardon. So sorry. I didn't know . . . Jane," Davey called to me as I braved another entrance. "Jane, darling, I didn't know you were going to come into the room at that moment. Very sorry. Really."

" 'If a sportsman true you'd be,' " the other person intoned. " 'Listen carefully to me/Never, never let your gun/ Pointed be at anyone/That it might unloaded be/ Matters not the least to me.' It's worth remembering."

The speaker was Mrs. Benefer's husband, Tom, one of the gamekeepers on the Sandringham Estate. Davey, handing him the shotgun, grimaced in a I-can't-believe-you're-reciting-doggerel-to-me fashion.

" 'You may hit or you may miss,' " Benefer continued, undeterred. " 'But at all times think of this/All the game birds ever bred/Won't repay for one man dead.' It's a fine poem." He said it unsmilingly, as though one wouldn't presume to disagree.

"Yes, it does rather make 'Ode to a Nightingale' seem like one of those young-man-from-Nantucket thingys, doesn't it? Now, are we finished?" Davey reached for his black tailcoat, which was draped over a nearby chair.

"Nay, barely begun." Benefer took the gun from Davey's other hand. "A course at Purdey's is what you need, lad, so's you don't go kill someone." He scowled.

"What on earth are you doing?" I asked Davey, having advanced into the Ballroom, which was now, presumably, safe to advance into.

"His Royal Highness wants the lad to be loader in tomorrow's shoot," Benefer replied instead.

"You?" I suppressed a giggle.

"Ha ha," Davey said miserably, brushing at some imaginary lint on his black trousers.

Benefer just shook his head with dismay. He was a big man, strongly built, probably only in his early forties, but a sort of ruined splendour nonetheless, the raw Norfolk weather having turned his face brick-red, his hair to unkempt straw thatch, his hands to knotted wood.

"Out in that awful cold," Davey continued, whimpering. "And Father snapping my head off. I can just hear him. He'll be in the most foul temper, I know it."

"Not if you do as instructed."

"Why can't he load his own gun?" I asked.

"Because someone has to load one gun while His Highness shoots with t'other. I've told you, lad. You've been coming to Sandringham for—what?—more than six or seven years now. Have you been paying no attention?"

"To shooting, I most certainly have not!"

"Paid attention to the bag, I can see." Benefer winked at me and then glanced somewhere in the middle of Davey's physique which, it was true, was beginning to strain the fabric of his scarlet waistcoat.

"Yes, pheasant is truly delush," Davey allowed, sucking in his stomach. "Goes ever so nicely with Mother's vintage Krug. But I expect I shall soon be rather off pheasant." His brow crinkled. "I wonder if I shouldn't consult my Staff agreement. I don't remember 'loader' under 'footman's duties.'"

"Why you of all people?" I interjected, shivering a little. The Ballroom was rather chill and just a trifle damp. "Everyone else got the 'flu?"

Davey shrugged. "I suppose so."

"'Make a man of him,' His Highness said to me," Benefer explained.

"How rude!" And then Davey added unhappily: "I'm probably to be one of Father's endless improvement projects. Sandringham kitchens. Reclaimed marshes at Wolferton. And me."

"Don't be a misery," I countered. "It might be fun."

"I don't think I approve of blood sports. I'm going to join the anti's and—" He halted in mid-sentence. "Oh, I'm sorry, Tom. I forgot about . . . you know . . . Aileen's sister."

Benefer just shook his head impatiently. "Just go get your coat."

"Why would I need my coat?"

"We're going outdoors."

"Whatever for?"

"So's you can practise, you gormless twit. Did you think we were going to use the Ballroom?"

"But . . . but, it's *raining*!" Davey wailed, pointing toward the nearest window, a frame for a study in grey.

"Rain won't kill you. There'll probably be rain to-morrow, too. Now, get your coat, lad." Benefer shot me a look of amazement as Davey folded his tailcoat over his arm. "Heaven help HRH with you as loader."

I couldn't help snickering. Davey put on a hurt expression. "I think you're *both* awful," he declared and flounced toward the door to the corridor. Benefer and I burst into laughter. Getting a smile out of an East Anglian was usually a challenge, so pulling a laugh out of Benefer felt like a triumph.

"And put something decent on your feet, too! Can't have you tramping about in black pumps with buckles," Benefer shouted.

"Wait. Davey!" I called, darting after the footman as he disappeared through the door, reminded of my original reason for being in the Ballroom.

"What?" he said coldly, turning.

"Here." I pulled a small white envelope from the pocket in the front of my uniform. "Would you give these to"—I dropped my voice. I was still on the Ballroom side of the door—"You-Know-Who." I pushed the envelope at him through the opening.

He regarded the envelope askance as if it was a summons to small claims court. "What is it?" he said suspiciously.

"Tickets on the National Lottery and, um, just a little note about something else. Here. Take it."

"You give it to her."

"Davey, you're the one in attendance on Her Majesty."

"Hmph."

"Oh, come on, don't be crabby. We were just having a laugh. You're very funny." I leaned through the door and impulsively pecked him on the cheek.

"I wasn't trying to be funny." But he had thawed under the mighty power of the Kiss. Davey's moods, bad ones being infrequent, usually pass like summer squalls anyway. "Mother having a flutter on the lottery now, is she?"

"Margo, actually," I whispered as he took the envelope and put it in his trousers pocket. "By the way," I added, HRH's name suddenly recalling me to another something I had overheard outside HM's study Wednesday. "Do you know if Queen Mary, the Queen's grandmother, was a little, oh . . . light-fingered?"

"What? When playing Barcarolle on the Bösendorfer?"

"No, silly. As in 'take things without permission.' "

"Ah. Well, I'm told Her late Majesty was a bit, as you would say, 'light-fingered.' Um . . ." He looked anxiously down the corridor. "You do have an odd way of asking odd questions at odd times. Look, I must go, darling. Ask me again later. I have to fetch my coat, as you well know. I wonder if one can be a loader and carry an umbrella at the same time?" he mused, retreating down the corridor. "No, I'd need three arms, and only vicars carry umbrellas in the country. Oh, to be in London, warm and snug at the Bag O'Nails, with a voddie and T and—"

I shut the door on his lament and turned back to the Ballroom and the remaining figure inside. Tom Benefer's tweed-jacketed back was to me. He had placed the shotguns side-by-side on a red couch nearby and was staring out one of the tall windows toward the box hedge, a black shape without sunshine to animate the green. I could almost sense his discomfort being indoors and his impatience to be out in the weather that made the rest of us yearn for a cosy inglenook, a roaring fire, and a good book.

Benefer was friendly enough. Most of the outdoor staff on the Estate aren't as preoccupied as the indoor staff with rank and station, perks and privileges, and the whole panoply of snobbery and sycophancy which they take so *veddy* seriously and I find more of a laugh and a half. Perhaps being much in nature leaches self-importance from the human character. Is nature more democratic than human society, then? Beats me.

I glanced around the Ballroom. It's a cavernous sort of place, plainer than its counterpart at Buck House, much of the cream-coloured wallspace above the dado devoted to artful displays of swords and shields and daggers and the like from India, given to the Prince of Wales in the 1870s during a state visit, but looking more like booty brought back from some imperial adventure, which I suppose the state visit was in a way. With the two small cannons at one end, a gift from Emperor Napoleon III and Empress Eugénie in 1855, the place has an oddly militarist atmosphere for a room in which you might expect there to be balls in the grand manner, sweeping music, sweeping gowns, sweeping emotion. (I blame those historical romance novels I read as a young teen for these idiotic thoughts.) In fact, the Ballroom is given over to rather dull events these days, such as last weeks's buffet party for the Estate employees and their spouses where, I'm told, everyone stood around and chitchatted while nibbling canapés, sipping some concoction and waiting to be circulated toward the Queen like bees queuing for royal jelly. In one corner was a Christmas tree nearly twenty feet high, unlit and rather drear in the cold midday light, topped with a huge silver star, and down one side were long trestle tables still covered with starched linen where members of the Royal Family had stacked their gifts for the great unwrapping on Christmas Eve. The gifts were whisked away Boxing Day. Mostly, the Ballroom is used as a cinema, as it appeared it would be that evening. I noted an alignment of chairs facing a decorative Chinese screen that would be replaced later by a silver screen.

"What," I asked, "are they showing this evening?" I knew what it was. The remake of *Miracle on 34th Street*. The information was posted in the Staff lounge. But I wanted to worm my way into Benefer's frontal lobes without seeming as if I was too inquisitive, and this seemed like a decent opening gambit. Heck, it was the only opening gambit.

"Mmm," he replied, turning his head slowly toward me as I approached. I seemed to have pulled him away from some reverie. He regarded me blankly from under tobacco-coloured toothbrush eyebrows.

"I just wondered what film they were going to be showing this evening."

"Don't know," he said as if the idea of watching a film on a winter evening had never occurred to him. "I'll be in bed. Shooting day tomorrow."

"Back to normal."

"Aye, back to normal." He smiled briefly as if glad of the idea and turned back to the view. A bird of some nature was flitting about the hedge. I wasn't getting very far. And then I thought of a way in.

"So, you go to bed early when there's a shoot the next day."

"Much wants doing before the guns assemble."

"These shoots are sort of the culmination of the working year for you guys, I guess."

"Aye, that they are."

I thought of Tuesday's events. There were to have been two more drives scheduled for after luncheon, but that had ended with the discovery of the body of Jackie Scaife. "Must be really crummy if a shoot gets spoiled," I said.

"Aye," he agreed, noncommittally.

"Were you at the panto?"

Benefer turned his head away from the window and gave me an up-and-down look. "The panto? No. Aileen were, though. Weren't best pleased with her sister's performance."

"I heard. Sorry about her death."

"Oh, aye." He managed to convey in two words a whole world of regret and, oddly, skepticism, to which I reacted with a twitch of the eyebrows. "Murder, you mean," he said gruffly in response.

"The anti's—"

"Weren't bloody anti's."

I started. "Who, then?"

A shadow fell over Benefer's face. "Don't know," he said.

"But the ARF's really turned sort of terrorist," I argued. "And your sister-in-law was dressed as the Queen, a kind of provocation—"

"And Jackie was getting at them in other ways, the letter to the newspaper and that bloody fur coat and all, I know, I've heard it."

"What about the threatening letters she was receiving from ARF?"

Benefer grunted.

"Who, then? Who would want to kill her?"

He took what seemed like a long time answering. "Don't know," he said finally in his curt manner.

I thought about the different motives for murder—greed, thwarted love, revenge, and the like—and how little I really knew about the victim. 'Vivacious' was the word Hume Pryce had used to describe Jackie, but 'vivacious' had the effect of a euphemism; it could mean anything from 'charming' to 'tarty' depending on who was using it, and what did it mean when a man like Pryce was using it, the man who couldn't wait to get back to his girlfriend in Nives? Perhaps Jackie was too tempting, or was a temptress, to use a really awful old word. Mrs. Benefer had made her sister seem irresponsible, a drifter in life, moving about the U.S. in search of . . . what? Fame & Fortune, the usual thing people went to America in search of? Or was she running away from something? Was she an adventurous woman or frightened woman? Bold or just brassy? The downstairs gossip from some of the old-timers cast her in less than a flattering light, but then they had spent their lives folded away in a little corner of rural England all their blessed lives. Maybe I was just reacting to some of the old farts and fartettes around the Big House, but some of what I had heard about Jackie in the last few days had made me want to admire her, in a way. She had to have had some daring.

"So," I said to Benefer while he continued to wait for Davey, "what was your sister-in-law like?"

He thought a moment and then replied: "She were pitiful."

"Really?" This wasn't at all what I'd expected to hear. I said, "But everyone says she was, like, the life of the party, the belle of the ball—that sort of thing."

"She were a bit of an actress, Jackie were."

"But why 'pitiful'?"

Benefer ran gnarled fingers through his hair. "She weren't getting what she wanted, I don't think. She always wanted the high life, the city, folks with fancy houses and motors . . ." Words seemed to fail him. It was as if even the concept of wanting these things was beyond the pale of his understanding. "Jackie were always like that. When I first knew them as girls, she and Aileen would pore over these flash magazines, and pop stuff on telly and all. Well, Aileen weren't like that, really. She were just indulging Jackie, of course, being

practically like mother to her—" He stopped suddenly.
"When I go up to London now—any of them big cities,
don't matter which—I can't wait to get back, you know.
The crowds. So many foreigners now, it don't seem like
the same country. I keep looking out for English faces.
Do you know what I mean?"

The question didn't seem to require much more
than an ambiguous grunt. I would have replied in the
negative anyway. I like London's cosmopolitan atmosphere. I can't imagine what the capital would be like
without Indians and Caribbeans and Arabs and Greeks,
the whole world walking by as you wait at Oxford Circus
for the Tube.

"But why," I asked, nudging the conversational
boat back on course, "did Jackie return to England after
all those years in the States?"

"Aye, that's the question, isn't it? What were she
doing back here, poor cow?"

"She never said?"

"Not so's you'd say exactly. Time for a visit, was
all she said. At least to me. Might have said something
else to Aileen."

I felt discouraged. Tom was either obtuse or he
was keeping things back—not that he owed me an explanation, of course. But surely, if a relative arrived on
your stoop nearly two decades after she'd departed for
the high life overseas, she'd have some sort of explanation.

"Did she seem—oh, I don't know—worried? sad?
disappointed? Oh—and were you given any advance
warning? A letter, perhaps a phone call?"

"Just showed up. One evening in September, I
think it were. We'd just finished our tea. She'd hired a
cab from Lynn. There she was, two suitcases and that
fur coat under the porch lamp."

"Must have been a surprise."

"It were a surprise, all right," he said ominously,
and then gave me a discerning look. "Say, you're sticking your nose in a bit, aren't you?"

"Well, Tom," I countered, (So nice not to have to

worry about 'sirring' the Estate workers) "you're the one who said he didn't think it was the ARF."

He shrugged. "Aye, that's true. I did."

"I'm just trying to figure it out, that's all."

Benefer seemed to accept this. He pulled up the sleeve of his sweater to reveal a hairy arm. "Jackie were up to something, though," he said pensively. "She acted real cheerful but . . ." He looked at his watch. His brow furrowed. "Where is that lad? How long does it take to put on a coat, find a pair of boots? There's no use skiving. His Highness wants this done proper."

"But what, Tom? You said Jackie seemed cheerful but . . . ?"

"Oh, I don't know. You'd catch her in a certain light. Not so young anymore, was Jackie, if you cared to notice. Still had that bounce, but she had to work at it. And she was working at something. I don't know what. She were out a lot, away for days sometimes. Made Aileen burn, like our cottage were a doss-house or something. Bit edgy, Jackie was. Not enough to do. That's why this panto were a godsend even if it were taking the mickey out of the Royal Family. Or so I hear."

"Funny returning to Norfolk," I mused. "If she really fancied city life, you'd think she'd pick London if she was going to come back to England."

"Didn't hardly know anyone in England anymore but us. A few others, maybe. Not much money either, not so's you could live in London. Oh, she acted like she were flush but I think she were pinched. Cadged a bit off me in the last few weeks, for Christmas and all. Said she was having trouble getting her bank in America to send her her money."

I thought of Hume Pryce's description of Jackie at the cashpoint at King's Lynn, having been cheerless but for the attention-magnet of her fur coat.

"And you didn't believe her?"

"Didn't know what to believe. Still don't. And don't believe she were done in by these animal-rights loonies."

"You seem awfully sure."

Benefer had resumed his gaze out the window.

The rain seemed to be allayed somewhat. The grey had turned a lighter shade in patches. "No, it were something closer to home," he muttered darkly. "Something to do with Manchester." He shook his head as if trying to rid his mind of something.

"Why Manchester?" I asked, confused.

But in profile, his face was unreadable. "It's nothing," he said dismissively, and then looked again impatiently at his watch. "I'm going to roust that lad, he can't be far." He turned abruptly toward the Ballroom door. "Mind nobody takes those Purdeys," he called over his shoulder.

"But . . ."

Damn, I thought. What might Manchester have to do with anything? Curses, I amended. Lines from a song in an old musical thrashed their way into my head, unbidden: 'Manchester, England, England/Across the Atlantic Sea/And I'm a genius, genius/I believe in god/And I believe that god believes in Claude, that's me.' *Hair* was the musical, the choice of our English teacher, an old hippie, for our high school production. Our parents had had fits, and the red pencil had gone through half the text and a third of the songs. A fully clothed, drug-reference-deleted, and thoroughly innocuous production left this little chorus member with no musical memory but for 'Manchester,' the dittiest of the show's ditties.

Fortunately, the needle on the mental turntable didn't stick because, in one of life's Molière moments, as soon as Benefer exited stage left, Davey made an appearance stage right, at one of the Ballroom's tall windows latched so that it may be used as a door. He was wearing a long navy overcoat but on his feet were a pair of green wellies, and on his head an absurd-looking bobble-hat. I pointed (how rude) and giggled while Davey, hands on hips, and a vexed expression twisting his chubby features, appeared to mouth something.

"What?" I said, moving toward the glass.

More fishy mouth movements. I pressed my ear to the glass.

"Where is he?" I could hear.

"Gone to look for you," I shouted.

"Damn and blast," came the muffled rejoinder. Davey looked up at the sky, which accommodated him by sending a splash of rain onto his countenance. "Open the door!"

I grimaced. The latch looked perfectly ordinary but I worried that if I unhooked it, a bell would sound a warning or a light would flash in the security control room. Of course, this often happened. False alarms were rife. People were always opening some window or some door they oughtn't have, or accidentally running a dust-cloth over one of the little red panic buttons located in some of the rooms, forgetting that when Her Majesty was in residence, security went into higher alert. In theory. Sometimes an officer would pop along eventually and give you a weary lecture. Often nobody did and you figured the door or window either wasn't securely sealed or someone assumed it was a false alarm, or someone was asleep at the wheel, so to speak.

Anyway, as I hesitated, Davey began stamping his feet on the path, raising little torrents of rainwater and mouthing furiously, "Let me in, let me in."

"Oh, all right," I mouthed back at him just as furiously. Tentatively, I undid the latch and then, wincing, pushed down on the handle. My ears pricked up. No bell, no sound, no discernible change in the hum of the Big House. I pulled back the door to admit a blast of wind, a gush of rain, and Davey stepping over the stoop, bringing the smell of wet wool with him.

"Thank you, darling."

"We'll probably have security down on us like we were the west Norfolk branch of ARF." I shut the door.

Davey waved a dismissive hand. "They're all having elevenses, they'll never notice."

"Why didn't you come back the way you left?"

"I borrowed these from Eric Twist." He pointed to his footwear. "Fancy him having *green* wellies. Who does he think he is? Anyway, the pig didn't bother to clean them properly and I didn't want to track mud through. I was only thinking of you, darling," he added witheringly.

"Thank you ever so much," I responded with matching insincerity, adding, "Maybe I should go find Tom and tell him you're here." It might give me an opportunity to continue my conversation with the gamekeeper.

"Wonderful. I'm looking for him. He's looking for me. And before long, I'll have to look for you to tell you to stop looking for him. This'll turn into a farce."

"Watch the carpet. You're dripping."

"Bother," Davey said and sank down onto the floor, splaying his legs. "What film are they featuring tonight?" he asked disconsolately, head in hands.

"Miracle on 34th Street."

"Ugh. How vomitingly saccharine." He looked up. "Fancy a drink at the Feathers this evening?"

"As it happens, I already have a date at the Feathers."

"Ooh, who's the lucky one, then? Not Buckyboos, surely. I saw your handiwork earlier, by the way. I once had a frock that shade of red."

"The 'date' is with my father."

"Oh." Davey sighed. "Poor you. Poor us." He pressed his back against the door and looked up to the pewter sky. " 'Very flat, Norfolk,' Noel Coward once said. Very *dull*, would be nearer the mark. *Achingly* dull. Horribly, achingly, bollocks-rattlingly dull."

"Oh, don't go on again. It's not that bad."

"You've changed your tune, Janers. You couldn't wait to get back to London last year." He paused in thought. "Of course, there was that film bloke to get back *to*, wasn't there?" he said slyly. "What was his name again?"

"Neil. Neil Gorringe. You know perfectly well."

"And? You can tell Davey, sweetheart. Here, rest your weary head on my tender, albeit somewhat damp, bosom and unburden yourself." His voice grew all creamy. "Your confidences will go no further."

"Ha! There's a laugh. Why don't I just throw in pictures of me without my knickers so you can sell it to *The Sun*?"

"That's very hurtful, Jane. I would never do something like that."

"No, that's true. You wouldn't. I'm sorry." I backtracked. It was true. Davey may be the veritable switchboard at Buck House Gossip Central, but he knows when to hold 'em and when to fold 'em, to drag in a gambling metaphor kicking and screaming; that is, Davey is judicious when judiciousness is called for. Last year, he inadvertently witnessed the resolution to a murder at Buckingham Palace and, like the other characters in the drama of it all, has kept his counsel. He is, as he likes to say, loyal to Mother.

Davey had just happened to hit a nerve, that's all. Neil Gorringe was camera assistant on *The Queen's House*, a film produced about the running of Buckingham Palace which had shown on telly in the late spring (and which included a shot of yours truly stickhandling a Hoover down the Picture Gallery). I saw a lot of him during the filming backstage at Buck House and for a time following, but things just seemed to peter out after a while. I think it was the petering-out that cheesed me off. I'd rather have had some sort of formal uncoupling or great purging slanging match but, no.

Well, I rationalized, Neil, being in the film biz, was obliged to travel about in his work, and who knew what other women he met? Men are pigs, but Neil was a rather nice pig on the whole, so I was still a bit miffed. I knew he'd gone up with a crew to the Orkneys or the Shetlands or some godforsaken northern reach of the kingdom in the late summer to film endangered somethingorothers. He might still be there, for all I knew. I related as much to Davey.

"Poor you," he said again. "Oh, well, just think, darling: Norfolk's the Côte d'Azur compared to the Shetlands this time of year."

"There's a consoling thought."

Davey eyed me suspiciously. "I thought you thought being here wasn't that bad this year?" I must have made an unconvincing gesture for he added: "You *are* up to something, aren't you? Marks and Sparks bags from Mother. Questions about the Duchess of Windsor's title. And then Queen Mary's fondness for *k*nick*k*nacks *k*not her own. I'm sure it all ties together somehow. But how?"

"Nice-looking shotguns, don't you think?" I replied, tap-dancing over to the Purdeys on the couch and gesturing like a demented quiz-show hostess in an effort of distraction.

"You could buy a nice cottage in Norfolk for the price of one of those beastly things. Now, tell Davey about your sudden interest in Queen Mary."

"I just wondered if she was a bit of a klepto, that's all."

"S'truth, she was. Or 'tis said she was. A constant peril to the country house set. She would take a fancy to her hostess's favorite baubles and bibelots and either slip them into her handbag or make such a to-do admiring them that her hostess found herself forking them over. Her late Majesty's ladies-in-waiting would later post the purloined trinkets back to their owners, although—you'll like this—there's a story that after Queen Mary died in the 'fifties a great removals van drove out of Marlborough House on a returns mission. Sounds a bit over the top to me."

"Wonder if it runs in the family?" I mused, running my hand over the silky wood and fine engraving of the gun's stock.

"Kleptomania!" Davey looked aghast. "Of course not. What would give you such an idea?"

"I'm a bad person and I have evil thoughts," I replied deflectingly.

"Tosh. Although . . ." Davey pulled off his hat. "It's my theory—and it's only a theory, darling—that if you're good—you know, good good good, and all the time, too—then you have to have some sort of release. I mean, *I'm* good as gold—as you know—but I have my little . . . hobbies. Queen Mary was the height of moral rectitude and duty fulfilled and suchlike, so her occasional bouts of gewgaw pinching, I figure, were her way of running amok as much as a royal personage can."

"Makes you wonder if HM has some secret vice."

"Mother? Really, Jane! What an appalling suggestion!"

"It's *your* theory, Davey. I'm just giving it another application." Davey has a fierce loyalty to Mother, as he continually refers to the Queen. I'm sure there's fertile ground here for some psychologist, given that he calls his biological mother, who runs a B & B in Stratford-upon-Avon, by her first name, Sylvia.

"I wonder whether HM doesn't at least have a soundproof closet hidden away," I continued. "Somewhere she can scream her lungs out. I mean, if I had to spend my days christening ships and touring factories and listening to lord mayors drone on and on, I'd go around the twist. I'd need some sort of release. But HM doesn't exactly sweat it out on the StairMaster, does she? Or mix a vat of martinis after a long day at the walkabout, or kick the corgis when she gets home. How does she vent, I wonder?"

"She's good, is Mother."

"I thought your point was the bad had a way of slipping out, like jelly from a sandwich."

"There are exceptions." Davey sniffed. "You look skeptical, my dear. Well then, I daresay *puzzles* are one of Mother's diversions from a life of routine and duty."

"Meaning . . . ?"

"Meaning the last time there was a spot of unpleasantness deathwise at Court, Mother took a rather keen interest and you, if I'm not mistaken, found yourself acting as Mother's dogsbody."

"I'm not sure if I find 'dogsbody' an attractive phrase."

"Why is Mother interested in the unpleasantness at the Dersingham Village Hall, if a humble footman and corgi-minder with a desire for an uncomplicated yet sybaritic life may ask?"

"Well, Jackie Scaife was murdered on Her Majesty's Estate."

"As well I remember." Davey shuddered. "Still . . ."

"And she was dressed as Her Majesty. You know very well this has given the Royalty Squad fits. I'm surprised my opening this door for you hasn't sent them charging in . . ."

"I'm not sure if all this quite explains Mother's personal interest."

"Er, no. I suppose it doesn't. Actually, I don't know why HM has a bee in her bonnet about this."

"You're the Bee in her bonnet, ha!"

"Speaking of headgear, Davey, when the police questioned you the other day, did you describe to them what Jackie was wearing?"

He frowned up at me. "No, they didn't ask. They could see for themselves, of course. 'Headgear'? You mean the Spitting Image effect? The headscarf and tiara? Is it important? Darling, should I have spilled the beans?"

I drew in a breath. "What beans?"

"I don't know what beans. Are there beans?"

"No," I said shortly.

"Oh, there are beans, all right." He sighed. "Well, I shan't spoil your fun. I wouldn't want my penchant for *scandale* to expose Mother to anything exposingish. And where is that Tom Benefer? It'll be time to serve luncheon before very long."

"Still looking for you, I'll bet. What were you doing in here, in the Ballroom, of all places, playing with these rifles in the first place?"

"Shotguns, darling. Do get it right. And to answer your question: I don't know. I think Tom was doing some work in the Gun Room when Father accosted him and *suggested* me for loader. This seemed like the nearest empty room, although I had no idea we were to go outside." He unbuttoned his coat. "Getting rather warm in here."

"Isn't the Gun Room Mr. Boughton's business?" I asked, referring to the man responsible for the upkeep of the several display cabinets full of Royal firearms, from Prince Albert's muzzle loader to George VI's duck gun.

"Oh, normally. But Mr. Boughton's another felled by 'flu and Tom, of course, knows something of this business. And he's handy."

"West Newton's aways a bit," I said, referring to the location of the Benefer cottage.

"No, Tom's staying over here at the Big House this year while Mother's in residence. Staying over with Aileen, I mean of course, silly me."

"That's a bit odd."

"Not really."

I looked at Davey. "What do you mean?"

"Darling, did you think Aileen was going to leave her sister and her husband *alone together* at their cottage in West Newton?"

"Why not?"

"Ho ho. You don't know, do you?" Davey grinned Cheshire-like. "I'm surprised you haven't gleaned this. It's rather rich. Juicy as a *filet mignon*, in fact. Here, sit next to me and I'll tell you a little story." He patted the floor beside him.

"Oh, brother." I sat. The floor was cold and Davey's coat still damp.

"Once upon a time, back in the days when—oh, when you were probably still in nappies and I was but a tot with a growing pash for platform pumps, when Callaghan was Prime Minister—I think—and Mother was just settling into middle age, there was to be a wedding on the Sandringham Estate. Young Tom Benefer, bachelor, late of Whitewell, was to marry younger-still Aileen Scaife, spinster of this parish or whatever ecclesiastical jurisdiction we're under, and they were to live happily ever after here in dankest Norfolk, he helping to raise fowl for slaughter, she helping to keep Mother's home neat as a nunnery.

"One day, however, the bride-to-be's younger sister, a fetching thing, hoved into view after a trip somewhere or other, to take up her modest role in the wedding party. Now, young Tom was a lad who liked to put it about a bit. And Jackie—well, she was a lass with a zest for life and a few scruples loose, if y'know what I mean. One day, on the virtual eve of the wedding, Tom and Jackie were caught *in flagrante delicto*, a shag *al fresco*, I am reliably told, among the sugar beets or the vining peas or somewhere equally uncomfortable. And they were caught by none other than—can you guess? Is it beyond your deductive powers?—Aileen Scaife, betrayed and broken-hearted sister, soon to be Mrs. Thomas Benefer."

11

AT FIVE O'CLOCK at Sandringham House everything stops for tea. Well, the Royal Family and guests stop for tea, in the Main Drawing Room. We downstairs types stop at the self-serve canteen-style Servants' Hall for a cuppa if we get a moment. I didn't have a moment. Normally, by that time of day, I would have had a moment but, late in the afternoon, we got word belatedly that one Royal had made a right royal mess of one of the chairs in the Dining Room at luncheon and who would make a stab at cleaning it before table was set for eight-thirty dinner? Having drawn the short straw, I supposed I could, but having the Royal Family taking tea on the other side of the doors connecting the Dining Room to the Main Drawing Room made my task a little more difficult than it might have been.

The mess in question appeared to be some sticky

dessertlike object, a crêpe suzette perhaps. It had landed kerplunk on the seat and splashed sauce on the back of one of a set of Regency chairs around the dining room table. Fortunately, the fabric and wood were not so rare or fragile as to demand the services of a restoration consultant. All that was required was to gently rub the green and gold fabric carefully with upholstery cleaner and a sponge, which I did quiet as one of the mice that are also inhabitants of royal residences. I wanted to switch on my little Hoover Dustette to collect those crumbs dried around the chair not amenable to hand-brushing, but even the dinky Dustette has a noxious whir that I was sure would rise above the tinkle of fine china and civilized conversation and disturb HM's tea-time peace. So I stood around like a lemon for a while, absently running a soft cloth over the surface of the table and the sideboard—which didn't need cleaning but training will out—and strained to hear the conversation next door. Alas, the door was thick enough to prevent verbal seepage, although I could hear the occasional hearty guffaw belonging to the Duke of York, whose estranged wife I think turned into a bit of a Hooray Henry.

The Dining Room is a rather odd shade of green, somewhere between the colour of French mints and the filling of a key lime pie, a design element to which I had given little thought until Hume Pryce had offered his critique at the Feathers. However, he had visited Sandringham House on a bright summer day. In the depths of winter, I could understand full well why someone decided to take a paintbrush to the place. Except on special evenings when candles blazed for formal dining, how utterly gloomy the dark, dark wood must have made the Dining Room seem. Even with a lamp each side of the sideboard switched on, the room in late afternoon seemed drear, abandoned, unloved.

As I went about quietly tidying things that didn't need tidying, a task which took about ten percent of my brain power, I couldn't help thinking with the remaining ninety percent about Davey's disclosure of an act of whoopee between Tom Benefer and Jackie Scaife in the remotish past.

"What happened after that?" I had asked Davey.

"Had a ciggy and languished in love's afterglow?"

"How could they? They had been caught."

"Yes, so they had. Well, it seems as if nothing happened, really, did it? The wedding went ahead as scheduled. And here it is, twenty-odd years later and Aileen and Tom are still shackled together."

"You'd think it would have ruined everything, wouldn't you? Imagine coming across your fiancé and your sister—"

"—having a bonk."

"That would have ended it for me. I'd have sent him packing. Out the door. You're gone, mister."

"Forgave him, I suppose Aileen did."

"I suppose," I said reluctantly. But, I wondered as I rubbed at one of the blue, white, and gold Minton plates decorating the sideboard, did Aileen forgive her sister? I tried to imagine how I would feel if, for instance, I had been the one engaged to marry Mr. PotatoHead back on the Island (not that he's any great catch in my opinion, but I'm speculating here) and I had come across him and my sister, Julie, doin' the nasty in some potato patch or wherever. I would be devastated. I would feel utterly betrayed. As I told Davey, I would have shucked my fiancé faster than I could shuck an ear of corn, but what do you do with a sibling? You're the fruit of the same womb. The chances are good your mother will invite you both to the same Christmas dinner. Oh, I thought, if one of my sisters ever tried something like that on me, there would be aitch e double hockey sticks to pay and it would be big-time, too.

And yet, here's old Aileen. She marries the creep. And she keeps up a cheerful—or I assume cheerful—correspondence with the viper sister who hotfoots it (one presumes) to America and then lets said v. sister stay in her home upon her return to the auld sod. She's either a remarkably forgiving woman or . . . ? Or what? It occurred to me that a person might derive a curious kind of power from being the wronged party.

You could play the martyr. Passive-aggressive on a grand scale. Did Aileen forgive Tom his trespass, to get all biblical about it? Or did she have something to hold over him all these years? And what about Jackie? Did Aileen's magnanimity depend on an ocean's breadth? And did it all start to wither two minutes after Jackie stepped through the Benefer cottage door one early autumn eve? Well, who knew? But the thoughts did bring a flush of pink to one's little grey cells.

I began idly to run a cloth over the filigreed edges of a rather sumptuous golden clock dead centre on the mantelpiece. Five thirty-five, the hands read. Surely, teatime couldn't go on much longer. If only the Royal Family had maintained Edward VII's custom of Sandringham Time, I thought; then it would be five minutes after six and teatime would be over.

I was leaning against the mantel, thinking about this, sighing and wondering whether I should just hop it and finish my skivvying later, when Davey popped through the door from the corridor that runs through the centre of the Big House and connects all the main rooms. He was carrying an electric kettle and he looked distinctly harassed. This clearly wasn't his day, what with the gun-loading lesson in the damp and all.

"Bother and phoo," he muttered, hastening around the tapestry screen that conceals the door and heading for the serving stand next to the sideboard. "Wherever's that power point?"

"What's the problem?"

"This silly kettle won't boil," he explained, bending to find the socket beneath the serving stand. "Mother'll be asking for it any moment. The power point in the serving kitchen's buggered . . . I think," he said with a short grunt as he plugged the kettle in.

"There's lots of other sockets in the kitchen."

"They're making raspberry tarts, Jane, if you know what I mean. One could die in there! Were baked beans on the luncheon menu? I don't recall. At any rate, I'm not venturing in again without a gas mask." Davey pressed his ear to the kettle and smiled with relief. "Oh, good, the kettle does work."

"It's such an odd way to do things." I was referring to the Queen's fondness for making the tea herself. Well, not so much her fondness for making it herself—it could just as easily be brought from the kitchen—but the manner of her making it. Card tables are set up and pushed together in the Main Drawing Room, covered with tablecloths and napkins and Queen Alexandra's favorite Minton tea service, and soon weighted down with brown bread and butter, local preserves and jams and honey, sandwiches of chicken or egg or cucumber with all the crusts cut off, sponge cake and chocolate cake, scones and biscuits and so on—truly a groaning tea table. And, of course, there's tea, the beverage. HM sits at one end with an ivory-handled silver kettle which rests on a stand with a paraffin burner underneath. The kettle tips and releases the boiling water into a silver teapot containing a special blend of China and Indian tea from which HM eventually pours the national beverage (or is that beer?). Of course, if you waited for a paraffin burner to boil water, the *Nine O'Clock News* would be over and you'd still be waiting. This is where Davey, or whichever footman is on duty, comes in. He boils the water in a real electric kettle and then shimmers into the Drawing Room and replenishes the silver kettle on the burner.

"Wouldn't it be easier," I said in a low voice just in case we could be heard next door, "if Her Majesty just boiled an electric kettle herself and forgot all this bother with the paraffin thing?"

"But Jane, it's tradition!"

"Sandringham Time was a tradition and that's not done anymore."

Davey opened his mouth to reply but the lamps either side of the sideboard flickered suddenly, drawing our attention away. At the same time, the kettle hesitated in its boisterous climb to boil, and then, before we had time to ponder this failure, the Dining Room was plunged into darkness. "Oh!" we exclaimed in unison, hearing an echo of our dismay in the room beyond. And then, just as suddenly, the lights snapped back on and the kettle resumed its mindless chore.

"Whatever was that?" Davey glanced around the room as if he expected further baths in the murk. A chorus of 'aahhs' filtered from next door.

"Maybe something's wrong with the mains," I supplied, knowing nothing about electricity other than what I had learned in grade nine industrial arts, which wasn't much. "I still think my letting you into the Ballroom this morning should have set an alarm off or something."

"Oh, come on. Boil, you stupid thing," Davey admonished the kettle.

"A watched pot never boils." I just made that up.

"This pot will boil or I shall thrash it. By the way, what are you doing in the Dining Room this time of day?"

I pointed to the Hoover Dustette and the upholstery cleaner. "Someone made a mess at luncheon. Mrs. Benefer isn't exactly on top of things these days—understandably—so we're just dealing with it now."

"It wasn't me! I didn't spill. You know where I was, catching my death . . ."

I shook my head and pointed to the door to the Drawing Room. "It was one of Them," I mouthed.

Wisps of steam issuing from the mouth of the kettle recalled me to something I had been thinking about earlier. "Speaking of traditions and all," I said to Davey, "don't a lot of the positions and jobs and so forth on the Estate run in families? Passed from father to son, mother to daughter and the like?"

Davey appeared to consider this. "Yes, they do tend to, I think, now you mention it. It's really its own little world out here."

"But Tom Benefer's not from here originally, is he?"

"No. He was raised on the Whitewell estate in Lancashire, I believe. It's part of the Duchy of Lancaster."

"Wonder how Tom wound up a gamekeeper on Her Majesty's Estate in Norfolk, though?"

"Aileen and Jackie's father was one of the Estate managers here, I'm told. I guess Tom married in. Oh, good, kettle's boiling. Thank you, darling." Davey patted the lid as the instrument switched itself off. "And I daresay Tom married up," he added as he bent under the serving stand to pull the plug.

"It's a good job, isn't it?"

"Oh, lovely job, I suppose, if you're at all"—he rose and pulled a face—"the *outdoorsy* type, which, fortunately, I am not. Besides, I don't think there is a growing demand for gamekeepers, at least not on private estates. Private estates are a rather diminished commodity, these days." He quickly gathered up the cord and headed for the door. "Just think, Jane, if there were no Royal Family, wherever would I get a job? I don't think you'll find 'footman' posted at the Jobcentre."

"I suppose some fabulously rich American might find you . . . decorative."

"Perish the thought."

Teatime didn't last that much longer, despite the second—or was it a third?—pot poured by Her Majesty, and finally I could hear a stir of movement next door. After tea, Family and guests usually repair to their rooms for what we below-stairs types gratefully refer to as the silent hour to gird themselves for the next bout of holiday feasting: drinkies then din-din. I had plugged in the Dustette, stretched the flexible cord to the max, maneuvered myself under the dining table with its several walnut leaves added, and prepared to get the bit of hoovering done smartlike so I could get on with my own meal and thence to Dersingham to meet my father.

And then the electricity conked out again.

Damn.

I waited, expecting the light to be restored at any second. Unfortunately, the seconds kept flying past and still no light.

Well, there was some. As my eyes adjusted to the darkness, the Dining Room windows, though heavily draperied, began to glow softly, an effect wrought by the security lamps outside. I was thinking how like empty film screens these phosphorescent oblongs seemed, each waiting for an animating figure, when a silhouette silently emerged from the shadows to the side, causing me in alarm to almost hit my head on the underside of the table. At the same time, unseen but heard, the door to the Main Drawing Room opened and another silhouette slipped into view.

"I say, anybody there?" The voice of the second apparition was very nearly jolly.

And then the lamps snapped back on and phantoms turned to shapes once more.

"Oh, it's you, Inspector," the same voice continued, delighted. It was Lord Thring, whose grey flannel trousers I could see through a thicket of chair legs. "We were wondering if the, er, blackout was intended for the Drawing Room alone."

"No, sir, I believe more than these west rooms have been affected. But the source of the problem has been found and there should be no more disruptions this evening." Paul Jenkyns's voice was calm and reassuring in a practised sort of way though Lord Thring didn't sound like he needed to have his little hand patted.

"Oh, very good, then." A trace of disappointment edged Lord Thring's reply. What with there being a virtual moratorium on shooting parties the last two days, Lord Thring, I figured, was probably becoming bored and eager for a little diversion.

Lord Thring's flannels began to flap their way back to the door while Jenkyns's dark blue crisp-pressed trousers neatly breaking on burnished black oxfords marched in the other direction but before blue trousers could exit, the flannels turned and inquired, "Jenkyns, isn't it?"

"Yes, my lord."

"Welsh name."

"I believe so."

"You don't look Welsh. Too tall, for one."

"No, my lord. My people are from these parts."

"My father dealt with a Jenkyns. Had a shop at King's Lynn. Related at all?"

"I was raised in Hunstanton."

"Ah, the seaside. Lucky man. There are always so many pretty young women by the sea."

"Yes, your lordship." A smile broke through the tone of Inspector Jenkyns's professional reserve.

"Well, I won't keep you, Inspector. Good evening."

"Good evening, my lord."

I could hear Inspector Jenkyns close the door behind him and I expected Lord Thring to make his exit similarly. But the flannels hesitated a moment, then made their way toward the table under which I was still crouched like a cat in a carry-box. One of the chairs near me was pulled to its side and two sensibly shod feet arranged themselves in front of it. My heart beat a little faster. I felt foolish and oddly complicit. I hoped his lordship was just cooling his heels for some reason. But to my dismay, like a lopsided moon, Lord Thring's florid face suddenly loomed below the rim of the table, about six inches from my own, his grey hair hanging like a carpet fringe. "And speaking of pretty young women . . ."

"Oh!" I exclaimed, feeling myself flush. "Good evening, my lord."

"And good evening to you, my dear. Are you enjoying yourself under there?"

"I'm just finishing a bit of tidying up. I'm sorry to have . . . you know . . ." I contorted my face in an apologetic fashion.

"On the contrary, it is I who should ask your pardon. I'm evidently disturbing your work. However, I would like to talk with you if you have a moment."

My heart sank. I knew what this was going to be about.

"And I wonder if you wouldn't mind coming out from there," his lordship continued. "I'm finding this position really rather uncomfortable. I'll have a crick in my neck."

Lord Thring's face, impeded by the balloon of his stomach from resting comfortably anywhere near his knees, was becoming as red as the red cashmere sweater swaddling his ample flesh. I quickly backed out, drag-

ging my Dustette after me, and popped up on the other
side of the table, nearly tripping over the cord still attached to the power point.

"Mind the Minton," his lordship warned as I
swayed against the sideboard. "Perhaps you could make
use of a chair."

I pulled the nearest one out and sat down contritely, grateful not to have broken anything.

"Can't be two American housemaids in Her Majesty's employ . . ." he continued.

"Canadian, my lord."

"Of course, Canadian. I do apologize. Hiring
Americans would be most odd, now that I think of it.
My dear, you needn't look so pained, I'm not going to
scold you . . ."

"It's not that, sir." I had planted my backside on
the very chair I had washed not half an hour earlier.
That's why I was looking pained. There was damp seeping through my uniform.

"Yes, well . . ." My response prompted a ripple
of consternation on his plump features and a sweep of
the hand across the brow, an attempt to rearrange the
hair that flopped schoolboyishly across its furrows. Lord
Thring had a large face, handsomely square in youth, I
presumed, but now relaxed into soft dewlaps and rosy
hillocks which, for some odd reason, made me think of
the swagged draperies Lady Thring had chosen for the
drawing room windows of Barsham Hall. His countenance was, on the whole, a cheery one, and he wore a
cheery expression. He would have made a good Father
Christmas, if he was ever moved to be one for his estate
workers. But for the eyes. Lord Thring's eyes were
small, hard, and black. Whether they were quite so
button-hard under other circumstances, I didn't know,
but the variance with his expression was not encourag-
ing.

"At any rate," his lordship continued, "you *were*
the young woman who slapped my stepson, I believe."

"Yes, my lord. But he was in my room and he
wouldn't leave and he was coming on to me and—"

"My girl," he cut in, "as I say, I'm not here to scold you. I'm sure your version is perfectly plausible."

"It's not a *version*. It's the truth."

"Yes, yes. Quite." Lord Thring shifted uncomfortably in his chair. My protest provoked a certain wariness to his eyes which I found rather strange. "Well, I'm sure it is as you say. My stepson is rather . . . he's somewhat immature, I suppose one could say. I'm sorry if he frightened you."

"He didn't frighten me. He just . . ." I wanted to say, 'harassed the *hell* out of me when I was feeling particularly crummy,' but phrased it in a way I thought might enlighten the likes of his lordship: "He just didn't behave as a gentleman should." To myself, I sounded very silly. I managed to suppress a giggle by biting my lip.

But Lord Thring interpreted my gesture otherwise. "Please don't cry, my dear," he said hastily. "Buchanan was being a beast. You had every right to defend yourself. Of course you did. There, there." Jovially: "He's not the first young man to be slapped by a fair maiden, ho ho." He waited while I effected to recover and then said with a heartfelt sigh, "I just wish you *hadn't* hit the boy, that's all."

Good god, I thought. You'd think I'd k.o.'d the twerp in the first round and sent him off for brain surgery.

"It's upset his mother, you see," his lordship continued. "Mothers, don't-you-know. Overprotective creatures."

"Lady Thring has already spoken to me about the incident," I responded stiffly.

"Ah! Oh, I see." He pushed his hand slowly through his hair.

"And her ladyship's asked me to apologize, too. Which I *will not*," I added as his eyebrows rose in hopeful response. My damp bottom was making me snappish.

"Oh, couldn't you try?"

"No."

"Think about it, perhaps?"

I thought about it. "No. Bu—Mr. Walsh should apologize to me."

"Perhaps we can effect a compromise. A mutual apology."

"Well . . ." I replied, thinking: What a lot of fuss over nothing! "I suppose . . ."

"Oh, good!" he said heartily. "Do so dislike rows at Christmas time."

Who had been rowing, I wondered? Mother and son, I bet. Or perhaps the Marquess and Marchioness, over how to handle the bundle of teenaged joy her ladyship brought into the marriage? Nevertheless, I was feeling somewhat at sea. For Lord Thring to concern himself at all with a tiny incident involving one of HM's housemaids and his stepson, Lady Thring must be a real gorgon, or a real something, in private. Otherwise, why concern yourself? Bucky was big enough and ugly enough I would have thought to handle his own problems.

Lord Thring leaned forward across the table in a confiding sort of way. "And should my stepson misbehave in your presence while we're staying at Sandringham, I do hope you'll come to me."

"Your lordship, if I may say, your stepson shouldn't ever be in Staff quarters at all."

"Yes, of course you're right. I'm afraid Buchanan hasn't quite got the hang of things."

I was beginning to get impatient. It wasn't just the bit of hoovering left to do, it was the wet seat. I was feeling all squirmy. But Lord Thring didn't seem that anxious to leave. He ran his hand again through his hair, allowed a tight smile to cross his face, and said:

"You must then be the young woman who gave assistance to Her Majesty during some, er, incident last year, was it? There was a Canadian involved, I believe."

"I was sort of at the right place at the right time." Right place at the *wrong* time, actually. Sadly. "So I was able to help a bit."

Funny, HM mentioning the murder at Buckingham Palace to Lord Thring. Family members, I could understand, particularly members of *that* Family, who if they didn't know the meaning of discretion before, had certainly learned it in the post-Squidgygate/Camillagate period. But Lord Thring? Oh, well, he was an old friend.

"A one-off, I expect," his lordship continued with a kind of steely bonhomie. "Not something one's likely to find oneself embroiled in a second time."

"Shouldn't think so," I lied.

"No, of course not." He seemed to be reassuring himself. What an odd old duck he was. "Well," he said, leaning one arm on the table and levering himself off the chair. (Standing, he's thin and tall but with a great ball of a stomach like he swallowed his Christmas dinner whole and hadn't digested it.) "Now that the electricity seems to be working, I'd better get on with things. Thank you, my dear, for hearing me out."

I rose as well, so grateful to get off the damp, and made a mental note to replace the chair with one against the wall before leaving, lest a member of the Royal Family get diaper rash. But as Lord Thring turned, the door to the Main Drawing Room opened and the Queen herself stood framed in the entrance, wearing the tweed skirt and pink sweater of the morning, a corgi attending her feet.

"Affie, there you are," she said, as I bobbed in a curtsey and Lord Thring made an apologetic gesture. "Come along, I've toasted another muffin. The last one, and you may have it."

His lordship stepped around the corgi, who regarded his trouser legs with sufficient interest to provoke the Queen to address the dog in a low warning tone. She began to close the door but as she did, she gave me a lingering look. I wish I could say what HM's look expressed, but I can't. It was just . . . a look.

12

" 'ARE YOU LONESOME TONIGHT?' " I warbled to my father a few hours later as I plunked myself into a seat at the Feathers and removed my jacket. My father eyed me suspiciously over his pint of Woodforde's.

"I didn't know people your age were that keen on Elvis." This from Hume Pryce whom I had bumped into entering the lounge bar. He was fetching some drinks.

"We're not," I replied cheerfully. "At least I'm not. But Dad here is, so there's an entire file drawer in my brain filled with snippets of Elvis lyrics. One of the awful legacies of childhood, I guess. Maybe I should bring a charge of abuse . . ."

"I saw him in Las Vegas once, a few years before he died," Pryce said, placing drinks in front of each of us.

"You're a lucky man." My father's face wore a stoic expression. "I never did get to see the King live—"

"Poor Dad, he had three daughters instead. Like Lear, speaking of kings."

"—what was it like?"

"Oh, really very interesting." Pryce sat down and lifted his glass. "Cheers. Anyway, I was travelling—"

"Ahem!" I ahem'd. I couldn't bear to hear another Elvisian reminiscence. "I have an announcement."

They both regarded me solemnly, my father with a reproving frown for interrupting my elders.

"In 1961," I began in a speechifying sort of voice, "Mr. Elvis Presley was invited to perform before Her Majesty the Queen at the Royal Command Variety Performance at the London Palladium. Also invited were, well, a whole bunch of people whose names I forget. Unfortunately—well, *amazingly*—Elvis passed up the opportunity. He declined the invitation. The King did not perform for the Queen. Her Majesty has in fact and in truth never met Mr. Elvis Aaron Presley. Ha! There! Did you know that?"

"No," said Pryce in a puzzled voice, thinking I had addressed him.

"Dad?"

"Yes, I knew that. The question is: How do you know that?"

"How do you *think* I know it?"

My father took a longish quaff of his bevvy. "Okay," he said at last. "I believe you." He didn't look all that happy about it.

Pryce's eyes moved from me to my father and back. "Some private family matter, I expect."

"Mmm," we chorused and lapsed momentarily into silence.

I glanced around the lounge bar. Only a few folk were in attendance: One elderly gentleman, who had captured the table nearest the fireplace, was dozing, his grey head fallen to his chest like a slumbering egret; at another table a dour middle-aged man in a tweed jacket was squashed piggy-in-the-middle between two smartly dressed older women, who might have been his mother and his aunt, each leaning forward aggressively, mouths working overtime in whispered argument. The fire was cozy, the lights soft, the woodwork fairly glowing, and I should have been glad to be snugly removed from the dirty weather outside the pub's mullioned windows, but for a kind of dull tension in the room. My father was grouchier than he ought to have been over the Elvis thing—he didn't even pursue Pryce's remembrance of the King at Vegas—and Pryce, for all his attempt at cheeriness, looked strained, the skin around his bony face taut and pale.

Next door, the public bar seemed jolly and lively by contrast, the chatter and laughter coming in waves, though only a portion of the more spartan room was visible beyond the interceding figure of the barman working the taps: It was like admiring a marvellous party through the slit of a letter box. I could see elbows poised as darts were aimed at an unseen target, hands lifting glasses to invisible faces, backs of heads of those seated. I felt an urge to switch places—I suspected some members of Staff were among those in the public bar—but then my eyes alit on the back of a particular head. There was something about the shape—or was it the hair colour?—that seemed familiar and, at the same time, troubling, as if a less than happy memory were associated with it.

"Problem, Bird?" my father asked, pulling me by the psychic hair roots back into the room.

I shook my head and hoped at the same time to shake my memory loose. It didn't work. Tricking the mind by distracting it was the ticket, so I said to Hume the first thing that came into my head: "I thought you'd have gone to Nevis to join your girlfriend by now. Sun, fun, et cetera."

"Er, no," he replied bleakly. "I expect I'll be here a while yet." He glanced at my father with an unhappy expression. "I'm to 'keep myself available,' as the expression goes."

"You're always better off coming clean." It was

Dad's Voice of Conscience. If I had heard it once, I'd heard it a million times.

"I'm not sure I *feel* better off," Pryce said. "Your father, Jane, must be rather good at what he does. Steve Bee. Clairvoyant Copper."

"There's nothing mysterious about it," my father said evenly. "It's my experience that people don't always tell the whole truth. On Tuesday, after you told my daughter and me Jackie Scaife had been murdered, you said 'she was still in costume when she died.' In fact, you'd told me the same thing earlier when I first met you at dinner. But the police weren't releasing many details at that point because of fears for the Queen's safety . . . All it took was a question to the landlord here . . ."

"Which was?" I said with rising curiosity.

"I asked the landlord whether Hume had spent the entire evening after the show at the village hall here in this room or"—he gestured toward the public bar—"in there. And the reply was that Mr. Pryce had gone up to his room a little before seven and didn't come back down until almost an hour later. It was something any one of the people you were sitting with could have told me, Hume, if I'd known who they were."

"I didn't know Temple could be so bloody perceptive," Hume muttered as he lifted his glass.

"People who run bars grow sharp eyes and ears or they get out of the business. Besides, they're the only ones *not* drinking."

"I might have *needed* to be in my room for half an hour," Hume insisted.

"To do what? There's toilets down here."

"To make a phone call."

"You could have stuck to that story."

Pryce sighed. "Acting was never my forte. I suppose that's why I dabble in directing. Still, I think it was rather unkind of you to be suspicious of me."

"Force of habit. Also, a habit of the Force. No offence. Next round's on me."

I had been listening to this exchange unable to get

a word in edgeways. Unrecorded above are the 'but's . . .' that dribbled from my lips to no effect.

"Hume went back to Village Hall Boxing Day night," my father explained at last.

It was not exactly a comprehensive explanation. For 'but' I exchanged another conjunction: "And . . . ?" I said. "And . . . ?"

Hume cast his eyes quickly about the room and said, dropping his voice, "I found Jackie"—he looked down at his hands and cleared his throat—"dead."

"*You* did?" I was startled. "About what time?"

"Sometime after seven, or thereabouts."

"More than two hours after the panto was done," I mused. "But why . . . ?"

"Because it was more than two hours after the panto and no Jackie," he replied with some vehemence. "It wasn't like her to miss the fun. She said she was meeting someone, but I'd assumed she was bringing that someone to the pub with her. Besides, I'd been made responsible for the hall and then there were those threats Jackie'd been receiving so I began to worry a little bit. Finally, I excused myself and went out."

He stared at the amber liquid in his glass as if it was an LCD screen across which events were being replayed. "The lights were still on when I arrived. The place was blazing. Well, it had been blazing when I left. The door was open, unlocked, so I went in and called out. But there was no response. I thought something was odd, so I looked in the kitchen and the side rooms, switching off most of the lights as I went. And finally I went up on the stage and there she was, lying on that litter. I thought she had fallen asleep . . ."

"So did we."

"She hadn't removed her makeup and so . . . well, she looked healthy enough. Until I touched her." He frowned. "I had tried shaking her, you see . . ." His voice trailed off.

"Why didn't you report it right away?"

"I just couldn't take it in," Pryce replied, running a hand through his hair. "I couldn't understand how she could be dead. She had no congenital illness that I knew of. I supposed she could have simply popped off. It happens. Dicky heart or the like. But then it occurred to me she might have been . . . killed after all. You know—murdered. She certainly didn't look as though she had been attacked or . . . whatever. But I remembered those threatening notes she had received and then . . ."

"Yes?" I prompted.

Pryce glanced at my father, who had remained impassive throughout his narrative, silently sipping his ale, and then me. He coloured slightly and continued. "I heard a noise. I'd fastened the entrance door behind me when I went into the hall, but I was sure someone was trying to open it. I had returned to the main room by this time and I could hear—or thought I could hear—footsteps crunching on the gravel just outside. So . . . well, I suppose I panicked, really. I went for the back door as quietly as I could and . . ." He shrugged. "And made my escape. As it were."

"Did you turn out the lights in the stage area?"

"Yes."

An awkward silence descended on the table, a void filled by snoring from the man by the fire, the chatterfest of the two old dears, and the boisterous clamour from next door. Pryce shifted uncomfortably in his chair.

"I thought my being there, alone—you know—with the . . . body would look rather suspect. And I suppose I didn't want to have to hang about here in Norfolk if there was going to be some sort of investigation, what with, as you say, sun and fun beckoning elsewhere. I thought, too, it might be ARF loonies." He sighed, affecting a pose between shame and nonchalance. "I know, I was being selfish *and* cowardly. It was a stupid thing to do. But, anyway, there you are. I've confessed and I'm not sure I feel one whit better." He added defensively, "If your father wasn't so perceptive, I would probably have got away with it."

Dad frowned. "With what? If you had no connection with this death, then you had nothing to worry about."

"Tell that to the Guildford Four."

"A famous false-arrest case in Britian, Dad," I explained to smooth the creases of mystification on the paternal brow, then hastily, lest the old man take offense, asked Pryce if he had any idea who might have been loitering outside the hall.

"None," he replied promptly.

"Not even whether it was a man or woman? Maybe from the heaviness of the feet on the gravel?"

He appeared to think about it. "Sorry. I have no idea. I didn't really pay much attention. It all happened in a few seconds."

"Was there a car in the parking lot?"

"I wouldn't know. I'm afraid I went up the street rather quickly. You see, after I went out the back door, I couldn't very well go around the hall and into the parking area. The hall's windows overlook it. I turned the other way, hopped over the wall, and walked through that woods, that undeveloped property, future housing estate or whatever it is, next door. Then I crossed the street to the church side and came back here."

"There was nobody around?"

"Dead, I'm afraid. Sorry, poor word choice."

"The street lighting here is pretty minimal," my father commented.

"It's certainly not London," Pryce echoed, gesturing to the window behind us, its inky mullions reflecting more of the pub's mellow interior than enabling any light from outside to enter.

"There's really no proper lighting in the hall parking area, either—other than an old incandescent lamp high above the entrance door, and I'm not sure that was even switched on—so if there had been a car there, I'm not certain I would have seen it, even if I had looked over that way.

"But"—Pryce raised a finger—"*but*, I'm sure I would have *heard* a car—you know, tires on gravel, a door slamming shut and the like."

"So, whoever it was must have walked from some other place in the village."

"Or," my father added, "came from further afield

and parked nearby. You didn't recognize any vehicles in the vicinity, I guess."

"I really wasn't looking," Pryce said drily, before lifting his glass and draining his pint. Somewhat rebuked, my father drained his.

"Another? Bird?"

"Ta, pater. Just a half."

"Didn't Jackie tell you she was going to meet someone?" I asked after my father had shifted his bulk toward the bar, empty glasses in hand.

"I assumed that someone would be along shortly. Remember, it's a couple of hours later that I decided to go back to the hall. If Jackie had intended to meet someone a fair time later, why not meet him—or her—here at the Feathers?"

"A need for privacy?"

Pryce shrugged.

"Or, perhaps, it was someone worth waiting for, no matter how long it took."

"I'm sure I don't know."

Of course, I thought, in the suspicious sort of way that was becoming my wont, the period between six-thirty and seven-thirty nevertheless remained within the estimated time-of-death parameters already established. Jackie could still have been alive at seven-thirty. It was possible. Was it possible the person she had actually been waiting for was Hume Pryce? Had he cooked up this story when my father had suggested there might have been a gap or two in his tale of Boxing Day night?

I smiled at the director across the table. While he wasn't quite the nonchalant Trustifarian having-a-lark-playing-panto-producer he had seemed the other night, he wasn't exactly a perspiring, frightened, about-to-be-arrested killer, either. Of course, I had been fooled in this regard before, notably last year when I had the unhappy experience of discovering that one of my comrades, a friend in fact, had poisoned another friend, a footman at Buck House. The killer had seemed perfectly normal, up until the end. Such revelations can leave you a little shaken in the trust department, believe me.

I realized my reverie had left me with a smile growing tighter by the second, as if my jaw were experiencing cramp. Pryce was beginning to stare. Well, what was I thinking of? What could his motive be anyway?

"Are you well?" he inquired.

"Sore tooth." My permanent excuse, it seemed.

"Is there a Royal Dentist at Sandringham?" This from my father who had returned, drinks in hand. "Sorry. Just asking. I thought you said hundreds of people work for the Queen."

"Hundreds do, but there's no dentist hovering around on the off-chance Her Majesty chips a tooth. It's not exactly the court of the Sun King, you know."

"*Do* you need to go to a dentist, Bird?"

"No, I'll be fine." I shot him a put-a-lid-on-it look.

"Did Louis XIV have a dentist in attendance?" Pryce lifted his glass, then hesitated with another thought: "*Were* there dentists in those days?"

"I think barbers pulled teeth in those days," my father replied.

"George Washington had wooden teeth. I remember some advert on telly when I was in the States made a point of it. For tooth polish, I think."

Oh, bugger George Washington and his timber clappers, I thought and interjected, hoping to steer the conversation away from things dental: "What'd the police say about your . . . new information regarding Boxing Day night?"

"Not terribly much. Don't wander off, they said." Pryce regarded my father darkly. "I think they're more troubled by the Animal Rights Front, anyway. When I talked to them earlier today, they were pressing for more details about the threatening notes Jackie had been receiving, and what she'd said to me about them, and so forth. Not that I could remember anything more than what I had told them the day before. I expect having the Queen in residence at Sandringham is making them rather anxious."

"They've tightened security around the Big House. We're on amber alert," I added, unhappily aware of the consequence to me personally. And then, like day following night, the Duchess of Windsor's tiara popped into my head, cursed thing.

"By the way, where did Jackie Scaife's 'Queen' outfits come from?"

"A costume hire I know in Cambridge."

"Tiara, too? Er, jewellery generally?"

"Hats, wigs—all of it. They're very good. Royal looky-likey isn't *un*popular. Of course, Jackie had a few bits and bobs of her own which she brought with her from the States."

"Like her own tiara?"

My father gave me a sidelong glance as Pryce turned his attention to his beer.

"Odd you should ask," he said after taking a long draught. "We hired one for the royal banqueting scene at the beginning of the second act where the Queen of Hearts is to appear in full regalia. But I do think she must have used one of her own, after all. It looked rather different when she came out on stage. And I'm sure it was the one she was wearing when I saw her . . . well, when I saw her later."

"So Jackie doesn't, or didn't, wear the tiara on-stage until the second act."

"Yes, I believe I did say that. I must say, you do seem rather consumed by this tiara."

"It's a girl thing."

The two men stared at me.

"You wouldn't understand."

A suitably diverting comment, I thought, the mysteries of femininity having their uses. But Pryce had given me an idea, a far-fetched idea, but an idea nonetheless. And good ideas vis-à-vis the death of Ms. Scaife seemed to be as scarce as pheasant's teeth, speaking of teeth again.

"Did she wear the tiara for the rest of the panto?" I asked.

"No. For most of the second act, Jackie wore this acidulous yellow two-piece, with a matching yellow hat and yellow sensible shoes—she really looked marvellous. Just like Her Majesty at a walkabout. You know, if you saw your own mother in the street in such a bizarre

ensemble, you'd think she'd lost her mind. Anyway"—
Pryce snickered—"Jackie carried this enormous yellow
handbag. And in it, she had a bottle of seltzer, which she
would take out and spray the audience at opportune
moments. It was absolutely hilarious. Jackie looked so
like the Queen, and you found yourself imagining the
Queen—the real one—soaking some nob—whoosh!
splash!—at Ascot or the State Opening of Parliament or
somewhere. Whoosh! Whoosh! Really, it was too
funny." He leaned his head back and laughed out loud.

Well, I guess you had to be there, although I have
to admit my fancy was tickled a touch. I wish I *had* been
there. (For other reasons, too, of course.)

"Well," Pryce said, his face dropping, wiping a tear
from the corner of his eye, "I guess you had to be there.
I expect panto is really a bit too English for others to
enjoy."

"No, I saw one last Christmas in London. It was a
riot. I loved it." And, I thought, if only Pryce knew
seltzer—soda water—was just what the Queen *did* carry
in her purse. It was the first line of defence against
corgis who piddled on Axminsters.

"Pantos are fun, aren't they? Bad luck with this
one, though." He looked all philosophical. Then started.
"Oh, sorry, to finish answering your question: Jackie
wore the tiara again in the final scene, the wedding of
the Prince of Hearts—a bloke in a Charles getup, huge
ears with a flapping mechanism, wonderful—and the
Princess of *Di*-amonds—ho ho! We played about with
the standard script. Our Chuck and Di weren't quite as
convincing as our Queen, but, oh well, you can't have it
all."

"But when I found Jackie, or we found her—when
you found her, too, I guess—she was wearing the *Country Life-, Horse & Hound-* sort of stuff. Barbour, wellies,
and so on."

"She wore that clobber early in the first act. I
thought it would make the connection to Sandringham."

"I wonder why she put those clothes on after the
play was done, though."

"Keep warm probably. Jackie was having trouble

reacclimatising herself to English winters. She had taken off the posh frock from the wedding scene, and she was waiting for someone, so . . ." Pryce twisted his hair into a temporary ponytail. "Fortunately, we didn't have to hire those things. Practically everyone wears those sorts of clothes around here, so Jackie was able to borrow. The Barbour might have been her own, in fact, though I usually saw her in that provocative fur coat."

"She didn't take the makeup and wig off after, though."

"No. That is odd, I grant you."

A sudden eruption of laughter in the public bar drew our attention away for a moment. Something on telly, I expected. There was one above the bar and my watch said it was just after nine o'clock, the right time to switch from the *Nine O'Clock News* on BBC1 to a comedy on BBC2. And there was that head again! So familiar! But who was it? And why didn't it turn around to look at the screen like normal people? If only I could match the hair with a face.

"What were you doing at the hall this afternoon, by the way?" I heard my father say to Hume. "I noticed you outside when I went past in the car. The police cordon's still up, isn't it?"

I turned back in time to see Pryce nod. "But I was allowed in to sort out the costumes and effects, which need to be returned to Cambridge and a few other places. I expect, Jane, the police have kept the tiara along with the other things Jackie was wearing," he added teasingly.

I acknowledged the ribbing with a smile but it was more of an I've-got-a-secret smile. I knew the police had the tiara, and they had it by a more circuitous route than Hume could ever know about.

"And I expect they have the sceptre, too, now that I think about it. Gosh, forgot about that sceptre." He smiled at me. "Please don't tell me sceptres are a 'girl thing,' Jane."

I tried to think. Did Barbie have a sceptre? Well, I knew she didn't have an orb. Cheerleader Barbie had a baton. That was *like* a sceptre, long with a knobby bit at one end. "I think they're probably more of a boy thing," I replied instead.

"Ah, Freud. But sometimes, Jane, a sceptre is just a sceptre. However, in this case, a sceptre is a priest."

"Oh, I see. A riddle. Is this akin to a raven being like a writing desk? . . . *Alice,*" I added to decorrugate their corrugated brows, *"in Wonderland.*"

"You've a clever daughter here, Steven."

"Don't I." The paternal-unit regarded me more with worry than pride, which was itself worrying. "So how is a raven like a writing desk, Jane?"

"Who knows? It's a paradox, I guess. But how can a sceptre be a priest?" I turned to Pryce.

"When administering extreme unction to a monarch? You're not RC, are you? Neither am I, actually. Well, the sceptre was a priest; that is, it was made from a priest."

"I hope the priest wasn't alive at the time."

Hume laughed. "No. The priest in this case was inanimate. It's . . . well, it's just a stick, really. A heavy one. Fishermen use them, apparently, to give the *coup de grâce* to fish without spoiling their appearance. I gather they're used in shooting, too. Some poor bird falls out of the sky, not quite dead, and the priest is used to dispatch it. And if you're still wondering why it's called a 'priest,' it's because the motion of delivering the blow imitates a priest performing the Last Rites. Black humour, I suppose.

"Anyway, Jackie brought the priest in. Her idea. It wasn't very long, perhaps eighteen inches, with one sort of club end and the other end rather sharp—for cleaning the fish, I expect. Jackie bought some Styrofoam balls at a craft shop in Lynn, glued on some sparkle dust, and, *voilà,* she had a sceptre."

My father and I looked at each other in a are-you-thinking-what-I'm-thinking sort of way. And we both looked at Pryce, who didn't seem to be thinking what we were thinking at all, or at least was feigning not to.

"What is it?" he said, recoiling. "You both look like you've discovered cold fusion."

"Did you tell the police about the 'priest'?" my father asked quietly.

"I've only just thought of it this minute."

"The victim died from a blow to the back of the head—"

"Oh? . . . Oh! The priest!"

His surprise: real or fake? It beat me. But the eyes, bright and large as a baby's were pretty good.

"—and I don't think the weapon's been found," Dad continued.

Pryce blinked rapidly. "I'm sure I didn't see the sceptre when I was packing things this afternoon at the hall. Although I was really only concerned with the items on the list from the costume hire. Where, I wonder . . . ?"

Where, indeed, I thought. How difficult would it be to dispose of such a thing? Throw it in the sea? Bury it? It could be anywhere.

"But was it there Monday night?" he asked himself, creases of perplexity appearing around the bridge of his nose.

"You mean when you went back to the hall to find Jackie?"

"Mmm. The props stayed on a prop table in the wings. Now, did I see the sceptre when I walked past looking for Jackie? Or am I thinking of a rehearsal evening earlier?" He stared upwards as if looking for shapes in clouds. "I can't remember. Might it be important, do you think?"

"Might," my father allowed.

"Perhaps the anti's used the priest as an ironic gesture, given that it looked like the Queen's regalia."

"That presumes ARF knew the priest existed, knew it had been turned into a sceptre." And presumes it's ARF at all, I thought, but kept my counsel.

Pryce spun a finger around the rim of his beer glass absently. "I was just thinking," he said, as an eerie ring emitted under pressure from his rhythmic rubbing, "in the banquet scene, very near the end, Jackie made an odd sort of fluff with her lines. More of an ad-lib, really. I had hoped to do some 'notes' later and mention it to her but, of course, I didn't have the chance. I say," he amended, looking up, "I think that man is going to fall into the fireplace if someone doesn't right him soon.

"Malcolm," he called to the figure wiping the bar with a white cloth.

"Do you remember what the ad-lib was?" I asked as Pryce directed the barman's attention to the snoring o.a.p.

"Not quite. The original line has something to do with the Queen of Hearts threatening whoever stole the tarts and demanding said tarts be found . . ."

But I had stopped listening. As the barman shifted himself, I glimpsed the noggin nagging at my mind turned in profile, instantly recognizing in the blunt features someone I knew, and wished I didn't know.

"Bugger bugger bollocks," I blurted.

"Jane!"

"Oh, heck, then."

"Whatever's the problem?" Pryce inquired.

"Oh, hell, he's seen me." The profile had turned full face.

"Who?"

"Don't look, don't look! Oh, too late." The someone I knew and wished I didn't know was rising from his chair. There had been a moment of perplexity, then recognition had illuminated his face. "It's a reporter with the *Evening Gazette*," I hissed. "The guy with the sort of oat-colored hair. His back was to us."

"Is he a reporter?" Pryce looked dismayed. "I saw him arrive late this afternoon. With luggage. He's staying here, I think. And you know him?"

"He's one of the tabloid terriers on the Windsor watch. Gosh, I haven't seen a paper in days. Has there been stuff in about Jackie's death?"

My father nodded.

"I don't need this," Pryce said firmly. "If you two will excuse me . . ." He drained his beer, leaped from his seat, and slid through the doorwell just as the unwelcome figure greased in, his face wreathed in smiles, his hand clutching his pint to his chest, the condensation spotting his tie.

"Just follow my lead," I muttered to my father. "Hello there," I said to Macgreevy. "How are you?"

" 'Allo, Stella, luv. Nevah bettah." He cocked his thumb at my father. " 'Oo's the geezah?"

"The geezah's me old man. And why are you doing this Cockney routine?"

"Four hours in megaboring Norfolk and I have to do something to entertain myself. Sorry about the 'geezah' bit, sir. May I sit down?"

It wasn't a request. He plunked himself down in Pryce's vacated seat. "Fancy meeting you here, Stell."

"Well, you know who my employer is. Dad, this is Andrew Macgreevy. From the *Evening Gazette*. Right? Still?"

"You don't read my prize-winning prose? I'm very hurt."

"And this is my father, Steven Bee."

"Stell, I didn't know you were married?"

"I'm not."

"But your surnames are different. Rigby. Bee."

"You must have misheard, Mr. Macgreevy. This is my father, Steven *Rig*by."

"How do you do, Mr. *Rig*by. What brings you to this not-so-green and not-always-pleasant land?"

"I came to visit my daughter." My father regarded our new tablemate blandly and me with a glint of concern, probably for my mental health. On my first encounter with Macgreevy, more than a year earlier, I had seized on a pseudonym, hoping it would deflect his noseyparkeristic tendencies. Foolishly, I had chosen the name of a character on *Coronation Street*—Stella Rigby. A minor character but a memorable name for viewers of the long-running British soap. Macgreevy knew perfectly well what my real name was, but he wouldn't relent. Neither would I, actually.

"And what brings you to Norfolk, Mr. Macgreevy?"

"Andrew, please, Stella. We're old mates. 'Nother round? Stell? Mr. R.?"

"Actually, we were just on our way—" I began.

"Oh, yes? Where to? Got tickets to the Royal Dersingham Opera? There's so much to do here, isn't there?"

"I'm driving my daughter back—"

"Of course. But Stell and I haven't seen each other in such a long time, have we, luv? Stay a while longer. How is Her Maj, Stell? 'Nother tense Christmas at the Big House? At least Di pushed off before they sat down to nosh. Must have cheered them enormously." He swirled his beer around in his glass and smarmed like a nightclub greeter.

"You'd know more than me. I didn't get here until Boxing Day."

"Oh, yeah?" Macgreevy narrowed his eyes, assessing me. "Hmmm."

"So, why *are* you here? The Royals going in and out of Sandringham Church may be a photo op but it can't be very newsworthy."

"Come on, Stell. You know why I'm here. A murder on Her Majesty's Estate? Animal-rights nutters lurking about? Rumours—unconfirmed—the victim was tarted up to look like Her Majesty the Queen? The whole national press is swarming. I booked the last room in this bleedin' place."

Oh, joy, thought I. A plague of locusts with Nikon zoom lenses.

"And," Macgreevy continued, leaning forward conspiratorially. "I hear tell the body wasn't found by security doing its usual sweep. Some members of Staff made the gruesome discovery at the village hall. A couple of footmen, I hear. And, in the vicinity, a young woman, slim, dark-haired—you've grown yours since I saw you last, Stella—wearing a white uniform. A housemaid, my source says."

"And what would your point be?" my father interjected, regarding Macgreevy with the sort of granite cool that cops cultivate. I always hate it when he directs this ofttimes irritating *reasonableness* at me, but, boy, it's fun watching him do it to someone else.

"My daughter tells me there are quite a number of housemaids at Sandringham House," Pater continued without a trace of rancour in his voice. "Most of them are young, and odds are the majority of them will have dark hair instead of blond, given that blondes are a minority in society, even in England. And, as I understand it, people who work for the Queen sign a letter of confidentiality. I think I know my daughter, Mr. Macgreevy, and I doubt she would break that oath to supply you with information, even if it was for what you reporters call 'background.' Also, there's a police investigation going on in this village. Should my daughter have any information that might shed light on this crime, I'm sure she knows her first responsibility is to the proper authorities."

Whew! I thought. But I wasn't sure Macgreevy understood he had been read the riot act vis-à-vis me. During Papa's pronunciation, the reporter's face had grown all hooded and peevish like a child's, but when it came to an end, he smoothly turned his attention back to me and said cheerfully: "Rumour has it Her Maj was in the vicinity. Know anything about it?"

"I think we'll be on our way," Dad said, rising abruptly.

"Just doing my—"

"I know, Mr. Macgreevy, you're just doing your job. You're welcome to it."

"Ten quid says your father's a cop, Stell." He let his eyes travel my father's height, six feet plus. Then he smiled. "What? Not betting? Be seeing you," he called after us. "Oh, and who was that bloke sitting with you?" He cupped his hands over his mouth.

"Just a local," I cupped back.

"A likely story."

"I hate reporters."

We were upstairs in my father's room and he was reaching into the wardrobe for his coat while I sat on the bedspread flipping through a couple of papers he had bought at a newsagent's earlier in the day, *The Times* and *The Daily Telegraph*, each of which carried restrained accounts of Jackie Scaife's death below the fold on page one.

"Mom's a reporter," I responded unthinkingly to my father's rare burst of animosity. Or was. She's an editor with the Charlottetown *Guardian*, not that the newspaper of a city with less than fifty thousand people has a huge staff.

There was silence but for a metal hanger scraping along the bar of the wardrobe.

"I didn't mean your mother, Bird," he said softly.

I looked up. He was shoving his arm purposefully into the sleeve of a navy blue parka. He *did* look like a cop. Sigh. No getting away from it. But it was the little pause that troubled me more. The *significant* little pause. However reasonably and rationally and unemotionally my father presented to me his separation from my mother after nearly thirty years of marriage, I knew (my whole generation knew, for it seemed like most of my friends' parents had been to, or were heading to, Splitsville) all kinds of nasties percolated away in subterranean depths that could bubble up through the surface calm unexpectedly. Hates reporters, eh?

Macgreevy was fairly off-putting, it was true, but Macg. seemed to have got up the ancient paternal-unit's backside fairly sharpish, which was odd. You'd think having a reporter for a wife all those years would have inured him to such people. A cop and a reporter was not a marriage made in ideological heaven, true. While Dad was busy *maintien*ing *le droit*, to mangle the RCMP's real motto, *maintiens le droit* (uphold the law—*not* 'they always get their man'!), Mom increasingly over the years, or at least it seemed to me, was questioning *le droit*—a kind of reporter-y thing to do but not one inclined to charm your police officer husband. Still, they seemed to get along on the credo & convictions front, or at least agreed to disagree, not that I was paying a huge lot of attention, being a somewhat—but not completely—self-absorbed teenager person for much of the time.

"Are you coming? Bird? Hello. Dad to Bird. Come in, Bird."

"Sorry."

"You can keep those papers if you like."

" 'S'all right. I got the gist."

"We'll take these stairs," he said, indicating a door leading to a set of fire stairs. "It's actually quicker to the parking lot, and if you want to avoid your reporter pal . . .

"Hume came and went to the village hall this way," he added as he pushed the door against a volume of chilly, damp air and we descended the stairs. The wind had fallen in ferocity and a few stars were noticeable for the first time since I had arrived in Norfolk, portending perhaps a clear day for the shooting party.

"And you thought that was odd."

"Yes and no. The employees here all seem to use them. That door's open half the morning. They don't seem to mind the cold the way we do—"

"Weird, considering how cold Canada is."

"—and it is a quick way across the lot here and over there to the hall." Dad pointed vaguely into the shadowy distance as we crossed the parking area. "Hume probably wanted to get there quickly without going through the pub and being diverted by his friends. And I can understand why he came back up this way, if he intended to keep quiet about his discovery. But it seems just a little . . . furtive."

"But you were skeptical about him earlier. Thanks, squire." He unlocked the passenger side.

"Just the way he acted when we—you and I— were having a drink with him the other night," he said, moving around the boot of the Vauxhall and stepping into the driver's side.

"I thought he was just reacting to your being a plod . . . a Mountie, I mean."

"Maybe."

"It's freezing. Give us some heat, Dad."

He turned the ignition and switched on the fan. "But I think he's still holding something back."

"You're getting interested in this, aren't you?" I remarked gleefully. "Finding wintry Norfolk . . . megaboring?"

Dad glanced in the rearview mirror, prepared to shift into reverse, but then seemed to think better of it.

"I'm worried about you, and what you seem to be getting yourself involved in."

"Accepted the results of the Elvis Challenge, have you? Hee hee."

"It's a police matter, Jane."

"I think they're on a wild-goose—or perhaps in these parts, -pheasant—chase. And so, I might add, does a certain person who happens to be my employer."

"You noticed in the paper, I hope, ARF has claimed responsibility."

"I did. And I say phooey. Some wacko could have phoned that in. Or ARF could be just taking advantage of something they didn't do, lazy sods."

My father was silent a moment, looking out the windscreen toward the wet carrstone wall separating the street from the parking lot. "Well . . ." he began, sounding reluctant. "As it happens, you might be right. From what I hear, the investigation is going less well than hoped. There's no arrest in the offing, and there's some grumbling about the direction, or the target. But whoever is responsible, I don't want you involving yourself. Homicide isn't a game."

"I'm a big girl."

"Not that big, from my perspective." He shifted the car into reverse. "And why," he added, glancing at me as he turned his head to check the parking lot was clear, "is your *employer* taking such a personal interest?"

"Well, she feels a responsibility toward the people on her Estate, for one thing . . ."

"Yeah, so . . ."

"Dad, turn left instead of right. Let's just take a look at the village hall."

"It's darker than Cavendish Bay on a moonless night. You're not going to see anything."

"It might trigger something. Who knows?"

"You haven't answered my question, Bird."

"About my *employer*, oh?" I was gratified to see his hand push the turn signal down rather than up, but I wished he hadn't asked. I really didn't know why and I said so.

"But there is something bothering her," I added,

as we drove the short distance between the Feathers and the village hall.

"Then why doesn't she talk to the police about it?"

I laughed. "They probably haven't asked her opinion. Anyway, HM has to be careful. She couldn't be seen interfering in an investigation. And besides, she's been doing the same job for a gajillion years. I think she enjoys the break in the routine, the puzzle, the challenge . . ."

"With a little help from her housemaid."

"Well, she doesn't have the freedom of movement. I don't think being a monarch is all it's cracked up to be."

We had turned into the parking area, an ill-kempt patch of gravel and thin grass. Below a single dim outdoor lamp fixed under the eaves the double doors opening into the hall lay in shadow. Taped across, a sunny yellow cordon, denying egress, was plainly readable, however: CRIME SCENE. DO NOT CROSS. I stepped out of the car, and my father struggled from his seat, muttering, "I don't know what you think you're going to find."

"I just want to see what it's like in the dark. After all, the murder took place after dark. Switch the car lights off, Dad."

It was odd how isolated the village hall was. English villages are compact compared to North American towns, and Dersingham was really no different. But some peculiarity of planning or hazard of history had set the village hall down, solitary as a tomb, in a reach of land that seemed to blend into the very night itself. To the west and south, beyond a sheep pasture, a few pinpricks of light indicated the presence of cottages. To the north, the thorny crowns of winter trees, grey on grey, loomed over the Hall's silhouetted roof. Only to the east was there proof you were not a lone figure in a nightshrouded meadow: Streetlights cast a feeble light on St. Nicholas' Church and the graveyard behind the low wall on the other side of the roadway down which the rare car hurtled, its headlamps tracing a laser path in the road before roaring off in the distance. Half a dozen people could be lurking around here without being seen, I thought. Only the lamp over the doorwell even came close to breaking the promise of concealment, a situation easily remedied with the flick of a switch. I said as much to my father.

"If the inside lights were on—and I understand they were when Hume arrived—then there would be more illumination here outside the hall," he commented, as we walked past, toward the west side of the building. "Do these windows look right into the hall itself, or into some other rooms?"

"Right into the hall. But the drapes might have been drawn. There would still have been some light in the sky when the panto started at two-thirty. The drapes were pulled back for the aborted shooting luncheon.

"And this," I continued, turning the corner to the west side, "is the exit door behind the stage. Davey rushed out here after . . . Dad?"

He wasn't following me.

Then I heard a sound, coming not from behind me as I expected, but from the wall and the woods in the shadows ahead. "Dad?" I said more tentatively, wanting to believe he had somehow raced around the building from the other side. But my father wasn't the sort to find humour in scaring the bejesus out of someone. The sound continued, a kind of scrabbling, a scrunching of dead leaves and hot breath, faintly heard. I could feel my heart thumping as I peered into the middle distance.

"Bird?"

So startled was I by my father's voice that I banged my head against the brick and called out in pain. Just then, out of the shadows, a shadow blacker still leaped through the air toward me.

NEXT MORNING, I awoke with a start. The alarm clock
wasn't the culprit. Dreaming was. In this particular
dream, or nightmare as it was, I was tearing through a
tangled sunless forest, pursued by I knew-not-what, one
hand desperately clinging to something spiky on the top
of my head, the other gripping the satiny folds of a
gown, a ballgown of nineteenth-century vintage, volumi-
nous and encumbering, its weight and mass dragging at
me even as thorns and branches of surrounding trees
slashed and shredded the fine material. I was guided in
my piteous flight through the darkness by a light like a
coalminer's lamp, a clarifying beam that bobbed and
swayed with each movement of my head. The source
was, I realized with the sensible illogic of dreams, a diamond tiara glowing with its own inner fire, my beacon in
my ordeal and yet—horror swept me like a tide—the

true object of my pursuer's passion. Finally, my lungs heaving, my legs aching, I burst onto a midnight shore that seemed to disappear into a void. Inky, oily water lapped at the edges of my tattered gown. A starless sky turned my moment of exultation into one of hopelessness. In that moment, a creature vaulted out of the abyss, knocking me into a kind of ooze, covering me with a smothering, punishing heat, sending the tiara twisting and twirling over and over into the darkness, its light trail dazzling until a horrible sucking plucked it from my dream world. The creature shrieked but did not release me. I kept pushing and pushing against it, feeling the sinewy lengths of an animal's body but sensing a human intelligence, a face somewhere in the blackness above my own face. I desperately flailed my arms in a vain attempt to fling off my attacker and rise through the murk into some light, some calm that I knew existed beyond this fearsome state, but I only sank deeper and deeper. And then, just as my scrabbling fingers were able to distinguish the outline of the face, I was suddenly thrust into a dark room, its corners and shapes dusted with very faint light. The images of horror dissolved like sugar in tea and I realized, with a swell of relief, that I was awake. My eyes were open, I had flung the covers off, and I was staring at my own window in my own room brushed by the first glimmer of the approaching dawn.

This was not an auspicious start to the day, I thought as I lay there, drenched in perspiration, the oppressive aura of the nightmare lingering as the few remaining images were drawn into oblivion. The trigger, of course, had been last night's disturbance back of Dersingham Village Hall. But, as triggers to bad dreams went, it was really pretty benign. What had lunged toward me in the dark was not some homicidal maniac, some crazed rapist, but a dog. A big black and rather frightening dog, to be sure, but not a canine bent on a vicious attack. Its front paws had pitched into my chest, pinning me against the wall, but its wet nose had merely snuffled around my face avidly for a moment, its tongue curling luridly over its teeth, before dropping to the ground and wriggling over to give my father an olfactory hoovering. Then it bolted off into the night.

"A dog like that shouldn't be running free," my father muttered. "Are you okay?"

"Yeah, just scared me for a moment," I replied, having rediscovered the pleasure of breathing. I wiped at bits of dirt and twigs left on my coat by the dog's paws. "Funny, there was a black dog that darted into the stage area of the hall after we discovered the body Tuesday—a Lab."

"That was a Lab."

"Really? I can't imagine one of the Queen's dogs being on the loose like that at night. She's got about twenty or so gundogs at the Sandringham Kennels and her guests' dogs board there, too, and they're all supposed to be extremely well trained."

"The Queen can't be the only person with Labrador dogs in this part of the world."

"There is that. I presumed Tuesday's dog had belonged to one of the guns, had slipped its tether or something when they arrived for the shooting luncheon. I guess that one"—I pointed vaguely in the direction of the dog's vanishing—"belongs to some villager."

"It must. It seemed high-strung for a trained hunting dog."

"So was the Tuesday one, in a way. Unless this dog was the ghost dog they say haunts the grounds around Anmer Hall. It was real, wasn't it? I didn't imagine this?"

"It was real."

"Oh, well, a coincidence, I guess."

But as I lay under the bedclothes, luxuriating in the moments left me before the alarm finally went off, I wondered: Was it a coincidence? Could it be the same dog?

Such questions soon found themselves deposited in an unmarked mental file folder because Mr. Alarm finally went off and I was thrust into the day's skivvying before you could say Sophie Rhys-Jones. It was much later in the morning, when I had gone to the Linen Room to fetch another fresh set of sheets for one of the guest bedrooms, that I came across Aileen Benefer and was confronted with something almost as startling as having a dog leap out at you in the dark.

The Linen Room is more substantial than the sort of closet thing you might have in your home furnished with sheets and towels sufficient for a family of 4.2 or 3.7 or whatever the average size is nowadays. The Linen Room at Sandringham House, like similar rooms in the other royal homes, is actually a *room* into which you can walk and move about. It's more reminiscent of a linens shop, or perhaps a discount linens shop, because the shelves extend nearly to the ceiling and the goods— bedclothes, bathroom towels, table linens, etc. etc.—are piled high under strong light such that the place is a torrent of white & bright, a detergent adman's dream. True to the conscientious Mrs. Benefer, everything is neatly labelled and categorized and inventoried and so on, such that there is no loss and no waste. (The Queen even insists the good bits of old sheets be sewn together to make do. HM is a very 'waste not, want not' sort of monarch, though she's hardly likely to fall into the 'want' category.) Given the number of people—Royal Family, guests, Household, and Staff—who need to be supplied with fresh linen on a regular schedule, the task of organizing and control of the Linen Room is not one to be taken lightly.

That's why it was so startling to switch on the overhead lamp, turn a corner, and come across Mrs. B. slumped in a scattered heap of bedlinen on the floor. She blinked against the sudden burst of light, but made no effort to rise to her feet and reassert her sense of decorum. This wasn't the Mrs. B. I had come to know and . . . respect. Certain members of Staff you might find sleeping it off in some cranny somewhere, but Mrs. B.? She'd always struck me as a potential poster girl for the Christian Women's Temperance Union.

"Are you okay?" I asked tentatively, sniffing the air for the sour odour of booze.

Mrs. Benefer lifted her face. Her expression was so

harrowing I actually staggered a half step back. She looked positively shattered. There were dark circles like bruises around her eyes and her skin had the tautness of cling film around a bowl. But liquor I could not smell, only the odd sweet odour of linens that have shrouded a thousand sleeping bodies.

"Are you okay, Mrs. Benefer?" I repeated, more urgently, crouching down. Had she had an accident? Was she ill?

"She slept with him, you know," she announced, staring at me glassily, her voice threadbare.

The non sequitur left me nonplussed. I made a sort of strangled reply.

She nodded to herself. "She slept with him all right."

She? Him?

"Who?"

Mrs. Benefer struggled to focus on my face. "My sister, of course," she said finally. "She slept with him."

Oh, Lord, I thought, she's snapped.

"Mrs. Benefer, maybe you should go have a lie-down."

"I am lying down."

"But Mrs. B.," I reasoned gently, "you're lying down in the Linen Room."

"Oh, am I?" She looked around vaguely.

I followed her eyes. She must have entered the room in the dark, pulled the sheets from their shelves, and made her impromptu bed. She couldn't have been lying here very long, I thought. The Linen Room attracted a certain amount of traffic. Surely someone else would have noticed her.

"Come on, Mrs. Benefer, you'd better get up. What would Her Majesty say if she found you like this?" Not that the Queen was likely to wander into the Linen Closet, but I hoped the magic title would rouse her spirit.

"Oh, let me lie here a while." She closed her eyes. "I'm so very, very tired. I haven't been able to sleep, you know."

"I know. Losing your sister and all."

Poor Mrs. B. I felt at a loss. I couldn't lift her. I couldn't seem to budge her. And I didn't want to raise an alarm and cause her embarrassment.

"She was sleeping with him, you know."

"I know. You said."

"Everybody knows. Laughing behind my back." Her eyelids flew open. "They think I did it, don't they?"

"Mrs. Benefer, they—if by 'they' you mean the police—think the Animal Rights Front is responsible. Now calm yourself."

She gripped my arm abruptly. "I don't have an alibi."

"I wouldn't worry."

"I drove to Cromer, you see. Afterwards. I don't know anybody in Cromer. Not now."

Cromer is a seaside town about forty miles east along the Norfolk coast.

"You mean after the panto you took a long drive?"

"I had tea in a chippy." Her voice rose with hope and then fell despairingly. "Oh, they won't remember me, they won't remember."

"Sure they will. If you remember the time you were there."

She stared at me, unseeing. "Half six, half six, half six," she chanted.

Mrs. Benefer's distress over the issue of alibi was troubling, but it couldn't help spark my curiosity. Dad had suggested the ARF trail wasn't exactly burning with clues. If attention was to turn elsewhere, where better than the bosom of family, the site of so much murderous intent? Tom and Jackie had had an affair, I now knew. One could easily presume Aileen's enduring resentment. And at least a few people knew that Aileen had quarrelled with Jackie after the panto, though the notion seemed to be they had quarrelled over Jackie's supposed affront to the Queen. 'She slept with him,' Aileen had said. But she had changed the tense, hadn't she? *She was sleeping with him.* Past imperfect. Aileen wasn't so much referring to the ancient past as to the recent past. Was it possible Tom and his sister-in-law had resumed their affair? The uncharitable thought rose in my head: Suppose Aileen had lashed out physically at her sister that night, had truly finally snapped, and this episode of incoherence and denial was but its echo.

"Mrs. Benefer, we really need to get out of here," I said, trying unsuccessfully to peel her fingers from my arm. "Maybe I should go and find your husband, then."

Oh, damn, I thought as soon as I said it, Tom Benefer's out with the Royal Family and the Thringys and the whole shooting party kit-and-caboodle. When I was in the upstairs bedrooms earlier, I'd heard the barrage, like a distant war, muffled by the trees and the brickwork of the Big House.

"We had our honeymoon in Cromer, Tom and me," Aileen said dreamily, relaxing her grip and closing her eyes. "I forgave him." She smiled and seemed to drift off for a moment, and then those eyes, like those of a demented dolly, snapped open again.

"But she was pregnant!" she cried, as though giving voice to some interior conversation. "She told me she was pregnant. You bastard!"

"Mrs. Benefer!" I shouted.

"Oh! Where's . . . ?" She blinked at me in an unfocused sort of way and said in a childlike voice: "She was pregnant, you know."

"I do know, actually."

"Oh?" Sorrow accentuated the incipient lines around her mouth. "I'm not able to have children. Maybe that's why he took up with Jackie."

"Mrs. Benefer, you're worrying yourself over nothing."

"Do you think so? Oh, I'm so tired, so awfully tired."

"You shouldn't rest here."

"Although I suppose it *could* be anyone," she babbled on, oblivious. "Anyone in trousers. She liked anyone in trousers. Always did. Maybe it was that director fellow—"

Hume Pryce?

"—he was her type. Or Paul. Oh, they were all her type, really—"

"Paul?" I said out loud.

"—but Tom was with her in Manchester. He denies it but I found the ticket stub in that coat of hers . . ."

"Paul who, Mrs. Benefer?"

"Mmmm?"

"Paul who?" I pleaded, giving her shoulder a little shake as she appeared to be nodding off again.

"Jenkyns," she replied smartly, as if she had had a moment of lucidity. But her eyes drooped.

"Her Majesty's PPO? *Inspector* Paul Jenkyns?"

"Mmmm. Must rest."

"No! I mean, you should rest. But not here." Oh, don't conk out now, I thought, giving her shoulder a more urgent shake. "Mrs. Benefer, what about Paul Jenkyns and your sister? You mean they've been having an affair?"

She blinked. "No. No. When they were teenagers. He was very young. Younger than Jackie. Mature for his age. So handsome." She smiled but it was like a smile on a fading photograph. "Mother was gone. Jackie was a law unto herself in those days."

Mrs. Benefer closed her eyes once more. Poop. Such an interesting titbit. But in gossip, as in jewellery, all that glitters is not gold. Apparently. Mrs. B. didn't appear disposed to further revelations, and I was becoming increasingly concerned about the unmanageability of her kipping in the Linen Room. It was lucky for me that the next person to breeze in was Heather MacCrimmon.

"Oh, thank God. Come over here and help me."

"What are you doing down there, Jane? . . . Oh!"

"Mrs. Benefer's not well," I said, rising, adding sotto voce whispered from the side of my mouth, "I think she's having a bit of a breakdown."

"Poor Mrs. Benefer," Heather murmured. "Well, a nice cup of tea and she'll be right as rain."

"Oh, *puh-leeze*, Heather. A nice cup of tea, indeed. A nice cup of tea, two Prozac, and sleep for a week, maybe . . ."

"Hmph," she continued dismissively, "Mrs. B. has

a wee episode every year. It's Her Majesty. She gives Mrs. B. the collywobbles."

"She didn't act like this last year."

"I've been in service longer than you."

"Mrs. Benefer's sister has been murdered, remember."

"Oh, aye, there is that." We both glanced down at our supine boss. "She does look poorly."

As one, we dropped to our knees on the bed-clothes and picked an ear each. "Mrs. Benefer!" we chorused.

"Mmmm?"

Heather glanced at me impishly. "You could slap her."

"Very funny."

"Here, then, let's get her sitting up."

Each of us grabbed a shoulder and pulled her forward. Mrs. Benefer obliged by opening her eyes and registering a little more understanding of the situation.

"Mrs. Benefer, we're going to take you to your room now," Heather fairly shouted.

Mrs. B. winced.

"Put your arms around our shoulders, Mrs. Benefer. Mrs. Benefer!"

"Are *you* feeling strong enough for this?" I addressed Heather. "I thought you had 'flu?"

"I got sick of being sick. Here. Heave to." And with a grunt or two we got Mrs. B. unsteadily to her feet.

"She *is* a bit far gone, isn't she?" Heather whispered over her head as we led Mrs. B. to the Linen Room door. "Ought we to tell someone, do you think?"

"Tom," Mrs. Benefer muttered. But whether she was registering Heather's question or following her own train of thought was difficult to discern.

"He's with the shooting party," I replied, in case it was the former.

"I suppose he could be got on the mobile," Heather said doubtfully.

"That would sort of raise the alarm, though. I mean if we want to be discreet . . ."

"Oh, aye." Heather struggled for the door handle,

opened the door a crack and peeked out. Satisfied the coast was clear, she added, "Oh, well, nice cup of tea— she'll be fine."

We did manage to get old Aileen to her room without too much bother. Once on her feet, she seemed to come more properly to attention and like a patient supported by two nurses we toddled down the hall passing only Nigel Stokoe en route to elevenses in Servants' Hall. He disinterestedly interpreted our mission of mercy as the sober leading the inebriated—hardly a novel sight among Staff, particularly at Christmas, even in late morning. Heather volunteered to mind Mrs. B. for a bit, make the silly tea, while I went back to the final chore *du jour* on my rota: tidying Buchanan Walsh's room.

The good news was that Bucky was out with the other guns blasting defenceless birds to kingdom come and wasn't likely to interrupt me in mid-skivvy as his mother had the day before. The bad news was that his bedroom, smaller and plainer than the Marchioness's, was, predictably, a pig's breakfast. Untidier even than the Duke of York, Bucky had left yesterday's attire from sweater through tie and belt down to unmentionables like a trail of haberdashery breadcrumbs leading the intrepid scout to the loo and back. He had eaten all the Bendick's mints and scattered candy wrappers over a bedside table next to empty tins of lager.

The bed looked hurricane damaged—bedclothes awry—and I wondered at first if Bucky had actually got lucky. If Davey Pye has any envy of housemaids it's this: We can act as Clio's chambermaid (skivvy to one of the nine Muses, apparently) with neat opportunities footmen lack to peek into wardrobes, inspect personal correspondence, open diaries, and sniff the bedclothes. Frankly—*really!*—I never, well, rarely, engage in that sort of activity. It's like your second week working in a chocolate factory—you lose all interest in the chocolate. And besides, intensive snooping is time-consuming and there's the danger of getting caught. You rarely glean anything of real interest anyway.

Davey doesn't believe this.

Still, I did sort of give Bucky's bed the once-over. Other than crumbs of what looked like cheese-and-onion-flavoured crisps—evidence, along with the lager, that he snuck in his own private stash to Sandringham—he appeared to have slept unaccompanied. While I rejoiced for womankind, I also hoped the turbulence in the bedclothes wasn't evidence of a seizure. A bottle of pills stood on the bedside table, next to the tins of lager. Dilantin, the label read. Some anticonvulsant medicine, I guessed, considering the probable foolishness of adding alcohol to the mix. On the other hand, I thought, an epileptic's life is probably a closely monitored life, perhaps obsessional where triggers are concerned. Maybe Bucky, in his thoughtless way, was just seeking to discover the limitations of his disability.

Or am I getting soft? I wondered, thinking of his late-night harassment as I removed the old sheets and began the process of remaking the bed. It was when I was on my knees doing my fabulously tight hospital corners, gleaned from a brief period as a candy striper at the Queen Elizabeth Hospital in Charlottetown, that I noticed a satchel tucked well under the bedframe. In the under-the-bed shadows, it appeared to be an olive-drab canvassy-looking thing, not very large, not very elegant. I could see it was firmly fastened with two leather straps but it hardly looked impregnable. I stared at it for a moment. Something Hume Pryce had said had been bothering me and I wondered if relief might possibly lie in the satchel. Could it? It was a long shot. And fiddling with Bucky's property was a breach of privacy.

Ah, but then the Muse descended—Clio, that is—and she commanded me to let my fingers do the walking among the embryonic dust bunnies (which, of course, never get beyond the embryo stage at Her Majesty's residences). Who was I to argue? So I extended my arm as far as it would go and after some intense scrabbling snatched the bag and pulled it forward along the carpet and into the light of day. There was not much weight to the bag, which was a cause for disappointment, but there was definitely something lumpy inside, a cause for cheer. I pirouetted over to the door to make sure it was shut, then jetéd to the window to make sure no one was standing on one of the little wrought-iron balconies, which was rather paranoid of me, and then, safely in the middle of the room, pulled at the satchel straps.

Well, who's a clever girl, then? I had wondered if there had been a link between Bucky's seizure during the first act of the panto, his subsequent withdrawal to a side room, and Jackie Scaife's second-act appearance on-stage in the royal banqueting scene with a slightly altered piece of costuming. And damned if I wasn't right. What I pulled from the canvas clutch felt hard and cold and spiky and yet somehow more fragile than I would have expected. It was, of course, a tiara.

This time I resisted the temptation to try it on. When you've had champagne it's hard to go back to beer, they say; and when you've had the Duchess of Windsor's wedding tiara perched on your noggin it's hard to give a fig for a rhinestone jobbie from some costume-hire. They also say you can't tell the difference between diamonds and rhinestones. Ha! The jewels that I fetched to Cartier's and back blazed with an incandescent life. They stopped your breath, filled your heart with awe. The paste copy I held up to the window merely twinkled cheesily. There was no fire within. There wasn't even kindling to burn. It was little more than an adult-sized version of Princess Barbie's headgear from bygone days. Like the Duchess of Windsor's, however, this diadem featured several large centre stones and a number of filigrees of smaller ones, but that was where the similarity ended. From afar, in an audience composed of people whose familiarity with diamonds ended at the chips in their engagement rings, nothing would have appeared unusual. And if any of the other actors had noticed the difference, they, like Pryce, would have figured the substituted tiara was one of Jackie's props in her looky-likey kitbag.

The dilemma for me, however, was: Now that I'd found the real fake, what was I going to do? Beyond the questions of (a) what the heck had Bucky Walsh been doing with the Duchess of Windsor's tiara back at the village hall in the first place and (b) what the heck had he planned to do with it in the second, was the simpler and more persistent question, the one I kept coming back to: What the hell did the tiara, or tiaras, rather, have to do with Jackie Scaife's murder, if anything? Was it possible Bucky had returned later that evening to the village hall when he had discovered the switcheroo? In attempting to reclaim his prize, had he attacked Jackie? He was good at attack—to that I could attest. But if he had attacked her, why wouldn't he have taken back the blinkin' *real* tiara? On the other hand, perhaps he had never discovered the switch at all, never opened his satchel, merely crammed it under his bed when he arrived at Sandringham. That might explain his relative indifference to the murder at Dersingham Village Hall. Or was it feigned indifference?

What to do? I couldn't ignore what I'd found. On the other hand, taking it straightaway to the police might be rather overreacting. And mightn't going to the police about Bucky be interpreted in some quarters as payback time on my part? I wasn't supposed to be nosing around in guests' luggage anyway. The Marchioness would be savage. Even Her Majesty might not be too chuffed. I needed advice.

I looked at my watch. Nearly noon. Damn. The person from whom I needed the advice, Her Britannic Herselfness, would not be in the Big House. She would be on a horse somewhere. She liked to go riding precisely at ten-thirty. Then she and the other lady guests would be taken by Land Rover to join the shooting party at the timber lodge at Flitcham hill, now mercifully free of graffiti and, one hoped, nasty surprise corpses. Then HM and ladies would join the guns for the rest of the afternoon. Then back for tea. Then drinkies. Then dinner. There was hardly an unscheduled minute in between.

Fortunately for the shooting party, the weather had cleared to a good degree. While the sky retained its sullen pewter cast, the heavy mist shrouding the stark trees and fields had lifted to reveal a landscape of warmer russets and browns. The apparent clemency had come at a price, however. Overnight, the temperature had fallen below the freezing point, the steady, persistent dripping rain had dwindled and hardened, leaving patches of the countryside powdered with fine dustings of snow. What looked no colder was in fact colder still. But, I thought, at least the ground would be hardened, less mucky, for I was suddenly determined to walk it. 'You must be me to know if anything should not seem quite right,' HM had said to me the day before. It would be odd for a housemaid to make an appearance at a shoot, but I had an ostensible rationale: to fetch Tom Benefer to see to his wife.

14

GETTING TO THE SITE of the shooting party was surprisingly easy. I'd half expected some burly security types to come crashing down upon me as I made my way, but none appeared to be in evidence, which was odd. I had prepared myself to talk my way forward. And I kept my eyes peeled for the antipoaching trip wires which fired blanks, but I supposed those had been removed in advance of the Royal progress. You hardly had to machete your way through Dersingham Woods, either. Unlike some primeval Canadian forest, barren of human footfall, this woodland showed the hand of man in its deliberate plantings and beaten paths, its copses and coverts. It was, in its way, as tiny and tidy as England itself, tinier and tidier than even tiny tidy Prince Edward Island.

The air was chill and while the wind was not sending daggers through you, it nevertheless had a pitiless bite. I wore my MEC jacket over a fleece with a pullover sweater underneath for extra warmth, and I pulled the hood up, which I thought would not only protect my ears from the chafing cold but camouflage me as well from the Nikon zoom lens crowd who might very well be lurking about. (I didn't need Macgreevy or one of his reporter pals to get the wind up.) Still, I could have used one of those windproof Barbour jackets but, oy, the price of them—more than a week's wages! On my feet I had my dependable Docs, but what I really needed were some leggings. I had tugged on a pair of jeans but something underneath would have been nice.

The sound of a horn in the distance, then a muffled answering whistle further on alerted me more precisely to the whereabouts of the shooting party. A few seconds later, I could hear the faintest clatter of sticks and odd whooping and whistling noises—the sound of the beaters pushing their way through the undergrowth, tapping the tree trunks, frightening the birds from their hiding places so they would take flight in their panic.

Someone bellowed "Over!" and immediately the first crack of a gun rent the air, causing me to jump with fright. There was another shot, a few more shots, and then it seemed as if war had broken out on Her Majesty's Estate. An interminable blasting away, a veritable roaring fusillade seemed to go on and on. I certainly won't have any trouble finding them now, I thought, as I quickened my pace toward the source of the din, scrunching the dead leaves underfoot, feeling the wind prick my cheeks, and noting the occasional feathered creature overhead lucky to have escaped death.

After a few moments' brisk stepping, in which the barrage did not let up, indeed grew louder and seemingly more urgent as I approached, the shooting party came suddenly into view through a tangle of pines. My eyes went immediately to the sombre sky scattered with birds caught in anxious flight careening piteously to earth. I had arrived at the edge of a copse at an angle oblique to the spectacle and could see past clusters of waiting figures, silent and alert, toward the busy guns marshalled before a thicket, each aiming his barrel resolutely into the air while a loader behind struggled to keep up, breaking and reloading like a madman. It seemed like a sea of waxed jackets and green wellies, Norfolk tweeds the dun colours of the wintry countryside, black Labradors springcoiled at heel. A sour smell in the air, raised by the spent cartridges, assaulted my nose; the relentless racket of the gunfire hammered my ears. It was all quite unnerving in its way and instinctively I edged back into the underbrush as if seeking safety. Something shiny and metallic caught my eye amid the dead leaves and I worried for a moment I had stepped into some poacher's device, but when I stooped to examine it, grateful for the distraction from the slaughter, I saw that it was a wristwatch, a rather delicate, finely wrought instrument that appeared nevertheless to have been exposed to the elements for some time. The crystal was a bit cloudy and the surface, stainless steel or silver or, perhaps, platinum, was blemished with fine scratches. There was an inscription on the back, but it was obscured by caked mud. A presentation watch, I figured as I tried scraping at some of the adhering dirt, and then, as I was about to put it in my pocket, something happened.

There was sudden silence. The shooting had stopped.

As if on cue, the tableau dissolved. The guns, shotguns cocked in the crook of their elbows, began to gravitate toward each other for conversation while their loaders joined with other Estate workers swarming to the task of gathering the pheasant carcasses from the nearby grass and stubble. The dogs, on command, sprang forth to retrieve downed game in more distant parts, happy and eager to be released. Off in the distance I could see part of a convoy of Land Rovers, an old canvas-topped truck I assumed carried the beaters to and fro, and another wagon to which some workers were already carrying braces of pheasant. There was something oddly affecting about the scene. I felt as if I was about to walk into a time warp and join an Edwardian drama. Too bad my clothes were so ordinary, but then, I thought as I stepped out of the undergrowth and on to the crisp winter grass, the other women visible weren't exactly dressed in Edwardian finery either, opting instead for practical Barbours and overpants. Only the men—a few of the guns and gamekeepers—wore costumes of a more timeless nature: Norfolk jackets, knickerbockers, and gaily coloured wool socks.

I could see Prince Charles in a tweed cloth cap talking to his elder son, Prince William, who seemed to have really grown in the year since I last clapped eyes on him and was now considered old enough to join the shoot. Prince Edward, similarly chapeau'd, was standing in a knot of people including Prince Andrew and Lord Thring, his bulk resting on a shooting stick, while Peter Phillips, Princess Anne's son, neat buzzcut and all, had the misfortune to be stuck listening to Bucky, who was still wearing his Gunfenders, earplugs to prevent hearing loss (although I wondered, in his case, if they didn't allay the sharp noises, like those in the panto, that might trigger an epileptic attack). Bucky's back, fortunately, was to me. A little further along I noted Prince Philip leaning aggressively toward Davey Pye while poor Davey, looking quite out of place in an ill-fitting sage-coloured jacket, stared morosely at the Purdey he was holding. I expected he was being made a man of. Finally, at the far end, a lone figure—and a complete surprise—a woman. In the quaint world of shooting parties women are for spectating—occasionally acting as beaters or working the dogs—but they're not for participating in the main event, the shooting itself. Yet here was Lady Thring, shotgun cocked in the arm of a deep-brown-hued Barbour, blond hair cascading from beneath a chic matching trilby, a Hermès scarf wrapped around her neck, even at a distance looking for all the world like she was to the manner born. Her ladyship looked fairly gleaming, in fact. She made everyone else's tweeds and waxed jackets look like tat. And maybe for that reason, and because she was a woman in this essentially male preserve, she had not drawn her own little coterie. Even her loader had wandered off, though Pamela appeared to be signalling impatiently with gloved hand toward some bewildered figure wandering the undergrowth, head down.

I seemed to attract no particular attention, but virtually everyone was concentrated on some task of his or her own anyway. Inspector Jenkyns, bareheaded and half a head taller than nearly everyone else, frowned at me from afar, but someone nearly as large in a navy jacket had engaged the Inspector in conversation so he didn't hasten to impede my progress. Anyway, I was intent on finding HM. I found her soon enough, a tiny figure swaddled in her own sage-green waxed jacket with hood, a pair of 'relaxed-fit' matching overtrousers, and old black boots. She was holding what looked like a short shepherd's crook in one hand, tooting a whistle, while a Labrador wiggling excitedly by her side roared off into the deepest part of the coverts and began snuffling about in the undergrowth, the Queen continuing to direct it from afar with her whistle and a series of hand gestures. The dog would look up expectantly and then dive into the foliage where Her Majesty indicated. The spectacle was quite amazing. I arrived at HM's elbow just as the dog returned with its prize—a plump pheasant—and laid it lovingly at her feet. Then HM raised the whistle and the process started again.

"Oh, hello, Jane," Her Majesty said, glancing at me with mild surprise through her owly spectacles. Her grey curls peeked from the side of the hood as she turned her head. Her pink face glowed with exertion and, probably, the pleasure of working the dogs. "What brings you out here—oh!"

The Queen drew in her breath sharply.

"Your Majesty?" I said, startled.

"In your hand, Jane. What have you got?"

"Oh, I'm sorry, Ma'am. I forgot I was holding it. I found this when I was walking here. It looks like some old watch." I placed it in Her Majesty's outstretched hand.

The dog returned with another pheasant but the Queen ignored his anxious snuffling. "My watch!" she exclaimed, examining it, pulling off a pair of green woollen gloves to better feel its surface. "It's my watch! How extraordinary. Wherever did you find it?"

"Just over there in those bushes, Ma'am." I pointed in the direction I had come from.

"But it's incredible! I lost this, oh, I can't tell you how many years ago. Miles from here, too, I thought. It was a gift from the president of France when I was a girl. He gave it to me not long before the war, and it was of great sentimental value. I wore it on my wedding day. I was so sorry to lose it."

"You nearly had the army out looking for it, as I recall," said Princess Anne drily. She had been working the dogs nearby and had walked over when she heard her mother's cry.

"Yes, well, I did love this watch. I'm so pleased . . . Oh, Ben," she said, addressing the fretting dog by her side. "Off you go." She blew the whistle and the black Labrador raced away. "But how, I wonder . . ." she continued as she directed Ben.

"Perhaps a bird, Ma'am," I filled in. "Attracted by the shininess, then dropping it later when it proved inedible or not useful."

"Very likely," Princess Anne agreed.

"Philip!" the Queen called. "Philip, come here!"

His Royal Highness released Davey from his hectoring and trudged over. He appeared rather pale and drawn and in not too good a humour. Davey, noting my presence, mouthed "Help!" behind HRH's back, and made a whimpering face like an unhappy terrier.

"Yes, what is it?" Prince Philip said tersely.

"My watch. Do you remember?" The Queen lifted the timepiece to her husband delightedly.

He peered at it down his long nose. "I remember you nearly had the army out looking for the bloody thing."

Princess Anne suppressed a smile. The Queen's face fell. "I did *not* 'nearly have the army out,' " she said quietly. "Philip, if your arthritis is bothering you so, why don't you go home?"

"I have my hand-warmer. It's that bloody idiot footman . . ."

"Then you shouldn't have chosen him in the first place. I don't think he's . . . suited to sport."

"Mmph," said His Highness, as if unwilling to concede the point.

"Well, anyway, I'm very pleased, Jane," she said, turning to me as her husband trudged back to the bloody idiot footman and her daughter to working the dogs. She slipped the watch into her jacket pocket.

"But you're here for another reason, I expect," she continued, as she sent the dog off on another pheasant-fetch.

"Ma'am, it's about a different piece of jewellery. I've come across another tiara."

And I quickly outlined the circumstances of finding the fake in Bucky's room earlier (with apologies for snooping) and my quandary over what to do.

"And so you think young Mr. Walsh here was the original possessor of the Duchess of Windsor's tiara?"

"I know he seems an unlikely owner of such a thing, Ma'am. And I don't know where he could have got such a thing *from* . . ."

"Given that it was stolen fifty years ago."

"Yes, Ma'am."

The Queen rewarded Ben with a pat, sent him on his way again, then glanced thoughtfully in the direction of the guns, toward Bucky and Lord Thring, as I tugged at my hood to keep myself as anonymous as possible. People were beginning to move in a single direction, toward what I presumed would be another stand.

"I think, Jane," she said, "that you shall have to tell Lord Thring what you've found. There's really no other choice."

This time I took a glance at his lordship, a surreptitious one and a doubtful one. "Ma'am, I suppose there's the option of telling the authorities . . ."

"I think that should come from Lord Thring," HM said firmly.

Okay, you're the Boss, I thought, but wondered a bit at this strategy. It presumed, for one, that his lordship would tell the police. His alleged distaste for his stepson indicated he would. His devotion to his stepson's mother indicated he wouldn't. And then there was the question of his lordship's doing what you might call the right thing. Would he? I supposed he would. He *was* HM's friend.

"But I would suggest not telling his lordship now," the Queen warned. "After tea, during the quiet hour."

The Lab returned, a black massing of energy writhing excitedly about the Queen's person, tail high and wagging, tongue out as he awaited further instructions. So nice, I thought, not to have to beware the corgi's ankle-seeking lunge.

"Is there anything else?" HM inquired, placing the whistle in the same pocket as the watch and tapping the ground absently with her crook.

"Actually, yes," I replied, "although . . . well, I think Your Majesty is *really* going to consider me a terrible snoop. I mean, I really wasn't snooping, I just happened to—"

"Walk with me."

The Queen moved on as she spoke. I followed.

"Well," I began, glancing around to see that no one was within earshot, "Jackie Scaife was receiving threatening notes composed of cut-out letters from magazines and the like . . ."

"Yes, I know."

"Well . . ."—I sort of gulped mentally—"I happened to find a torn piece of paper with cut-out letters and numbers in . . . um, Lady Thring's suite."

The Queen's eyes peeked at me from the edge of her hood. "Really," she replied. I couldn't appraise her tone. Surprise? Worry? Displeasure? Satisfaction? It was rather like her use of the word 'interesting' in conversations with ordinary folk during walkabouts. Was she interested, or was she just being nice?

Anyway, I blathered on, in for a pound as well as a penny: "It was just a scrap of paper, really. I don't know where the rest went."

"Down the loo, likely."

"Er, yes, Ma'am."

"What were the numbers and letters?"

"There was an *S* and a *T* on one line. And a six, a two, and a seven just below."

"A six, a two, and a seven," HM repeated. "Part of a . . . telephone number?"

"Perhaps, Ma'am. Not enough numerals to track anything down, though."

"Unless it's part of the prefix—0627."

"Hadn't thought of that. If it was a prefix, it could indicate a town or village or area."

"Or it might be part of an address."

"Or that, Ma'am."

"Or a date. Let me see. Six, two, seven. The sixth of February . . . oh, how odd! The sixth of February is my Accession Day—the date in 1952 I was proclaimed Queen."

It *was* odd. Worrying, even. Particularly when clues suggested they might lead back to Her Majesty herself. If it was a date on that scrap of paper, why that date?

"Do you have the piece of paper with you?"

"Ma'am, I left it in my room. But there was a tear by the number seven, if you're wondering about the seven."

"So it could be the sixth of February in one of the years in the 1970s. If it's a date at all, of course. And then there's the *S* and the *T*. Much more difficult, so many possibilities. Although . . ."—the Queen paused—"I'm reminded of Sandringham Time."

"You mean when the clocks were set ahead half an hour."

"I'm surprised you know about that, Jane. My uncle David had the practice stopped when I was a girl."

"Somebody mentioned it to me recently, Ma'am." But who? Caroline Halliwell, of course! The Marchioness had alluded to it when explaining her delay in returning to the Duke's Head Boxing Day evening.

". . . so," Her Majesty was saying, "it could refer to six twenty-seven Sandringham Time, which would be, let me see, five fifty-seven Greenwich Time." She shook her head. "Does seem rather unlikely, though. Such a precise time. I thought I was the only one beholden to such scheduling."

The Queen tapped her stick into the frozen ground with each step as we walked. I could see a few curious glances coming my way, but I tried to keep my head down a bit without looking too ridiculous.

"Ma'am, I can't help noticing that her ladyship is among the guns."

"Lady Thring's an excellent shot. She trained in America, I believe," the Queen said noncommittally.

"Could she be under threat from the anti's, the ARF?"

HM glanced over to a small clump of trees past where Lady Thring had joined her husband in their progress to the next stand. They appeared to be sharing a laugh, Lord Thring haw-hawing heartily, his great head thrown back, her ladyship looking both amused and somehow proprietorial in the way she linked her free arm in his.

"If Lady Thring has been threatened by such people, she has not passed such intelligence on to me. I suppose it's possible . . ."

Her Majesty's voice trailed off. A sudden snarl of anger and a flash of teeth took everyone's attention as a black and a yellow Labrador contended with each other over some issue in their doggie world. The fray was short-lived. Two dog-handlers reacted sharply and the dogs were parted, the yellow one to strut around stiff-legged, hackles raised and leg cocked, while the black, tail between legs, loped off in another direction. More people seemed to be milling about than I had first noted from my hidey-hole in the woods, some of them, I presumed, beaters, an assortment of men of all shapes and sizes in a variety of clothing from anoraks to Barbours, various Estate workers, some of them making their way to the beaters' wagon, others moving on foot to the next wood. In the throng I noted Tom Benefer and was reminded that one of my reasons for intruding upon the shooting party was to alert him to his wife's collapse. But he was some distance and the Queen, who had become unexpectedly the target of a very frisky, very affectionate black Lab, couldn't very well be left abruptly. Protocol mandated she dismiss you.

"Get away," the Queen said as the dog leaped up and tried to lick her face, its weight very nearly toppling her. "Whose dog is this, I wonder?"

"Ma'am, I don't know how you can tell the difference. They look so much alike."

"You soon come to tell them apart if you're involved with dogs at all, Jane. Now, get away," she commanded the dog again, pushing at it gently with her crook. The dog took the hint and bounded off into the crowd. "Perhaps it's one of Affie's," HM added, watching after it with keen attention. "Not well trained, though."

I, too, watched the dog disappear. In doing so, my eye was drawn to a certain figure in a group of men that had stopped in its progress, his familiar face in profile to me, his balding head a beacon.

"Yoiks," I said. Not an expletive I use often.

"Yoiks?" echoed the Queen.

"My dad, Ma'am. My dad's just over there with that bunch, just over there to the left. He's wearing the blue coat—it's a parka, really." It was a parka, my father's familiar blue winter parka. So it was he who had been talking to Inspector Jenkyns earlier. Why hadn't I made the connection? Simple. I never expected in a million years to see my dad among those attending or serving at Her Majesty's shooting party.

"What on earth is my father doing here?" I blurted nonetheless.

It was the sort of rhetorical question for which HM had no answer. But one crazy answer macheted its way into the jungle of my mind: *He's come to petition Her Majesty to send me back to Canada. He must be stopped!*

Fortunately, a cooler head prevailed. Mine. However unhappy my father was with my 'career-path,' such as it was, he wasn't the sort of person to intervene with one's employer. Or so I thought.

We, the Queen and I, were soon upon the group and my father, catching my eye, detached himself and joined us. I suddenly found myself in a social situation I wouldn't have dreamed of a year ago.

"Your Majesty, may I present my father, Steven Bee. Dad, Her Majesty the Queen."

Like, as if he didn't know who she was.

"I do hope you're enjoying your stay in England, Mr. Bee." The Queen switched into her walkabout conversation mode.

"Yes, I am enjoying it, thank you . . . Your Majesty."

I must say, it was rather fun to see my father a bit gobsmacked for once.

"I understand you are with the Royal Canadian Mounted Police, a staff sergeant."

"Yes, Ma'am. With the Charlottetown detachment."

"How very interesting. I was last in Charlottetown in 1973, for your province's Centennial."

"Yes, I remember it well. I was part of the honour guard."

"Oh, were you?" HM appraised my father as if trying to place the face. "Oh, well, it is more than twenty years ago, isn't it?" She laughed. "You're a fan of Elvis Presley, your daughter tells me."

"Yes, Ma'am."

I looked from one to the other, our breaths co-mingling in the frosty air. What I was hearing wasn't exactly Wildean repartee, but I knew I was going to find the encounter memorable, not the least because it would eliminate any lingering doubts—Elvis Challenge be damned—dear old Dad had over my involvement with certain unpleasantnesses happening in the vicinity of HM the Queen. So there! Ha!

But then I heard my father say: "Ma'am, since I've been here, I've been trying to encourage my daughter to return to Canada and go back to university and get her education—"

"Dad!"

"I wonder if Your Majesty has any advice for a girl who won't see sense."

The Queen smiled and shook her head. "I'm not one to advise on university education, Mr. Bee. I've never been, you see. Nor to any school, really. I was taught at home.

"But," she added, noting my father's disappointment. "I don't think you need worry. Jane has an independent spirit and good common sense and I'm sure those qualities will serve her well in life in whatever she decides to do. It's served me well. Your doing, I expect. Yours and your wife's. I think you've done a fine job with Jane."

"Thank you, Ma'am," my father said. Slightly humbled, I thought. I could have hugged HM except, of course, such a thing would have been a major no-no.

"And, anyway," the Queen continued, "in the end, it's probably better to let children find their own way, at least to a degree. My son resigned his commission with the Royal Marines some few years ago, to his father's very great disappointment. But he wasn't at all happy, and now he's much more satisfied with his work. So, there you go."

HM increased the wattage of her smile. "Now, I must have a word with one of my guests. Good luck to you, Staff Sergeant." And she trudged off in her big wellies, a tiny figure with two excited black dogs for chaperones.

"Nice try," I said when HM was out of earshot.

The paternal-unit shrugged. "I thought since you wouldn't listen to a head of family, you might listen to a Head of State."

"You're a *co*-head of family, Dad. Remember?"

"I said *a* head of family, *a* head, not *the* head." He stamped his feet to shake off the cold. "Anyway, Bird, she gave you a nice endorsement. I guess I should be happier, but I wish you weren't here."

"Here here?"

"No. Here, as in England."

I couldn't get into this battle. "Why are you here?" I asked instead. "As in here here."

"The local constabulary is putting on a show of

strength, part of the increased security. I asked if I could tag along. And they agreed."

"They checked you out surely."

"Of course." He eyed me knowingly. "Checked you out, too."

"What do you mean?"

"How do you think you got through these woods without being challenged?"

"But I work here."

"No, you work *there*." He jerked his head to one side. "In that big red house."

"You mean, *you* made it possible for me to reach the shooting party . . . unmolested, so to speak?"

"No, not completely. You're known to some of the other security staff, but I helped. You were observed. You could have been turned back."

"Oh." I felt oddly deflated and a bit weirded-out. I'd thought I had been rather clever reaching the shooting party on my own. It was a bit creepy knowing I had been watched while being blithely unawares.

"When I realized it was you I saw talking to the Queen's minder I should have known."

"Her what?"

"Paul Jenkyns, her PPO—Personal Protection Officer."

I thought about Aileen Benefer's earlier mutterings about her sister and Jenkyns and teenaged love, or lust, or whatever it might have been, and quickly recounted the morning's Linen Room follies for my father.

He glanced over at Jenkyns. We had arrived at a new stand of timber in front of which a general winnowing was taking place, the guns each with his (and her) loader solemnly taking up pegged positions with a kind of military intent along a line; the ladies, some keepers, other staff, security, and dogs falling behind as spectators would to the main action of a premodern battle. Jenkyns stood aloof, a few yards behind Her Majesty, bareheaded, capless, hoodless unlike the others, as if to hide such silvery magnificence was a crime against beauty.

"Of course," I concluded, "this romance or whatever was two decades ago. And Jackie'd been in the States for most of the time after."

Although as I said this I couldn't help remembering the powerful feelings of teenaged love, the exhilarating ups, the devastating downs, the sense, when it was over, you would never experience anything like it again. Might it have had some lasting effect? Do the effects last even unto the fourth and fifth decade of one's life— or beyond? Alas, being barely into my third decade, this was a subject upon which I had little perspective. It flitted across my mind to discuss this with the old man, but there are some things which are just too squirm-making to talk about with your father, this being one of them.

"And he's married in the interim, I suppose," I heard my father say.

"He's too much of a muffin not to be snapped up by someone. Handsome, Dad," I quickly explained, responding to his puzzled expression. "He's very good-looking, don't you think?"

"Mm, maybe."

"Of course, there's the skin-deep thing, I suppose."

"Yup."

"His wife is someone from the area, I'm told. Daughter of the Lord Mayor of King's Lynn, la-dee-dah. I overheard Jenkyns tell Lord Thring yesterday that he grew up in Hunstanton. Which is odd, because I was sure I'd heard he grew up in Lynn."

"What about the state of his marriage?"

"No idea, really. But I guess being a policeman's wife isn't exactly . . . oh, sorry, Dad."

"What about being a policeman's daughter?" he asked.

The question was unexpected. "It was *fine*, Dad. I'm not complaining." Well, it *was* fine. Prince Edward Island doesn't exactly seethe with crime so my father's profession did not bring unceasing worry and alarm to our family life. There were a few times of anxiety when I was very young and he was a less office-bound officer, but my memories of the events were wrapped more around my mother's ministrations, her attempts to smooth the situation. It is, I think, harder on the wife, or spouse as the case may be.

"Anyway," I continued, "being a PPO to members of the Royal Family probably brings its own strains. Jenkyns spends more time with the Queen than he does with his family. And then there's all the glamorous occasions he has to attend while on duty, not to mention living in a Palace and travelling in limos, and going on international trips. After all that, it must make family life in a poky semidetached somewhere seem pretty dull at times."

"They're on duty for how long a period?"

"Eight days at a time, I think."

"And what do they do the rest of the time?"

"What they call 'recce' trips, for one thing. If the Queen is going to open a hospital wing in Bristol, for instance, the PPO and a bunch of other security types will scout it out in advance, travel the route the Queen will travel, check the surrounding buildings and so on. But, Dad, you've had to do some of that stuff at home."

"But not at this level."

The hubbub of conversation that had been swirling around us for some time abruptly, as if by common but unspoken consent, ceased. An anticipatory stillness settled on the assembled, broken only by the twittering of smaller, unsuspecting and unwanted birds, and the ceaseless rustle of the treetops in the wind off the North Sea. My father bent closer to my ear. In a low voice he asked, "When did Jenkyns come on duty this time around?"

"I don't know," I whispered, surprised. "He was with the Queen Tuesday morning when we found Jackie dead, and he's with her now, Friday, so . . ." I shrugged.

The sour tone of a horn's blast cut the air. An answering whistle from somewhere deep in the woods followed. We were abjured to silence by nothing more than the growing atmosphere of alertness, even of tension, as the advancing beaters, crashing through the undergrowth, tapped the tree trunks, whooping and whistling and stamping the ground in a way that seemed, as it hadn't earlier when I was at a distance, somehow savage, almost unearthly, certainly unsettling. A few foolish songbirds streaked from the trees, screeching, but the guns were not deceived. They remained silent and alert, waiting, their Purdeys aimed high in anticipation. Then, as before, someone—a beater—shouted "Over!", one beautiful bird burst from the high branches with a drone of wings, curling to the right at the corner of the wood. The crack of a single shotgun—Lord Thring's—shattered the stillness. I recoiled instinctively. The bird seemed to hang suspended in the air, before plunging to the snow-stippled grass with a heartrending thud, an inert mass of feathers. Immediately after, another bird soared into view, then two more, then, suddenly, the sky was full of pheasants and isolated shots quickly turned to a fusillade. The air reeked of spent shot, the beaters kept up their noise-making, the loaders struggled to keep up, and the pheasants, those few unable to streak across the sky and find safety in another wood, thumped to the ground in a deadly rain.

Not every kill was clean, however; nor was every shot calculated to send the victim falling safely distant. You had to remain alert. One or two pheasants crashed so near to hand that spectators, including the Queen herself, were obliged to step quickly from the bird's trajectory. One poor bird, its wing shattered, flopped helplessly about on the ground until one of the keepers reached down and twisted its neck. Even at a distance I thought I could hear the crack, and I winced.

The carnage continued. It was a full five minutes before the barrage seemed to slow. Another bird plummeted from the sky, landing this time only a few yards from where I and my father were standing. It, too, had not been cleanly killed and, impotently, I watched it flap its feeble wings and raise its poor neck. One beady eye stared up—accusingly, it seemed. Tom Benefer, who had been standing not far behind us, moved smoothly to the fore, pulled back his open Barbour, and from his belt removed a stick with which he dispatched the poor bird in one swift blow to the head.

It was not the ease with which he did the deed that grabbed my attention, nor its cold-blooded effect. It was the cosh itself. It was a longish thing—the tip of it, I realized, had been visible just below the edge of Benefer's coat. And it was the tip end by which he grasped the instrument, or, rather, just below the tip end because the tip, glinting in the air from the ball of his fist, appeared rather sharp. The other end, however— the piece which came crashing down on the pheasant's skull—was bulbous and black, heavy-looking, surely a club end, as Hume Pryce had described it. Tom Benefer was holding a priest and his movement was truly, in a perverse way, like the sprinkling of holy water. But was it *the* priest?

I had no time to investigate the blunt instrument which may have ended Jackie Scaife's life because at that moment something else happened. The shots had been growing more infrequent in the last minute or two. Pauses erupted, tantalizing episodes of blessed silence, which the ears perversely filled with their own ringing. The dogs, panting at heel, strained with anticipation as the slaughter slowed. Everyone seemed to take on a new alertness. As I watched Benefer scoop the dead pheasant from the ground, I heard a single shot somewhere down the line. There was a second of silence, then another, final, shot. But no horn succeeded this volley. Instead, the air was filled with a new sound, horrible yet unmistakable. It was a howling that penetrated to the very soul.

A dog had been shot.

15

THE REST OF THE AFTERNOON, I'm told, was a rather solemn affair. Lord and Lady Thring suddenly—and quite reasonably—had some other business (the dog) to attend to. Prince Philip was so vexed he had himself driven back to the Big House. Davey told me later that day HRH's arthritis was the real reason behind his particularly foul mood; the incident with the dog was more a handy excuse to make an exit. The Queen soldiered on, as she is wont to do, and, after the shock and its aftermath, and at the Thrings' insistence, determined sentiment favored a continuation of the day's shooting. That didn't make things any jollier, however.

The dog's distress had shattered the mood of the shooting party in a way, I think, Jackie Scaife's death had not. The latter had been little more than an inconvenience to all but those of us behind the curtain at

Dersingham Village Hall that day. Regret was more for the postponed lunch. Few knew the victim. I'm not sure how many knew the dog, but everyone had been party to the accident.

There had been an odd stillness at first, as if people could not grasp the relationship between the final shot and the animal's howl of pain. My attentions had been turned toward Tom Benefer; I had missed the moment. But when I jerked my head in the direction of the commotion, I could see Lord Thring, his gun lowered, staring into the underbrush, and everyone else staring at Lord Thring.

"Oh, Affie," I heard the Queen murmur sorrowfully, for she had moved within my earshot, "how could you!"

As I was told later—for people talked of little else—his lordship, believing a bird to be flying low through the corner of the wood nearest which he stood, had followed its movement with his shotgun. There had been no bird, or else the bird had got away. The movement had been that of a dog, a young black Labrador, unleashed, unfettered, not well trained. But, for all that, it was puzzling that Lord Thring could make such a ghastly mistake. He was, as had been said, the second-best shot in England (who was the first remained a mystery, as did the method of determination). He had been a fixture in shooting parties for forty years or more. And he knew dogs. He owned them. He trained them. He was a judge at field trials in England and America.

'You may hit or you may miss'—Benefer's little poem came back to me in altered form—'but at all times think of this/All the game birds ever bred/Won't repay for one *dog* dead.'

Well, at least the dog wasn't dead, which was a mercy. When everyone pulled out of paralysis, there was a general motion, like a tide, toward Lord Thring, whose face seemed to have lost as much blood as the wounded dog was giving forth from its hindquarters despite the ministrations with a bunched handkerchief by his lordship's loader kneeling at its side.

"What kind of shooting do you call that, man!"

Prince Philip snapped, his face black with anger, as we all looked down at the handkerchief, for a moment so clean and white against the dog's black fur, now turning crimson with unseemly speed. Lord Thring's plump features twitched as if he had been stung. Lady Thring glared at HRH. The rest of us, Royals and commoners, remained impassive as stones, awed by the unhappiness of the occasion. A few turned away from the sight.

The beaters were starting to come out of the woods, drawn with greater haste by the dog's pained keening. "Don't crowd," Meacham, the head gamekeeper, taking control, warned the growing numbers as one of the larger men silently removed his coat and laid it, waxed side up, on the ground to form a litter. The coat was slipped under the animal, then lifted with tender care to a Land Rover which a more enterprising member of Staff had thought to drive from its parked position some few hundred yards away. The Thrings, minus Bucky, caught my eye and gave me a cold smile, huddled with Her Majesty for a moment, then made their own way across the clearing toward the cars. With kennels at Sandringham and the Sandringham Stud on the Anmer Road, there was no worry for lack of veterinary assistance.

An atmosphere of gloom descended. Because the wounded animal was out of our ken, the routine of retrieving the dead pheasants resumed. Some of the pickers scooped up the carcasses by their lifeless necks and conveyed them to the appropriate gun peg for counting; others, the Queen among them, worked the dogs with whistle and patted canine heads encouragingly as each found and fetched the bird marked out for him. Conversation, however, fell to cheerless murmurings. Leaving my father to join some of his new security buddies, I walked over to Tom Benefer. He was walking the line, inspecting the kill, occasionally dropping to collect spent cartridges.

"Could I look at your priest?" I asked, stooping to help him with the latter task, making myself useful. "That's what it's called, isn't it? A priest?"

"Aye," he replied, taking a handful of cartridges

from me and placing them in a leather bag strapped around his person. He opened the side of his coat and pulled the instrument from a kind of holster attached to his belt. "It were me father's," he said as he passed it to me.

While the implement didn't lie heavy in my hand, it nevertheless felt solid. And lethal. I beat the cosh end against my open palm—I had removed my gloves—and winced a little at the pain. Fish or fowl would certainly be made short work of. But what about something larger?

Benefer had moved further down the line toward the next peg where the pheasants lay in a tidy midden near a scattering of spent cartridges. "You didn't loan it to your sister-in-law by any chance, did you?"

His toothbrush eyebrows crinkled together. "Jackie?" he replied. "No." But it wasn't a firm negative. Something about his tone invited me to further inquiry.

"Had it gone missing, then? Recently?"

Benefer slowly dropped cartridge shells, one by one, into his bag. He seemed to be thinking.

"Aye," he said at last, looking away from me toward the mound of pheasants. "Thought I'd lost it. Had it for Prince Charles's grouse shoot in November then . . ." He shrugged. " 'Twere gone."

"But here it is." I made absolution motions with the priest. "It *is* the same one, isn't it?"

"Aye, 'tis. Not many like it in these parts."

He turned his back to me and pushed on. There was a general gathering movement, like a battalion preparing to decamp. Some of the guns were strolling toward the Land Rovers, revved and ready to convey them in warmth to another part of the Estate. Some beaters were already climbing into the beaters' wagon, a well-used army-style wagon with a green canvas top pulled over a frame to keep out the elements. Other Estate workers carried pheasants already collected and counted over to the game cart to be tied in braces and hung on rails. Still, a few lingered. I could see my father in conversation with a couple of lookalike plods, one of whom was gesturing in the direction of the recent accident, as if attempting to reconstruct the scene of the crime. Princess Anne was attempting to master some of the dogs, their excitement apparently unquenched by the morning's activity, while, nearby, the Queen, tucking an escaping grey curl back into her scarf, appeared to be in earnest conclave with Inspector Jenkyns.

"Then how did you manage to find your priest if it had been lost?" I asked, following Benefer to the next peg.

"Odd, that," he replied. "It found me."

We waited while a number of workers divided the birds among themselves and left for the game cart. I realized I was beginning to shiver. Despite my best efforts to dress warmly, the damp cold was beginning to seep into my bones.

"It were at Dersingham, at the village hall, Tuesday," Benefer continued in his halting way. "Her Majesty and Their Royal Highnesses and all were to have their grub in the hall, but we were going to go down the pub, what with the usual arrangements at Flitcham all buggered, bloody sabs. Outside the hall, one of the dogs—one of his lordship's, I reckon; weren't one of ours—came past with my priest in its mouth." A look of remembered surprise crossed his face.

"Do you know where the dog found it?"

Benefer shook his head. "It were a bit muddy-like. But undamaged otherwise. Could have been anywhere."

"The dog wasn't leashed?"

"Nay. One of his lordship's, I'm sure. I don't know why it weren't on a lead. Should have been. Barely more than a pup, too. That one won't be winning any championships. Poor training. Something wrong with it up here." Benefer tapped his forehead. "And now it's been shot."

"You mean it's the same dog, the one that was shot here and the one with the priest Tuesday?"

"Oh, aye. Might be wrong. Don't think so, though."

And was it the same dog that burst onto the stage

when we found Jackie Scaife's body? And the one that jumped up on me back of the village hall only the night before? If it had been, it could mean the dog had been loose, unkennelled, for half the week, likely larking about all over the Estate. How many black Labradors in the general area were left to their own devices? Not many, I would have thought. Surely none. Even the villagers who owned them would keep them constrained. Gundogs were valuable—'purpose-built' canines. And in this neck of the English woods, most of them were well trained and well housed.

"What's this to do with Jackie?" Benefer asked in a lowered voice as we drew nearer to the Queen and Jenkyns, still in conversation.

"Oh!" I exclaimed, for the dog thing had diverted my thinking. "I don't know if you've met this Hume Pryce person, the guy who organized the panto, but I met him at the Feathers and he said Jackie showed up at rehearsals with a priest and I don't mean an employee of the Church of England . . ."

"Shhh." He lowered himself to pick up a few cartridges.

"What?"

"Don't talk so loud. Her Majesty doesn't need to be troubled with this."

Seemed to me like unwarranted concern—in fact I knew better than anyone it was unwarranted concern—but it was too late anyway. The Queen had turned at my sudden exclamation—sound carries so outdoors—then noted the priest which I was brandishing excitedly in the air like one of Shakespeare's bare bodkins.

Benefer rose at HM's approach and doffed his cap. Jenkyns remained a respectable few feet removed, restraining a dog by its lead.

"Ma'am," I said with more intensity than I intended, "I think . . ." Then the notion overwhelmed me: I was holding the murder weapon. I shuddered, not from cold this time but from horror. The very thing clutched in my hand had not just eased some wounded bird's passage to the next life, it had crashed into the skull of a vital human being. In my mind's eye, slo-mo, I could see the weapon swinging, swinging through the shadows toward a woman's vulnerable flesh.

The priest fell from my hand to the hard ground with a dull thud. The Queen glanced at it, then at me, her blue eyes mirroring with concern what must have been horror in my own brown orbs. "Jane, you think . . . ?" she prompted.

I blinked, casting off the traces of the vision. "Ma'am, I think that . . . *that*"—I gestured to the priest as Benefer bent to reclaim it—"was used to kill Jackie Scaife."

There was a stunned silence. I looked from the Queen, whose eyebrows had risen marginally above her glasses, to Benefer, who flushed suddenly, to Jenkyns who watched me over the Queen's head with a Jurassic stoniness. Only the dog's rhythmic panting and the rustle of wind through the tree branches returned me fully to the present.

Nervously, I continued: "You see, the murder weapon has never been found. That thing"—I gestured again to the priest—"was found outside the village hall on Tuesday after the guns and the keepers and everyone arrived. According to the panto director, Jackie had contributed a priest to fashion a sceptre for her getup . . . er, raiment, Ma'am. Meanwhile, Mr. Benefer had been missing his priest the whole time . . . ."

I looked to Tom for instant agreement but he shifted his gaze as mine met his. Adjusting his cap with bare fingers white with cold, he suddenly seemed a man with better things to do. "Mebbe this isn't mine," he said and held the stick forth as if he were the Archbishop of Canterbury about to hand Her Majesty her sceptre at Coronation.

"You just said there weren't many like it around here!"

"Oh, aye, I did that," he muttered, withdrawing the instrument.

"Tom, *is* that thing yours?" the Queen inquired gently.

"Yes, Ma'am."

Her Majesty continued: "Then, if it was found

outside the village hall, why wasn't it given to the authorities? Paul, perhaps you should take it."

"It wasn't so much found outside the hall as it happened to sort of *come past* the hall," I explained, since Benefer seemed to have come over all mulish.

"I'm not sure I understand."

"What I mean, Ma'am, is that a dog came past carrying the priest in its mouth, so the priest could have come from further away."

"It never occurred to me it might be a murder weapon, Ma'am," Benefer interjected as Inspector Jenkyns joined our circle with the restive Labrador. "I were just glad to have it back."

"A dog, you say." The Queen looked down thoughtfully at the canine between her and Jenkyns. "A gundog? A retriever?"

"Aye. A black Lab."

"One of ours?"

"I don't think so, no, Ma'am."

"An unfamiliar dog intruded on us on the stage at the hall," the Queen mused, glancing at me then at her detective. "But, Paul, I believe you took the animal outside."

"Yes, Ma'am," he replied.

"Then the dog's discovery—if we can call it a discovery—of the priest came *after* your sister-in-law's body was found." Addressed to Benefer, it was more a quest for assurance than a question.

"I reckon so, Ma'am."

"What did you do with the dog?" The Queen addressed her detective.

"Ma'am, I believe I handed it to one of the keepers."

"It must have got away, then. It was a rather unmanageable dog, as I remember."

"Were his lordship's, I think, Ma'am. Same what was shot here just now. Same dog."

The Queen was silent, the corners of her mouth turned inward. She appeared deeply disappointed. Benefer shifted uncomfortably from one foot to the other, the priest still in his hand.

"Did Lord Thring remove the priest from the dog's mouth?" I wondered aloud, wanting both to fix the scene outdoors that morning in my mind and to draw out the conversation so a distracted HM would not dismiss everyone prematurely.

A palpable tension had arisen in the meantime; remembering that both men had had affairs with Jackie Scaife and each likely knew of the other's involvement, I wondered if I wasn't catching an ancient whiff of *eau de* testosterone. I had thought at first that Benefer was merely uneasy in the presence of Her Majesty, as so many are, but the unease had moved quickly through coldness to a kind of hostility as he gave Jenkyns the critical eye. The latter, turned icily handsome and remote as a prince in a fairy story, met the gamekeeper's glance with a flicker of disdain, then bent in one fluid motion to adjust the dog's collar and lead. As he did so, he replied offhandedly to my question: "No, I took it from the dog. But I returned it to Tom."

"I'm afraid we may be keeping people waiting," the Queen interjected, looking toward the convoy of vehicles queued in the middle distance. "Paul, you will see to that priest, won't you."

It was a command, not a question. But Benefer continued to maintain his grip on the instrument.

"Tom," Her Majesty prompted.

"Er, Ma'am, it won't do much good to police now. I've had me hands all over it, and I've used it . . . on birds, that is . . ."

"But the police might at least be able to match it to the wound," I contributed. "Or there might be other information on it."

Benefer turned obstinate for a long moment, his lips squeezed to a thin line, his feet rooted to the frozen ground. Then, wordlessly, he handed the priest over to Inspector Jenkyns, who received it cautiously, holding it dangling by the smaller, sharper tip. Minder and minded then departed for the waiting Land Rovers.

Why, I wondered, had Tom Benefer been so keen to retain possession of the priest? Surely as a murder weapon it superseded in horror the sentimental value it might have as a reminder of his father.

"You'll get it back eventually," I offered as he continued to stare after the retreating figures.

"Eh?"

I repeated myself. Benefer made a vague dismissive gesture. He seemed to be in a galaxy far, far away. "Here," I said at last, jabbing at his hands to give him some more of the cartridges I had scooped from the earth.

"What brought you here?" He looked at me as if for the first time.

The angels? I thought. Was this a cosmological question?

"Don't often get housemaids out on a shoot." The irritation in his voice was undisguised. "You shouldn't be here."

"I came to tell you Mrs. Benefer doesn't seem very well," I countered with a half-truth. Well, quarter-truth. I briefly explained the circumstances I found Mrs. B. in earlier that morning.

Benefer received the information solemnly. "She goes a bit funny when Her Majesty comes up from London," was his response, a discouraged one.

"I've heard. But I think she has a little more on her plate this year, Tom."

"Aye," he said. But his attention drifted back to the figures in the distance. A cold gust of wind sent a shiver through me.

I returned to the Big House some time later, passing, as usual, through the kitchen courtyard with its surround of outbuildings used, or once used (in more ancient days), for some of the bleaker tasks of keeping up a country house—laundry, for instance. While Staff make egress to the Big House through the entrances off the kitchen courtyard, the Royal Family and guests venture that way usually only when they've been up to wet and mucky things like spending the day blasting away at God's winged creatures. There are rooms to remove wet coats and muddy boots, deposit guns and related paraphernalia, and generally ease one's way back into civilization as we know it. It was from one of these rooms that I passed, after removing my own coat and boots, that I heard a sort of muffled snuffle. Not a doggy-type snuffle but a human one, the type demanded by oxygen starvation after a jolly good cry.

Lord Thring had apparently been having a j.g.c. When I peeked in, he was slumped on a wooden bench like a beached walrus, one wellie on, one wellie off, mopping Niagara from ruddy cheeks.

"Oh, dear," he sniffed damply, rubbing his red-rimmed eyes to better take in my presence. "I'm a little overcome."

"Is there anything I can do, your lordship?"

"No," he replied miserably while trying hard to compose his features in a semblance of a patrician poker face. "I'm sure I'll be quite well in a moment."

"Will the dog be okay?" I felt sorry for Lord Thring, and assumed the earlier mishap was the source of his unhappiness.

His lordship's face began to crumple at the word 'dog' but he managed to stay further tears. "Jet will mend. Only the leg was wounded. Fortunately."

"Oh, then it was your dog. Some people were wondering."

"Not well trained, I'm afraid." He sniffed loudly. "More of a pet, really. I shouldn't have brought him. Poor mite."

"My lord, you didn't somehow lose him earlier in the week by any chance?" I thought there had to be some reason for the dog's sudden and strange appearances. Shooting parties aside, the dog should have been in the Sandringham kennels.

Lord Thring stopped mid-honk in a strenuous cleansing of the nasal passages. "Er . . . no . . . er, well, yes, in a way I suppose." He completed his ablution and muttered through his handkerchief, "At Dersingham Hall."

"Boxing Day, at the panto?"

He refolded the piece of white cloth with the care afforded a new little treasure. "No," he replied with a flicker of annoyance. "The next day. At the luncheon. The aborted luncheon, rather."

"Poor thing, it must have got awfully hungry."

"No, Jet was found later that day. He was only gone a few hours. Well, there was rather a lot of confusion what with, you know . . ." He twisted on the bench trying to repocket the handkerchief without rising.

He's prevaricating, I thought. There can't have been two black Labradors on the prowl? The one that leaped out at me the previous evening at Dersingham Hall had to have been Lord Thring's, surely. But why would his lordship lie?

"My lord, may I sit down a moment?" I thought I might as well get this tiara folderol over with, particularly if his lordship had a propensity to fudge. If HM arranged a little meeting, it might give him time to think up something, if there was something to be thought up, that is. His l-ship indicated a chair opposite while he pulled at his remaining boot.

"When I was cleaning earlier," I began, feeling not a little trepidation, "I came across something . . . unexpected . . ."

"Yes," he said, straining.

"In Bu . . . Mr. Walsh's room . . ."

"Ooph!" The boot fell to the floor with a rubbery thud as Lord Thring fell back against the wall. "Aah. That's better."

"It was a tiara."

The words hung in the air like a sour note.

"A tiara," Lord Thring repeated dully.

"A paste one. Costume jewellery."

"I see. But I'm not sure, my dear young woman, if I understand the significance. My stepson is probably involved in some"—he frowned—"amateur theatrical or the like. At Cambridge."

I thought that possibility as remote as the Queen abdicating to a life of mahjong in Miami and my face must have shown it.

"Well, what then?" his lordship said with a hint of exasperation.

"Jackie Scaife, the deceased woman, was wearing a tiara in the panto," I explained all in a rush, anxious to get it over with. "But it wasn't paste. It was genuine."

And I told him the story of the tiara's provenance, the tie to the Duchess of Windsor, the theft at Ednam Lodge (which he recalled), the certainty the diadem was gone for good and then its sudden inexplicable reappearance. Throughout, Lord Thring's expression grew increasingly cross. It was like watching Father Christmas realize he had had all his savings in Barings bank. Making the link to Bucky and his postseizure recovery in the committee room of the village hall, however, was the final straw.

"It's impossible! Utterly impossible!"

"But, sir, it's the only explanation."

"Nonsense!" he boomed. "That woman could have got her hands on the Duchess's tiara somehow. She was utterly unscrupulous!"

"But, sir, what was your stepson doing with a paste tiara in his satchel?"

"In his satchel! Were you snooping in his private things?"

"It was sort of open. I peeked in." I really do hate lying, but in my defence, m'lud, I plead the greater good.

Lord Thring eyed me suspiciously. "The reason I'm telling you this, my lord," I continued before I could be upbraided further, "is because the police need to be told. The tiara could be important to their investigation."

"To a murder by a bunch of animal-rights extremists?!"

"Well, if not that, then to solving an important jewel theft."

"My dear woman, that was fifty years ago. And the thief has confessed. You just said his name, a Richard Dunphie."

"But it isn't known who fenced the jewels. And it isn't known who bought them off the fence."

"This is ridiculous!" his lordship exploded, rising

suddenly. "I've a mind to tell Her Majesty about your impertinence!"

Then do, I thought grimly. I was about to make a final plea, though: If he didn't tell the authorities about Bucky's cache then I would have to. Unfortunately, the Marchioness stepped into the frame of the door at that very moment.

"Oh, you're still here, are you, Affie darling. I'd wondered where you'd got to. Are you feeling better?" Pamela was wearing the brown tweed trousers she had been wearing outdoors—no bulky overtrousers for her!—a creamy Shetland sweater, and a Puffa jacket of honey hue that nicely set off her blond hair. "Come upstairs now," she added with a silky drawl. She hadn't seen me, I realized.

Then she did. I rose. Her eyes glittered ominously.

"It's nothing, my dear," his lordship declared before she could open her mouth. "We were just having a chat."

"This is the one, you know. The one who *assaulted* our son."

Assaulted? How things escalate. I'll be blamed for Bosnia next.

"Pammy, my dear, we were just talking about that. Weren't we?" he added, hard button eyes demanding my compliance.

"Um . . ."

"And she is prepared to apologize to Buchanan."

"I should damned well say so!" her ladyship snapped before I could open my cakehole to protest (even if I had been considering the option for strategic reasons). "Imagine the Queen, of all people, having servants who behave like this one!"

Ooh, it's that word 'servants.' HM never uses it. We're *Staff.* It is such infuriating utterances which fuel the ire, making one braver than one might be in other circumstances. Ignoring the issue of the Slap & the Apology (possible pub name for the S & M crowd), I asked instead:

"Your ladyship hasn't been receiving threats from animal-rights zealots by any chance?"

"Of course I haven't!"

"My apologies."

"Words I expect *you* to convey to my precious Buchanan."

"Why would you ask such a question?" Lord Thring interrupted, creases of mystification warping the bridge of his rather pudgy nose.

I looked from one to the other, unhappily aware I was about to supply them with more evidence of being a stickybeak extraordinaire.

"Because when I was cleaning yesterday morning I found in her ladyship's suite a scrap of paper with cut-out letters and numbers from magazines pasted on it."

There was a sharp intake of breath from both husband and wife.

"I found it by accident," I added hastily, hoping to stave off a tongue-lashing.

But the Marchioness did nought but glare while his lordship frowned deeply, appearing more dismayed than angry. He looked off into the distance, through a window that framed a rose-colored octagonal tower, in Edwardian times the game larder, since converted to public loos for the tourists.

"I mention this," I continued, following his eyes but noting nothing more than the bare trees and grey sky, "because the last person on the Sandringham Estate receiving letters with words made from cut-out bits from magazines was—I'm sure you must know—"

Lord Thring's eyes locked with mine.

"—was killed."

16

THE THRINGS DID NOT care to discuss threatening letters, snipped-up magazines, or deceased persons any further. "No, we did not know that woman had been receiving any such thing," Lord Thring announced as he and his lady wife swept from the room.

I don't know how they could have *not* known. Such details had surely swept through the villages on the Estate by this point, gathering momentum as they passed from tongue to tongue, reaching at last the ears of the high and mighty, among them, the Thringys. For all I knew, particulars of the threatening notes had been printed in the national press, although I confess I couldn't recall such details in *The Times* and *The Daily Telegraph* I had perused in my father's room in the Feathers only the night before.

I was beginning to feel inordinately frustrated.

Given that the ARF lead was about as dry as the wit of the Duke of Edinburgh, one could only come back to the usual suspects in the case of murder, which so often turn out to be, alas, one's nearest and dearest. Could it be Aileen, feelings of betrayal rekindled after so many years, desperate to get her sister out of the picture? Or Tom? He had painted an unflattering portrait of his sister-in-law when I talked with him in the Ballroom, but was it a deceit? Had he and Jackie taken up where they had left off two decades ago, to some sort of very bitter end? Was Tom the father of the child the autopsy revealed Jackie to be carrying? Aileen seemed convinced her sister and her husband had had an assignation in Manchester. Tom, too, had mentioned Manchester but the context was obscure, darker, angrier, as I recalled.

Some of the Thring wealth came from property in Manchester, it was said. Did ownership require Lord Thring's presence in the Lancashire metropolis? I thought both Thringys were behaving with less confidence than their position in society afforded. He had been both anxious to talk with me and strangely tentative during our encounter in the Dining Room; she had been passionately defensive over the topic of threatening letters.

My mind went back to the scrap of paper found in the Marchioness's loo and so, when I returned to my room, I brought with me a copy of the British Telecom phone book for King's Lynn and District borrowed from the footmen's lounge, prepared for one of those horribly boring elimination tasks. If the numbers—six, two, seven—referred to the prefix of a phone number, it would probably be located in the list of local and national codes in the front, although as I began to run my eyes over the columns and columns of UK villages, towns, cities, and their phone codes, I wondered: Would a blackmailer be wise to put down a telephone number?

I'm afraid my eyes glazed over rather quickly— especially when I found no match for the city of Manchester or immediate vicinity—so, to stave off sleep, I got off the bed and went to the window. Everything out of doors seemed unusually still. The branches of the trees along the path to Sandringham Church, playthings of the North Sea winds, rose bold and stark into a sky that had turned from its usual winter slate to a softer, paler grey, the harbinger, I was sure, of snow. The only movement I could see, as I turned my attention from the horizon down to the footings of the Big House, was Davey, in black coat, struggling along the walkway parallel to the west front with a passel of corgis. He reminded me of a plaster figure in one of those saint's day parades in Latin countries, helplessly swept up and borne along by the teeming mass. It was difficult to tell who was walking whom, corgis or footman.

I was a little surprised to see him returned from the shoot so early, back to his usual duties, but there was a question I thought he might be able to answer. Though not exactly cheered by the notion of once again venturing outdoors but also aware Davey would probably be busy with other work once the shooting party returned to the Big House, I grabbed my jacket, tore down the stairs, out through the kitchen courtyard and around the south end of the building, until I found Davey & dogs idling near the Nest, a small summer-house an admiring courtier built for the widowed Queen Alexandra, Edward VII's wife.

Davey brightened when he saw me. In the few minutes since I had noticed him along the path, he had become entangled in the dog leads, and looked more like someone tied to a stake with the expectation of being set fire to, than a plaster saint shouldered through the streets of a Spanish village. "Help!" he whimpered, swaying like a tree about to topple. Just in time, I managed to loosen the offending leads and free him from plunging into the sea of golden fur.

"Thanks. Would you be a love and take some of the little blighters?"

"Not *that* one," I said, recognizing Joan, the most prosaically named of the eight, and the one most fond of my tender lower limbs. All corgis seem alike to my nondiscerning eye, but Joan is distinguishable by the particularly snappish look about her expression. She is a dog with Attitude.

"Where are you walking?" I added as I took the lead and found myself jerked in two directions at once. You wouldn't think such small dogs have such power in their little legs.

"Your choice. The Estate isn't exactly beset with fun-filled destinations."

"The church, then."

We crunched our way across the frozen lawn to a point where it joined the church walk, the dogs, once directed, leading the way and vying with each other for some kind of position in the doggie hierarchy, their fat little white-furred bottoms bouncing up and down provocatively. Davey meanwhile cheered his early release from the shooting party thanks to a certain grumpy royal consort. "But what a simply ghastly experience," he went on. "The cold. The noise. Father shouting. You have no idea. Oh! But you do. What *were* you doing there among the careening pheasantry anyway?"

I kept mum about the tiara in Bucky's room and told him instead about Mrs. Benefer.

"Poor dear," he clucked.

"She was quite loopy. She even said the Queen's minder had been one of Jackie Scaife's lovers."

"Really? Which one? Jenkyns? Ooh, I didn't know that. Do you think it's true?"

"I don't know why she'd say it otherwise. Anyway, it was when they were teenagers."

"Sounds like our Ms. Scaife did put it about a bit."

"Jeez, Davey, you're as bad as other men. 'You're a tease if you do and a slag if you don't.' "

"Do and don't do what?"

"Do or don't do *it*."

"Oh. *It*." Davey stopped and grimaced. One of the dogs had squatted at the base of a towering Scots pine, one of a dozen marshalled to make an arbour over the pathway, and left a little souvenir. "I could pretend I didn't see that."

"Are you sure you want to spoil Her Majesty's walk to church Sunday?"

"Mother spends time around horses, you know, Jane. She's certainly seen worse. Oh, bother!" He took a plastic bag from his pocket and from the bag, a scoop. "If only the Royal Family liked cats," he sighed, getting down on his haunches and doing the necessary. "At least cats do it in litterboxes."

"It?"

"The other *it*."

We walked on, through a pair of wrought-iron gates, and into a clearing. Off in the distance to our right, across a road, was the restaurant, souvenir shop, and cafeteria closed to the public since October. Ahead, the lych-gate of the church with its brown tile roof looked like a rustic temple near lost amid heavy conifer branches. It was along this part of the church walk the masses gathered in late December and January to watch members of the Royal Family go to Sunday service.

"When did Inspector Jenkyns come on duty?" I asked.

Davey thought a moment. "Tuesday morning. When we found . . . you know. Why do you ask?"

"My father was interested to know, actually. Wondered how the PPOs are scheduled, and so on. Professional interest," I added, dissembling a bit. "I wonder where Jenkyns spent Christmas?"

"In London, in the bosom of his family, I should think. Although I seem to recall his wife's family lives in King's Lynn, or somewhere about."

"They do."

"So perhaps the hols were spent in these parts. It would be more convenient. Being a PPO puts such a strain on a marriage."

"Someone told me Jenkyns was from Lynn, too, but I heard him tell someone he grew up in Hunstanton."

"Ah, the seaside. What better place to meet girls. Or boys, as the case may be. Myth! Spark! Stop that!" He tugged at the leads to reassert mastery over a couple of corgis who had elected to scrap over something. A few snowflakes began to flutter down from the darkening sky. "I lost it at the seaside one summer," he added dreamily.

"It?"

"Among the many its of which we have been speaking. It was at Weston-super-Mare. He was French."

"No kidding? I lost *it* to a French boy, too. Well, Quebecois. Close enough. Cavendish Beach, PEI. I had my first summer job at a restaurant there. He was a bus-boy trying to improve his English."

"And did he?" Davey purred.

"*Absolument!* My French improved, too."

Davey grinned slyly. "You never quite forget first love, do you?"

"No," I had to admit, though I didn't care to remember some of the aftermath, notably the flurry of idiotic missives I sent Quebec-bound afterwards, the content of which made me burn even now with embarrassment. "Did you keep up? Write? Visit?"

"Not really. His English was rather poor."

"And your French?"

"Poorer still."

"I wonder how it would feel to meet again?"

"Could be quite wonderful."

"Or very disappointing."

We had reached the lych-gate and were idling the dogs by the steps. "Shall we take a turn through the graveyard?" I asked, noting the little waist-high gates were unlatched. "I've never really had a chance to look around."

The dogs were eyeing us expectantly. Forward or back? Left or right? Davey shivered. "Let's turn back. I'm getting chilled."

"Oh, pooh. Don't be such a weenie."

"Mind your choice of words. Most of these little dears have yet to perform their little functions."

But I was already through the gate with my bunch, who seemed greatly pleased to snuffle at new phenomena, notably the white fence posts lining the walkway to the church's south porch.

"And I don't fancy scraping it off grave markers!" he called after me. "Oh . . . all right, then."

"See!" he said a moment later when he had caught up with me and one of his charges began to squat on the nearby lawn. "Here. Take this."

I took the lead from him, while he ducked under a length of chain linking two of the posts. Next to me, resting on a weathered wooden pole, was a simple metal plaque inscribed with plain lettering. *'The White Stone Memorial,'* I read, wondering at first to what it was referring and then realized it was a grave under the east window of the church about ten yards away marked with a white cross.

ALEXANDER JOHN CHARLES ALBERT

Third Son of Albert Edward
Prince of Wales

and ALEXANDRA

Princess of Wales

Born 6th April 1871
Died 7th April 1871

"Poor mite. Look, Davey. He only lived a day."

"A few hours, really." Davey slipped back under the chain and joined me, retrieving his lead.

" *'The Red Memorial,'* " I read aloud. We both glanced at a much taller marker, a red stone cross, indicating the nearer of the two graves under the east window.

JOHN CHARLES FRANCIS

Fifth Son of King George V
and Queen Mary

Born 12th July 1905
Died 18th January 1919

"Would have been one of the Queen's . . . uncles, I guess. Gee, he was only . . ."—I calculated quickly—"thirteen when he died. How sad! Poor king and queen."

"He wasn't very well."

"Oh? What was the problem?"

"Epilepsy."

"Really? Like Bucky. But—age thirteen!—people don't die of epilepsy, surely?"

"Well, I guess they didn't have the drugs and things to control it that they have now. Besides, I think Prince John was also, you know, mentally challenged. Anyway, he spent the last few years of his life away from the Family, at Wood Farm, with his own Household, so maybe he became too much to handle. Oh, Phoenix, no!" Davey glared at the dog with disgust then stooped once again below the chain. "Your lot," he muttered to me, "must be constipated."

But I wasn't paying him much mind. I put my tongue out to catch a snowflake then asked: "Was he born with it? Prince John, that is?"

"With epilepsy?" Davey rose, making a moue at the contents of his plastic bag. "I'm not sure. I don't think so. I think he sort of—well, you can't exactly *catch* epilepsy, I know that. He developed it, I suppose. Or something caused it. If one of those genetic predisposition thingys is involved, I've never heard of any other member of the Royal Family with it."

I continued to gaze at the grave markers. I was having one of those odd sensations, like those that accompany a floundering attempt to remember somebody's name. You want to scratch your brain, but can't, of course.

"Come along, Jane dear, you're the one who wanted to go round the church."

Pulled back from the plaque by a couple of eager corgies, I glimpsed the clock high on the church's west tower. Nearly four o'clock. The afternoon was already beginning to close in. By contrast, the colors of the stained-glass windows took on a soft glow, evidence someone was within or the lights were being kept on for the holiday season.

"What might cause epilepsy, if it didn't just develop on its own somehow, do you think?"

"I haven't a clue, Jane. Brain tumor? Accident? Blow to the old bean?"

"Might one of those be the case with Prince John?"

"Really, Jane," Davey said, stopping by the south porch, "I'm not *The Royal Encyclopedia*."

"Well, I'm crib notes compared to you. Think!"

"There's a good doggie. How convenient. Look." He pointed to an arrangement of grates near the doorwell, upon which a dog, Joan, was voiding her bladder. "Oh, yes, Prince John," he murmured, noting the pique undoubtedly settling along my face.

"Well . . ." The strain of thoughts made his eyelids flutter. "I've never heard a brain tumor mentioned. Accident? Perhaps . . . oh! There was a rather wicked nanny in the picture, I've heard tell."

"A wicked nanny?" I echoed, peering at the carved stone angel in a niche over the entrance holding a baby. Odd, an angel holding a baby. Wasn't that part of the Madonna's job description?

"More of a sadist, really," Davey was saying. "When Prince Edward was a baby—the Edward who became the Duke of Windsor, darling—"

"Yes, I know! I'm not a complete dud at English history."

"—the nanny used to pinch him and twist his arm before bringing him into the drawing room to see his parents. This would send him into crying fits, of course, and his parents, the future George V and Queen Mary, would grow so uncomfortable they would have him taken away again."

"How awful! Why?"

"Unhealthily besotted with the child, I gather. Or jealous of his parents. It went on for years, apparently, before the King and Queen found out. The same nanny—at least I think it was—also ignored Edward's younger brother, Bertie, who became George VI. Gave him irregular feedings while riding in bumpy carriages so that he had chronic stomach trouble all his life, not to mention a terrible stuttering problem. Or so I've been told by the old dears around here."

"I think they'd call it child abuse today. So much for the vaunted English nanny."

"I'm sure she was an exception, Jane. Now whether Prince John, the youngest brother, had the wicked nanny who might have done something, well, abusive, I just don't know. What date did that marker give for Prince John's birth?"

"Nineteen . . . Five. I think."

"Hmmm, that has to be a decade after the other two were born. The wicked nanny must have been banished by then. Oh, surely." He tilted his head. "Or, perhaps not. Although, come to think of it, I believe I've heard Prince John had a rather *nice* nanny. He wouldn't have been sent to live at Wood Farm with someone cruel, I shouldn't think. Although, on the other hand, they say Queen Mary was a somewhat *distant* mother. Sorry, Jane. Prince John is less a page and more of a footnote in the Windsor saga."

It didn't matter. I had stopped listening. Davey had given me an idea, or at least half an idea, and I felt suddenly exhilarated. It was like being handed a tiny golden key. But which door, I wondered, might it unlock? There was really only one practical way to find out, and it would require me to do something I really didn't fancy doing.

"Jane? I say, did you want to have a peek in the church?" Davey interrupted my little reverie. "It's quite lovely. Outside it seems just another little Norfolk church, but inside it's Aladdin's cave—a solid silver altar and suchlike. Here, I'll hold the dogs."

The word 'dogs' seemed to cause a little stir among those so-named, but my attention, which had been rather absently focused on the decorative Christmas holly bordering the curve of the south porch's tudor arch, moved to the porch's dark recess, toward the great oak door that led into the church. It was opening with painful slowness. A thin creaking noise sent Davey's neck to turning and we both waited for someone to appear. It was like watching paint dry.

Finally, a face peered around the edge of the door, a ghostly visage in a halo of rich golden light, a startling sight until it became apparent the light was the glow of the church's interior, and the face belonged to someone familiar.

It was Aileen Benefer.

"Ah!" she exclaimed softly, moving full into the doorway and hugging herself as if the transition to the cold outdoors was too much to bear. Her Barbour jacket was rolled up her arms. "I wasn't sure who was there."

"Just us, Mrs. Benefer. Davey and me. And a few dogs. Um, how are you feeling?" I was very surprised to see her up and about, and at Sandringham Church, no less. I had assumed after Heather and I had got her to her room earlier in the day that she would remain tucked up horizontally in one place for some goodly period of time.

"Quite well, thank you," she replied, closing the door, her voice rather too bright.

The corgis, tongues exposed, regarded her expectantly. She seemed to hesitate, as if anticipating an ankle assault. Instinctively, Davey and I drew the dogs back by their leads.

"I must be getting back now," Mrs. B. continued. She skirted the inside of the porch and came into the cold grey light.

"Are you sure you're all right?" I asked.

Though the disconcerting vagueness of the morning had vanished, I wouldn't have said she looked aces. Her skin was waxy and her eye sockets seemed almost battered. But my earnest solicitation served more to irritate her. Her brow darkened and she replied firmly, "Jane, I'm fine. I expect to see you on time tomorrow morning."

"Yes, Mrs. Benefer," I replied as she turned and made her way quickly down the path.

Davey shrugged. "Quick recovery."

"Hmph. I know she's quite religious but what was she doing in church on a Friday afternoon, I wonder?"

"What do most people do in church?"

"I don't know. Pray?"

"Of course."

"How do you know Aileen was praying?"

"Her tights were bagged at the knee."

"Very clever."

Davey received my accolade with an indulgent smile.

"But," I continued, "did you note anything else about what she was wearing?"

The smile faded. "That green really isn't her colour?"

"No, silly. Her jacket. It didn't fit very well. It was about two sizes too small."

17

READER, I APOLOGIZED to him. Bucky, that is. During the silent hour, the interlude between tea and dinner, I went to his room.

"Wadda ya want?" he asked with enormous charm, when he saw who it was at the door. A black tie was loose around his collar.

"I'm sorry I slapped you," I said quickly and then, attempting to salvage a little dignity, added: "So hard."

"Oh, yeah?" His tone was suspicious. "My mother get to you?"

"She made a few suggestions."

He snorted.

"And . . ." I was about to append. But something was sticking in my throat and it wasn't one of those pesky fishbones that so bedevil the Queen Mother.

"And?"

"And I wondered if you'd care to join me at the Feathers tonight." There. I said it. And I didn't throw up. "After the Queen goes to bed, or whenever you can get away."

Bucky's expression went from peevish to pleased in a thrice. Indeed, there was something vaguely triumphal around the edges which was significantly offputting. Ergo, my caveat, as follows: "Don't get the wrong idea."

"Yeah, yeah, whatever."

"Now, isn't there something you'd like to say to me?"

His face was as blank as a slate.

"I apologized to you," I supplied. *"Therefore . . . ? And . . . ?"*

"Oh, yeah." He stepped back from the door. "C'mon in."

I hesitated.

"Look, I got your point. I'm not gonna hit on you. I just don't want to talk where other people can hear everything." So inside I ventured.

"So, anyway," he continued, closing the door behind us. "Like, sorry about being so weird the other night. I just . . ." He shrugged helplessly. "You know . . ."

Not really. But I supposed it was about as much articulation as Bucky was able to render in the contrition department. Anyway, my eyes were doing a little lo-impact aerobics trying to see if there was anything different about the room, an exposed satchel perchance, or, better yet, a rhinestone tiara glittering feebly on the dresser. But if the Marquess and Marchioness had confronted sonny-boy about this curious contrivance earlier in the evening, he didn't seem agitated or bothered in any way.

"Are you looking for something?" he asked, not at all warily, moving to a mirror to fiddle with his tie.

"Sorry. Just me being a housemaid. You tend to see things others don't. Dust, for instance."

"Damn these ties."

"Bucky, much as I hate to drag up the past, especially when it's been put to rest so recently, there's still something I was wondering about regarding the Slap. I thought your mother—her ladyship—was a bit over the top about it all. I mean, you're a man, I'm a woman. This *thing* happened. I don't think of it as a huge big deal but she sure did."

Bucky's hand had gone to his cheek. "She's just like that. I don't know why." He rubbed at the skin though the mark had vanished since Wednesday. "She's always been that way."

"So if you got in a fight at school or something, she'd . . . what?"

"Give hell to the parents of whatever kid I'd been in a fight with. It was real embarrassing. But it didn't happen that often after a while. Word got around. Parents told their kids not to get into fights with me."

Such overzealous protection. Was it just lioness behaviour, as Lord Thring suggested earlier, or was the behaviour triggered by a particular incident? The latter was the target upon which my intellectual faculties were drawing a bead.

"Anyway," he said, turning from the mirror and reaching for his dinner jacket, "how are we getting there?"

"To the Feathers? Your car, I guess. I sure don't have one."

"I don't have one, either."

"You don't?"

"No. They won't let me have one. My mother's afraid I'll have a seizure while I'm driving. And Affie thinks my having a car is expensive and unnecessary. Of course he's practically got a fleet of cars and the two of them are spending big bucks redecorating Barsham Hall, or haven't you seen the magazines?"

"Could you have a seizure driving?"

"Well, it's possible," he said grudgingly. "There's times you can be going down a country road and the way the light filters through the trees, it can be sort of like a strobe light, you know. And that could trigger something. Or you could have a seizure for some other reason.

But I usually know when I'm going to have one, so what are the chances?"

"Why don't you just buy a car on your own?"

"With what money?"

"Peel it off your mother."

"Hah."

"Or get a job."

"I will. When I get back to the States." He looked at his watch. "I better go and make nice for a while. Let's see, dinner's at eight-fifteen—"

"Or eight-thirty if the Queen Mother keeps to habit."

"—hell, I don't know when I can get away. I can't use the headache excuse."

"I'm sure Her Majesty will retire early." After the day's debacle, my bets were on an early night for much of the Royal Family. "And my guess is Princess Margaret won't be doing the Cole Porter songbook till two in the morning. She's down with a chill."

"I heard. Maybe ten-thirty? Is that too late?"

"No," I said, lying. "Meet me at the Jubilee Gates. We'll have to walk. It's not far."

"I know. I lived at Anmer Hall for a couple of years when I wasn't away at that stupid school."

By late evening, the wind off the Wash had risen anew, whipping into stinging pellets the afternoon's gentle confetti snow that had hardened into thin drifts along the edges of the lifeless gardens, the outbuildings, and stone wall surrounding the grounds. Tree branches lost from view in the embrace of darkness snapped and groaned. We were alone, Bucky and I, trudging along the roadside, heads lowered into the wind, my torch the only illumination but for the occasional passing car. The temperature had dropped, too, and the chill had taken on a biting edge. Despite the extra layers under my jacket, loitering at the Jubilee Gates for my guest (!) had set me to shivering, so I was grateful to be moving, cheered by the thought of a cozy pub fire at the end.

Bucky just seemed grateful to be free of the rituals of the Big House.

"No fucking charades, thank God," he exclaimed when we were past the gates and the sentry. "Everybody was acting so weird anyway."

"Sort of a strained atmosphere, was it?"

"Yeah, you could say that."

"Probably the incident with the dog."

"I guess. Prince Philip didn't show up for dinner. Affie kept giving me these looks down the table. The only one doing much talking, other than the Queen, was Charles. And it was blah blah blah architecture, blah blah blah organic blahblah.

"He's so *boring*," he shouted to the wind while I wondered how a chap such as Bucky kept up his end in conversation with members of the Royal Family, or did they stick him at the gah-gah end of the table? "No wonder Di dumped him. God, I'm glad to be out of there."

"Any trouble getting away?"

"Na. The Queen went to bed early like you said she would. My mother wasn't happy about me leaving the house but I just told her, 'Look, I'm going out. That's all there is to it.' They're worried about this terrorist crap. Even whatsisname, the Queen's detective, got into the act. Wanted to have me driven to Dersingham, and driven back."

Ooh, for a warm car! I thought as the wind laced into my cheeks.

"I can't wait to get out of this fucking country!" Bucky shouted. "I'd do anything—anything!—to get away."

"Have you told them yet?"

"No. Soon. I've got a few things to do first." He kicked at a stone along the road. "Look, I really am sorry about the other night. I deserved the slap. I don't know why I told my mother it was you. But she would *not* let up about it, and I couldn't think of any good story for this big red mark on my face. I mean, I guess I don't have much imagination. Anyway, it won't happen again."

The road to hell being paved with etc. etc., I was disinclined to believe his little promise, at least in its universal application. Specifically—and despite the 'aw shucks, ma'am' routine, which I could have lived without—I did believe him. Otherwise I wouldn't be trudging through the moon-shrouded starless *peopleless* winter gloom with him.

"So, Bucky," I said with a feigned (and, one hoped, convincing) nonchalance, "what was it like growing up in the States?"

We were passing the Norwich Gates and I was eager to get to my Nancy Drewing before we were swallowed up in the Friday follies at the pub.

"Great!" he replied, dashing across the road ahead of me in advance of a passing car. I directed the torch to the back of his Barbour and followed.

"North Carolina—the first colony to break with Britian!" he continued, apropos of what I'm not sure but could guess easily enough.

"You said something about Durham County— Walshes of Durham County. Isn't there a city, Durham?"

"We lived aways south in Moore County, near a place called Southern Pines."

"On a plantation, y'all?" I drawled, coming over all Miss *Scah*let.

Bucky was silent. I flashed the torch in his face. He flinched.

"Bucky?"

"No, we didn't live on a *plantation*. Would you turn that thing away?"

"I thought your family was big into agriculture." I redirected the beam to the centre strip in the road. "Walsh-Rayner."

"They are, tobacco mostly. But . . . My mother and me, we sort of lived apart. They weren't real happy about stuff, the family, that is. I guess part of it was Mom having me and not being married. She was pretty young and they're still real conservative in the South, or were back then."

"So, what did they do? Kick your mother out?"

"No, not really. I mean, my folks have always been okay to me, although . . ."

That his folks had been less than okay to his mother was left hanging in the cold Norfolk air.

"Anyway, I'd spend parts of summers with them in Durham. I think maybe it was my mom wanting to be on her own. There was some sort of big to-do around the time she was pregnant with me. Or so I've heard. They never really told me much."

"And your mother never remarried. Or married, I mean."

The clumping of our respective Docs filled the void. "There were different guys interested," Bucky replied, finally. "But she was real busy with the stud—the horses, I mean—and the kennels, building her business."

And then one day the Marquess of Thring (or the Earl of Chudleigh as it was then) showed up at a field trial for Labrador retrievers. How veddy *interesting.*

"Why did she marry your stepfather, then?"

"Dogs and horses, I guess. What else?"

What else? Marrying an English lord would be a fine up-yours to the snooty Walshes of Durham County from a woman who had probably suffered opprobrium at their hands.

"It wasn't Affie's money, if that's what you're thinking," he continued, while I listened to the toe of his boot connect with another stone. In truth, I had thought just that, and I supposed others had, too: Lady Thring, prototypical gold digger, money her main motive, the title a sweet little bonus.

"My mother had built up her own business. She wouldn't take family money. Well, she had a small trust. So do I, come to that, but I don't see any of it until I'm twenty-one, another year and a half away, dammit!

"Anyway, Mom said she wasn't interested in marrying him, but Affie kept hanging around, and flying back and forth and telephoning, then bringing my mother to England and so finally—"

"She gave up her business?"

"No. Someone runs it for her back home. See! I'm still saying 'back home.'"

"Your mother's adapted, though."

"She actually loves it here. She's got more energy than I've got. Like decorating Barsham Hall. The place is so huge and cold, I hate it, but she couldn't wait to get her hands on it. And there's different boards she sits on. All the charity stuff. Even organizing that dumb panto-mime."

Or delegating the organizing, I thought, reflecting on Hume Pryce's comments. We clumped along the road in silence, the bitter wind biting our skin. My trusty torch told me we were near the bend in the road that led downward to Dersingham. A faint orange glow in the sky indicated the presence of life.

"What did your mother do with you while she was working?" I asked.

"There was school. And we had a housekeeper since I was about five. A real nice woman named Carmelita. She was great. I wanted Mom to bring her here but Carmelita has family in the States and couldn't come . . ."

"No, I mean when you were really young? Did you have a nanny or an au pair?"

"Yeah. It's kind of hard to remember. We had quite a few for a while. I think when my mother was first on her own, things were pretty crazy for a while. Mom's kind of bossy, you may have noticed, and she doesn't like it when things aren't done just right. That's why Carmelita was so great. She knew just how to handle my mother. Caroline's good at it, too."

"So you don't remember any of these nannies?"

"Like, I was three or four years old when the last one left," he replied irritably. "Who took care of you? Didn't your mother work at something?"

"She's a journalist. But she took some time off when I was born, I think. My grandmother lived nearby, and there were my two older sisters, so we didn't have to bring anybody in."

I felt increasingly impatient. Establishing that Bucky had had an au pair when he was small was useful, but I needed more. Oh, why couldn't he have a recovered memory like everybody else seemed to have these days!

"I guess anyone your mother hired would have had to learn how to cope with your epilepsy."

He groaned. "Not that again. I've had to hear about my fucking *'disability'* ever since I can remember. I wish everybody would just forget about it. Lots of people have it. It's no big deal. But there's some out there who still think it's this weird thing, like you're crazy or wacko or something."

"Dark Ages thinking, I know," I clucked sympathetically. "I'll bet it was lousy for you in school, the way kids can be."

"Worse here."

"Did you always have it?"

"As far as I can recollect."

"But do you remember a first time you had a seizure?"

We were turning into Dersingham, the windows of the Feathers like little golden lozenges tantalizingly aglow in the middle distance. Under the feeble light of the first street lamp, Bucky's profile came into sharper relief. I noted incipient annoyance and a runny nose. I switched off my torch.

"Sort of, I guess," he replied finally, running his glove under his nose and sniffing. "I remember being in this ambulance. And I was in the hospital for a while, I think. For tests."

"Was anyone with you when it happened?"

"I don't know! I don't like to think about it."

"Try."

"Why?"

"Just indulge me."

"You didn't indulge *me.*"

"Oh, give it up, Bucky."

We plodded along for a minute. My ears were starting to sting in the cold. Then he muttered peevishly, "I think it was one of the nannies, then. Probably scared the crap out of her."

"Your mother wasn't around?"

"No. I don't know. I just remember sort of falling against something in the hallway. Then it's a blank until the ambulance."

"And nothing happened before the seizure took place? You didn't, say, fall on your head? Or maybe . . . get hit on the head?"

"I don't remember," he mumbled.

"The nanny wasn't English, by any chance?"

"I don't remember! I *do not* remember! I don't think I was even three years old. What is with you anyway?"

"I'm just interested, that's all. I have an older sister who's becoming a doctor so . . . you know." Actually, *I* didn't know, but it was the only excuse I could think of. Fortunately, Bucky seemed to accept it as a plausible reason for my persistent interrogation.

"You weren't born in early February, by any chance, were you?" I continued in the persistent interrogation vein.

"No. In June. 1975."

"Not June second?" Could it be? Was the 6 2 7 an American-style date arrangement, the month coming first?

"June ninth."

"Damn."

"Do you want to know my sign?"

"Er, sure. Gemini, isn't it?"

"Yeah," he replied glumly.

I suppose it would have behooved me to make a wrong guess so Bucky could have the pleasure of correcting me.

Being a Friday and late in the evening, the Feathers was as jammed as a Bakewell tart. When we rounded into the hotel's courtyard, Bucky headed immediately for the Stable Tap, as it's called—a handsome brick-and-stone stable, separate from the hotel proper, that had been renovated and given over to darts, pool, and, as the sign genteelly put it, 'pub games.' The place was really more of a videogame arcade, and while it was sometimes lively and fun on a dreary country eve, it wasn't really the place in which to have a good natter.

"C'mon, Jane," Bucky pleaded when I demurred from the idea of spending time amidst ringdingdinging machinery, the blare of overamplified music, and the bawl of what one might regard in a sour moment as Dersingham's more loutish element. "They got a great new game in here. C'mon. Please, please. Just for a little while."

His wheedling tone was all too reminiscent of past (mis)adventures. However, he had set me on alert for another reason. "How do you know there's a new game in there?"

"Because I was here after the pan—" He bit his lip.

"After the panto? You came here? I thought you said you went to a club in King's Lynn to meet some friends?"

"Sorry, miss, I guess I just misspoke." He grinned at what he thought was cleverness. "I meant to say here. Anyway, are you coming in here with me or not?"

"Not."

"Well, I'll just play a few games and join you later."

So, I thought, entering the hotel on my own, grateful for the rush of warmth, Bucky had spent time after the panto here. In Dersingham. He had had a different story Wednesday night. Misspoke indeed.

As I walked down the narrow hall to the lounge bar my mind went back to the famous tiara. Why did Bucky carry it with him to Dersingham, to the panto, in the first place? And when did he first notice a switch had been made, that he had with him a rhinestone clone, not a glittering original? I had reasoned by this time that Bucky could only have secured the Duchess of Windsor's tiara from a certain familial source, and I had begun to think this, too, was HM's reasoning. It would explain something about her air of circumspection on the subject.

However, none of this stolen jewellery business could sufficiently divert me from my current scenario: that on a cold winter's eve in a village hall in Norfolk the Marchioness of Thring had come face-to-face with the woman who, years before, had abused or neglected, or in some way had been deemed responsible for, her beloved son's affliction. Her ladyship must have recognized her nemesis even under the makeup and costuming contrived to turn a relatively young woman into the parody of an aging monarch. Did they meet afterwards? Caroline had mentioned her ladyship had been unexpectedly late returning to King's Lynn Boxing Day evening. And Jackie had told Hume she was meeting someone that night. Was that someone her old employer, Pamela Walsh of Moore County, North Carolina? And did that encounter lead to you-know-what? *'Mothers, don't you know.'* Lord Thring's words came back to me. *'Overprotective creatures.'*

Granted, there were some untidy bits to this accounting, and I did rather dread broaching it as an hypothesis to You-Know-Who, but I was nevertheless rather pleased with myself as I bounced into the lounge bar.

That is, until I bumped into Andrew Macgreevy, my favorite Fleet Street hack.

"Hello, Stell, whatta ya havin'?" He had a pint of something sloshing in one hand, a cigarette in the other, and a mad grin on his face.

"A jeroboam of Bolly would go down a treat," I replied, tugging at the zipper of my jacket. "Or would you get into trouble if they decided to vet your inflated expense account?"

"Not if I can prove the information's worth the money. Saw you at the shoot this morning, by the way."

"Oh, yeah?" Damn, I thought. Those bloody camera lenses. "Well, half the Staff's down with the 'flu, so you end up doing all kinds of odd and sods around here. Including," I added just to ward him off, "carrying messages to Her Majesty."

"And what sort of communication would you be conveying to Her Maj, pray tell?" Macgreevy rocked back on his heels and appraised me blearily as I removed my jacket. I realized he was half-corked.

"Watch it. You're spilling."

"Have this one, Stell. I'll get another. Go on, luv, I haven't touched it."

"Oh, all right," I said ungraciously, flipping my jacket over my arm and taking the glass with the other hand. "But neither beer nor Bolly, you will not get me to break my Staff agreement."

The problem with accepting a drink from Macgreevy was the obligation it cast to continue conversing with him. On the other hand, I noted, casting my eyes about the smoky room, there was nowhere to sit. I waved to my father who was occupying a table near the window with a bunch of men of similar mein—coppers, I could tell at a glance. Dad waved back. Hume Pryce was holding court on the other side of the room by the fireplace with a pair of married but bored-to-tears thirtysomething-type matrons. He took no note of me. And, when a few punters parted the way Red Sea–like, there was Davey and Nigel at their own table. "Yoo-hoo," they called out in tandem above the din, gesturing for me to join them. I made a move but Macgreevy, who had had time to fetch a lager, caught me by the arm.

"Don't go. We were just getting reacquainted."

"Read your story in the *Gazette* earlier." I had, actually; earlier, while waiting for Bucky to finish dinner. And I had perused a few of the other papers, too. "Pickings must be slim. But I must say you have a talent for breathing new life into old facts."

"From you, high praise indeed." Macgreevy lifted his glass in a mock salute, squinting through the smoke of his cigarette. "Still, new facts would not go remiss. A confirmation the Queen was among those who stumbled—I speak that metaphorically—across the deceased would be a nice Christmas prezzie from a certain member of Her Majesty's Staff to a certain humble scribe upholding the Great British Public's right to know."

"Well, there's one detail you humble scribes don't seem to have glommed onto," I said in a deflecting sort of way. I was referring to the tiara, of course, no mention of which had appeared in the newspapers to my knowledge. I could only guess the authorities were withholding information on this rather scrummy detail, journalistically speaking, for reasons of their own.

"What's that, then?" Macgreevy affected nonchalance, planting his lips on the edge of his beerglass but keeping his eyes glued to mine.

"Now why would I tell you?" I began to edge away. I was regretting opening my mouth. Teasing a Windsor watcher is perilously akin to bear-baiting.

"You were there at the village hall, weren't you." It wasn't a question. "C'mon, Stell. Tell." He raised his voice to be heard above the din. "I could arrange a fee."

"I wasn't. I won't. And no, thanks," I shouted over my shoulder, heading for Davey and Nigel's table.

"Hello again, Andrew, old love," Davey said cheerily, looking past me. Macgreevy had followed on my heels. "Chatting up our favorite intrepid housemaid? . . . Er, our favorite housemaid, rather."

I squeezed next to Davey. Macgreevy peered down at the three of us with a mixture of irritation and amusement. "You lot," he said, wagging two ciggy-gripping fingers at us, "are an impediment to the journalistic enterprise. So's this whole bloody village, come to that."

"Andrew," Davey said, brushing ash from the table, "as I may have mentioned in the recent past, we'd be happy to talk to you about anything except Moth—except the private life of Her Majesty the Queen, her family, her heirs and successors, her Household and Staff. And we haven't anything to say about the murder here in the village because we don't know anything you don't. Isn't that right, Nigel?"

"Abtholutely," Nigel mumbled drunkenly.

"Nigel, sit up. There's a dear. So, Andrew, how may we help you otherwise?"

"If I wasn't one to maintain friendly contact with my 'sources,' I would happily suggest you three sod off."

"But of course, Andrew, you would never engage in such unpleasantness."

"Of course not. One day, you may change your minds."

Davey put a finger to his chin thoughtfully. "Isn't there some metaphor about hell and the possibility of its freezing over? Jane?"

"I do believe there is." I smiled up at Macgreevy. He smiled back. Though he never for a moment looks crushed by the negative effect he has on people, I actually felt a little sorry for him. Journalists and thick hides go together, but thick hides can be insensitive casings that cut you off from the feeling world. "Oh, and thanks for the drink," I called halfheartedly as he edged back into the crowd.

"Tried it on with you already this evening, had he?" I asked Davey when Macgreevy had gone.

"Indeed, yes. Plied us with pints, most of which have found their way down Nigel's gullet, I might add. Still, no joy for our Andrew Macgreevy, poor boob." Davey waved a hand to take in the room. "He's been about as welcome around here as a sexually transmitted disease. They all have, really."

"They?"

"There's been a bunch from the national press wandering around making nuisances of themselves. They've mostly gone."

"Andrew got the only remaining room here at the Feathers."

"He's not such a bad chap, really. Fancies you, I think."

"Oh, nonsense."

Davey made demurring noises while slurping his lager.

"He does *not* fancy me! He's just after the main chance, that's all."

"Whatever you say, darling."

"He's got ten years on me! And he's not even very good-looking."

"Oooh, but ever so *forceful*, don't-you-think."

"He's just rude, that's what he is. Oh, sod off, Davey." He had started laughing in his beer, spraying droplets across the table. "I'm not sitting with you!"

"Don't be cross, darling. Nigel, tell Jane I didn't mean it. Nigel!"

Nigel opened his eyes very wide. "Whaaa?" he asked in a startled slur.

"Never mind, go back to sleep. Don't know why he's so tired. I'm the one who spent all morning in the bitter cold being tongue-lashed for my inadequacies in sport." Davey's hand shot out to catch Nigel's head before it hit the table. "There are days one *does* question one's loyalties."

Some little time later I noted Hume Pryce had been deserted by his tablemates so I went to join him, happily deserting mine. Davey had decided I was *la belle dame sans merci* vis-à-vis Macgreevy and had turned sulky when I refused to countenance such silly talk. As it happened, something Mrs. Benefer had said in her delusional episode that morning had found a small resting place in my cranium and I thought Hume might be able to offer a confirmation. Not that it detracted from my central thesis of the moment; it's just that one hates loose ends.

"Still here, I see."

"Until they make an arrest or say otherwise, I presume," Pryce said glumly as I sat down. He had removed his glasses and was rubbing his eyes.

"I was wondering something," I began. "When did Jackie take on the role of the Queen of Hearts in the panto?"

"We had auditions in late October so it must have been shortly after that."

"But you weren't rehearsing every day?"

"Oh, no. We really didn't begin in earnest until a few weeks ago. This is just a little country production. There were some rehearsals in November and a few of us would drive up from Cambridge. And, of course, there were other things to organize, the sets and costuming and so on."

"So anyone in the panto would have had a chance to get away for a time if they wanted to."

"Yes." He blinked at me. Rubbing had accentuated the web of fine lines around his eyes obscured when his glasses were in place. He looked unaccountably tired. "Why do you ask?"

"I wondered whether Jackie had been away, gone on a trip or something."

"Not in December, anyway." He removed a tissue from his pocket, blew on the lenses and his glasses and began polishing. "Do you think this has something to do with her death?"

"No. Well, not really. It's just that Mrs. Benefer thinks Jackie went away with some man. Thinks it was her husband, actually."

"It wasn't me, if that's what you're thinking."

"No . . ."

"They've had no luck with the animal-rights loonies," Pryce continued, unhappily gesturing with his glasses toward the table containing my father and his new cronies. "So they'll be nosing about elsewhere before very long . . ."

"Already started, I think."

"Well, as I explained to the police earlier this week, there was nothing but a professional relationship between Jackie and me, and between her and everyone else in the cast, as far as I know. I liked Jackie. She was attractive. And, in other circumstances, perhaps something might have happened between us." He shrugged and put his glasses back on. "But nothing did."

"You tried."

"I suppose one could say a little flirting was going on. There was just something about her. She seemed to invite it. Nothing would have happened anyway. I have Helen in Nevis. Anyway, the more I put my mind to it, the more Jackie seems . . . seemed, rather, a woman with something else on her mind. She wasn't using the panto to give herself a social life. She didn't really seem to be at loose ends, though I know she hadn't a proper job or prospects and she'd saddled herself with family she didn't necessarily get along with."

"Did Jackie go away somewhere in November?" I asked, returning to my original inquiry.

"Mmm?" Pryce took a sip of his drink. "Yes. I believe she did. She mentioned she had been in Manchester for a few days. Wouldn't be my holiday destination, Manchester."

"Did she say why she'd been there?"

"Visit a friend. Probably wouldn't have mentioned it if I hadn't asked where she had managed to find a lemon-yellow handbag. Is this important?" The firelight danced on the lens of his glasses.

It was my turn to shrug. Could Jackie have gone to Manchester with her brother-in-law? It did seem an unlikely place for a tryst. Still, Tom Benefer had grown up on the Whitewell estate, one of the Duchy of Lancaster estates, so Davey had said, and Whitewell was only about thirty miles north of Manchester. The area was more or less Tom's old stomping grounds. But Manchester was ringing some other bell for me, and not just that awful song from *Hair* either. But which bell? I shook my head to clear the cobwebs.

"What?" I said. The cobwebs clung and Pryce was on to something else.

"I was saying, I believe I've managed to recall the change Jackie made to the line at the end of the banquet scene in the *Queen of Hearts*. In the original, the Queen—Jackie—refers to the King of Hearts, and the fact that the stolen tarts must be found and says, '. . . His Majesty will give the culprit a thorough beating with his own fair hand.'

"But what Jackie said, I think, is this: '. . . *her ladyship* will give her *child* a thorough beating with her own fair hand.'

"Most peculiar, really. I didn't have much time to consider it, because the scene was at an end and we had to prepare for the next."

I must have been staring because he shifted uncomfortably in his chair.

"I wonder now," he continued under my gaze, "if

it had something to do with Pamela, as she was the only wife of a peer in the audience, the only 'her ladyship.' I don't see how, though."

As it happened, I did. And it turned my theory right on its head.

18

UNFORTUNATELY, I DIDN'T have an opportunity to give this gleaming bit of information the mental airing it deserved, because Bucky had weaved his way unsteadily to the table I was sharing with Hume Pryce, flopped into a spare seat like a wet puppy, and then playfully slugged Hume in the shoulder.

"Hi, cuz," he whooped.

"Hello, Bucky," Pryce said with little enthusiasm, rubbing his arm. "Oughtn't you to watch your alcohol intake?"

"Ah, shut up. I'm fine."

I looked from one to the other. "Are you two related?" I asked, startled. There was, I supposed, a faint resemblance: something about the eyes, perhaps; the blueness of faded jeans, a slight downturning at the corners.

"Kissin' cousins," Bucky declared. "Where can I get a drink around here?"

"We're remotely related," Hume sighed. "I'm a second cousin—well, maybe more of a third cousin—to Pamela. And I believe you've had quite enough," he added sharply, addressing Bucky.

"You never mentioned this before."

"You didn't ask. And I hardly think about it. Pamela and I share—what?" He paused in thought. "Actually, I think we share two sets of great-great-grandparents. A rather remote connection, so I don't know her that well. And, really, it's been years since I saw her last."

"But you told us you met her at the King's Lynn Festival last summer."

"Yes, I know. But before that. Pamela and I first met in my more hippie-ish days, I guess you could call them. I had arrived in America after the usual destinations of the time, Marrakesh, Crete, Goa, Nepal, a side-trip to Australia in my case. I thought I'd keep going: cross the U.S. from California to New York and stop and visit the long-lost rellies in North Carolina en route. And so I did. I had a very pleasant time as I recall." He smiled softly.

"Your great-grandfather invented some device that helped in the tobacco industry . . ." I struggled to remember our conversation earlier in the week.

"Yes, that's the connection, you see. But it gets a bit muddled. My great-grandfather, the inventor, made a business partnership with an American in the tobacco industry. But, as it happened, each man married the sister of the other. To seal the bargain, I suppose. Well, one hopes there was *some* love involved. Anyway, there you have it: a family relationship tenuous as well as confusing."

"When did you travel in the States?"

"That time?"

"Don't look at me," Bucky interjected, alighting on our conversation suddenly like an excited bug.

"If you say so." Hume turned to me. "Oh, it would have been . . . 1974. Yes, that's right. I remem-

ber there being nothing but that Watergate business on
the telly."

"February?" I asked, still thinking of the scrap of
paper found in the Marchioness's suite and the possibility it might refer to a date in the 1970s. "Or June?"

"No." Hume's eyebrows twitched. "Late summer.
I remember watching Nixon's resignation speech. I'm
sure it was in, let me see, August of that year. Why on
earth would you think of February?"

"Watergate's ancient history to me."

"Yes, of course it is," he said drily while continuing to regard me with mild perplexity.

We had skimmed Watergate in twentieth-century
world issues in high school but a refresher in late
twentieth-century American history was not my purpose
in asking. Hume's earlier revelation about Jackie's ad-lib
in the *Queen of Hearts* had cast a different light on the
relationship I believed the deceased had had with the
former Pamela Walsh. I was certain now Jackie had been
an au pair in America and Bucky had been her little
charge. One day, went my reasoning, when Bucky was
around two years old, there had been an unhappy 'incident.' Not long afterwards Bucky had had his first
seizure. The guilty party, I had been assuming, was
Jackie, then a young, restless, and probably impatient
woman; that Lady Thring had recognized her one-time
employee even under the makeup and costuming of the
panto (perhaps Jackie had even impersonated the
Queen's voice in those early days in North Carolina) and
had been overwhelmed with rage to once again see the
woman whose assault had brought on her son's affliction.
My fevered brain had imagined Jackie fleeing Moore
County one step ahead of the law, travelling from place
to place, job to job, lest she be found out, living the life
of a fugitive. I imagined, too, Lady Thring nursing a
hatred against Jackie all these years, and that their meeting after the panto was finished at the village hall to
have been acrimonious, explosive, and, finally, fatal.

Now the shoe seemed to be on the other foot.
Nearly two decades ago, *Pamela Walsh had hit her own
child*, and hit him hard enough to do lasting damage.

Perhaps she had lashed out this way only the once, but it had been enough, and it had been witnessed. Casting Lady Thring as the perpetrator helped to explain at least one item that had been worrying me: the fragment of the letter I had found in the Marchioness's suite, a fragment that for all the world looked like part of a blackmail note.

As I sat there in the Feathers, the rest of it came to me in a flash: Jackie Scaife had fled nothing in 1970s America. She had been described as restless, and restless she was, leaving her employ with Pamela Walsh and going on to other ventures in other places, following the sun, having fun, and arriving finally where I guess so many wanderers arrive, at the edge of the continent, in California. Tom Benefer described his sister-in-law as less the vivacious, pleasure-loving creature others seemed to think she was. He thought her, rather, as being pitiable, the sparkle more a masquerade. Had she come to the end of something in California—the end of an affair, a job, money, hope?

I found myself imagining her in some West Coast city sometime in the summer receiving yet another of Aileen's dutiful letters with clippings enclosed. Perhaps some of the letters never reached Jackie over the years, perhaps she only skimmed them and tossed them aside, but perhaps this time something caught her eye. Since becoming Marchioness, Lady Thring had attacked Barsham Hall with decorating gusto and her (or, rather, her designer's) handiwork had been both fodder for some of the tonier magazines and spark to press controversy over a restoration deemed in some quarters to be less than faithful. Might Aileen have included a piece about the Thrings in one of the letters, complete with a picture of her ladyship graciously inviting readers to her swell digs? I imagined Jackie seeing the woman she knew as plain old Pamela Walsh, a person estranged from her own family, suddenly transformed into the wife of an English lord, fabulously wealthy, no doubt, and evidently intent on reflecting the life and style of the English aristocracy. What charity were the proceeds from the panto to go toward? The British Epilepsy Research Trust, of course.

What a perfect blackmail target the former Pamela Walsh had become!

As for the time of Hume Pryce's sojourn in America, I had wondered at first if it coincided with the cut-out numerals on the bit of paper in Lady Thring's suite, presuming they reflected part of a date, 6 February 197—? But I quickly realized Bucky's birth and, more particularly, the events around his first epileptic seizure were well *after* the Watergate summer. Would Jackie have remembered so precisely the date of an incident in—what?—1977 or 1978, even if it was disturbing and abhorrent? Somehow I thought you might better be able to attach a calendar date to some event in your own ordinary life if it coincided with something more dramatic and memorable—a public event, for instance. Pryce remembered the time of the North Carolina visit because it coincided with Nixon's resignation as president of the United States. Jackie may have remembered when Pamela struck her son or when he had his first seizure because it coincided with some other event. But 6 February, the anniversary date of HM's accession to the Throne, would hardly go remarked upon by the American media. *That* had to be a coincidence.

Still, I thought bleakly, as I turned my attention back to my tablemates, the outcome was the same. Murder. I glanced at Bucky. Or, rather, at Bucky's back. He had gone to fetch himself another drink. I decided to join my father at his table and made my apologies to Pryce. Bucky was soon chatting up a young woman who had wandered in from the public bar. I had caught his eye a moment before; I thought he would join us, but a hooded expression fell over his face as he assessed the people I was sitting with. The woman, apparently, was a safer bet.

My father offered to drive us back. It was late. Time had been called, and the few other members of Staff who had ventured to the Feathers from the Big House that evening, including Davey and Nigel, had already made their leave. We—Bucky and I—were waiting in a kind of strained silence in the tiny vestibule opening onto the courtyard for my father to get his coat from his room. I don't know what was flitting through Bucky's brain as he drew pictures with his finger in the condensation formed on the squares of glass in the door, but mine was ruminating on the conversation at my father's table earlier. A conversation, I might add with justifiable pique, in which I played little part, having been cast by the middle-aged and male, into the seen-but-not-heard limbo of children everywhere. Being my father's *adult* child apparently buttered no parsnips.

I realized, however, as I absently brushed some iridescent flecks from the corduroy collar of Bucky's coat (an intimate gesture I immediately regretted for the suggestive grin it produced) it was the *absence* of something in that conversation that was niggling at me. The talk, of course, had strayed toward the murder, the floundering investigation into ARF, the paucity of leads, the seemingly pristine homicide setting, the possibility of drawing the inquiry closer to the deceased relatives and friends and such. I listened politely like a good little girl and thought with some satisfaction, *Ha! I'm a damn sight closer to the truth than you guys!* But now it struck me as odd there had been no discussion of one element I thought would have excited a bit of conversation and speculation even if its connection to the murder was ambivalent.

Feeling a bit 'sans merci,' I waited until my father returned from his room and we were gathered into the Vauxhall.

"So," I announced, twisting around to get a better view of Bucky sprawled across the back seat as one in ungainly sleep, "now that my father—who I may have neglected to mention is a staff sergeant with the Royal Canadian Mounted Police—and I have you in the car, let's talk about the tiara."

Bucky's eyes flew open. I smiled at him. "What?" he muttered, his eyes darting between my pearly whites and the back of my father's head. "What are you talking about?"

"The tiara in your room at the Big House."

"Bird!" my father growled warningly as we pulled out of the parking lot.

"I don't know anything about any tiara."

"There's a rhinestone tiara in a satchel under the bed in your room."

Bucky's tiny mouth opened and closed fishy-fashion but no word emerged.

"A rhinestone tiara was hired for the panto. It's gone missing," I pressed on.

"Then somebody must have stuck it under my bed," he responded at last, having recovered enough sensibility to pout.

"Meanwhile, the dead woman was found with a real tiara on her head. Real diamonds. Worth heaps of pounds."

We left the dim lights of Dersingham behind and sped into the darkness. Bucky became a ghostly presence in the back seat, silent yet radiating a palpable tension.

"I don't know anything about any tiara," he reprised. "Real *or* fake."

I turned back and stared unseeing at the dark wall of trees by the roadside. "When did you notice the switch, I wonder?" I said half to myself. Then I answered myself: "At the Feathers, of course! You were meeting someone there. That's why you wanted to stay behind in the village after the panto. That's why you brought the tiara with you to Dersingham in the first place. That's right, isn't it, Bucky?" I squirmed against the seatbelt and pushed my face around past the headrest, squinting to see in the gloom. "C'mon, Bucky. You pinched that tiara from someone. I think we both know who. And you brought it with you to the panto in your satchel because you were going to meet someone that night. Someone who—"

"—receives stolen goods," my father supplied.

"Look, Bucky, you've been telling me you've got no money of your own. And you want to go back to the States. This is how you were going to finance it. Do you know anything about the provenance of that tiara?"

"The wha . . . ?"

"Its history, the original owner, that sort of stuff."

There was a long silence.

"No." He was sullen.

"Then you admit you stole the tiara, the genuine one?"

"I'm not admitting any damn thing. I don't know the whatsis—provenance—of any tiara. What would I know about tiaras?"

"I'm surprised his lordship hasn't talked to you about all this. He knows about the tiara in your room."

"Oh, yeah? How would he know that? Oh, Jesus, you've told him, haven't you? You little—" He caught himself, no doubt aware of my father's presence. "You just did this to get back at me."

"Dad, could you sort of pull over by the side of the road for a minute?"

Nice to have your father obey your commands. We stopped alongside the stone wall just past the Norwich Gates. A faint illumination from the security lights seeped into the car and cast a sickly light on Bucky's features.

"I did not do this to get back at you," I replied emphatically to his accusation. "There's been a murder on the Estate and the victim was dressed as the Queen and wearing a tiara. I could have told the police what I found in your room, but I thought it would be better to tell your stepfather with the hope that maybe he at least could keep you from getting into trouble."

"And then you bring your father, a Canadian cop, into it?"

"I'm on vacation, son."

"Then what were you doing at the shooting party? And don't call me 'son'! I'm not your son!"

"Calm down, Bucky," I remonstrated. "Nobody's going to haul you off to the scrubs over this. I'm guessing you didn't steal the genuine tiara from the neighbour down the street. It belongs to your stepfather, doesn't it? Lord Thring's not going to shop you for theft."

"You're talking about murder, not stealing! What does this tiara have to do with murder?"

I turned my face away to look at my father. Well, what *did* it have to do with the murder? By now (and with considerable dismay, given Bucky's presence in the car), I believed Lady Thring the perp. in the death of Jackie Scaife. Yet the tiara remained a puzzle. What was Lord Thring doing with an immensely valuable piece of jewellery stolen fifty years ago from the Duchess of Windsor? Did he undergo a shock of recognition when Jackie Scaife arrived on stage with it perched on her head? Did Lady Thring know of its existence, its provenance? Did she recognize it, too? Was it—and this was a wild thought—the blackmail ransom itself, paid in the form of jewels, not cash, worn brazenly by a triumphant blackmailer? Was Bucky *un*involved?

"Probably nothing," I answered Bucky with misgiving while my father switched on the car's interior light. "The tiara has probably nothing to do with the murder. But it is connected with a murder *victim*. And," I added with emphasis, as if this justified the third degree, "it's an unsolved crime in itself."

"Okay, I swiped some jewellery off Affie. Satisfied? But it's not like the crime of the century. He probably wouldn't have missed it, if you hadn't opened your mouth."

"That's not what I mean. The tiara, the genuine article, was itself stolen. From somebody else. Half a century ago. You didn't know?"

His vacant expression told me he didn't. I gave him a brief history of the Duchess of Windsor's wedding tiara and the theft at Ednam Lodge.

"Affie with stolen property, huh?" he said when I had finished. Delight swelled in his voice. "Now isn't that just real interesting."

My father frowned in disgust. "You said 'some jewellery' earlier. Does this mean you've stolen more than a tiara?"

Bucky squirmed. "I've taken one other piece, that's all."

"From where?" I asked. "Didn't your stepfather—or your mother, since she's more likely to wear the stuff—notice missing jewellery?"

But Bucky didn't answer. He stared at me blankly as if deep in thought or daydreaming.

"Bucky?"

His eyes rolled back slightly. Then he blinked and refocused on me. "What?"

"Are you all right?"

"Yes," he said with annoyance. "I'm fine. Um . . ." He blinked again. "They were in a safe," he explained. "Just like in the movies, in a wall safe behind a picture. In the library at Barsham."

"And you have the combination?"

Bucky scowled. "I happened to overhear Affie saying the numbers as he worked the dial one day. I think he was reading from a piece of paper. I was in a big chair turned toward a window. He didn't see me. I tried it later when he left. This was, like, last winter."

"But your stepfather must have noticed pieces missing."

"There's heaps of stuff in that safe. Morys, Affie's dad, was a crazy old coot, collected all kinds of things. You should have seen Barsham Hall before my mother got her hands on it."

"You mean the late Lord Thring, your . . . stepgrandfather, so to speak?"

"So to speak, yeah," he groused.

"So the tiara might have belonged to the *late* Lord Thring, not the present one."

"Well, it might be Affie's stuff. I don't know. Affie might have put it in there himself. But I don't think so. Anyway, as I said, there was a lot of it. So last summer, I took one small piece, a ruby ring. No reaction from the old folks, so I thought I'd try for another. Since Affie was driving up here to Norfolk early the day after Christmas to check on the new kennels he's been building, I decided to join him rather than go later with my mother."

"Tiara's kind of big, isn't it?"

"I just grabbed it first thing. Someone was coming down the hall, so I had to be quick." He shrugged. "I figured, to hell with it, nobody's noticing this stuff missing. I'll make a killing on this one and get back to the States in style."

"You've been selling to someone in the area, though, haven't you? Someone in King's Lynn?" My father had adjusted his rearview mirror to get a better look at the back-seat occupant.

"Maybe. Look, I'm not telling you anything about that. I could get into worse trouble."

"You're in trouble enough."

Bucky pouted and said nothing. My neck was starting to get sore from twisting around, so I snapped off the seatbelt and got up on my knees, digging my chin into the headrest.

"What did he—presuming it's a he—say when you pulled rhinestones out of your satchel?"

Bucky glowered. "He laughed. I was totally pissed off. I couldn't figure it out."

"You lied about going to a club in Lynn that night. You *were* at the Feathers. You've said." Bucky didn't respond. "So did you go back to the village hall by any chance?"

"Yeah, I . . ." He stared up at me. "No, I . . ."

"You *did* go back, didn't you?"

There was no daydream or deep thought in his stare this time. A violent panic registered instead.

"I . . . I didn't go in," he stammered. "I didn't! You see, I thought I saw my . . ."

His eyes widened further. "Oh, God. I've got to get out of here."

Suddenly he was struggling with the latch.

"Saw who?" I shouted as he scrambled out the door. "Saw who?"

But he slammed the rear door with a fierce crunch and began to run up the road to the Jubilee Gates, his coat flapping in the icy wind.

"What brought that on?" my father asked with paternal equanimity when I had sat back properly in my seat.

"I think he saw his mother at the village hall the night of the murder. Who else could it be?" I found myself for the moment unaccountably thrilled and saddened at the notion. It seemed to confirm everything I was thinking.

"What I meant was, what brought on this interrogation?"

"Was I interrogating Bucky?"

"Sounded like it to me."

"Well, then, how was I?"

I caught his smile. "Not bad, Bird. Not bad at all." He pulled the car back onto the road. "Am I to understand you think that boy's mother was involved in this homicide?"

"Yes." And I quickly told him why as he drove me the remaining few hundred yards to the Jubilee Gates in the wake of Bucky's fleeing figure. "And," I finished, "her lady's maid, Caroline Halliwell, says the Marchioness was much later than expected returning to the hotel in Lynn."

"What about the threatening note found in the deceased's pocket, the one from the animal-rights terrorists?"

"Well, okay, my hypothesis doesn't account for everything. But even your friends at the table earlier were doubting terrorist involvement."

"And this tiara business?"

"My reason for interrogating Bucky? I don't know where that fits. Or if it fits at all. But I couldn't help noticing the subject never came up earlier. Is *nobody* interested that a chunk of diamonds and platinum once belonging to the Duchess of Windsor has been found intact after fifty years? Or are the investigators keeping the information to themselves for some reason?"

My father regarded me solemnly as I groped for the door handle. I could see just past his face through the gates to where Bucky, after a brief conversation with PC Nesbitt, was disappearing into the shadows surrounding Sandringham House. I wanted to catch him up and ask him if he wouldn't mind filling in the blank in one of his last utterances.

"You haven't told anyone else what you're thinking, I hope?"

"No."

"Bird, I'm still not happy with you involving yourself in this business."

"Don't worry, Dad."

"Just . . . would you wait a minute!" Cold air rushed against my skin as I prepared to bound from the car. "Just keep your ideas to yourself for the time being. Will you do that for me?"

"Well . . . yeah, okay," I replied reluctantly. There was one person with whom I fully intended to share my idea, but dear old Dad didn't need to know that.

"I mean it, Jane. You can't go around making accusations without being able to back them up. You've got some pretty powerful people in there." He gestured toward the Big House. "I don't want you in trouble. Or in danger."

I always know the old man's serious when he abandons the nickname. Still, I thought as I dashed down the path into the tunnel of looming trees, I supposed he was right. I would have to be careful: I certainly had no *physical* proof to back up my supposition. I reflected, too, in a self-admonishing sort of way, that perhaps I was becoming too pleased with myself over my clever hypothesis. Was I tempting fate and forgetting there would be real consequences for such people as Bucky, Lord Thring, and, I daresay, for Her Majesty? I was not a little worried over the latter's reaction; in fact, as I drew closer to the House, I felt a little fillip of trepidation over what the morrow would bring. I would have to make my case quickly. The Things were leaving Sandringham Sunday, and then they would be gone to America.

Sandringham House, or at least those nooks and crenellations of the south end visible to me as I approached, appeared unusually lifeless. No light shone from any window, though most times, however late the hour, some member of Staff was up pottering about, engaged in one obscure duty or another. Now, only outdoor security beacons casting pools of light around the snow-scattered kitchen courtyard suggested a winter night like all winter nights. I hesitated, wiping my boots unnecessarily along a porcupine-brush bootscraper, staring up at the windows like black eyes in the rosy brickwork. It was at that moment I felt a tiny stab of anxiety. Something was not quite right.

And then, as if on cue, a figure stepped noiselessly from the shadows near one of the entranceways. My heart did a somersault. But it was only one of the policemen on security duty doing a regular round. "Mind how you make your way, miss," he said as he approached. "The mains have gone again."

I should have felt grateful relief but for some reason a sense of unease clung to me as I groped my way along the narrow back corridor guided only by the ghostly rays of intermittent amber security lamps. The House was silent as a tomb but for the occasional creak and sigh of a great old structure settling into another bitter Norfolk winter. No familiar figures flitted by. All the doors were shut tight. Was it something in the air, then, I wondered, sniffing gently as I neared the south entrance of the kitchen? Was the most ancient of senses playing a trick on me? All I thought I could smell were the phantoms of cooking odours from the evening meal, yet something more alien lingered: Visions of pheasants from the morning's kill slipped unbidden into my mind. The wounded dog, too. I should have pooh-poohed such groundless fears but I couldn't. Some presentiment urged me forward, into the kitchen.

That's when I heard it: a soft groan emanating from the other side of the kitchen's north doors, followed by vague scuffling sounds like that of an animal trapped behind a heavy door. At the same time, there was a sudden snap. Lights flashed on along antiseptic countertops, taking the kitchen from near gloom into half-shadow. As quietly as I could, I removed my boots and made my way across the frigid floor on stocking feet, my breath quickening with every step. At the door, which leads to the Gun Room, and beyond, to the Dining Room, I hesitated, feeling a sort of dread spreading from my stomach outward to my limbs. I steeled myself and then, with all my might, pushed through the swinging doors and burst into the room.

Bucky gaped at me, his eyes ablaze. In his arms, like a baby, was cradled something I had often passed my dustcloth over, a shell fired by the Boers, cone-shaped, ominously black, very heavy, mounted on a polished steel stand and refitted—I thought this absurd and kitschy—as a clock. I knew the inscription by heart. It had been fired on the fifty-eighth birthday of HRH the Prince of Wales, 9 November 1899, and later presented to Edward and Alix by a captain of one of the regiments fighting in the Boer War.

But the clock in Bucky's arms held my attention but a moment. For at Bucky's feet was something much more devastating. Or, rather, someone: a figure in a Tattersall check shirt, face down on the green carpet. There was a trickle of blood running from a wound at the back of the head and, I realized, looking at the speechless Bucky again, a smear of blood along the clock face and on Bucky's gloved hands. The figure was discernible. The straw-colored hair and the ruddy skin in quarter profile gave me the clue.

It was Tom Benefer.

OVER THE FIREPLACE at the south end of the Main Drawing Room is a full-length portrait of Queen Alexandra as Princess of Wales, painted toward the end of the nineteenth century. Her slender willowy figure is sheathed in a ballgown of ivory lace, olive-green and antique-gold, sombre colours mirrored in the autumnal hues of the pastoral setting in which she is posing. Her face, a perfect oval, appears as fragile as porcelain. Said to be a woman of great charm, greeting visitors with a radiant smile, Edward VII's consort gazes from the portrait down the length of the Drawing Room to a looking glass above a second fireplace with eyes that suggest not gladsomeness but traces of sadness, anguish, yearning kept in dignified check. I used to wonder at the mood until I was told the miniature the Queen holds in her right hand is of her eldest son, Albert Victor, later Duke of Clarence, who died at age twenty-eight, only a few years before the painting of Alix was completed.

Another mother with an unprepossessing son, I reflected, staring up at the portrait as I sat waiting sorrowfully in a damask-covered Louis XV armchair next to the—cold, of course!—fireplace. Prince Albert Victor—Eddy, as he was known—died at Sandringham, of influenza, it was reported. But gossipy types among Staff versed in Royal minutiae say syphilis carried off the prince who, had he lived, would have succeeded his father, Edward VII, as king. Eddy was thick as two short planks, lazy as an anvil, but with sufficient reserves of energy to excel at his favorite pastime—sex. Some even claim him Jack the Ripper. Frankly, despite Eddy's being royal and all, I don't really think he was the sort of guy you'd want to bring home to meet your parents. Still, his mother was devoted to him as only mothers can be: She left his room at Sandringham untouched for years after his death.

I was really sitting thinking all this in part to distract myself from the horror and confusion of the Gun Room. Even as I sat in the Main Drawing Room, I could hear the murmur of voices, mostly male, on the other side of the double doors, a continuation of the (barely) controlled anxiety that had overtaken the security staff in the face of this terrible breach. Someone had been murdered, not just on the Sandringham Estate, but in Sandringham House itself, only a few hundred feet down the stairs and up the main corridor from the Queen's bedroom replete with resident Queen.

I had sounded the alarm or, rather, I had gone to fetch the nearest officer, the one who had startled me in the courtyard earlier, and he had brought the full force of the security staff to bear on the situation. In seeking help, I had left Bucky unattended. "I . . . he . . ." he had gibbered, ashen, gripping the Boer clock like a madman when I came upon him in the Gun Room. After he was able to find his voice, he said he had navigated his way through the kitchen because he, too, had heard a distant groan and in the dark of the Gun Room had bumped up against something solid yet squishily pliable. When the lights snapped on, he saw with terror he had stepped on the body of Tom Benefer. The groan I had heard was of Bucky lifting the heavy clock. It had been used to crush Benefer's skull. The groan Bucky had heard had been Benefer's last for we both seemed to know without even thinking that he was dead. There was ice in the air, something metallic in the odour, the awful sight of blood on the carpet. I could feel my stomach start to heave as Bucky jabbered on breathlessly. "I didn't do it!" he kept sobbing.

I didn't know what to believe.

What I couldn't believe, though, was the *fact* of Tom Benefer's death. I could make no sense of it. Was it utterly unconnected to Jackie Scaife's death? But how could it be? They were brother- and sister-in-law. They were once, briefly, lovers. (And lovers again recently?) Their deaths were within a few days of each other. And yet, if their deaths were connected, it completely violated my hard-thought-out assumption that Pamela, Marchioness of Thring, was the figure at the heart of the first murder. I felt as though someone had taken the nearly completed jigsaw puzzle in the Saloon and thrown all the pieces into the air. Leaning helplessly against a wall in the Gun Room after I had returned with the officer and the place began to fill with large men of the uniformed and plainclothes variety, I could only mutter to myself, 'It doesn't make sense.' I must have looked stunned as an oyster for before very long the Queen herself opened the door to the Main Drawing Room and half-pushed me through. 'Go and sit down,' she commanded in a low voice. 'You've had a shock.'

Sandringham may appear a sizable country house but it's not so big a commotion in one of the central rooms in the wee hours of the morning doesn't eventually awaken its slumbering occupants and send them struggling downstairs to see what the bother's all about. There was a certain jostling of Royals and commoners in assorted sleepwear rubbernecking in the passageway on either side of the Gun Room, obliging a kind of crowd control on the part of security. Finally, the Queen herself had descended, wearing a comfy tartan housecoat,

effecting a kind of parting of the way and a certain edgi-
ness among the luckless security staff who, had this
been a Tudor reign, would surely have feared for their
heads. HM looked as grave as her own good self laying a
wreath at the Cenotaph on Remembrance Sunday. She
circulated among Staff and Family speaking in hushed
tones before wending my way and steering me into the
Main Drawing Room, closing the door behind me.

A table lamp either side of the fireplace was
switched on, creating a sanctuary of warm golden light
among the shadows of the long room. A slight odour of
pine pervaded, a reminder of the Christmas tree at the
other end, its jagged shape limned by a trickle of light
that seeped over the many chairs, tables, and curio cabinets to the far corners. How pointless Christmas trees
are after the big day, I thought in my misery; how lifeless they appear in the dark. But, try as I might, these
thoughts proved no distraction. Like filings to a magnet,
my mind rushed again and again to the murders.

No outsider committed this crime, I was sure. No
member of ARF could have slipped into the House in
the wake of a heightened security alert, however easy it
had been to slink across the lower reaches of the Estate
and trash Her Majesty's lodge at Flitcham. Yes, I know
there had been security breaches publicized and unpub-
licized in the past, but a security breach this time? And
to target—of all people—Tom Benefer? Not likely.

An air of desperation, of frenzy even, clung to this
second death. Tom Benefer was a gamekeeper, after all;
a man of the open air who spent much of his time outdoors. If one were intent on killing such a man, how
much easier and safer it would be to kill him in his
milieu, when he would be alone in some corner of the
Estate, masked by trees, concentrated on his conser-
vancy work. But to commit such a heinous crime in the
Gun Room, virtually the heart of Sandringham House,
while the Royal Family was in residence and in blissful
sleep, was grippingly brazen. There was a crudeness
about the act, too. Jackie Scaife's body had been moved
after she was murdered in the village hall, laid out in
decorous fashion. But the murder in the Gun Room sug-

gested haste, impulse, surprise. The means were similar. Blunt instruments in each case. But that clock! You couldn't get a blunter instrument.

I shivered. Still, I thought, despite the disparities in style—ludicrous application of the word, but there you go—these murders had to be connected. Yes, I was sure of it. I was on the point of rising, to rejoin the fracas, go to my room, whatever, when the door began to open. I expected to be questioned by the authorities but was hoping they might wait until the next day or, rather, until the later hours of this particular morning after I had had a chance to sleep. I felt bone-weary—the shock, I suppose, as HM suggested. It had been, to say the least, an eventful day. But the foot that eased its way through the opening crack was not shod in a size 14 black Oxford but, rather, a pair of navy slippers. It was the Queen. I rose quickly and curtseyed. I realized I was still wearing my jacket and holding onto my boots.

"Your Majesty," I said.

The Queen shut the door behind her with a quiet click. She looked unseeingly about the room, tapping one finger against her chin. At last her eyes alit on my humble presence, she broke whatever royal reverie she had been in, and bade me sit down, settling herself into a sofa chair the other side of the fireplace. The lamplight softened the lines around her eyes and mouth as her face settled into its familiar composure. I would have thought her unruffled by the turn of events but for her eyes. The blue of them, so startling bright and crystalline on first close encounter, had hardened to stone. She was, I knew, very, very angry.

"What doesn't make sense, Jane?" she asked without preliminaries. "I'm sure I overheard you muttering in the hall that something didn't make sense. Of course, this death doesn't make sense. Most cruel," she added with some vehemence, "but I think you were on to something else."

"Ma'am, I'm sure Mr. Benefer's death is linked to Jackie Scaife's somehow but I just can't make sense of it. I'd already come to a conclusion about the Scaife murder. I was *so* sure! But then this . . ." I shrugged helplessly.

"What had you concluded?"

I must have blanched. I had half dreaded this moment, telling HM that I posited the wife of her friend and Norfolk neighbour, a guest in her own home Christmas week, had killed a woman. Now, in the face of this latest offense, my confidence in my brilliant theory seemed to ebb like the tide in the Bay of Fundy.

Meanwhile Her Majesty's eyebrows were doing an impatient little dance around her forehead. "Jane . . . ?"

"Well, Ma'am, um . . ." I sputtered sputteringly. Finally, I gulped and spit it out, if one can do such things in rough sequence. I told her that I believed Jackie Scaife had been an au pair for Lady Thring, or Pamela Walsh as she was then, in America in the middle 1970s; that Bucky had been physically abused in such a way that triggered epileptic seizures, which continued to this day; and that the abuser had not been the au pair, as I first surmised, but the very mother of the child herself. I said I thought Jackie had been blackmailing the Marchioness with this knowledge, knowledge that would damage both the relationship between mother and son and Lady Thring's position in Society. How the Marchioness had responded to this blackmail at first I couldn't say, but I told HM I thought Jackie's murder had probably not been premeditated. I mentioned the altered verse in the performance of the *Queen of Hearts.* Surely a provocation, I said, perhaps a desperate one by a woman whose more conventional blackmail strategy was failing to get a response?

"The fragment of paper with the numbers on them, you mean. You believe Lady Thring was receiving blackmail letters."

"Yes, Ma'am. I thought the numbers might refer to a date after all. Perhaps Jackie remembered exactly when Bucky—Mr. Walsh was hit or pushed or whatever. Or when the first seizure occurred."

"She would have to have had a very good memory."

"When Your Majesty mentioned this morning that the 6 and the 2 in 627 coincided with your Accession Day, 6 February, I wondered if Jackie mightn't have remembered the incident because it did coincide with a public event. My parents and their friends, for instance, all know exactly where they were and what they were doing when President Kennedy was shot," I added, reflecting that if I heard another Boomer's reminiscence on this subject I was going to scream.

"But anniversaries of my Accession Day would most certainly go unmarked in America," the Queen pointed out. "And there is the problem of the *S* and the *T*."

"Well, it was just a thought . . ."

"Although . . ." Her Majesty had that sort of light-bulb-over-the-royal-head look. "I receive a number of letters from America, and I have noticed they do tend to date their correspondence with the month first, the day second, then the year, rather than the day first, then month and year in ascending order the way we do. Ours makes more sense, I think."

Of course, I had thought of this already. "That would be June 2."

"Curiously, the date of my Coronation—June 2, 1953."

"Ooh!" It was my turn for the light bulb. Something from my grandmother's collection of Royalty books came to mind. "Your Majesty's Silver Jubilee in . . . um . . ." I'm a dud without a calculator.

"Nineteen seventy-seven."

"Yes! That would be about right," I said excitedly. "Bucky would have been around two years old, I think. Jackie would remember the date, June 2, 1977, because of the celebrations for your Jubilee Year. There would be items on television in the States. Jackie was an Englishwoman. She grew up on the Sandringham Estate. So the public event—the Jubilee celebrations—and the private act—the abuse of Bucky . . . Mr. Walsh—would remain linked in her mind."

The Queen frowned. "I think you're stretching the bounds of coincidence, Jane. Besides, the Jubilee

Year commemorated twenty-five years from Accession, not Coronation. The highlight of that year, 1977, which the Americans might have taken notice of, took place on June 7, not June 2. I drove to St. Paul's for a Thanksgiving service in the State Coach."

"Oh." My light bulb dimmed.

"Not that I'm dismissing your argument." Her hand sought her neck unconsciously. But her trademark three strands of pearls were absent as, of course, they would be if you were rudely awakened from your slumber. "But that fragment of paper seems inconclusive. Those numbers might as easily indicate a train schedule or . . . let me see, a street address, or . . . a hymn in a hymnal . . . a sequence of numbers for the National Lottery . . ."

"But, Ma'am," I pleaded. I had invested a lot of thought in this hypothesis and was feeling rather let down. "The numbers and letters were cut-out bits from magazines. That suggests blackmail to me."

"Yes, there is that," she agreed. "But it's not much to go on, is it?"

"Her ladyship returned to the Duke's Head in King's Lynn after the pantomime much later than expected. At least according to Caroline Halliwell."

"Yes, well, none of this is conclusive proof, is it?" HM demurred. "And then there is this appalling incident tonight which you yourself point out would seem unconnected."

"Mr. Benefer may have seen or heard something that put him in danger, Ma'am. He told me he wasn't at the village hall Boxing Day evening for the panto—he wanted to get to bed early for the next morning's shoot—but he may not have been telling the truth."

Her Majesty looked unconvinced. "That clock presented to my great-grandfather looks extremely heavy to me. Could a woman lift it?"

"I've read that people can do really incredible things under duress," I replied hopefully. Well, it was true! But it was also true the clock was bloody heavy. The last time I dusted the top of the ledge on which it sat, I had to really put my shoulder to it to budge it.

"Men have that upper-body strength thing of theirs that makes them occasionally useful," I continued, "but a woman frightened or angry can be just as strong." I reflected on the Slap and flexed a mental bicep.

The Queen smiled a little smile. "You are determined, aren't you, to fault my houseguest."

I grimaced and pulled my head below the hood of my jacket like a turtle. I cast about for a new hypothesis.

"Ma'am, I believe the tiara that was stolen from the Duchess of Windsor, the one Jackie Scaife wore at the panto, belongs to Lord Thring," I said promptingly for another idea had come on deck.

"Yes, I know." The Queen sighed.

I must have looked startled for she amended her statement: "I should say, rather, I'm not at all surprised. The possibility had suggested itself after my sister surprised me with the tiara on Wednesday morning. When you told me this morning—or yesterday morning . . ." She glanced over the top of her glasses at the gilt clock on the mantelpiece. "When you told me Buchanan was in possession of a paste tiara and that there must have been an exchange, I could only come to the conclusion that the young man had taken the genuine tiara from his stepfather. I'm sure, Jane, you must've arrived at the same conclusion."

"Yes, Ma'am, I did. Well, I did *finally*. But . . ." How to put this: Why the circumspection about the tiara in the first place? Why the constrained atmosphere? Why oblige *me* to tell Lord Thring of the booty under his stepson's bed?

The Queen pursed her lips, emphasizing the little frown lines. She was staring at me, though it was more like looking through me. I think she was trying to make up her mind about something. She was. Finally, she said: "As you probably know, Jane, Affie—Lord Thring—is quite an old friend of mine. We've known each other for, oh . . . many, many years—more years than I care to remember, really. He grew up virtually next door. In the early years of the War, before he joined the Navy, he'd visit when my sister and I were staying at Windsor. I recall we even got him to perform in one of our Christmas pantomimes." A smile crept along the fine lines at the corners of her mouth. "He was an ugly stepsister in *Cinderella*."

"Were you actually *in* the panto yourself, Ma'am?" I was intrigued.

"Mm, yes. I was Prince Charming. Margaret got to be Cinderella." The smile widened, lighting up her face. "Affie was very amusing—you wouldn't think it. My father just roared." HM blinked, momentarily perplexed. "What was I saying? Oh, yes, Affie: how long we've known each other. Well, he was an equerry to me for a time in the late 1950s, before his first marriage. He travelled with my husband and me to India during our tour in 1961, and so on. And, of course, we share a number of sporting interests." She paused, a certain cheerlessness pulling at her features. "Yes, it *has* been a long time."

Her Majesty sighed and continued:

"Lord Thring's—or Chudleigh as he was then—appointment as equerry was met with a certain unhappiness in some quarters. But, as I said at the time to certain of my advisors, the gods may visit the sins of the fathers upon the children, but *I'm* not about to.

"You see, father and son didn't get along awfully well. Morys—Affie's father—was rather pro-German before the War, publicly so. He was part of a set of sympathizers who thought Hitler was"—Her Majesty frowned deeply—"a fine fellow on the whole. This set sometimes gathered at Thring House in London and occasionally, I think, at Barsham Hall. The German Ambassador may have joined them at times. I don't quite remember the details. At any rate they were all for appeasing Hitler, though by the time the War began, most of them had changed their views. Not Morys, however. He remained unrepentant.

"He was a terrible man, really. Brutal to his wife—Affie's mother—too, I'm told. I remember her as a wonderfully gentle woman, a devout Roman Catholic, always doing good works for the tenants on the Barsham Estate or for people in the nearby villages. She died

before the War started. Poor Affie. And then his father
behaving so badly . . ."

Her Majesty shook her head in silent disapproval.

"Finally Affie felt obliged to publish a piece in *The
Times* to make his own views known, to separate himself
from his father. I'm afraid the public rebuke completely
severed whatever was left of their relationship. I don't
think the two of them have spoken more than a few
words to each other over all these years. And Morys
lived a jolly long life.

"But Lord Thring and I never discuss these matters. He finds it all too painful, I'm sure. Indeed, the
topic of his father's embarrassing sympathies and in-
trigues has never arisen, but for a little flurry of public
interest when he was appointed equerry. It's all in the
past." HM frowned. "Or that's what I would have
thought."

The Queen paused, and glanced at me in an assessing sort of way. Then she sighed. "As it happens,
Morys was friendly with my uncle David—King Edward
VIII, as you know. And my uncle also mingled with
some of the people in Morys's set, which, in retrospect,
was probably not very, well . . ."

She didn't finish the sentence. Or couldn't. But I
was able to draw my own conclusion: Edward had probably not been very wise in these friendships. Davey had
once told me some historians thought the Duke of
Windsor had taken a cheerier view of National Socialism
than he ought to have.

"Anyway," HM continued after a moment, "I do
believe Morys attended my uncle's wedding to Mrs.
Simpson in France in 1937. I think Lady Thring had
died by that time. All this, too, is in the past. I'm not
sure the sort of relationship Morys maintained with my
uncle and his wife over the years, and I'm not certain
Affie would know, either. Again, it's the sort of subject
that doesn't arise in conversation."

As Her Majesty talked, something began to stir in
my brain. If Lord Thring had been deeply estranged
from his father, a father who in the past had been a
disgrace to King & Country, to what lengths might he go

to keep that past well buried? Might he have realized, at the panto, that the sparkling tiara Jackie Scaife was wearing on her head was none other than the one he thought was hidden in a safe at Barsham Hall, which he had inherited from his father? One that he had already somehow identified as having once belonged to the Duchess of Windsor and acquired through theft, another source of disgrace? Might he have returned to Dersingham Village Hall that evening at some propitious time to retrieve the diabolical thing and . . . ?

It was too shocking.

"So you see," the Queen was saying, "when this tiara reappeared nearly fifty years after it had been presumed taken apart and sold off, I began to worry a little about Lord Thring. And after you found the paste version in his stepson's room, well . . ."

"I did tell Lord Thring about both tiaras as you suggested, Ma'am. He was . . . a bit put out with me."

"You see, I was rather hoping he would come and tell me about all this. How did he come to have the Duchess's wedding tiara? Affie would have concerns about his good name, his family's reputation given the unpleasantness before the War, but he would also be concerned about one and one's family. However, he's not brought the subject up. And I'm very worried he may have done something . . . foolish."

Understatement of the season. "Oh, surely not, Ma'am," I said sympathetically but, as I said it, I suddenly remembered Hume Pryce saying he was sure he heard someone trying to open the doors of the village hall when he went back Boxing Day night. Might it have been Lord Thring? And would Lord Thring's presence explain the manifestations of that spectral dog?

"And besides," I continued, refraining from voicing these thoughts to Her Majesty, "there's still Tom Benefer's death to account for."

But even as I said this, other factors flickered in my mind like fairy lights on a Christmas tree. Benefer and the priest at the village hall the day we found Jackie's body, for instance. The black dog had been playing with the priest. Lord Thring's dog. Then

Benefer and the priest—again—at yesterday's shooting party. Had Benefer put two and two together? Had Lord Thring seen the gamekeeper calculating and read suspicion in his face? Lord Thring was not a young man. But he was a big man, a man who liked the outdoors. He was elderly but he was not soft. He could have picked up that heavy clock and . . .

My mind was buzzing. Even the tiara thing, I thought, could be beside the point. Lord Thring may simply have been being perversely chivalrous. He might not have recognized the tiara at all. He may simply have sought to meet his wife's blackmailer and, well, things went fatally awry.

I must have *looked* like my mind was buzzing, all wide-eyed and openmouthed, for the Queen was scrutinizing my face with concern. She was twisting her wedding ring, a sign that she was either angry or deeply stressed. The latter I thought. Hoped.

"They say most murders occur in the home, Ma'am," I said tentatively.

"Well, this is *my* home!"

"I mean, among family members."

"Yes, of course." HM's brow darkened. "One can't help being aware that the victims are both the sister and the husband of my Housekeeper."

It was an unhappy awareness, indeed. Could it be true? Was it this simple after all? A mere domestic situation that had spiralled out of control, fuelled by jealousy and recrimination? Hume had said the sisters were arguing when he'd left the village hall. Could old Aileen, repressed and pious, have finally burst a vessel and hit her sister, perhaps without meaning to, thus sending herself over the edge mentally? Jackie's enfoldment into the Benefer household had been regarded with amusement by others on the Estate in the know, but the characters in the drama—one of them, anyway—must have had to swallow a certain amount of pride in the name of charity. Finally, it might all have been too much: the reminder of past infidelity, the suggestion of infidelity resumed, the taunting of animal-rights extremists, lampooning Her Majesty in a public performance. Had Aileen and Tom subsequently argued?

"That clock is *very* heavy," the Queen reiterated, as if she had been following my train of thought.

"Hell hath no fury, Ma'am." I thought even as I said it that it was sort of a sexist thing for Shakespeare to say.

The Queen regarded me curiously. "Like a woman scorned? *Has* Mrs. Benefer been scorned?"

"Well, not exactly scorned, I guess, Ma'am, but . . ." Did HM not know? She was not immune to the enticements of gossip, it was often said; indeed, it was also said there was little scuttlebutt among Household and Staff that didn't eventually reach the royal ears. Davey even claimed to collect bits just to amuse Her Majesty when he came a'corgi-collecting. But, of course, not every piece of idle talk would necessarily find a permanent home in one of HM's little grey cells. She only spent six weeks a year at her Norfolk home. And perhaps people would have thought the scandal before the Benefer nuptials too dark and unhappy for Her Majesty to hear. Or too salacious. At least in those days of yore, the 'seventies. Of course, these days, we were all living in the wake of the Prince of Wales's blatherings on the goggle box about his irretrievably broken-down marriage and general Seventh Commandment–breaking, so what *wasn't* taboo?

"Not exactly scorned as betrayed," I explained to the Queen. "Tom more or less betrayed his wife-to-be before they were wed."

And I told HM the whole story as it had been told to me.

"I see," she said solemnly when I had done. "The past certainly has the power to intrude on the present in terrible ways. It's very sad."

"But, Ma'am, the thing is: Mrs. Benefer thinks it's all started up again. She was raving a bit yesterday, I'm afraid. I found her in the Linen Room and she seemed to be having some kind of breakdown. Anyway, she was insistent that her husband and her sister had gone off

together to Manchester—of all places. She said she had
found a ticket stub in his jacket. Or her jacket. Or some
body's jacket. It seemed to be proof enough for her that
they had gone off to have a . . . a . . ."

"Tryst?" Her Majesty supplied, a glint of amusement in her eyes. "In Manchester?"

"Well, Tom Benefer grew up on the Whitewell estate so . . ." I suppressed a yawn. It did seem awfully
late.

"I was in Manchester earlier this month. I can't
say I would choose Manchester if I was . . . well, anyway . . ." HM cleared her throat and reached down for
her handbag. Only there was no handbag, of course. "I
think it's time we—"

But I interrupted. I had a glimmering. "Manchester? Your Majesty was in Manchester?" The
wretched song was starting to bubble in my brain again.
'Oh, Manchester, England, England/Across the Atlantic
Sea/And I'm a . . ."

"Yes. It was a bit of a peace mission, actually. Apparently I said something unflattering about Manchester
to a student when I was visiting Russia earlier this year.
'Not such a nice place' I *allegedly* said. I really don't
remember, but the damage was done so, anyway, it was
off to Manchester to make amends. My husband and I
had a very busy day there. Marked an anniversary of the
Co-op movement, opened a bridge, a new barracks, a
new sixth form house at a school of music . . ."

The ceilings in the Main Drawing Room of Sandringham House are notable for their trompe l'oeil
paintings of the sky. It is a summer sky, not a winter
sky: a soft robin's-egg blue with fluffy clouds of pink
shot through with gold. It is not a Norfolk sky; it's
barely even an English sky. It is a celestial sky, a
heaven from which might descend angels to commune
with us more material beings. I looked up at the ceil-
ing-sky, resplendent even in the pale light of the table
lamps. O hark the herald angels sing! And they're sing-
ing to me.

"But, Ma'am," I said excitedly, my heart racing

with the sudden and new realization. "If Your Majesty was in Manchester that means . . . !"

But, oh! How dreadful it was. It was someone close to the Queen after all. I was sure. Or at least as sure as I could be.

20

NEW YEAR'S EVE for the Royals and guests had been planned for Her Majesty's timber lodge at the top of Flitcham Hill. This was wonderfully convenient because it allowed the Queen to neatly arrange for two separate parties to be Land Rover'd over to Flitcham after dinner at the Big House, the smaller of the two parties, however, to tarry in the Saloon for a time at Her Majesty's request. This meant a virtual exodus before ten o'clock of most of the members of the Royal Family and a few of the members of Staff selected to serve midnight nibblies and open the vintage Krug. I expect the bunch of them felt more than happy to greet the new year in surroundings as humble as those at Flitcham, for Tom Benefer's death had brought to Sandringham House not only a pall but a nasty case of creeping anxiety. Security had been topped up yet

again, but the chief beneficiaries of the revamped polic-
ing were members of the Royal Family who nevertheless, I was told, felt less than comfortable in the charged
atmosphere. Staff members had no personal protection
officers or corridor officers for their safety so furtive hud-
dlings and paired duties were the order of the day while
the notion lingered unvoiced that one of us, familiar as
we were to each other, had to be some kind of a homicidal maniac. Of course, speculation ran to the murder
earlier in the week at Dersingham; the familial connection between the victims did not go unremarked and the
tide of pity for Aileen Benefer began to ebb through the
day as she grew into an object of conjecture. It didn't
help that she remained unseen and unheard. Under police guard, said one. A suicide watch, said another. I
knew differently, but said nothing.

My thoughts were elsewhere, to another among
the guests and Staff at Sandringham House, and to a
certain nonhousemaiding task I needed to complete before the sun set that New Year's Eve day. I was at once
less affected by the general apprehension and more concerned for my own predicament. It had occurred to me
during my wee-hours audience with HM that I myself
might have been in danger over the last day or so, might
be yet. The Queen, herself, cautioned me to beware as I
departed the Main Drawing Room, Docs in hand, only
to find myself ushered to the police presence where I
reiterated for the record my experience of the murder in
the Gun Room. I didn't speculate on the identity of the
killer with the police, but then I wasn't *asked* to speculate. If I had been asked, I wouldn't have been able to
say because I was lacking sufficient evidence. Such was
Her Majesty's concern as well.

In the Main Drawing Room, as the clock on the
chimneypiece struck two A.M., I had quickly, and with
not a little disquiet, outlined for the Queen the new
revelation, such as it had come to me from on high,
metaphorically speaking. She received these views and
others that came to me all of a rush stony-faced, her lips
pinched. There was a long silence in which she pushed
her wedding rings around her finger with greater and

greater speed until they were practically whizzing. Finally she stopped, removed her glasses, and cautiously rubbed at lower lids grown puffy for want of sleep.

"I expect you're thinking, too, of the incident at the shoot," she said with some reluctance. "I thought something was wrong. And their behaviour was indeed strange. And yet . . ." Her Majesty yawned suddenly, her blue eyes watering with the effort. "Well, let's see what you and your father learn tomorrow—or this afternoon, rather—in King's Lynn, Jane," she added, putting a hand to her mouth to suppress a further yawn and glancing toward the clock. "I'll make that telephone call after luncheon. That should establish an alibi at least, or the lack of one. We simply can't do with mere conjecture."

The air in the Saloon was chill when I stepped into the room that evening. I was wearing a short black dress—unhappily, not a smart cocktail frock for a New Year's party—but a variant of the housemaid's uniform, the style worn by those senior housemaids chosen to personally serve Her Majesty's lady guests with breakfast in bed during their stays at Sandringham. The black uniform has puffy sleeves and a hemline higher than our regulation white attire, and even without a frilly lace cap I couldn't help but feel a little like a maid in a French farce. A borrowed item, the uniform was a bit on the tight side so that the volumes of cold air released into the two-storey-high room by the members of the Royal Family departing for Flitcham through the entrance porch seemed to whip through the thin fabric in a way not even the cheery log fire blazing in the hearth could allay. But, perhaps, too, I was feeling chilled in a more fundamental psychological sense. My afternoon in King's Lynn had been both refutation and confirmation, turning my theory once more upside down.

In my hands was a silver tray. I was doing footman's duty. It was the excuse for my presence, the real footmen either serving at Flitcham or at the Staff New Year's Party in Servant's Hall. Though I had wielded

many a tray in my waitressing days at Marilla's Pizza
back on the Island, and tangled with many an exacting
customer, I had never served postprandial imbibements
in quite such fraught circumstances, or to such highborn
clientele. I hesitated at the door after stepping into the
room from the corridor. I could see Princess Margaret
reclining on a couch turned at an oblique angle toward
the fireplace, part of a woolly green and blue tartan rug
covering her from foot to neck littered with slips of paper that she was examining intently in turn. Propped up
against a cluster of Queen Mary's embroidered pillows,
Her Royal Highness looked a little like an invalid,
which she was, in a way. Her chill had been keeping her
in her room where she had been taking all her meals,
but at Her Majesty's insistence she'd managed to strug-
gle down to the Saloon.

On a couch opposite with an orange poppy floral
pattern, the backs of their heads to me, one grey-haired
and thinning, one blond and sleek, Lord and Lady
Thring sat in muted conversation while next to them,
slumped in a chair of his own, was young Buchanan, the
fingers of his left hand drumming the plump upholstery
of the arm. There was no one else, not even a corgi; but
for the Thrings' murmuring and the crackle of the fire,
silence lay upon the room like a soft blanket. Table
lamps glowed softly against nascent shadows in the high
moulded ceiling overhead, casting pools of light over the
oak wainscotting, the seventeenth-century Brussels wall
tapestries, the blizzard of Christmas cards, and sprays of
the Queen's favorite chrysanthemums. It was, in its way,
an indelibly cozy scene, the wind and rain battering the
window, while inside all was golden and tranquil.

Or so it seemed. There'd be tears before bedtime,
I knew. At the very least.

Princess Margaret turned her head from the fireplace and caught my eye, light glancing off a pair of
round tortoise-shell glasses. Her look of inquiry caught
the Thrings' attention, aborting their conversation. Lady
Thring glanced over her shoulder, skewering me with
her great brown eyes. I shivered and stepped forward
with the tray, offering first Her Royal Highness the glass

of hot water with fresh lemon and honey she had requested, then the others coffee and brandy in order of gender and rank. Lady Thring continued to stare at me as I dipped the tray, Lord Thring retaining a patrician poker face while Bucky eyeballed my legs greedily and everything above my neck sourly. One glass remained on the tray. I stepped away from Bucky's glance and hovered by a small pie-crust table, unsure quite what to do.

A moment passed. The clock on the mantel whirred and clicked then politely tinkled the time: ten o'clock. As the last note echoed, outside the room could be heard a skittering of nails along hardwood and a muffled yelp. Hark! the herald corgis bark, I thought, as the golden furballs trotted through the central arch into the Saloon white snouts gleaming, little pink tongues hanging like sausages in a butcher's window. The Queen followed immediately behind wearing a sky-blue dress shimmering with pale silvery blue dots, her trademark three strands of pearls, a large sapphire brooch set in diamonds, and an expression on her face of complete calm. Everyone but Margo rose to his or her feet and made the minimal acts of deference, small neck bows from the men, a perfunctory curtsey from Lady Thring. The Queen took a crystal glass of Malvern water from my tray as I bobbed, caught my eye with a meaningful glance, and moved purposefully toward the fireplace.

"Any luck, Margo?" Her Majesty asked, lifting the glass to her lips.

"None, I'm afraid," HRH replied in a croaking voice, plucking another National Lottery ticket limpidly from her lap and examining it against a piece of paper sufficiently translucent to allow me to see six numbers scrawled on the front. The draw had been live on BBC1 earlier in the evening. I expected she'd got a member of Staff to jot down the winning six numbers.

"No, wait, I believe this one's got three correct numbers! Three's something, isn't it?" She looked expectantly over her glasses at her sister, then at the Thrings.

"Ten pounds, I think," the Queen replied, seeking the Thrings' confirmation, then mine when they proved uninformed about such matters.

"Yes, Ma'am, that's right—ten pounds."

"Oh," Margo said disappointedly, dabbing at her nose with a lacy handkerchief.

"Do sit down, everybody," the Queen said. "You, too, Jane," she added, gesturing toward a Regency chair beside the couch on which HRH was lying.

"I'm sorry to ask you to stay behind," the Queen added, sitting herself down on a wing chair near the fire while the corgis stood vigil near her feet. "I hope you don't mind, but I have something rather urgent I would like to discuss." She sipped thoughtfully at her water, glanced at Margo who was gathering her lottery tickets together like a scattered deck of cards, and frowned slightly. She continued:

"The topic was tactfully avoided at dinner but, of course, as you know, there was a dreadful incident here last night. Or in the early hours this morning, rather. It's very, very disagreeable to have someone murdered in one's own home, although"—HM glanced at me—"it's not the first occurrence, nor the first time one has involved oneself."

"But surely, Ma'am, the murder of one of your gamekeepers is a police concern," Lord Thring boomed. Rather too heartily, I thought.

"Yes . . . well . . ." the Queen demurred. "In their zeal to protect me from a perceived terrorist threat, the police have, unfortunately, tended to overlook one or two items—items closer to home, so to speak. It's true I wouldn't normally intrude but I was rather brought into it, you see. Earlier in the week.

"Margo? Would you care to explain?"

"Lilibet, I'm really not *feeling* awfully well."

"My sister," the Queen sighed, turning to the Thrings, "removed a certain piece of evidence, or potential evidence, from the scene of the crime Tuesday morning at the village hall at Dersingham."

"I've said I didn't know she'd been murdered!"

"I know. I'm not blaming you, Margo. You thought the woman's costuming was . . . demeaning to one."

Lady Thring, who had planted the seed of this panto, shifted uncomfortably and wiped at some imaginary speck on the cappuccino-colored crepe Bruce Oldfieldy-looking frock she wore.

"At any rate," HM continued, "the thing removed was a piece of jewellery, and I'm sure it's no surprise to most people in the room now, that that piece of jewellery was a tiara, and not any old tiara either. Certainly not a paste tiara. But a very valuable set of genuine stones."

Seated across from me, Bucky slumped in his seat and glared malevolently at me. Lord Thring's eyes, too, flicked in my direction. Only Lady Thring appeared detached.

"The question," the Queen continued, tweaking a corgi with her foot, "was what a woman of ordinary means was doing with such extraordinary jewels. The assessed value of the stones alone would be hundreds of thousands of pounds, but the tiara also has a unique provenance: It once belonged to the Duchess of Windsor."

"My goodness! Really?" Lady Thring exclaimed, reaching for her brandy.

The Queen regarded her curiously.

"I   I didn't know, Ma'am," Lady Thring said in startled tones, her free hand fluttering to a set of diamonds at her throat, "Should I have?" Bucky, too, regarded his mother curiously. He shot up in his seat. "Buchanan? What is it, darling? What *is* going on?" Pamela raised a nervous hand to stroke her hair. "It's like you all have a secret."

The Queen shifted her scrutiny to Lord Thring. "Affie?" she said, her expression inviting him to explain.

"Oh, my dear," Lord Thring said with a deep sigh, taking his wife's hand after she returned the brandy to the small table in front of them, "I was hoping to spare you this . . ."

"Affie, you're frightening me now. What is it?"

"The tiara Her Majesty is referring to belongs . . . to me—"

"Oh . . . ?"

"—and I'm very sorry to say it's stolen property."

"I beg your pardon?"

"The tiara was stolen from Wallis soon after the war, Pamela," the Queen explained. "She and my uncle David paid a visit to England and stayed with friends at Ednam Lodge, near Windsor. When they were in London one evening, Ednam Lodge was burglarized and the Duchess's jewel case was taken. Quite a number of pieces of valuable jewellery were lost, including the tiara that my uncle had had Cartier make for their wedding."

"But . . . ?" Lady Thring gestured helplessly.

"You mean you don't know about this tiara, Mother?" Bucky interjected.

"No."

"But . . . I saw . . . I mean . . ." Bucky's face fought to master surprise.

"And do *you* know about it?" the Marchioness asked her son.

Lord Thring cleared his throat. "I'm afraid he took the tiara from the safe in the library at Barsham, Pammy."

"Now why would you do that, Bucky, honey?"

"For money," Lord Thring replied while Bucky's expression hardened to a scowl. "He has, I believe, taken at least one other item from the safe and sold it."

"Bucky, honey. Tell me this isn't true."

"If you tell me it's true you don't know anything about this tiara."

"Well, I just said I didn't, didn't I?" Her ladyship replied with exasperation. "What is going on? Affie?"

"Pamela, you're a little blind when it comes to the boy."

"Then why didn't you tell me he was taking things?"

"At first, I wasn't at all sure there was a piece missing. And then, of course, as I said, it *is* stolen property, which rather complicates the situation."

"But darling, what on earth are you doing with stolen property?"

"It seems," his lordship replied unhappily, fiddling with his cufflinks, "I inherited it."

"Oh," the Marchioness murmured, conveying in the single word a world of understanding.

"Affie," the Queen said, "when Margo insisted Tuesday morning the tiara was Wallis's, I'm afraid my mind went immediately to you or, at least, to your father. He was, I know, a great collector of unusual things, including jewellery. And I know you've told me in the past he wasn't immune to going to some lengths to acquire an item he might be keen on. And I did remember he was rather friendly with Uncle David, at least in the 'thirties. And then it was brought to my attention that the thief confessed to hiding the jewels on a boat at King's Lynn, and so, given that you were at the pantomime . . ."

Lord Thring expelled a deep breath. "Yes, I regret to say Morys did involve himself with some unsavoury types in acquiring things, although I've only realized the extent of it since his death. As you know, Ma'am, we were estranged almost since I was a boy. Suppose the kindest thing I can say is he followed his own path in life, but I found his political views, particularly through the run-up to the War, and during the War, to be deeply abhorrent. And, of course, he treated my mother so very insensitively. Repented nothing, too, which did not endear him to me. Anyway, mustn't dwell on this now. All water under the bridge."

"Not quite, I think, Affie," the Queen said gently.

Lord Thring blinked and snuffled. "Yes, you're quite right," he said with regret. "Suppose I'd hoped it was all water under the bridge after my father's death. But then discovering these jewels brought the past back with great force. At first I didn't understand what this . . . this cache was doing at Barsham Hall. Most of the family pieces are kept in a vault in London. I've an inventory, of course. Absolutely appalled when I realized who the original owner of these unlisted things had been, and how the tiara and the other jewels had come into my father's possession."

"How did you know they had once belonged to Wallis?" Princess Margaret asked.

"I didn't, at first, Ma'am. But there were some

letters in the same box as the jewels. There were one or two from Her Grace and one, I think, from His Royal Highness. From what I can gather from the letters, my father had managed to acquire a portion of the jewels stolen from Ednam Lodge—still in their settings—and offered them back to the Duke and Duchess, whether for sale or not, I couldn't say. But the letters indicate the Windsors didn't want them back. Her Grace thanks my father very kindly for his 'thoughtfulness' but in a later note His Royal Highness rather more firmly asks him not to correspond on the matter again. Odd, in a way. Thought she'd at least have wanted her wedding tiara back.''

"There were suggestions at the time that Wallis was somewhat overstating things for Lloyd's," the Queen said drily. "And having collected the insurance, she wouldn't have been able to wear the jewels again in public anyway. I think at the time Uncle David was still hoping for a responsible government post of some nature. I'm afraid the theft and the publicity around it put an end to that hope. What was it Wallis said to the press, Margo?''

"Oh, yes, what was it? Everyone was mimicking it at the time. She had been asked what she was wearing for jewellery the night of the burglary and she said something along the lines of 'A fool would know that with tweeds or other daytime clothes one wears gold and that with evening clothes one wears platinum.' 'A fool would know . . . !' " PM drawled in a parody of a Southern accent good enough to make the Marchioness flinch. "Good heavens, we were still being rationed eggs in those days! I don't think there was much sympathy for poor Aunt Wallis.''

"I expect they wanted to put the whole episode behind them," the Queen added. "They sailed for America not long after.''

"The letters were postmarked New York and Palm Beach," said Lord Thring.

"Affie, what were you intending to do with Wallis's jewels?" the Queen asked, sipping at her water while the corgis settled into sleepy piles before the fire.

"Don't know. Putting it off, really. Didn't know how I was going to avoid press attention. I suppose they should go to that charity the Duchess designated in her will—"

"The Pasteur Institute," PM supplied.

"—but any auction would bring out the blighters from the press. Don't need more stains on the family escutcheon."

"Then you must have had an unpleasant surprise the afternoon of the pantomime," the Queen said.

"Rather. Recognized it the moment the woman came on stage with the bloody thing blazing away on her head. Of course, thought the boy had something to do with it. Got hold of the combination somehow, did you?" Lord Thring leaned forward in his seat to catch Bucky's eye but Bucky had turned his attention to his coffee.

"Thought the only thing to do was to see if I could get the tiara back after everyone had left the village hall. Talk to the woman if she was still there—didn't know who she really was at the time—or root through the costuming. Fortunately, Pammy and I had each motored down from London in separate transport, so I drove around for a time until I thought most people had left.

"I had Jet with me. Parked off a ways and walked to the hall. I called out. Thought someone in charge would be there. But no one was about so I started looking and . . . and found this woman on the stage still wearing the tiara. Thought she was asleep, most peculiar. Then . . ."

Lord Thring sucked in his teeth. "I realized she was dead. I was so startled I dropped Jet's lead. Jet began misbehaving, and then I thought I heard someone else in the Hall—" He broke off. His face sagged. "Oh, dear, I've acted so very stupidly over this whole affair." He shook his head.

"There, there, darling." Lady Thring patted the sleeve of his dinner jacket.

"I suppose I lost my head, in a way," he continued mournfully. "Suddenly saw myself in the headlines. The woman seemed too young to have died of natural causes. And there was I, one foot away from purloined diamonds my own father had been hoarding for nearly half a century and which I was most anxious to keep hidden. 'They'll think I've murdered her,' I thought. So I left with some haste through the back door. Damned cowardly of me, I know."

"What about Jet?" the Queen asked.

"He followed me out the door but he went running off and I couldn't very well call him without calling attention to myself, so I had to leave him in the village and hope to find him later. Felt bad about that."

"Your lordship," I interrupted, "did Jet pick up anything from the stage area?"

Lord Thring's mouth formed a thin line. "Yes, it was that blasted priest, although I didn't know what it was at the time."

"Was it decorated?"

"No."

Just as I thought.

"When Jet reappeared outside the village hall Tuesday morning before luncheon, I was interested to see Benefer lay claim to the priest," Lord Thring continued. "And rather concerned when I later learned how the poor woman had died. It occurred to me the priest was the murder weapon and then, yesterday at the shoot, when Benefer began to brandish the damn thing—I saw him out of the corner of my eye and then Jet suddenly went for it—well, lost my head, I'm afraid . . ."

"Oh, Affie," the Queen said cheerlessly, "I thought it wasn't an accident. You're too fine a shot to make those sorts of mistakes."

"I don't understand," Princess Margaret said, then went into a spasm of sneezing.

"I could see the dog was heading for Benefer and the priest," Lord Thring replied, dismay clearly visible on his face. "People knew Jet was mine. Thought people might start to wonder why my dog was so taken with something they'd realize sooner or later was probably the murder weapon. Call attention to it, don't you know. Difficult enough to explain Jet's preoccupation with the village hall. He got away again on Thursday afternoon. Been running all over the Estate, I'm told. One of the beaters told me yesterday he'd seen Jet sniffing around the village hall. Then he suddenly appeared at the shoot. Feel awful. Worst thing I think I've ever done."

Throughout this, Bucky had been listening with increasing impatience, one leg jiggling maniacally. Now he exploded: "So what did you do? Send Mother back for the tiara that night instead?"

"Of course not!" Lord Thring replied sharply.

"But I saw you!" Bucky said to his mother.

"You couldn't have!"

"I saw you! I saw you through the window of the hall! I went back about seven or so to see if I could find the tiara and I saw you! You'd locked the door."

"Darling, it wasn't me. I've never heard of this tiara until this evening."

A kind of mulish consternation settled on Bucky's face. "But you were late getting back to Lynn. Caroline said you weren't back until after seven."

"I had a flat tire. Well, I did! Caroline has a nerve talking to you about this, Bucky." Her ladyship's eyes swept over the group. "It's as if you all don't believe me. I had a flat tire. I called the AA on my mobile but they were taking so long to send a truck, I thought I'd change it myself. The weather was dry that evening, and I've changed a tire before—I'm not like some women. But, as it happened, a nice little man saw my distress and stopped and helped me."

"Pammy, you should have called Caroline, or me."

"I'm afraid my mind was on something else," the Marchioness said curtly, glancing away. "What I would like to know, Buchanan, darling," she continued in a no-nonsense tone, turning to her son, "is why you have been taking your father's things—"

"*Step*father's," Bucky snarled through clenched teeth.

"Answer me!" she snapped.

"Like Affie said," her son mumbled. "For money."

"Bucky, you have all the money you could possibly need at your age. I've told you: I want you to grow up with some sense of financial responsibility. There's money held for you in trust. I don't want you thinking you can just go and do what you like with it. You have to use money wisely."

"The way you are with Barsham Hall?"

"Don't you sass me, young man. Not in front of Her Majesty and Her Royal Highness."

I think HM and HRH were finding this all rather galvanizing, the former, particularly, as though she might pick up some up-front American-style pointers on how to deal with ungovernable daughters-in-law. Of course, they both wore their well-practised po-faces during this exchange but, glancing at them, I thought I could see a sparkle of genuine extracurricular interest.

"I'm very sorry, Ma'am," the Marchioness said, turning to the Queen. "I had no idea our family problems would be aired here tonight."

"Quite all right," Her Majesty said briskly.

"I'm going home, Mother," Bucky said angrily before the Queen could add anything. "I'm going back to the States. I'm going to start a business or do something. And I'm going to find my father. That's why I really wanted the money."

Lady Thring closed her eyes, as if in pain. "Bucky, honey, we've been through all this. I thought it was settled . . . I'm so very sorry, Ma'am," she added again to the Queen.

"Where is he, Mom? Who is he? You know—so why won't you tell me?" Bucky's tone was urgent, as if having his mother trapped in the Saloon with the Queen of England would finally force her to grant what must have been a long-withheld wish.

"Bucky, shush now."

"I will not shush."

Lady Thring's face was rigid. "This is neither the time nor the place, Buchanan."

"My dear," Lord Thring said gently, a dash of sorrow in his voice that caught my attention, "you can't keep everything from the boy forever."

A silence would have descended on the room but for Princess Margaret's sudden sneezing jag.

"There's no point in looking for your father in the States, Bucky," Lady Thring said at last, reluctantly, her eyes narrowed. "Your father lives in England. He's English."

Mild surprise lit Bucky's features like a twenty-five-watt bulb, but it was nothing compared to the current that seemed to shoot through him when his mother completed the disclosure. "You'll find him just down the road, if he's still there. Your father . . ."—she forced the words out—"is Hume Pryce."

Bucky jolted upright in his chair.

"Who?" Princess Margaret croaked, oblivious.

"The director of the pantomime," the Queen murmured impatiently.

I supposed I should have been more surprised but I wasn't. Somehow it all came together, like a reverse film sequence of a shattered vase. It wasn't merely the physical resemblance between the two men, which was only slight, but the conjunction of calendar dates. Bucky's birthday fit: a little over nine months to the day an American president resigned his position. But what about those numbers and letters on the bit of paper found in Lady Thring's loo? That awaited resolution.

"But he's . . . he's a cousin," I heard Bucky moan in a kind of daze. "It's like, *incest*!"

"Nonsense!" Lady Thring crossed her arms. "We're third cousins or something. It's very remote."

I almost interjected that Her Majesty's husband was her cousin, too, (third) but realized the observation might not be welcomed in the circumstances.

"I'm sorry if this is causing you pain, Buchanan, darling," she continued, softening slightly. "Perhaps it was time you learned the truth after all."

"Does *he* know?"

"No."

"You never told him?"

She shook her head. "I knew what I wanted when I was eighteen years old. Or I thought I did. I wanted a child while I was young. And I wanted a business. I wanted my own life away from my family. I did not want a husband. Not at that point," she amended, patting Affie's hand. "I was ahead of the trends, I suppose. Girls are doing it now, having babies without a father in the picture, and without apology, too. And I don't mean lazy welfare mothers. I mean bright girls, smart girls. Girls with drive and ambition. Perhaps you all think less of me for what I did. My family was certainly horrified. But I've only ever had one regret.

"Hume came along at the right time. He was smart and funny and good-looking. He wasn't a local boy. And he was only in town for three weeks. I didn't expect to see him again any time soon. And, in fact, I didn't see him again until last July, at the King's Lynn Festival."

"I was with you!" Bucky exclaimed. "Why didn't you—?"

"I must admit I was more flustered than I thought I would be," Lady Thring carried on, oblivious. "Such a surprise to see him after nearly twenty years. I thought you might see a resemblance, Bucky. Standing so close. So I found myself just talking on and on about panto-mimes for some reason—I can't think how we got on the topic—and before I knew it Hume was organizing one here. In Dersingham, for goodness sake."

But Bucky's attention had strayed. He stared at his hands. "And you didn't stay behind after the panto Monday to talk to him, to Hume?" he asked suspiciously.

"I have no interest in cousin Hume, Bucky honey."

"But—"

"If I may," I said, interrupting, for an idea had come to me in the way that ideas do, without notice. "I wonder if it wasn't your *father* you saw at the village hall." Bucky's brow crinkled. "You see your mother—her ladyship, I mean—and Mr. Pryce have very similar hair colouring. Mr. Pryce wears his long—usually in a ponytail, but sometimes he undoes it. So if you took a quick look through the window of the village hall and spotted the back of a head with long blond hair you could be . . . confused. And the timing would be right. It's just a thought," I added hastily. The Marchioness was casting a gimlet eye at me.

But, to my surprise, she supported my supposition. "There. You see. I wasn't there. I've told you."

The detritus of a log, consumed by fire, tumbled against the andiron, sending off a blaze of sparks like fireworks beside Her Majesty's head. A corgi growled.

Bucky rose abruptly from his seat. "I'm going," he said petulantly.

"Bucky, where are your manners!" Lady Thring snapped.

"Ma'am," Bucky addressed the Queen, "can I go? I've got some stuff I need to think about."

The Queen caught my eye. A certain intelligence passed between us. "Of course you may," she said pleasantly to Bucky.

Bucky bowed from the neck, turned and exited the room.

"However, Pamela," the Queen said gravely, picking up the thread of Lady Thring's denial when Bucky had gone, "you did have a reason to return to Dersingham Village Hall that evening."

This time Lady Thring's attention to me was swift and hateful. HM, noting the sudden spin of her ladyship's head, continued:

"You musn't blame Jane. She was being diligent on my behalf. It wasn't her intention to cause embarrassment, nor is it mine. However, one found oneself drawn into this murder not simply because the deceased was dressed and made-up to look like one, but because, as I've said, the tiara she had been wearing landed—so to speak—in one's lap. I was rather concerned for you, Affie. Once I learned the tiara's history, I worried there might be a connection to your family. You really weren't behaving as your old self this week, and then the incident with the dog . . . well!" Her Majesty frowned, then added:

"We know the deceased woman was receiving

threatening letters, presumably from these animal extremists. The letters were composed of cut-out letters from magazines and newspapers. When Jane found the remains of a similar letter in your suite, Pamela, I couldn't help wonder at the coincidence. My concern deepened. I couldn't believe you would be . . . the active party in something of this sort. One could only assume you yourself were being terrorized—blackmailed, in effect."

Lady Thring examined her hands, her long smooth white fingers with their perfectly manicured nails painted the lightest shade of silver.

"Yes," she said quietly, "I was being blackmailed."

Lord Thring put his big hand over his wife's and squeezed.

"I started getting letters from that woman in October. They weren't composed of cut-outs from magazines. Not at first. They were just ordinary letters . . ."

"Signed?" I interjected.

"Yes, they were signed. I recognized the name of the young woman who had been, briefly, my au pair when Bucky was very small. Of course, she couldn't very well *not* identify herself. She was the only one who knew, you see. The only person who saw what I had done." In a tired voice Lady Thring asked: "Would I be right in assuming everyone knows what I am talking about? Ma'am?" She addressed the Queen.

"I believe so, Pamela," Her Majesty replied.

"Ma'am?" she repeated to Princess Margaret.

"I'm rather in the dark, I'm afraid," HRH said, drawing her rug higher around her shoulders.

"Pamela, if you'd rather not . . ." the Queen murmured.

"No, I've come to deal with it. It's taken a very long time. I've only just told Affie this week, and he's been very understanding." She smiled at him weakly. "You see, Ma'am," she said, addressing PM, "I hurt my child. I hurt him very, very badly. I am the cause of his epilepsy."

"Oh, dear," PM whispered throatily, suppressing a sneeze.

"I was so young—just turned twenty. I only had a little money. The Walsh Trust was not available to me until I was twenty-one, but I decided to go out on my own anyway without any help from my family. I had my baby—Bucky—and I was trying to make a go of a business, and the au pair, who was new—it was Jackie—was being less than satisfactory. One day, I just lost it. That's all I can say. I just lost it completely. I slapped my child. I slapped Bucky. Hit him so hard that . . ."

The Marchioness inclined her head to me. "You understand my reaction to what you did now?"

"Yes, your ladyship," I said contritely.

"I've been overreacting all my life to that one terrible mistake. Trying to do the right thing for Bucky. To make amends. I don't think I've succeeded."

"Does he know what you did?" PM asked.

"No. I've never told him. I . . . I just haven't had the courage. Maybe I will now. But he's had one shock tonight already . . ." She shrugged. "And there's no excuses for what I did. Stress is not an excuse for striking a child. If I'd done this thing today, I'd probably be under investigation. But in those days, people were only just starting to look into these things. Oh, I think the doctor suspected. I said Bucky had fallen against some furniture. I didn't say it was because I—*I*—had struck him so hard his head hit the newel post and that he might have a concussion.

"And a few weeks later, when he had his first seizure"—Lady Thring stared up to the clerestory windows with their stained-glass heraldic crests—"in my mind's eye, I'm the one taking him in the ambulance. But I know it was Jackie Scaife. She took him, and I was called to his little bedside later. The doctor in the emergency room told her the probable cause. It was confirmed later that a blow to the head had caused the seizure. And then there were more seizures, of course. Many more. By that time, Jackie had gone, left for some other job. She was crazy for boys and travel, that girl. And, after the seizures started, I needed some help with some nursing training, at least until we could get Bucky's seizures under control. Jackie left—on good terms, I thought—but I just put her out of my mind. I think I tried to forget there was one other person who knew what I had done.

"And then this fall these letters started arriving."

21

A CHORUS OF tiny chimes sounded as Lady Thring paused in her story. I glanced over HM's head at the clock. Ten-thirty. There was a faint rustle in the corridor and, almost as if willed by an off stage director, Aileen Benefer appeared in the doorwell. She was on the arm of Paul Jenkyns, leaning into him as someone might who had been in bed for a good long time and was only now finding her feet. While Jenkyns bowed his head smartly from the neck, Aileen fell into a wobbly curtsey the Queen's detective very nearly had to pull her out of.

"Your Majesty," Paul said smartly, echoed by Aileen in a quavering voice.

"Come in," the Queen commanded. "Please sit down, Aileen. And Paul, you'd better bring one of those chairs forward." She gestured down the length of the Saloon where another Regency chair sat between Queen

Alexandra's oak piano and the green baize table display-ing HM's Christmas jigsaw puzzle. Mrs. Benefer seemed to melt into the upholstery so recently vacated by Bucky. Where Inspector Jenkyns looked frankly dishy in his dark evening clothes, Mrs. Benefer in her drab shirtwaister and beige cardigan looked more like a dishrag, completely wrung-out, her features wan, hairdo undone and limp, her eyes dull and glassy.

Jenkyns placed his chair next to mine, all of us together virtually forming a semicircle with Her Majesty as our locus. The Inspector did not acknowledge me as he sat down, but I could sense his presence acutely, as if my aura, wispy and white at that moment of uneasiness, were glancing off his, a red and roiling thing invisible to the eye that saw only a man of practised composure. I found myself, inadvertently, leaning away from him, toward the couch upon which Princess Margaret was still ensconced like . . . well, like a princess.

"Please go on, Pamela," the Queen said, adding to the newcomers, "Lady Thring was just telling us about some letters she had been receiving."

"Yes, Ma'am," the Marchioness said uncertainly, eyeing the Inspector, then Aileen. She took a deep breath: "As I was saying, these letters started arriving. At first, I didn't take them seriously. I wasn't quite sure why a woman who had worked for me twenty years ago, whom I'd never seen again, was writing to me. I suppose I should have had an inkling. There was no return ad-dress but the postmarks, in most cases, were King's Lynn. A few from London, I remember. Manchester, once.

"I seemed to remember her telling me when she lived with us at Southern Pines that she had grown up on one of Your Majesty's estates," Lady Thring contin-ued. "Anyway, the first letter or two was friendly enough, or purported to be. But there was a . . . tone. And then so many more letters! First wheedling, then more and more threatening and abusive. Of course, she wanted money. I didn't know what to do. I had never told Affie what I had done all those years ago. I certainly had never told Bucky. And I'd only become patron of

BERT—the British Epilepsy Research Trust—last spring. I just tried to ignore it. Affie and I were going to be in the States after New Year's so I thought I might be able to escape everything.

"And then I went to the pantomime Boxing Day evening. I didn't recognize my former au pair at all. I arrived after Affie and my son, just in time for the show to start, so I hadn't even read the program to see the names of the performers."

"And then you heard her say something out of context in the second act," the Queen prompted.

"I don't know what the original line was, Ma'am. But she seemed to lean over the stage in her white satin gown and sash and stare right at me with those eyes. So like your eyes, Ma'am, if you don't mind my saying."

The Queen acknowledged the comment with a small frown.

"I won't forget it," Lady Thring continued. "She said: '. . . her ladyship will give her child a thorough beating with her own fair hand.' I had an awful shock. Suddenly, I could see through the disguise. I realized who it was! I wondered: Did people understand what she meant? I was so glad my poor Bucky was resting in one of the meeting rooms after his episode, so he didn't hear."

"And, I must say," Lord Thring added, "I was much too shocked seeing her in that tiara to think about what she was saying."

"I understood." Aileen spoke for the first time. Her voice was practically inaudible.

"You understood?" HM queried.

Aileen turned her head with painful slowness. "Ma'am, I believed my sister was trespassing against her ladyship. I didn't know why. Not at first. But at home one day I came across an envelope addressed to Lady Thring. I asked Jackie why she would be writing to her ladyship but she wouldn't tell me. Accused me of spying on her again. Spying on her? I wasn't spying on her. I was only ever trying to do what was right . . ."

"Aileen," the Queen said in a firm voice, for Mrs. Benefer seemed to be wandering.

"Yes, Ma'am?"

"The letter your sister wrote to Lady Thring . . . ?"

"Oh, yes, Ma'am. The letter. I found it in the pocket of Jackie's coat."

"Which coat, Mrs. Benefer?" I asked.

"The fur. I tried it on one day." Pinpricks of crimson blossomed on Aileen's cheeks as if her trying on the coat were a source of shame. She added quickly: "I'm sure there were other letters—"

"There were," Lady Thring said coldly.

"—but Jackie was more careful after I found the first letter, more secretive. Locking things in her suitcase. But I was uneasy. Then, at the pantomime, she directed those strange words to you, your ladyship. And strutting across that stage dressed up as Your Majesty. Oh, the shame of it!"

The effort of raising her voice seemed to drive Aileen further into the cushions of her chair. "I was never so angry," she intoned, half to herself, and then added: "They say these days you're to express your anger, but I never could do it. That wasn't how we were brought up. It wasn't proper. It wasn't polite."

The Queen fingered a strand of her pearls. "I'm told you had an unsatisfactory meeting with your sister after the pantomime was over," she said.

"Yes, Ma'am, I did. I waited until most everyone had left. She had an appointment with someone, Jackie said. 'Lady Thring?' I asked. But Jackie wouldn't answer. I lost my head that evening."

Head tilted forward, Aileen regarded us all sorrowfully from under an untidy fringe of hair. Her cheeks were mottled with red.

"I said everything I'd wanted to say to her for twenty years. And terrible things she said to me. God help me, I know she was my sister, but I didn't want her in my home. She was a thorn in the flesh. She should have stayed in America." Her face crumpled. "If only she had stayed in America, if only. It was my doing. I brought her back."

"But you just said you didn't want her in your

home." Princess Margaret's comment was muffled by her handkerchief.

"I didn't, Ma'am. And I didn't mean for her to come back to England at all. But she showed and wouldn't say why. Just moved in bold as you please. But after the pantomime Boxing Day, she told me why she came back. Thanked me. Mocked me. You see, all those years I'd kept writing to her. Sometimes I'd stick in clippings from papers or magazines to remind her of home. It was one from the *Tatler* I sent in the summer that caught her eye . . ."

"Oh, no," Lady Thring murmured.

"I'm so sorry, your ladyship. It was the article about the restorations at Barsham Hall. Jackie said she'd worked for your ladyship in America, and that you owed her money. I knew she was lying." She drew her cardigan tighter around her shoulders. "Jackie frightened me that night. She was triumphal—that's the only word I can think of. 'It's all coming together,' she said to me, 'everything I want. And you're not going to spoil it for me this time.' She said your ladyship had paid her."

"I most certainly did not," Lady Thring said with vehemence. "I gave her nothing. I did not respond at all to her . . . communications. Not even when she began sending these crazy notes with cut-out letters to intimidate me. She wanted a quarter of a million pounds! I was badly frightened when she pulled that little trick at the panto and while I was dealing with my son I thought about confronting her—"

"She said she was expecting someone," Aileen interjected.

"Well, I most certainly did not arrange to meet her. I left the village hall and drove back to King's Lynn. I had the flat tire and, while I was waiting, I resolved there and then that I was not going to give in to blackmail no matter what it cost in reputation. I'm bitterly sorry for what I did. But I can't undo it. I decided I would tell Affie and together we would figure what to do.

"I was going to tell him that night. But Affie, dear, you came in later, and you were so preoccupied—I know why now, of course. But my courage slipped then, and when we arrived here at Sandringham the next morning and I was shown to my room, there was a note waiting for me. With cut-out letters, no less. My Lord, I thought, this awful woman's invaded Sandringham House itself. That's why, Ma'am, I made my excuses from the shooting luncheon that day. I was shocked, although the note was quite peculiar."

"Did the note by any chance contain a passage from the Bible?" the Queen asked.

"Why, yes. Yes, it did, Ma'am. How did you guess? Or at least it was a reference to a passage from the Bible. The note was brief. All it said was: 'ST LUKE 627.'"

The Queen glanced at me. I must have looked *un peu* gobsmacked for in the midst of the seriousness of the occasion a tiny smile flickered about the corners of Her Majesty's mouth, which she quickly suppressed. So it wasn't Sandringham Time or the Queen's Accession date or her Coronation anniversary! It was a simple Bible verse. And yet, in the moment of my forehead-slapping stupidity, I had a glimmering of something else, the solution to a little irregularity that had been bothering me.

"I knew as a former convent school girl St. Luke didn't have sixty-two chapters," I heard Lady Thring explain, "so the number had to refer to the sixth chapter of the gospel, twenty-seventh verse. There wasn't a copy of the Bible in my suite, so after you all had gone to the shoot that day I went down to the library and found myself a copy of the King James version. The verse was one of the Beatitudes. I wondered if this woman who had been tormenting me had had a change of heart. I can only paraphrase—"

"I think you'll find my Housekeeper can supply you with the correct wording," Her Majesty interrupted. "Aileen?"

Mrs. Benefer's face lost what little colour it had had in the first place. In a quavering voice, she said as Lady Thring stared at her: " '*But I say unto you which hear, Love your enemies, do good to them which hate you. Bless*

them that curse you, and pray for them which despitefully use
you. And unto him that smiteth thee on the one cheek—' "

"Yes, thank you, Aileen." The Queen cut her off.
"I think we have more than the twenty-seventh verse
there."

"You?" Lady Thring snapped at Mrs. Benefer.

Aileen flinched. "My lady, I knew Jackie was sin-
ning against you. I was sure she would be caught. She
had been caught on occasions in the past. I hoped to
intercede. I hoped you would be merciful when the
time came."

"But why letters cut from magazines?" Lady
Thring's dark eyes flashed angrily. "It's just so . . . *dis-*
turbed. The last few threatening notes to me were composed the same way. Oh, don't tell me . . . ? It
wasn't . . . ?"

A silence fell over the Saloon, broken only by the
crackling flames and a sneeze from Princess Margaret. I
spoke up:

"The afternoon of the panto, Jackie took the
wrong Barbour from the Benefers' cottage."

I glanced at Mrs. B. for confirmation but she only
stared into her lap.

"She was wearing her fur coat, of course," I continued, feeling Inspector Jenkyns's eyes upon me, "but
she needed the Barbour jacket for one of her costume
changes. A Barbour Jackie's size had been borrowed
from a neighbour who was convalescing in hospital and
didn't need it. Jackie is—I'm guessing—a size or two
smaller than you, Mrs. Benefer?"

Aileen's head rocked in a barely perceptible nod.

"And I think at some point, while Jackie was at
the village hall, she realized she had taken her sister's
Barbour. I noticed the sleeves of the jacket Jackie was
wearing when we found her were well over her wrist,
down the back of her hand. Then, yesterday, when I
was helping one of the footmen walk the corgis, Mrs.
Benefer came out of the church. She was wearing a Barbour jacket but it was short in the sleeve. Her wrists
were exposed. The significance eluded me until now.

Mrs. Benefer, if you were sending Bible verses in cut-out letters, were you . . . ?"

"I wasn't sending notes to her ladyship," Aileen pleaded weakly.

"I don't think Jane is referring to that," the Queen commented.

"Do you mean," Inspector Jenkyns said coldly, leaning forward in his chair and directing his gaze at Aileen, "that you are behind these threats . . . these *supposed* threats from the ARF?"

Jenkyns had remained still as a statue during the conversation but his aggressive question to Mrs. Benefer brought a chillier dimension to the proceedings.

Aileen winced. Her eyes were bleak. "I told her she couldn't stop here forever. But she took no notice. Said it was her home as much as mine just because it had been our father's. And Tom . . ." Her bottom lip began to tremble. "Tom wouldn't do anything. 'She's *your* sister,' is all he said." Her hands writhed in her lap. "Yes, I sent the letters. I thought I might . . . frighten her away. She'd got herself noticed wearing that . . . that vulgar coat and writing letters to the paper. I was watching a film on telly one night—can't remember now what it was—but one of the characters was sending notes with letters snipped from magazines. It gave me an idea. I was that desperate."

"That must be how Jackie got the idea to send notes with cut-out letters to Lady Thring," I muttered.

"Such a letter was found in pieces in her jacket, Aileen," the Queen continued the thought. "Or, rather, *your* jacket. One presumes your sister found it that evening, and realized who was, in truth, the sender."

"Perhaps, Ma'am, Jackie had an inkling earlier," I suggested. "Mr. Pryce told me she showed him one of the letters and just laughed it off."

Mrs. Benefer bit her lip. Then she said in a small torn voice: "She tossed it in my face."

A mixture of astonishment, relief, and indignation descended upon the room with the realization that the official apprehension about an animal-rights extremist attack had been all for nought, precipitated by an an-

cient acrimony between two sisters, misinterpreted by
an officialdom already concerned for safety surrounding
the annual shooting at Sandringham and anxious there
not be yet another security cock-up.

"Ma'am." Lord Thring spoke gruffly, tugging at
his tie. "Can't help thinking you've pegged one of us as
a murderer."

No flies on you, your lordship, I thought, wishing I
could say it. The Queen didn't reply immediately but,
rather, drew in her lips as if she was settling her mind on
how to frame her response.

"I've doubted the ARF involvement from the beginning," Her Majesty addressed us, "but one is inclined to let security take its own lead. The victim was,
after all, costumed as one, so I suppose there was sufficient reason to be concerned.

"However"—the Queen lent emphasis to her
pause—"my Housekeeper's admission to fashioning
these letters has rather effectively put paid to that view.
So one is obliged to cast one's mind elsewhere. I know
calling you together like this is rather unorthodox, Affie—"

"Not like you at all, Ma'am."

"No, I suppose not, but circumstances do compel
one to change one's routine from time to time." HM
smiled.

"Unpleasant a prospect as it is," she continued,
the smile fading, "we must face the fact that Jackie
Scaife was murdered for reasons other than a newspaper
row with animal-rights extremists or her ability to impersonate me, or a convenient mixture of the two. Affie,
you went to considerable lengths this week to keep clos-
eted an old family skeleton. Pamela, you, too, had reason to fear a revelation from your past. And, Aileen,
you've neither forgotten nor forgiven your sister for what
she did to you before your marriage. Yes, I have been
told about the incident."

Her Majesty paused, absently running a stock-
inged foot along the chubby form of a snoozing corgi.

"What I've found remarkable is how profoundly
the past has managed to intrude upon the present. Each

of you has been haunted by something that happened twenty years ago—fifty years ago and more for you, Affie—and in each case this unfortunate woman, Jackie Scaife, sharpened your anxieties whether that was her intent or not. As for me—and for Margaret, too, I expect—it's remarkable how the Duchess of Windsor, gone nearly a decade now, still has the power to intrude upon our lives . . ."

The Queen's expression grew thoughtful. "If Mr. and Mrs. Simpson had never come to England, if Wallis had never met my uncle, how different might our lives have been, what do you think, Margo?"

"Uncle David would have married someone else, had children of his own," PM croaked.

"Our father might never have been King, might never have died so terribly young. I would not be Queen. We wouldn't be sitting here tonight. This would never have happened. There would never have been a special wedding tiara fashioned by Cartier for a Duchess of Windsor because a Duchess of Windsor wouldn't have existed. There'd have been no theft at Ednam Lodge, no jewels to fence, none for your father to buy, Affie. None for your son to take, Pamela. And none, Aileen, for your sister to wear at a village pantomime. And none, Margo, for you to . . . well, never mind."

HM turned from the glowering Margaret Rose. "Nevertheless," she continued, "however one thinks about this unhappy incident, one always seems to return to the tiara."

I found myself staring at Her Majesty. I know it's not nice to gawp at the Monarch in social situations, but I hadn't imagined her life in such circumstances before. But for an American divorcée she might well have been a minor Royal, living somewhere in the country probably, with her beloved horses and dogs, doing occasional light public duty in the manner of her cousins, the Kents and the Gloucesters, having a life in no way as beholden to duty and schedule and routine as it is as Sovereign. Did she never feel robbed? Robbed of the chance of a normal—or normal*ish*—life? Yet when she spoke, there was no bitterness, only the slightest wonder at the workings of time and chance.

"The tiara," the Queen continued after a pause, "was part of a costume. And the wearer of the costume was attempting to impersonate me. What I find curious, however, is that long after the pantomime was finished and the other actors had removed their costumes and makeup, left the village hall and gone home or to the Feathers, Jackie Scaife was still, I suppose one could say, 'in character.' I understand she wore a gown in the last scene, and had removed that in favour of more comfortable country clothes—perhaps she had slipped on the Barbour simply because the village hall is, as I recall, rather chilly—but she remained, nonetheless, much the way she appeared on the stage. The question is: Why?"

The eyebrows arched above the sparkling blue eyes.

"Apparently she was to meet someone," Her Majesty continued. "That's been mentioned several times and the presumption has been, I think, that the meeting was to be with you, Pamela; that Jackie felt sufficiently sure that her . . . *tactic* in the panto would convince you to stay behind. But you left without talking to her. So we come back to the original question: Why did Jackie Scaife continue her impersonation?

"The answer, I believe, is obvious. She was indeed meeting someone. It was not a meeting contingent on someone's emotional response to a series of threats but a *scheduled* meeting. And it was with someone who had never before seen her in the role of . . . well, me."

"Inspector," she said frostily, using his title instead of his name, "perhaps you'd care to explain."

There was a shocked silence. Heads swivelled from the Queen to Jenkyns as the possibility of a new and unheralded suspect emerged. But Jenkyns remained outwardly impassive, his hands folded on one knee. Sitting next to him as I was, however, I felt still the aura of anger.

"I understand," he replied obliquely, "that Your Majesty has been speaking on the telephone with my father-in-law."

"Yes," the Queen replied evenly, "I thought his worship might care to join us for tea one afternoon next month. He was most accommodating."

"He's deeply honoured, Ma'am. He phoned to tell me."

"I thought he might."

"And I understand, too, that your conversation covered a range of topics."

"We talked of schedules, actually, as our lives, your father-in-law's and mine, are somewhat beholden to such things."

"I see." Jenkyns examined the faces staring at him.

"Your father-in-law mentioned that you had left his home in Lynn Boxing Day afternoon at about six o'clock to take up your duties here at Sandringham. However, you were not scheduled to arrive until eight o'clock in the morning the next day and, in fact, did not arrive until that time. You seem to have an unaccounted-for absence."

"Paul?" Aileen said nervously.

"I spent the evening in Burnham Market, Ma'am. At a small hotel run by a friend of mine."

"I expect he would be able to confirm your time of arrival, would he?"

"Yes, Ma'am, he would . . ."

"Inspector?"

Jenkyns's nostrils flared suddenly. "However," he replied bleakly, "my arrival time wouldn't give me an adequate alibi. As Your Majesty has guessed, I was the one who'd arranged to meet Jackie at Dersingham Village Hall."

"If it's a guess, Inspector, it's a very good guess," the Queen observed.

"Oh, Paul!" Aileen gasped. She stared at him as if seeing him for the first time while Princess Margaret pushed herself higher against her pillows and exclaimed softly: "My goodness."

"I take it, Inspector, that you'd been somehow involved with Aileen's sister," the Queen continued.

"Yes, Ma'am. Jackie called me when she returned

to England a few months ago. I suppose Aileen had told her about me. Jackie and I met and . . ." He shrugged. His expression was grim. "May I ask how Your Majesty learned of this?"

The Queen nodded in my direction. "I think Jane may be able to help you there."

Jenkyns turned to me, his eyes narrowed. "I thought you might be behind this," he said with distaste.

I recoiled. Next to little me he seemed rather large and dangerous. "It was because of Manchester. Mr. Benefer muttered something about Manchester when I was talking to him on Thursday. And then on Friday, Mrs. Benefer said she'd found the remains of a train ticket to Manchester among Jackie's things. She thought her husband had gone off with her sister, you see. I didn't give it much thought until Her Majesty reminded me that she, too, had been in Manchester on an official visit at the beginning of this month. If Her Majesty was in Manchester that meant members of Staff, including at least one of her detectives, had to have been doing a 'recce' trip some weeks before."

"And, Inspector," the Queen interjected, "you were the detective assigned to that trip."

"But that doesn't mean—"

I cut him off. "Mrs. Benefer had also mentioned that you and her sister had been . . . close when you were teenagers. Besides, there was another clue—"

"Oh, my Lord!" This time Aileen cut me off. Her voice was ragged. "And I didn't believe Tom. He said he was going to visit family at Whitewell, but I wouldn't believe him. It was *you* she was meeting in Manchester."

"Aileen, you destroyed it for us the first time."

"You were fifteen years old, Paul. She was seventeen. It was . . . shameful. A disgrace."

"And she got her revenge on you, didn't she?"

Aileen stiffened as though shot with arrows. Her face was ashen. Oh, my goodness, I thought. Seducing Tom. That was the revenge. That's why she betrayed her sister with the man who was to be her brother-in-law.

Jenkyns gave Aileen a dismissive glance and folded his arms across his chest.

"Ma'am, I first met Jackie when I was fifteen, as Aileen has said. I was mature for my age, I suppose. We were in love. *I* was in love. Aileen broke it up."

"You were fifteen!" Aileen remonstrated again.

"My wife and I have been going through a bad patch in our marriage, Ma'am," Jenkyns went on, ignoring the protest. "Jackie was . . . well, it was wonderful to see her again. She always had a certain something, a tremendous vitality, a sense of fun—"

"Qualities that don't always last, Inspector, I daresay," the Queen interrupted.

Jenkyns shifted uncomfortably. The atmosphere was charged. Everyone stared at the Inspector.

"She had changed," he said reluctantly, meeting our eyes. And then more forcefully: "Of course, she'd changed. But I realized too late. There was a harder edge. Her expectations were different—but I guess they would be after all these years. She began to introduce the idea of marriage . . ."—he sighed—"that I should leave my wife. She said she was coming into some money—I realize now, Lady Thring, what she meant. But I didn't know then. She preferred to be coy about it. She began phoning me at home in London. My wife was starting to become suspicious.

"And then Jackie told me she was going to have a baby."

"The baby . . . oh!" Aileen moaned. "She said it was Tom's. She threw that in my face, too."

"It wasn't Tom's, Aileen. I doubt it very much. She told me on the phone last week that it was mine."

"And what was your reaction, Inspector?" Her Majesty asked coolly.

There was a tense silence. Jenkyns stared past the Queen and into the fireplace.

"I was, frankly, appalled, Ma'am," he said finally. "I was horrified. I had already decided I had to break it off, but this news added a dimension I wasn't prepared for. My marriage would not only be jeopardized but I began to realize my whole career would be, too. If there was scandal or trouble or fuss, my position as your detective, Ma'am, and with the RDPD as a whole, would be in trouble."

Grimly he continued: "We had arranged to spend Boxing Day night at Burnham Market. But I thought I couldn't go through with it. The affair would have to end and some arrangement made to . . . to end the pregnancy. She'd have to see this was reasonable . . ."

Jenkyns's expression tensed with the memory. "I drove to the village hall. We had arranged to meet there after six, after the panto was over and everyone involved gone. We couldn't be seen together, of course, so I parked a distance away . . ."

There was a rustle in the corridor, the sound of something soft hitting the carpet near the entrance, and Bucky reappeared in the Saloon, wearing his Barbour. A corgi raised himself and barked furiously at the intruder. The Queen reached down and patted the animal.

"Bucky, honey, I'm not sure we're ready to leave," Lady Thring said, noting his apparel and turning to the Queen for her endorsement.

"I was going to go to Flitcham on my own, Ma'am," Bucky explained, ignoring his mother and addressing Her Majesty. "But the security told me they didn't want guests leaving without a police escort so—"

"They suggested you wait here and go with the rest of us." The Queen finished the thought.

"Yes, Ma'am."

"Well, we shouldn't be too much longer, I don't think. Inspector Jenkyns was just telling us about Boxing Day afternoon. Inspector?"

Jenkyns frowned at Bucky. "Sorry, Ma'am. I was saying that I had arranged to meet Jackie after six, in the village hall. I didn't care for the idea of meeting her anywhere on the Estate. But she was becoming reckless. Her coming to Manchester while I was there was the beginning of it—the recklessness, I mean. You must believe, Ma'am, that I didn't arrange that. She knew I would be there, and so she simply appeared . . ."

"But you didn't send her packing, Inspector," the Queen commented.

"No, Ma'am. I . . . well, there are idle hours during recce trips so . . ."

Frailty, thy name is man, I thought, as Inspector Jenkyns appeared slightly humbled for the first time.

"As I was saying, Jackie insisted I meet her at the village hall. She said she had a surprise for me—I know what that was now, of course—but on the phone she wouldn't tell me. Just insisted. Said it would be fun." Jenkyns squirmed. "I was reluctant . . ."

"Your reservation at Burnham Market was for two, I expect."

"Yes, Ma'am. I suppose part of me remained in some sort of thrall. And yet, as I drove up from Lynn, I began to feel more and more that I was ensnared. I confess I was very angry by the time I'd reached Dersingham. Angry with myself, I suppose. But more angry with her . . ."

The clock on the mantel chimed the hour. Eleven o'clock. But though there were a few surreptitious glances at the mantel, fleeting time possessed no one in the room. Aileen's mouth had fallen open, a black hole in a bloodless face. She clutched her sweater tightly and stared at Jenkyns. Princess Margaret, I could see out the corner of my eye, was newly alert, her now-empty water-and-lemon stopped midway to her lips. Lady Thring rubbed along her fingers nervously. The Queen remained imperturbable, though there was ice in her blue eyes. Finally Lord Thring, colour rising to his face, boomed: "Do you mean to tell us, Inspector, that *you* killed this woman?"

Jenkyns's eyes swept over the assembled. He straightened in his chair and pushed along its arms with force as though he were about to vault from its confines. I could feel his tension and it made me apprehensive.

"No," he said at last, angrily, his cool broken. "No, I did not kill Jackie!"

THE FORCE OF Jenkyns's denial had the effect of shattering what little remained of hitherto civilized discourse. Everyone recoiled rather like deer in the vicinity of shotgun activity. Only the Queen continued to regard him with that long cool stare for which she is justifiably famous.

"I don't believe it!" Lord Thring boomed again. "You're lying. You'd a decent little motive. And—of course!—then you killed the gamekeeper. He must have known. He'd have seen you in Manchester!"

"My lord, I did not kill Tom Benefer. Nor Jackie."

"You mean you turned away from the village hall, after all?" Princess Margaret cleared her throat and added: "You didn't go in?"

"No, Ma'am, I *did* go into the hall."

"Well, then, there you go . . ." Lord Thring said, as if the matter were settled.

"I couldn't have killed Jackie," the Inspector continued forcefully, fastening his eyes on Lord Thring, "because she was *already dead when I arrived*!"

There was a silence as everyone digested this claim.

"Then why didn't you notify the police?" Lord Thring asked in skeptical tones.

Jenkyns hesitated. He splayed his hands along his trousers and stared at them. I noted the thick plain gold wedding band on his fourth finger.

"Because," he replied coldly, "the investigators would immediately question my presence and I had, as you say, my lord, 'a decent little motive.' They wouldn't be long in finding it, and even if I could prove I didn't kill her—and I *could* prove it—certainly my marriage would be over and likely my career at the Met would be . . . well, compromised at the very least."

He paused. A sudden gust of wind and rain hammered the windows. The Big House groaned in response.

"I went against everything in my training." Jenkyns ran an impatient hand through his hair, regret overtaking the anger in his voice. "I suppose in one way I panicked. I knew she'd raised the ire of local animal-rights extremists, and"—he glanced at Aileen—"she'd told me of receiving 'threatening letters.' So when I found one torn on the floor in the side room, the idea came to me: Put the pieces of the letter back into the pocket of her Barbour. I thought the investigators might then be diverted from the personal aspects of Jackie's life. For good measure, I used the sharp end of Benefer's priest on the fur coat—I'd picked it up on the stage—and then marked the letters *ARF* on the coat with a grease pencil."

"Did you know it was the murder weapon?" I asked.

"No," Jenkyns replied. "I didn't know. I found Jackie lying face down on the stage floor. She was obviously dead but there was no evident reason why and I didn't have time to investigate."

"Then it was you who placed her on that litter."

Jenkyns's eyes went to my own. There was just for a second a flicker of ineffable sadness.

"I did it without thinking. I just"—he shrugged—"picked her up and laid her down there . . ." He closed his eyes as though warding off the painful image.

"And Ma'am," he added, addressing the Queen, "you must believe me when I say I had no idea she was impersonating Your Majesty. I was too consumed with her death and its implications to understand why she was made-up that way. Only when we went onto the stage Tuesday morning did I realize . . ."

"Well, Inspector, you've certainly behaved cavalierly with the Queen's security," Princess Margaret said in a Lady-Bracknell-with-a-head-cold voice.

"No one's more aware of my folly than I, Your Royal Highness," Jenkyns responded. "In fact, I'd intended to make myself known to the investigators, hoping there'd be a way perhaps my wife might remain in the dark about my relationship with Jackie. But then late Wednesday evening I was confronted with a strange twist: I was asked to sort out a housemaid carrying valuable jewellery in a Marks and Spencer bag."

"Oh, not this tiara again," Lady Thing sighed.

"You reacted so strangely at the Jubilee Gates Wednesday when I explained whose tiara it was," I said to Jenkyns. "Almost overreacted, dropping it."

He eyed me unhappily. "Don't you think anyone claiming to have a tiara stolen fifty years ago from the Duchess of Windsor might be regarded askance?"

"I suppose," I said reluctantly. "But then there were other oddities as the week went on. Why, for instance, did the tiara angle fail to get into the papers? Were the investigators keeping it to themselves for some reason? I was sitting last night at the Feathers with my father and some of his new friends from the Norfolk Constabulary. They chewed over every detail of the Dersingham murder but no one said a word about the tiara. I mean, after all, it did once belong to the Duchess of Windsor. A pretty amazing part of the case, I would have thought.

"I began to wonder if you'd handed the tiara over," I continued, addressing Jenkyns, feeling rather brave. "Or, if you had, had you kept the tiara's provenance to yourself?

"Then something was confirmed for me last night: that Lord Thring's father had most likely been the owner for the last fifty years of the Duchess's tiara. I wasn't sure what that meant at first. But then I remembered I'd overheard Lord Thring tell you his father had dealt with a man named Jenkyns who had a shop in King's Lynn. You told his lordship you'd grown up in Hunstanton, which you hadn't. People around here tell me you grew up in Lynn. Why would you lie about such a small point?"

"How could you have overheard that?" the Inspector demanded.

"She was hiding under the table in the Dining Room, Inspector," Lord Thring said.

"I was cleaning something." Feeling myself start to blush, I hurried on: "Anyway, I began to ponder. A marquess wouldn't, I didn't think, 'deal with' a butcher or a greengrocer or the like. Staff would handle such mundane matters. Could the late Lord Thring have 'dealt with' a jeweller, I wondered? If you want to find a jewel fence, my father told me, look for a jeweller. And so we did, my father and I. This afternoon. We went to Jenx Jewellery on St. James Street. This was the other thing that made me think you'd been responsible for these deaths."

Jenkyns regarded me with something close to loathing. "Very clever. Nevertheless, my grandfather is dead."

"Yes, but the man who has the shop now is your cousin, Chris Jenkyns. And he apprenticed with your grandfather in more ways than one. He was quite talkative once my father got all RCMP-y with him."

"Is this true, Inspector?"

"Yes, Ma'am." Jenkyns answered the Queen more evenly. "My grandfather established Jenx Jewellery sometime in the nineteen-twenties. And, no, he wasn't always honest: The 'thirties and wartime were not good to him. But I'm not excusing his behaviour.''

Jenkyns seemed to study the tapestry above the fireplace as if the figure depicted, the emperor Constantine, might offer reassurance.

"Nor am I excusing myself," he continued. "Background checks are made when you apply to join the Met and—fortunately—nothing in my background appeared to be an impediment to my joining. But I was never certain whether my grandfather's . . . activities were unknown, or whether they were known and considered to have no consequence in determining my suitability. I never knew. I could never ask. When I applied to join the RDPD, I worried once again because candidates are even more stringently scrutinized. And by then there was my less-than-scrupulous cousin to consider. But everything seemed to be fine.

"Then I saw that tiara and was told about its background. I thought: 'It'll all come out—my family history, my earlier lack of candour.' There will be suspicion: another link to Jackie's death."

"But even if your grandfather acted as a fence from time to time, why would you assume he handled the Duchess's jewels?" Princess Margaret inquired.

"Because I knew he did, Ma'am. It was something of family legend, although it was my mother who told me when I was old enough to keep that kind of secret. You see, my grandfather kept an old boat that had belonged to *his* father and that was where the jewellery was kept while it was still 'hot.' Most of the jewels were taken from their settings and fenced later in London, but my grandfather was able to make an arrangement for part of the cache with the late Lord Thring, who was interested in rare and unusual things."

Silence fell. One of the corgis yawned so hard she squeaked.

"And what have you done with the tiara, Inspector?" the Queen asked, reaching to pat the dog. "Or perhaps I should say, 'tiaras.'"

"Tiaras, Ma'am?"

"I understand Bucky has the paste version that belongs to the costumer. Affie?" HM turned to Lord Thring.

"I'm sorry, Ma'am. Failed to deal with it . . . or him. Bucky must have it."

"The tiara's still under my bed in a bag." Bucky replied peevishly, looking straight at me. "I think."

"And Wallis's tiara?" the Queen asked of Jenkyns. "I had assumed you had returned it to the authorities after our discussion Thursday morning."

"I have it in my room, Ma'am," Jenkyns replied.

"And what were you planning to do with it?"

Jenkyns rubbed a finger over his lower lip. "I don't know, Ma'am. I . . . I've thought about tossing it in the sea, actually."

Princess Margaret gasped.

"You didn't think about following in your grandfather's footsteps?" Lord Thring remarked.

"No more than you would consider following in your father's, your lordship."

"The impertinence!"

Jenkyns's nostrils flared but he said nothing.

"You've two reasons for having killed that blasted woman," the Marquess continued heatedly, his face above his white collar like an aubergine on a Minton platter. "To protect your job and protect your marriage. You were at the village hall before any of us. You've as much as said."

"Affie, darling, calm yourself," Lady Thring said indulgently. But Lord Thring's repeated attempts to assail HM's minder had purpose. I could see that. His lordship knew where this inquiry was headed.

"Tom went looking for you last night," Aileen said with rising hysteria. She had been staring at Jenkyns with growing alarm. "He went looking for you! He said he was going—"

"And he found me, Aileen," Jenkyns interrupted angrily. "But I did not kill him." There was strain on his handsome features. The corners of his eyes were shot with blood.

"Look, this is ridiculous. I know it might look like

I had reasons to well and truly put an end to my relationship with Jackie. But the thought of murdering her to achieve that end never once crossed my mind. I was staggered when I found her lying there dead. Do you understand me? Staggered! As for that bloody tiara, it's just through a horrible stupid series of other people's venality—including Jackie's, I have to say—that it ever fell into my hands! I have no interest in profiting from that tiara. I wish I'd never seen it. But I didn't kill Jackie. And I didn't kill Tom. For any reason! Is there nobody who believes me?"

There was a dreadful silence. Everyone leaned away like trees before a blasting wind. Finally, someone spoke up. The familiar crisp tones cut through the atmosphere like a laser through crystal:

"As it happens, Inspector, I believe you."

The Queen regarded her detective with detachment. There would be no clemency for his unprofessional behaviour and he knew it. But he met her declaration with a thin smile and a grateful bow from the neck, as though the royal pardon had been granted nevertheless. Everyone else simply viewed Her Majesty with varying degrees of consternation.

"Are you quite certain, Ma'am?" Lord Thring mumbled.

"Quite certain, Affie," HM replied confidently, though her tone was cheerless.

Princess Margaret's head did a Wimbledon from her elder sister to Jenkyns and back. "For heaven's sake, Lilibet," she wheezed, "you're putting us all on tenterhooks."

The Queen turned her eyes to me. Her eyebrows had travelled to a spot just south of the sponge of grey curls and rolls on her head. It was a moment I had been anticipating with genuine dread. The herald angels in the Main Drawing Room in the early hours of the morning had played me false, or false*ish*. Too much Christmas eggnog, I venture. The drunken little golden towheads had imbued me with such enthusiasm for my own brilliance Her Majesty had even put aside her qualms and let me take my lead. That enthusiasm had swept me into Jenx Jewellery, agèd papa three steps behind. Everything Chris Jenkyns said seemed to confirm me in my convictions. And then Mr. Jenkyns—Chris—let drop something else which brought to me a flood of doubt and then, in a flash, a new understanding, this time aided and abetted by unbeings from the Christian Angels Temperance Union. I was absolutely sure this time. And this time there was going to be a tiny glittering bit of physical evidence. Her Majesty was both cheered and saddened by my gleanings when I met with her in her study briefly before tea. But she was confirmed in *her* own convictions, however unpleasant the consequences.

"It's sort of my doing that you came under suspicion, Inspector," I said haltingly, tugging at my skirt so I could avoid his eyes. "I've had a couple of false—I guess you could call them 'revelations'—along the way. One about Lady Thring and the threatening notes. The other was about you. There was your curious connection to the Duchess's tiara. And there was the Manchester connection, which I've explained."

I pressed on. "Mr. Benefer thought there was a connection to Manchester, too. I think he believed you were responsible for his sister-in-law's death but couldn't prove it so he kept mum. At yesterday's shoot, he was very reluctant to hand over the priest to you, as if he was sure you were going to destroy vital evidence—"

"Yes, I know," Jenkyns interrupted impatiently. "He told me. He *did* accuse me of killing Jackie." He turned to Aileen. "He came to my room late last night. I guess he couldn't sleep for thinking about it. At any rate, we talked and I think I was able to make him see that I wasn't responsible. My regret—my very great regret—is giving him the name of the person I thought *was* responsible. You must see, Aileen, that Tom wasn't in love with Jackie. I doubt if he ever was. He was concerned for *you*, how his foolishness so long ago had cast a shadow over your marriage and spoiled your relationship with your sister. I guess he wanted to make amends by helping to find her killer—"

"Well, then, who . . . ?" Princess Margaret began as Aileen buried her face in her hands and wept. But the

Queen raised a warning hand. "Let her continue, Margo."

"Sorry, Ma'am," I apologized to HRH. "I just wanted to say that when I was in the jewellery shop this afternoon, I had another sort of, well . . . revelation, I guess you might call it. Her Majesty had lent me a certain watch as a way of getting the owner's, Mr. Jenkyns's, attention and as a way of measuring his integrity—"

"That watch Monsieur Lebrun gave you before the War, Lilibet? The one that was found yesterday?"

The Queen nodded. "It's a little the worse for being out of doors all these years but the inscription on the back is quite readable once you scrape away some of the dirt."

"No one would mistake the watch was a gift from the president of France to Her Majesty when she was a princess," I continued. "The inscription tells the story. If Mr. Jenkyns were completely kosher then he'd kick me out or call the police or at least insist I return it to the rightful owner. But if he had any suspicions they evaporated pretty quickly. I mean, I don't look like a professional jewel thief, I don't think."

"No, you look like a housemaid," Bucky said with rancour.

"I simply told him I'd found the watch in a nearby field," I continued, ignoring him. "He was ready to trade until my fifteen-stone father and his warrant card came into the shop. Mr. Jenkyns was very cooperative after that. He gave us some of the history of the shop and its previous owner that we were seeking, but he also mentioned something else: that in the summer he'd bought a piece of jewellery off a young man who claimed to have lived on the Estate for a time.

"You didn't strike a very hard bargain," I added, turning my attention to Bucky, still standing between Jenkyns and Aileen, completing the semicircle. "He indicated he was happy to meet you again, even if it was Boxing Day night."

"Yeah, well, so, now you know who the guy was I sold it to," Bucky said sulkily.

Lord Thring regarded his stepson with worry and anger. "Why on earth would you go to Jenx Jewellery?"

"You pointed him out, Affie. We were walking down St. James Street one day a couple of years ago and you said your father liked to do business there. So . . ." He shrugged. "Well, how many jewellers do *I* know? I just took a chance."

"Bucky, honey, what are we going to do with you?" Lady Thring smiled weakly at her son. "You have been very naughty."

That, I thought with a heavy heart, was the understatement of the year, and one could say this with some confidence because the year had only about half an hour left to it.

"There was something else," I said, my heavy heart beginning to do leaden flip-flops. "Bucky, when you told me about showing the tiara to someone you'd arranged to meet in the Feathers after the panto, you said you 'couldn't figure it out.' You couldn't figure out what you were doing with a different tiara, a rhinestone tiara.

"But Mr. Jenkyns—Chris Jenkyns—told me you arrived at the Feathers 'somewhat in a state,' as he described it, and that after your insisting he meet you on Boxing Day you wouldn't show him what you had with you. 'Left it in the car,' you told him. You told him to wait a while, have a few drinks, and then you'd fetch what it was you wanted to show him. And you did. You went out. But you didn't go out to any car. You don't *have* a car. You went back to the village hall."

"Yeah, so?" Bucky's lower lip stuck out. "I told you I went back. The place was locked."

"What Chris Jenkyns said didn't strike me as significant until a little later," I persisted. "You must have known you had a fake with you *when you arrived at the Feathers*. You weren't surprised by what you had in your bag. *If* you knew you were carrying a fake, *when* did you know you were carrying a fake—that's what I wondered. I've seen both the tiaras. I've even"—I glanced guiltily at the Queen—"tried one on—the real one.

"There's a real difference in weight. The Duchess's is heavy, substantial, yet it's actually smaller in size. The rhinestone one is lighter but it's big and gaudy. It's shaped differently. Even hidden in a bag you can sense the difference, and, as it happens, I've lifted both in bags."

From the corner of my eye, I noted Lady Thring's expression. She was staring at her son with pale unsmiling intensity. Lord Thring, next to her, was listening with his eyes closed as if steeling himself against some inevitability. I took a deep breath.

"I think you knew right away, when you recovered from your seizure, that something wasn't right," I told Bucky. "I think you looked in your satchel then and saw a switch had been made. Maybe you even saw the performer wearing the genuine article go by—there were only two royal female parts: the Princess of Diamonds and the Queen of Hearts. So you waited at the village hall or outside the village hall to recover your property. Mr. Pryce left Jackie arguing with her sister, but once Mrs. Benefer had gone, there was no one in the hall but Jackie. Chris Jenkyns said you'd arranged to meet him at the Feathers at five-thirty. But you were late. It was after six when you arrived. So what were you doing from the time the panto ended at four-thirty until after six o'clock? Mrs. Benefer had to have left Dersingham by no later than five forty-five if she was in Cromer by six-thirty. You had opportunity."

Bucky looked at me warily, his eyes flickering with uncertainty. "You can't prove any of this."

"Inspector," the Queen instructed, "I wonder if you would examine the collar of our guest's jacket?"

Jenkyns rose, took Bucky by his left arm as he tried to lean away, and scrutinized the Barbour's corduroy collar. Bucky twisted his head to the right as though revolted.

"What do you see?"

"Well, Ma'am . . . some of the stitching appears worn. There's . . ." He peered more closely at the material. "Mm, there appear to be one or two tiny flecks of colour embedded in the waling."

Jenkyns stepped back, forcing Bucky to turn, so he

could better examine the collar in the lamp behind Princess Margaret's couch. This afforded me a better view, too. I could see two tiny pinpoints of reflected light as well as a thrush of colour rising along Bucky's neck.

"Rather shiny," the Inspector continued. "A commercial glitter, perhaps."

"So what," Bucky groused.

"I don't understand," Lady Thring cried, pushing herself forward. "What is this all about?"

"I'm sure forensics will find this very interesting, Ma'am," the Inspector said blandly above the Marchioness's remonstrations.

"That stuff must have got on there when I was wrapping Christmas gifts," Bucky protested, trying without success to see the collar of his coat, struggling against the Inspector's grip.

"In other words, you wrap gifts while wearing outdoor clothing," Her Majesty stated, echoing the general disbelief.

"I don't know. I don't remember."

"I'm afraid the person I told Tom I thought responsible for Jackie's death was you, Mr. Walsh," Jenkyns said coolly as Bucky continued to wriggle. "I'd no proof. But yesterday afternoon at the shoot, Her Majesty mentioned to me in conversation that a second tiara had been found—in your bedroom, Mr. Walsh—and that you were the likely victim of a switch at the village hall. I'm aware of your impulsive behaviour. The young female Staff regard you as a sex pest. It's well known you tried it on earlier this week with a certain housemaid who didn't welcome your advances. I saw Jackie's body where it had fallen in the village hall. She appeared to have been attacked from behind, suggesting a crude and impulsive killer."

"Get off me," Bucky cried.

"I think after talking with me, Tom went downstairs," the Inspector continued ruthlessly. "He knew you were spending the rest of the evening at the Feathers because I had told him so: If you remember, I had tried to persuade you not to leave the grounds. So I expect Tom waited for you, didn't he? To confront you."

Aileen stared up at Bucky, her wet and red-rimmed eyes filled with a magnification of the horror seeping into the room. Bucky tried one last time to wrench himself away from Jenkyns but failed. Slowly the stubborn set of his features transformed to those of a child whose ice-cream cone had tumbled onto the pavement, lower lip protruded, brows knotted, eyes petulant and uncomprehending. And like that same child on the verge of tears, Bucky suddenly flared: "She wouldn't give it back! It was mine! And she wouldn't give it back!"

What little colour remained in Lady Thring's face drained away. "Bucky . . ." she whispered uncomprehendingly.

"Well, she wouldn't!" Bucky wailed and jerked away from Jenkyns's reach.

"She said she was going to keep the tiara. And do you know why, *Mother*?" He spat the last word. "Do—you—know—why?"

Lady Thring stared at him, aghast.

"Instead of payment, that's why. Instead of *cash* payment. Oh, yeah, she told me she was blackmailing you. She told me who she was. *And what you did to me!*"

Lady Thring gave a strangled cry. "Bucky lamb, it was an accident . . . an accident!"

"I'm your child! You're not supposed to hit me! And leave me with some freakin' . . ." He seemed to grope wildly for the word. His arms flailed. "*Disability!*"

"It was an accident. You must believe me, darling, an accident. Mommy would never hurt you deliberately."

The two—mother and son—seemed to enter their own world of recrimination and remorse. The Queen, I couldn't help but note, sat stony-faced, mouth drawn to a narrow line, alert eyes following the players in the tragedy. The corgis, woken from fireside slumber by the battered voices, stood watchful, restrained by a regal hand.

"She said you hit me lots of times!"

"It's not true! It's simply not true! It happened once, oh, my darling, only the once. It was a horrible,

horrible mistake I've had to live with. Don't you know how it hurts me every time you're ill?"

"Hurts *you*!" Bucky shrieked.

"And now . . . oh, what have you done?" Her voice was anguished. "You've . . ." The realization that her son had killed not one, but two people, seemed to sweep aside the anguish over the sins of the past. Her eyes were transfixed with revulsion. "You killed a woman. Oh, Affie!" she cried.

"It was an accident!" Bucky said, putting a derisive spin on his mother's earlier defence. "Well, it was!" he added more emphatically. "She wouldn't give it to me."

"And was my gamekeeper's death an accident?" Her Majesty interjected in tones that could bring the glaciers back to East Anglia in a heat wave.

The familiar high and cutting voice had a transforming effect on the assembled. Bucky's face returned to its childish petulance. Aileen's body heaved as she broke into another jag of silent sobs.

"He accused me. Said he'd turn me in. What could I do?" Bucky pouted. "Ma'am," he added, though his sudden recall of etiquette seemed ludicrously beside the point.

Bucky's question deserved no reply. The Queen's sapphire eyes were glittering with unexpressed anger. My heart sank. I felt like such a puddinghead for my conduct in the Gun Room that night. So set was I upon another figure as the Sandringham Estate killer, I hadn't allowed myself to fully consider the bleedin' obvious: that a person with a murder weapon in his hands stands a damn good chance of *being* a murderer, not just some concerned bystander.

"But why," Princess Margaret asked, sitting upright, the rug fallen to her lap, "did you leave the tiara at the village hall?"

"I couldn't get it off her in time. She was face down. And then I heard someone come in. You!" He turned accusingly to Jenkyns. "So I got out the back door."

"What a cowardly episode," Princess Margaret

murmured, after silence had reigned for a few heart-beats.

"It was . . . self-defense," Bucky insisted, taking in our expressions of disgust and abhorrence. "She kept trying to hit at me with that . . . that sceptre-thing. Otherwise it would have been me!"

"But you were attacking *her*!" I argued, my encounter with Bucky Wednesday night in my room flashing in my brain. "She was just trying to defend herself!"

"She wouldn't give me that tiara!" he shouted again. "It wasn't hers! And she kept swinging that sceptre. The balls on the top and the bottom flew off. . . ."

"And hit you. That's how the glitter got on your collar."

Bucky looked at me wildly, barely cognizant of what I was saying. "Yeah," he replied. "The thing started to look real dangerous with that big fat black end to it. I kept trying to grab at it. But she just kept swinging and swinging it at me. And so finally I got it away from her. She ran, and . . . and I hit her as she turned away. We were on the stage. It was just a little tap. I mean, I just thought she was knocked out or something . . . and then . . ." He looked angrily at Jenkyns.

"And my husband?" Aileen said weakly, her hand at her mouth.

"He should've minded his own business!"

"You young idiot!" Lord Thring thundered.

"Well, he should've! What could I do!" The special pleading in his tone was obnoxious. "He just made me so mad, going on like that. I said it was an accident! But he wouldn't shut up. I tried to get away through the kitchens but he was talking louder and louder. So in the Gun Room—"

"When the lights went out . . ." I mumbled.

"That clock. It was *so heavy*." Bucky stared at the pattern in the oriental carpet as if reimagining the scene in the Gun Room. He glanced at me. "And then the lights came on, and there you were . . ." An idiot smile spread across his lips. "And you believed me!"

He blinked, raised his head, and regarded us with a kind of weird satisfaction. "You're all pretty dumb."

"Buchanan! Remember where you are!" Lady Thring had sufficiently recovered from shock to admonish her son for general rudeness and affront to the Sovereign.

"Oh, shut up, Mother. I'm so tired of you trying to turn me into one of these people—"

"Really!" Princess Margaret glared.

"—with the right clothes and the right schools and the right manners and all the fucking la-de-dah. I've had it up to here!"

"Buchanan, you've said quite enough."

"Oh, of course, it's more important that I should present the proper image, isn't it? I should *say* the right things and *do* the right things. Ever since we came to this country you've done this crap to me. Like I embarrass you or something. And sticking me in that awful school. And Hume . . ." His voice was filled with rage and bewilderment. "And now you're having another kid, aren't you? Aren't you?"

Heads swivelled to Lady Thring.

"How . . . !"

"Caroline, of course! Well, good luck with this one, Mother," Bucky screamed at her, bending into her face. "Good—fucking—luck."

There was a sudden crack, like the sound of a shotgun going off. I could see nothing, only Bucky snapping back and suddenly raising his open hand. The Queen's face caught my attention at the same moment. A fleeting expression of utter astonishment and outrage animated her features and she began to rise from her chair as Bucky's hand floated for a millisecond on high like a white bird caught in mid-flight. "Oh, my God, what have I done?" Lady Thring cried. "Oh, Bucky, Bucky . . ."

The hand came tearing down. But Jenkyns was quick. He grabbed Bucky's arm and with a kind of practised grace twisted it around and pinned it to his back. One of the corgis darted from HM's grasp and sank her teeth into Bucky's ankle. Bucky yelped, his whole body seemed to leap into the air. "Get off me, get off me!" he screamed, twisting and turning in Jenkyns's grasp, trying to kick the grunting dog with his unfettered foot while the other corgi yapped excitedly, waiting for advantage.

"I'm going back to the States, Mother!" he shouted above the melee, the Queen admonishing the dogs, Lord Thring pulling at their hindquarters. "Far away from *you*!"

"I think you'll be spending a good while longer in England, son," Jenkyns said coolly as the dogs returned triumphant to Her Majesty's side.

"Don't call me 'son,' you bastard! Jesus, my leg!"

"Ma'am?" Jenkyns indicated the corridor.

"Yes, please, Inspector."

"Get your hands off me! You're hurting me," we could hear Bucky muttering as Jenkyns half dragged, half pushed him into the corridor and into the nether regions of Sandringham House. Lady Thring sat as though petrified. And then, without warning, she alit from the couch and hurried from the Saloon, her long skirt gathered in her hands, calling plaintively after her son.

There followed a short and excruciating silence, broken only by Aileen's intermittent sniffling and the dogs' contented postcombat sighs. Finally, Lord Thring turned to Her Majesty and said in a hollow voice that could not mask his despair: "Ma'am, I'm so very sorry."

The Queen smiled bleakly. She shook her head sadly. "No more than I, Affie. No more than I."

"Should go to my wife."

"Of course."

"Goodness, Lilibet!" said Princess Margaret in a low voice after his lordship had retreated into the corridor and we had had another few moments to contemplate the course of events and allow our hearts to resume their normal rhythms. "How shocking! Poor dear Affie. And Pamela, of course, too. I doubt New Year's Eve will ever be the same for either of them again."

The Queen acknowledged the comment with a small gesture and glanced over her shoulder at the clock. "The year's nearly over," she sighed, fingering her pearls, "I suppose one must go to Flitcham. Actually, I think I'd rather see the New Year from bed this year. This has been simply dreadful!"

"They'll be expecting you, Lilibet. And there's just enough time."

"Yes, of course. Perhaps you'd help Mrs. Benefer back to her room, Jane. Aileen," HM added kindly to her Housekeeper, "this has been a most dreadful time for you. You must take a good long rest. We'll manage with the housekeeping somehow, won't we, Jane?"

"Yes, Ma'am," I agreed, rising to go to Mrs. Benefer. As I did so I happened to glance up at the minstrels' gallery at the north end of the Saloon, thinking I'd seen a flash of colour and movement through the oak fretwork. The Queen must have followed my glance for the next voice was hers and the tones were sharp: "Who's up there?"

There was a rustle. "Just me, Your Majesty."

The enunciation was unmistakable.

"What are you doing up there, David?"

"I'd wondered where Jane had got to, Ma'am. It's nearly midnight. I heard voices so I came looking. I thought Your Majesty had gone to Flitcham with—"

"Whatever is that on your head?" the Queen interrupted.

Davey had contrived to hide behind a bit of the decorative moulding at the side of the gallery but something glossy attached to his skull bobbled outward as he talked.

"It's fruit, Ma'am."

"I hope you're not wasting food, David."

"No, Ma'am. It's plastic fruit."

"I see. I wouldn't have thought you young people had even *heard* of Carmen Miranda." She sighed, then added under her breath to no one in particular, "At least he's not wearing a bloody tiara."

Epilogue

'NOBODY'S GOING TO haul you off to the scrubs,' I'd said to Bucky in my father's car the night of Tom Benefer's death. So much for my clairvoyant powers at that moment. Buchanan Walsh, once of Moore County, N.C., is now enjoying shared accommodation at an HM Government prison facility in northwest London, a not awfully convenient car-trip from Mommy and Step-daddy's home in Mayfair. It's likely to be some time before young Mr. Walsh returns to the United States, although perhaps by the time he's released, sometime in the next millennium, he'll have discovered how charming England can be.

On the other hand, perhaps not.

The Thringys, lord and lady, cancelled their new year engagements in America and holiday in the Carib-bean for obvious reasons. Their names, once occasional italic adornment to the society pages, vaulted overnight to screaming bold-type headlines on the front pages of every paper in the realm, broadsheet and tabloid. Few details of the murders failed to escape scrutiny, the attendant business of the Duchess of Windsor's tiara, like the unlucky Hope Diamond of ancient days, particularly capturing the public imagination. Lord Thring's fears for the soiled family escutcheon were fulfilled as readers picked up the diadem's ancient trail from Ednam Lodge to the vault in Barsham Hall to the village hall at Dersingham, adding 'bent,' 'dodgy,' and 'corrupt' to the vocabulary surrounding the villainy of his late lordship's unrepentant appeasement.

Inspector Paul Jenkyns's reputation was also a casualty, as he knew it would be the moment his father-in-law had phoned him with the delightful news that Her Majesty had *personally* invited him to tea. No longer a high-flyer in the RDPD, Jenkyns is said to have a desk job in some remote cranny of the Metropolitan Police bureaucracy. His marriage failed to survive the publicity, no surprise. None of this stopped his father-in-law, the Lord Mayor, from taking tea with the Queen, however. You'd think he'd have been utterly mortified. Poor Queen.

Of course, some details were nicely smudged over. The official line that Jackie Scaife's body had been found in the village hall by a meticulous professional security force was carried through to the arrest and conviction of Buchanan Walsh, who confessed to her murder, and to Benefer's, it was written, in the face of the Home Office forensic science service's insurmountable evidence and testimony from, notably, Chris Jenkyns. That the site of said confession was the Saloon in Sandringham House and the person leading the impromptu homicide inquiry was Her Majesty the Queen remained privileged, which suited all concerned just fine. Certainly neither the Thrings nor Mrs. Benefer nor Paul Jenkyns nor I had any desire to draw HM into unnecessary controversy. She gets enough of it. Poor woman hasn't had an *annus mirabilis* in years.

While concern was expressed over Jenkyns's failures, the Royalty & Diplomatic Protection Department and the Anti-Terrorist Branch of Scotland Yard were publicly given, on the whole, decent marks for diligent work while, in private, an internal inquiry advanced through the departments involved asking the usual questions: Who screwed it up this time? and who shall be roasted on a spit? In court, a little confusion arose when Chris Jenkyns insisted that a *Canadian* police officer with a female associate had questioned him in his shop, but this was dismissed as absurd. Only Andrew Macgreevy's ears twitched and he was on to me like baked beans on toast. I stonewalled, admirably, I think; from PEI, my father wouldn't take the call, and the resulting sidebar to the *Evening Gazette*'s extensive coverage of the Thring Shock Horror was the usual journalistic soufflé, built of air and fallen flat the instant it came from the oven.

Macgreevy has a talent for soufflés, though. New Year's Day, when I went to visit my father at the Feathers, he was barrelling out the door to hop it back to London, mightily cheesed off that he had blown his opp. to interview the perp., who had been wandering around the pub not more than a few feet away late Friday evening. This failure of prognostication didn't stop Macgreevy, however, from concocting a breathless personal eyewitness account exclusively for the excitable consumers of the always sublime *Gazette*. It was *thrilling*! Yawn.

The real problem I had was with my father. I'd suffered my third epiphany (I guess you could call it—Mrs. B.'s biblicality had a rub-off quality) outside Jenx Jewellery that Saturday afternoon. The meaning of Chris Jenkyns's story of the ever-impulsive Bucky's failure to immediately grant the jeweller a glimpse of his purloined treasure and his late arrival at the Feathers had only hit me with force when we walked back to the car park in Lynn. There were no boozy angels to misdirect me that time, only in my mind a few specks of glitter turning and twisting, scintillating in the light of a pub vestibule, drifting softly downward to adhere in their tenacious way to a coarse-haired mat covering a cold stone floor. Eagerly, I'd let my father in on my breakthrough.

I don't think I'd ever seen him quite so angry. I suppose there was some consolation in knowing he didn't disagree with my reasoning, but what really sent him over the edge was the awareness that less than twenty-four hours earlier I had walked alone, at night, in the cold, from Sandringham House to Dersingham with a man who was a murderer and that this—*this!*—was the very sort of reason he didn't want me living so far from home, in the corruption of the Old World, and that it was time to pack my bags and he didn't want any nonsense and so on and so on blah blah blah.

I calmly pointed out that I hadn't figured Bucky for a murderer at the time of our walk to the pub and that *he* hadn't figured Bucky for a murderer either when *he* had driven us back to the Big House. I also told him coolly that I could take care of myself, thank you very much, and, in support, I offered my able defence of myself when Bucky became rather too frisky up in my room earlier in the week. Bad move, Jane. Believing there are some things it's best a father not know, I'd neglected to pass along this information earlier. Alas, I only confirmed him in his sensibilities and the twenty-minute drive back to Sandringham was wintry, to say the least.

The emotional climate was balmier New Year's Day, however. Our small world had righted itself. Bucky was in custody and whatever peril I might have been in had vanished with him. As I said to dear old Dad over New Year's dinner at the Feathers, I was sure Bucky, cloaked in the conceit that none of Her Majesty's houseguests would be thought capable of committing a crime so foul, had smugly figured he had got away with, well, murder. Only near the end had he realized he had miscalculated. When I helped Mrs. Benefer back to her room, I noted a piece of luggage in the corridor outside the Saloon. That, I realized, had been the source of the soft thud I had heard just before Bucky had rejoined us. He hadn't been dressed and ready to proceed to Flitcham. He had been planning to quietly bug off un-

aware that Her Majesty had commanded the grounds be
sealed once the first party of Royals had left for the
timber lodge. So, I said to the aged parent, there really
wasn't much to worry about. He gruffly allowed that this
might be so and consoled himself with the expressed
thought that I was unlikely to find myself in such a
situation again.

Poor Father. As it happened, I did find myself in
such a situation again. At Windsor Castle, in the spring
of the following year. But, by then, my father was long
back in Prince Edward Island, too far away to know or to
worry. Unnecessarily.

And, while I'm tying up loose ends, you might like
to know Mrs. Benefer rallied quite quickly from her
double tragedy. I suppose you could say her faith had
made her well, or perhaps it was because her life was her
work; at any rate she had become a *genuine* martyr and
we girls were never more on our toes throughout HM's
January holiday. Hume Pryce couldn't wait to depart
Dersingham, and did so, New Year's Day. He came up
to my father and me as we were eating in the Feathers
and hurriedly wished us a semifond farewell. I could tell
he had no idea of his paternity, and I wasn't going to be
the messenger. I daresay he read about his relationship
to Bucky in Nevis and immediately lost his tan. The
Thrings were invited to Sandringham the next year. It
was a gracious act of support on HM's part, and while an
invitation from the Monarch is usually more of a command, the invitation was graciously declined and everyone knew why. Sadly, Lady Thring miscarried. The
stress, I suppose.

As everyone who reads newspapers or watches
telly knows, the diamond tiara was eventually returned
to the estate of the Duchess of Windsor and auctioned
by Sotheby's in aid of the Louis Pasteur Institute in
Paris. It didn't fetch the price it might have if it had
been auctioned with the Duchess's other jewellery in
1987 (these are the 'nineties, after all), but reading that
it sold at $1.1 million I still get shock thinking of myself
toting it around London in an old Marks & Spencer
carrier bag. The ultimate purchaser remained a secret, to

everyone's disappointment, but the rumour among Household and Staff is that Princess Margaret bought it, bringing it back into the Family, so to speak. Davey says HRH has always been miffed that the Queen, being the Queen, inherited all the great jewellery and that she, Margaret, had been obliged to borrow tiaras from her sister until she bought her own, the Poltimore tiara, in the late 1950s. Now, if rumour is true, Margo owns two. But she's never worn the Wallis tiara in public. And who can blame her, given the associations? Perhaps she bought it for private gloating, if she bought it at all. Who knows.

And, in smaller money matters, I was eventually paid back the money owed for the lottery tickets. I found a crisp £10 note in an envelope in my mailbox at the Buck House post office. It wasn't long after, though, that I overheard Davey worrying that Her Majesty owed *him* £10. I really think it's time HM carried a little money in that famous handbag of hers.

ABOUT THE AUTHOR

C. C. Benison is a Canadian writer.

If you enjoyed DEATH AT
SANDRINGHAM HOUSE,
you will want to read C. C. Benison's other
charming British mysteries.

Look for DEATH AT
BUCKINGHAM PALACE
at your favorite bookstore.

And in Fall 1997, look for
the latest Jane Bee mystery,
DEATH AT
WINDSOR CASTLE!

BANTAM OFFERS THE FINEST IN CLASSIC AND MODERN BRITISH MURDER MYSTERIES

C. C. BENISON

Her Majesty Investigates

____57476-0	DEATH AT BUCKINGHAM PALACE	$5.50/$7.50
____57477-9	DEATH AT SANDRINGHAM HOUSE	$5.50/$7.50

TERI HOLBROOK

____56859-0	A FAR AND DEADLY CRY	$5.50/$7.50
____56860-4	THE GRASS WIDOW	$5.50/$7.50

DOROTHY CANNELL

____56951-1	HOW TO MURDER YOUR MOTHER-IN-LAW	$5.50/$7.50
____29195-5	THE THIN WOMAN	$5.50/$7.50
____27794-4	THE WIDOWS CLUB	$5.50/$7.50
____29684-1	FEMMES FATAL	$5.50/$7.50
____28686-2	MUM'S THE WORD	$5.50/$7.50
____57360-8	HOW TO MURDER THE MAN OF YOUR DREAMS	$5.50/$7.50

Ask for these books at your local bookstore or use this page to order.

Please send me the books I have checked above. I am enclosing $____ (add $2.50 to cover postage and handling). Send check or money order, no cash or C.O.D.'s, please.

Name _____

Address _____

City/State/Zip _____

Send order to: Bantam Books, Dept. MC 6, 2451 S. Wolf Rd., Des Plaines, IL 60018
Allow four to six weeks for delivery.
Prices and availability subject to change without notice.

MC 6 1/97